"Will there be other Darkover novels?

"Oh, certainly, as long as editors keep buying them and fans keep wanting to read them . . .

"But I don't know what, or when, or how I will write all these things. I never know what a book is going to be about until I have written it, and sometimes even then I'm not very sure. I never know what a book is going to be about until it walks out of some darkness at the back of my brain and says 'Here I am; write me.'

"Oh, I can say to myself, 'Dammit, I'm going to write a book about so-and-so,' and force myself to write it.

"But my best books force themselves upon me. And many, many of them appear in my mind in the light of the bloody sun, or of the four moons of Darkover."

—Marion Zimmer Bradley
from *A Darkover Retrospective*
(included in this volume)

MARION ZIMMER BRADLEY

THE PLANET SAVERS
THE SWORD OF ALDONES

*→ rewritten
to be Sharra's
Exille*

ACE BOOKS, NEW YORK

Some portions of "A Darkover Retrospective" were adapted from an article
titled "My Life on Darkover," published in the amateur magazine
Fantasiae, edited by Ian Miles Slater, c/o The Fantasy Association, Box
24560, Los Angeles, Cal. 90024. Copyright © 1974 by The Fantasy
Association and used by permission of Ian Miles Slater.

THE PLANET SAVERS
THE SWORD OF ALDONES

An Ace Book / published by arrangement with
the author

PRINTING HISTORY
Ace edition / March 1980

ISBN: 0-441-67027-X

Ace Books are published by The Berkley Publishing Group,
200 Madison Avenue, New York, New York 10016.
The name "ACE" and the "A" logo are
trademarks belonging to Charter Communications, Inc.
PRINTED IN THE UNITED STATES OF AMERICA

10   9   8   7

CHAPTER ONE

BY THE TIME I got myself all the way awake I thought I was alone. I was lying on a leather couch in a bare white room with huge windows, alternate glass-brick and clear glass. Beyond the clear windows, was a view of snow-peaked mountains which turned to pale shadows in the glass-brick.

Habit and memory fitted names to all these. The bare office, the orange flare of the great sun, the names of the dimming mountains. But beyond a polished glass desk, a man sat watching me. And I had never seen the man before.

He was chubby, and not young, and had ginger-colored eyebrows and a fringe of ginger-colored hair around the edges of a forehead which was otherwise quite pink and bald. He was wearing a white uniform coat, and the intertwined caduceus on the pocket and on the sleeve proclaimed him a member of the Medical Service attached to the Civilian HQ of the Terran Trade City.

I didn't stop to make all these evaluations consciously, of course. They were just part of my world when I woke up and found it taking shape around me. The familiar mountains, the familiar sun, the strange man. But he spoke to me in a friendly way, as if it were an ordinary

1

thing to find a perfect stranger sprawled out taking a siesta in here.

"Could I trouble you to tell me your name?"

That was reasonable enough. If I found somebody making himself at home in my office—if I had an office —I'd ask him his name, too. I started to swing my legs to the floor, and had to stop and steady myself with one hand while the room drifted in giddy circles around me.

"I wouldn't try to sit up just yet," he remarked, while the floor calmed down again. Then he repeated, politely but insistently, "Your name?"

"Oh, yes. My name." It was—I fumbled through layers of what felt like gray fuzz, trying to lay my tongue on the most familiar of all sounds, my own name. It was —why, it was—I said, on a high rising note, "This is damn silly," and swallowed. And swallowed again. Hard.

"Calm down," the chubby man said soothingly. That was easier said than done. I stared at him in growing panic and demanded, "But, but, have I had amnesia or something?"

"Or something."

"What's my *name?*"

"Now, now, take it easy! I'm sure you'll remember it soon enough. You can answer other questions, I'm sure. How old are you?"

I answered eagerly and quickly "Twenty-two."

The chubby man scribbled something on a card. "Interesting. In-ter-est-ing. Do you know where we are?"

I looked around the office. "In the Terran Headquarters. From your uniform, I'd say we were on Floor 8 —Medical."

He nodded and scribbled again, pursing his lips. "Can you—uh—tell me what planet we are on?"

I had to laugh. "Darkover," I chuckled, "I hope! And if you want the names of the moons, or the date of the founding of the Trade City, or something—"

He gave in, laughing with me. "Remember where you were born?"

"On Samarra. I came here when I was three years old —my father was in Mapping and Exploring—" I stopped short, in shock. "He's dead!"

"Can you tell me your father's name?"

"Same as mine. Jay—Jason—" the flash of memory closed down in the middle of a word. It had been a good try, but it hadn't quite worked. The doctor said soothingly, "We're doing very well."

"You haven't told me anything," I accused. "Who are you? Why are you asking me all these questions?"

He pointed to a sign on his desk. I scowled and spelled out the letters. "Randall—Forth—Director—Department—" and Dr. Forth made a note. I said aloud, "It is —*Doctor* Forth, isn't it?"

"Don't you know?"

I looked down at myself, and shook my head. "Maybe *I'm* Doctor Forth," I said, noticing for the first time that I was also wearing a white coat with the caduceus emblem of Medical. But it had the wrong feel, as if I were dressed in somebody else's clothes. *I* was no doctor, was I? I pushed back one sleeve slightly, exposing a long, triangular scar under the cuff. Dr. Forth—by now I was sure *he* was Dr. Forth—followed the direction of my eyes.

"Where did you get the scar?"

"Knife fight. One of the bands of those-who-may-not-enter-cities caught us on the slopes, and we—" the memory thinned out again, and I said despairingly, "It's all confused! What's the matter? Why am I up on Medical? Have I had an accident? Amnesia?"

"Not exactly. I'll explain."

I got up and walked to the window, unsteadily because my feet wanted to walk slowly while I felt like bursting through some invisible net and striding there at one bound. Once I got to the window the room stayed put while I gulped down great breaths of warm sweetish air. I said, "I could use a drink."

"Good idea. Though I don't usually recommend it." Forth reached into a drawer for a flat bottle; poured tea-colored liquid into a throwaway cup. After a minute he poured more for himself. "Here. And sit down, man. You make me nervous, hovering like that."

I didn't sit down. I strode to the door and flung it open. Forth's voice was low and unhurried.

"What's the matter? You can go out, if you want to, but won't you sit down and talk to me for a minute? Anyway, where do you want to go?"

The question made me uncomfortable. I took a couple of long breaths and came back into the room. Forth said, "Drink this," and I poured it down. He refilled the cup unasked, and I swallowed that too and felt the hard lump in my middle began to loosen up and dissolve.

Forth said, "Claustrophobia too. Typical," and scribbled on the card some more. I was getting tired of that performance. I turned on him to tell him so, then suddenly felt amused—or maybe it was the liquor working in me. He seemed such a funny little man, shutting himself up inside an office like this and talking about claustrophobia and watching me as if I were a big bug. I tossed the cup into a disposall.

"Isn't it about time for a few of those explanations?"

"If you think you can take it. How do you feel now?"

"Fine." I sat down on the couch again, leaning back and stretching out my long legs comfortably. "What did you put in that drink?"

He chuckled. "Trade secret. Now, the easiest way to explain would be to let you watch a film we made yesterday."

"To watch—" I stopped. "It's your time we're wasting."

He punched a button on the desk, spoke into a mouth-piece. "Surveillance? Give us a monitor on—" he spoke a string of incomprehensible numbers, while I lounged at ease on the couch. Forth waited for an answer, then touched another button and steel louvers closed noise-lessly over the windows, blacking them out. The darkness felt oddly more normal than the light, and I leaned back and watched the flickers clear as one wall of the office became a large vision-screen. Forth came and sat beside me on the leather couch, but in the picture Forth was there, sitting at his desk, watching another man, a stranger, walk into the office.

Like Forth, the newcomer wore a white coat with the caduceus emblems. I disliked the man on sight. He was tall and lean and composed, with a dour face set in thin lines. I guessed that he was somewhere in his thirties. Dr. Forth-in-the-film said, "Sit down, doctor," and I drew a long breath, overwhelmed by a curious sensation.

I have been here before. I have seen this happen before.

(And curiously formless I felt. I sat and watched, and I knew I was watching, and sitting. But it was in that dreamlike fashion, where the dreamer at once watches his visions and participates in them . . .)

"Sit down, doctor," Forth said. "Did you bring in the reports?"

Jay Allison carefully took the indicated seat, poised nervously on the edge of the chair. He sat very straight, leaning forward only a little to hand a thick folder of pa-pers across the desk. Forth took it, but didn't open it. "What do you think, Dr. Allison?"

"There is no possible room for doubt." Jay Allison spoke precisely, in a rather high-pitched and emphatic tone. "It follows the statistical pattern for all recorded attacks of 48-year fever—by the way, sir, haven't we any better name than that for this particular disease? The

term '48-year fever' connotes a fever of 48 years' dura-
tion, rather than a pandemic recurring every 48 years."

"A fever that lasted 48 years would be quite a fever,"
Dr. Forth said with a grim smile. "Nevertheless that's the
only name we have so far. Name it and you can have it.
Allison's disease?"

Jay Allison greeted this pleasantry with a repressive
frown. "As I understand it, the disease cycle seems to be
connected somehow with the once-every-48-years' conjunction of the four moons, which explains why the
Darkovans are so superstitious about it. The moons have
remarkably eccentric orbits—I don't know anything
about that part, I'm quoting Dr. Moore. If there's an
animal vector to the disease, we've never discovered it.
The pattern runs like this; a few cases in the mountain
districts, the next month a hundred-odd cases all over
this part of the planet. Then it skips exactly three months
without increase. The next upswing puts the number of
the reported cases in the thousands, and three months
after *that*, it reaches real pandemic proportions and deci-
mates the entire human population of Darkover."

"That's about it," Forth admitted. They bent together
over the folder, Jay Allison drawing back slightly to avoid
touching the other man.

Forth said, "We Terrans have a Trade compact on
Darkover for a hundred and fifty-two years. The first outbreak of this 48-year fever killed all but a dozen men out
of three hundred. The Darkovans were worse off than we
were. The last outbreak wasn't as bad, but it was bad
enough, I've heard. It had an eighty-seven percent mor-
tality—for humans, that is. I understand the Trailmen
don't die of it."

"The Darkovans call it the Trailmen's fever, Dr.
Forth, because the Trailmen are virtually immune to it.
It remains in their midst as a mild ailment taken by chil-
dren. When it breaks out into a virulent form every 48

years, most of the Trailmen are already immune. I took the disease myself as a child—maybe you heard?"

Forth nodded. "You may be the only Terran ever to contract the disease and survive."

"The Trailmen incubate the disease," Jay Allison said. "I should think the logical thing would be to drop a couple of hydrogen bombs on the trail cities—and wipe it out for good and all."

(Sitting on the sofa in Forth's dark office, I stiffened with such fury that he shook my shoulder and muttered "Easy there, man!")

Dr. Forth, on the screen, looked annoyed, and Jay Allison said, with a grimace of distaste, "I didn't mean that literally. But the Trailmen are not human. It wouldn't be genocide, just an exterminator's job. A public health measure."

Forth looked shocked as he realized that the younger man meant what he was saying. He said, "Galactic Center would have to rule on whether they're dumb animals or intelligent nonhumans, and whether they're entitled to the status of a civilization. All precedent on Darkover is toward recognizing them as men—and good God, Jay, you'd probably be called as a witness for the defense! How can you say they're not human after your experience with them? Anyway, by the time their status was finally decided, half of the recognizable humans on Darkover would be dead. We need a better solution than that."

He pushed his chair back and looked out the window.

"I won't go into this political situation," he said, "You aren't interested in Terran Empire politics, and I'm no expert either. But you'd have to be deaf, dumb and blind not to know that Darkover's been playing the immovable object to the irresistible force. The Darkovans are more advanced in some of the non-causative sciences than we are and, until now, they wouldn't admit that Terra had a

thing to contribute. However—and this is the big however—they do know, and they're willing to admit, that
our medical sciences are better than theirs."

"Theirs being practically nonexistent."

"Exactly—and this could be the first crack in the barrier. You may not realize the significance of this, but the
Legate received an offer from the Hasturs themselves."

Jay Allison murmured, "I'm to be impressed?"

"On Darkover you'd damn well better be impressed
when the Hasturs sit up and take notice."

"I understand they're telepaths or something—"

"Telepaths, psychokinectics, parapsychs, just about
anything else. For all practical purposes they're the Gods
of Darkover. And one of the Hasturs—a rather young
and unimportant one, I'll admit, the old man's grandson
—came to the Legate's office, in person, mind you. He
offered, if the Terran Medical would help Darkover lick
the Trailmen's fever, to coach selected Terran men in
matrix mechanics."

"Good God," Jay said. It was a concession beyond
Terra's wildest dreams; for a hundred years they had
tried to beg, buy or steal some knowledge of the mysterious science of matrix mechanics—that curious dis-
cipline which could turn matter into raw energy, and
vice versa, without any intermediate stages and without
fission by-products. Matrix mechanics had made the
Darkovans virtually immune to the lure of Terra's advanced technologies.

Jay said, "Personally I think Darkovan science is over-
rated. But I can see the propaganda angle—"

"Not to mention the humanitarian angle of healing."

Jay Allison gave one of his cold shrugs. "The real angle
seems to be this: *can* we cure the 48-year fever?"

"Not yet. But we have a lead. During the last
epidemic, a Terran scientist discovered a blood fraction
containing antibodies against the fever—in the

Trailmen. Isolated to a serum, it might reduce the virulent 48-year epidemic form to the mild form again. Unfortunately, he died himself in the epidemic, without finishing his work, and his notebooks were overlooked until this year. We have 18,000 men, and their families, on Darkover now, Jay. Frankly, if we lose too many of them, we're going to have to pull out of Darkover—the big brass on Terra will write off the loss of a garrison of professional traders, but not of a whole Trade City colony. That's not even mentioning the prestige we'll lose if our much-vaunted Terran medical sciences can't save Darkover from an epidemic. We've got exactly five months. We can't synthesize a serum in that time. We've got to appeal to the Trailmen. And that's why I called you up here. You know more about the Trailmen than any living Terran. You ought to. You spent eight years in a Nest."

(In Forth's darkened office I sat up straighter, with a flash of returning memory. Jay Allison, I judged, was several years older than I, but we had one thing in common; this cold fish of a man shared with myself that experience of marvelous years spent in an alien world!)

Jay Allison scowled, displeased. "That was years ago. I was hardly more than a baby. My father crashed on a Mapping expedition over the Hellers—God only knows what possessed him to try and take a light plane over those crosswinds. I survived the crash by the merest chance, and lived with the Trailmen—so I'm told—until I was thirteen or fourteen. I don't remember much about it. Children aren't particularly observant."

Forth leaned over the desk, staring. "You speak their language, don't you?"

"I used to. I might remember it under hypnosis, I suppose. Why? Do you want me to translate something?"

"Not exactly. We were thinking of sending you on an expedition to the Trailmen themselves."

110 MARION ZIMMER BRADLEY

(In the darkened office, watching Jay's startled face, I thought, God, what an adventure! I wonder—I wonder if they want me to go with him?)

Forth was explaining; "It would be a difficult trek. You know what the Hellers are like. Still, you used to climb mountains, as a hobby, before you went into Medical—"

"I outgrew the childishness of hobbies many years ago, sir," Jay said stiffly.

"We'd get you the best guides we could, Terran and Darkovan. But they couldn't do the one thing you can do. You *know* the Trailmen, Jay. You might be able to persuade them to do the one thing they've never done before."

"What's that?" Jay Allison sounded suspicious.

"Come out of the mountains. Send us volunteers— blood donors—we might, if we had enough blood to work on, be able to isolate the right fraction, and synthesize it, in time to prevent the epidemic from really taking hold, Jay. It's a tough mission and it's dangerous as all hell, but somebody's got to do it, and I'm afraid you're the only qualified man."

"I like my first suggestion better. Bomb the Trailmen —and the Hellers—right off the planet." Jay's face was set in lines of loathing, which he controlled after a minute, and said, "I—I didn't mean that. Theoretically I can see the necessity, only—" he stopped and swallowed.

"Please say what you were going to say."

"I wonder if I am as well qualified as you think? No— don't interrupt—I find the natives of Darkover distasteful, even the humans. As for the Trailmen—"

(I was getting mad and impatient. I whispered to Forth in the darkness "Shut the goddam film off! You couldn't send *that* guy on an errand like *that*! I'd rather—"

Forth snapped "Shut up and listen!"

I shut up.)

Jay Allison was not acting. He was pained and disgusted. Forth wouldn't let him finish his explanation of why he had refused even to teach in the Medical College established for Darkovans by the Terran empire. He interrupted, and he sounded irritated,

"We know all that. It evidently never occurred to you, Jay, that it's an inconvenience to us—that all this vital knowledge should lie, purely by accident, in the hands of the one man who's too damned stubborn to use it?"

Jay didn't move an eyelash, where I would have squirmed. "I have always been aware of that, doctor."

Forth drew a long breath. "I'll concede you're not suitable at the moment, Jay. But what do you know of applied psychodynamics?"

"Very little I'm sorry to say." Allison didn't sound sorry, though. He sounded bored to death with the whole conversation.

"May I be blunt—and personal?"

"Please do. I'm not at all sensitive."

"Basically, then, Doctor Allison, a person as contained and repressed as yourself usually has a clearly defined subsidiary personality. In neurotic individuals this complex of personality traits sometimes splits off, and we get a syndrome known as multiple, or alternate personality."

"I've scanned a few of the classic cases. Wasn't there a woman with four separate personalities?"

"Exactly. However, you aren't neurotic, and ordinarily there would not be the slightest chance of your repressed alternate taking over your personality."

"Thank you," Jay murmured ironically, "I'd be losing sleep over that."

"Nevertheless I presume you *do* have such a subsidiary personality, although he would not normally manifest. This subsidiary—let's call him Jay—would embody all the characteristics which you repress. He would be gregarious, where you are retiring and studious; adventurous where you are cautious; talkative while you are taciturn; he would perhaps enjoy action for its own sake, while you exercise faithfully in the gymnasium only for your health's sake; and he might even remember the Trailmen with pleasure rather than dislike."

"In short—a blend of all the undesirable characteristics?"

"One could put it that way. Certainly, he would be a blend of all the characteristics which you, Jay, *consider* undesirable. But—if released by hypnotism and suggestion, he might be suitable for the job in hand."

"But how do you know I actually have such an—alternate?"

"I don't. But it's a good guess. Most repressed—" Forth coughed and amended "most *disciplined* personalities possess such a suppressed secondary personality. Don't you occasionally—rather rarely—find yourself doing things which are entirely out of character for you?"

I could almost feel Allison taking it in, as he confessed, "Well—yes. For instance, the other day, although I dress conservatively at all times—" he glanced at his uniform coat, "I found myself buying—" he stopped again and his face went an unlovely terra-cotta color as he finally mumbled "a flowered red sport shirt."

Sitting in the dark I felt vaguely sorry for the poor gawk, disturbed by, ashamed of the only human impulses he ever had. On the screen Allison frowned fiercely. "A—crazy impulse."

"You could say that, or say it was an action of the suppressed Jay. How about it, Allison? You may be th: only Terran on Darkover, maybe the only human, who could get into a Trailman's Nest without being murdered."

"Sir—as a citizen of the Empire, I don't have any choice, do I?"

"Jay, look," Forth said, and I felt him trying to reach

through the barricade and touch, really touch that cold, contained young man, "We couldn't *order* any man to do anything like this. Aside from the ordinary dangers, it could destroy your personal balance, maybe permanently. I'm asking you to volunteer something above and beyond the call of duty. Man to man—what do you say?"

I would have been moved by his words. Even at second hand I was moved by them. Jay Allison looked at the floor and I saw him twist his long we~ hands and crack the knuckles with an odd gestu.. ly he said, "I haven't any choice either way, doctor. I'll take the chance. I'll go to the Trailmen."

CHAPTER TWO

THE SCREEN went dark again and Forth flicked the light on. He said "Well?"

I gave it back, in his own intonation, "Well?" and was exasperated to find that I was twisting my own knuckles in the nervous gesture of Allison's painful decision. I jerked them apart and got up.

"I suppose it didn't work, with that cold fish, and you decided to come to me instead? Sure, *I'll* go to the Trailmen for you. Not with that Allison bastard—I wouldn't go anywhere with that guy—but I speak the Trailmen's language, and without hypnosis, either."

Forth was staring at me. "So you've remembered that?"

"Hell yes," I said, "My Dad crashed in the Hellers, and a band of Trailmen found me, half dead. I lived there until I was about fifteen, then their Old-One decided I was too human for 'em, and they took me out through Dammerung Pass and arranged to have me brought here. Sure, it's all coming back now. I spent five years in the Spacemen's Orphanage, then I went to work

14

taking Terran tourists on hunting parties and so on, because I liked being around the mountains. I—" I stopped. Forth was staring at me.

"Sit down again, won't you? Can't you keep still a minute?" Reluctantly, I sat down. "You think you'd like this job?"

"It would be tough," I said, considering. "The People of the Sky—" (using the Trailmen's name for themselves) "—don't like outsiders, but they might be persuaded. The worst part would be getting there. The plane, or the 'copter, isn't built that can get through the crosswinds around the Hellers, and land inside them. We'd have to go on foot, all the way from Carthon. I'd need professional climbers—mountaineers."

"Then you don't share Allison's attitude?"

"Dammit, don't insult me!" I discovered that I was on my feet again, pacing the office restlessly. Forth stared and mused aloud, "What's personality anyway? A mask of emotions, superimposed on the body and the intellect. Change the point of view, change the emotions and desires, and even with the same body and the same past experiences, you have a new man."

I swung around in mid-step. A new and terrible suspicion, too monstrous to name, was creeping up on me. Forth touched a button and the face of Jay Allison, immobile, appeared on the vision-screen. Forth put a mirror in my hand. He said "Jason Allison, look at yourself."

I looked.

"No," I said. And again, "No. No. No."

Forth didn't argue. He pointed, with a stubby finger. "Look—" he moved the finger as he spoke, "Height of forehead. Set of cheekbones. Your eyebrows look different, and your mouth, because the expression is different. But bone structure—the nose, the chin—"

I heard myself make a queer sound; dashed the mirror to the floor. He grabbed my forearm. "Steady, man!"

I found a scrap of my voice. It didn't sound like Allison's. "Then I'm—Jay? Jay Allison with amnesia?"

"Not exactly." Forth mopped his forehead with an immaculate sleeve and it came away damp with sweat, "God, no, *not* Jay Allison as I know him!" He drew a long breath. "And sit down. Whoever you are, sit *down!*"

I sat. Gingerly. Not sure.

"But the man Jay might have been, given a different temperamental bias. I'd say—the man Jay Allison started out to be. The man he *refused* to be. Within his subconscious, he built up barriers against a whole series of memories, and the subliminal threshold—"

"Doc, I don't understand the psycho talk."

Forth stared. "And you do remember the Trailmen's language. I thought so. Allison's personality is suppressed in you, as yours was in him."

"One thing, Doc. I don't know a thing about blood fractions or epidemics. My half of the personality didn't study medicine." I took up the mirror again and broodingly studied the face there. The high thin cheeks, high forehead shaded by coarse, dark hair which Jay Allison had slicked down, now heavily rumpled. I still didn't think I looked anything like the doctor. Our voices were nothing alike either. His had been pitched rather high. My own, as nearly as I could judge, was a full octave deeper, and more resonant. Yet they issued from the same vocal chords, unless Forth were having a reasonless, macabre joke.

"Did I honest-to-God study medicine? It's the last thing I'd think about. It's an honest trade, I guess, but I've never been that intellectual."

"You—or rather, Jay Allison is a specialist in Darkovan parasitology, as well as a very competent surgeon." Forth was sitting with his chin in his hands, watching me intently. He scowled and said, "If anything, the physical change is more startling than the other. I wouldn't have recognized you."

"That tallies with me. I don't recognize myself," I added, "—and the queer thing is, I didn't even *like* Jay Allison, to put it mildly. If he—I can't say *he*, can I?"

"I don't know why not. You're no more Jay Allison than I am. For one thing, you're younger. Ten years younger. I doubt if any of his friends—if he had any—would recognize you. You—it's ridiculous to go on calling you Jay. What should I call you?"

"Why should I care? Call me Jason."

"Suits you," Forth said enigmatically. "Look, then, Jason. I'd like to give you a few days to readjust to your new personality, but we are really pressed for time. Can you fly to Carthon tonight? I've hand-picked a good crew for you, and sent them on ahead. You'll meet them there."

I stared at him. Suddenly the room oppressed me and I found it hard to breathe. I said in wonder "You were pretty sure of yourself, weren't you?"

Forth just looked at me, for what seemed a long time. Then he said, in a very quiet voice "No. I wasn't sure at all. But if you didn't turn up, and I couldn't talk Jay into it, I'd have had to try it myself."

Jason Allison, Junior, was listed on the directory of the Terran HQ as "Suite 1214, Medical Residence Corridor." I found the rooms without any trouble, though an elderly doctor stared at me rather curiously as I barged along the quiet hallway. The suite—bedroom, miniscule sitting room, compact bath—depressed me: clean, closed-in and neutral as the man who owned them. I rummaged through them restlessly, trying to find some scrap of familiarity to indicate that I had lived here for the past eleven years.

Jay Allison was thirty-four years old. I had given my

age, without hesitation, as twenty-two. There were no obvious blanks in my memory; from the moment Jay Allison had spoken of the Trailmen, my past had rushed back and stood, complete to yesterday's supper (only had I eaten that supper twelve years ago?). I remembered my father, a lined, silent man who had liked to fly often, taking photograph after photograph from his plane for the meticulous work of Mapping and Exploration. He'd liked to have me fly with him and I'd flown over virtually every inch of the planet. No one else had ever dared fly over the Hellers, except the big commercial space-craft that kept to a safe altitude. I vaguely remembered the crash and the strange hands pulling me out of the wreckage and the weeks I'd spent, broken-bodied and delirious, gently tended by one of the red-eyed, twittering women of the Trailmen. In all, I had spent eight years in the Nest, which was not a nest at all, but a vast sprawling city built in the branches of enormous trees. With the small and delicate humanoids who had been my playfellows, I had gathered the nuts and buds and trapped the small arboreal animals they used for food, taken my share at weaving clothing from the fibres of parasite plants cultivated on the stems, and in all those eight years I had set foot on the ground less than a dozen times, even though I had travelled for miles through the tree-roads high above the forest floor.

Then the Old-One's painful decision that I was too alien for them, and the difficult and dangerous journey my Trailmen foster-parents and foster-brothers had undertaken, to help me out of the Hellers and arrange for me to be taken to the Trade City. After two years of physically painful and mentally rebellious readjustment to daytime living (the owl-eyed Trailmen saw best, and lived largely, by moonlight) I had found a niche for myself, and settled down. But all of the later years (after Jay Allison had taken over, I supposed, from a basic pattern of memory common to both of us) had vanished into the limbo of the subconscious.

A bookrack was crammed with large microcards; I slipped one into the viewer, with a queer sense of spying, and found myself listening apprehensively to hear that measured step and Jay Allison's shrill voice demanding what the hell I was doing, meddling with his possessions. Eye to the viewer, I read briefly at random, something about the management of compound fracture, then realized I had understood exactly three words in a paragraph. I put my fist against my forehead and heard the words echoing there emptily; "laceration . . . primary effusion . . . serum and lymph . . . granulation tissue . . ." I presumed that the words meant something and that I once had known what. But if I had a medical education, I didn't recall a syllable of it. I didn't know a fracture from a fraction.

In a sudden frenzy of impatience I stripped off the white coat and put on the first shirt I came to, a crimson thing that hung in the line of white coats like an exotic bird in snow country. I went back to rummaging the drawers and bureaus. Carelessly shoved in a pigeonhole I found another microcard that looked familiar, and when I slipped it mechanically into the viewer it turned out to be a book on mountaineering which, oddly enough, I remembered buying as a youngster. It dispelled my last, lingering doubts. Evidently I had bought it before the personalities had forked so sharply apart and separated, Jason from Jay. I was beginning to believe. Not to accept. Just to believe it had happened. The book looked well-thumbed, and had been handled so much I had to baby it into the slot of the viewer.

Under a folded pile of clean underwear I found a flat half-empty bottle of whisky. I remembered Forth's words that he'd never seen Jay Allison drink, and suddenly I thought "The poor fool!" I fixed myself a drink and sat down, idly scanning the mountaineering book.

Not till I'd entered medical school, I suspected, did the two halves of me fork so strongly apart—so strongly that there had been days and weeks and, I suspected, years when Jay Allison had kept me prisoner. I tried to juggle dates in my mind, looked at a calendar, and got such a mental jolt that I put it face-down to think about when I was a little drunker.

I wondered if my detailed memories of my teens and early twenties were the same memories Jay Allison looked back on. I didn't think so. People forget and re-member selectively. Week by week, then, and year by year, the dominant personality of Jay had crowded me out; so that the young rowdy, more than half Darkovan, loving the mountains, half homesick for a non-human world, had been drowned in the chilly, austere young medical student who lost himself in his work. But I, Jason —I had always been the watcher behind, the person Jay Allison dared not be? Why was he past thirty—and I just 22?

A ringing shattered the silence; I had to hunt for the intercom on the bedroom wall. I said, "Who is it?" and an unfamiliar voice demanded "Dr. Allison?"

I said automatically "Nobody here by that name," and started to put back the mouthpiece. Then I stopped and gulped and asked, "Is that you, Dr. Forth?"

It was, and I breathed again. I didn't even want to think about what I'd say if somebody else demanded to know why the devil I was answering Dr. Allison's private telephone. When Forth had finished, I went to the mir-ror, and stared, trying to see behind my face the sharp features of that stranger, *Doctor* Jason Allison. I delayed, even while I was wondering what few things I should pack for a trip into the mountains, and the habit of hunt-ing parties was making mental lists about heat-socks and windbreakers. The face that looked at me was a young face, unlined and faintly freckled, the same face as always except that I'd lost my suntan; Jay Allison had kept me indoors too long. Suddenly I struck the mirror lightly with my fist.

"The hell with you, Dr. Allison," I said, and went to see if he had kept any clothes fit to pack.

CHAPTER THREE

DR. FORTH was waiting for me in the small skyport on the roof, and so was a small 'copter, one of the fairly old ones assigned to Medical Service when they were too beat up for services with higher priority. Forth took one startled look at my crimson shirt, but all he said was "Hello, Jason. Here's something we've got to decide right away; do we tell the crew who you really are?"

I shook my head emphatically. "I'm not Jay Allison; I don't want his name or his reputation. Unless there are men on the crew who know Allison by sight—"

"Some of them do, but I don't think they'd recognize you."

"Tell them I'm his twin brother," I said humorlessly.

"That wouldn't be necessary. There's not enough resemblance." Forth raised his head and beckoned to a man who was doing something near the 'copter. He said under his breath "You'll see what I mean," as the man approached.

He wore the uniform of Spaceforce—black leather with a little rainbow of stars on his sleeve meaning he'd seen service on a dozen different planets, a different colored star for each one. He wasn't a young man, but on the wrong side of fifty, seamed and burly and huge, with

22

a split lip and weathered face. I liked his looks. We shook hands and Forth said, "This is our man, Kendricks. He's called Jason, and he's an expert on the Trailmen. Jason, this is Buck Kendricks."

"Glad to know you, Jason." I thought Kendricks looked at me half a second more than necessary. "The 'copter's ready. Climb in, Doc—you're going as far as Carthon, aren't you?"

We put on zippered windbreakers and the 'copter soared noiselessly into the pale crimson sky. I sat beside Forth, looking down through pale lilac clouds at the pattern of Darkover spread below me.

"Kendricks was giving me a funny eye, Doc. What's biting him?"

"He has known Jay Allison for eight years," Forth said quietly, "and he hasn't recognized you yet."

But we let it ride at that, to my great relief, and didn't talk any more about me at all. As we flew under silent whirring blades, turning our backs on the settled country which lay near the Trade City, we talked about Darkover itself. Forth told me about the Trailmen's fever and managed to give me some idea about what the blood fraction was, and why it was necessary to persuade fifty or sixty of the humanoids to return with me, to donate blood from which the antibody could be first isolated, then synthesized.

It would be a totally unheard-of thing, if I could accomplish it. Most of the Trailmen never touched ground in their entire lives, except when crossing the passes above the snow line. Not a dozen of them, including my foster parents, who had so painfully brought me out across Dammerung, had ever crossed the ring of encircling mountains that walled them away from the rest of the planet. Humans sometimes penetrated the lower forests in search of the Trailmen. It was one-way traffic. The Trailmen never came in search of *them*.

We talked, too, about some of those humans who had crossed the mountains into Trailmen country—those mountains profanely dubbed the Hellers by the first Terrans who had tried to fly over them in anything lower or slower than a spaceship.

"What about this crew you picked? They're not Terrans?"

Forth shook his head. "It would be murder to send anyone recognizably Terran into the Hellers. You know how the Trailmen feel about outsiders getting into their country." I knew. Forth continued, "Just the same, there will be two Terrans with you."

"They don't know Jay Allison?" I didn't want to be burdened with anyone—not anyone—who would know me, or expect me to behave like my forgotten other self.

"Kendricks knows you," Forth said, "but I'm going to be perfectly truthful. I never knew Jay Allison well, except in line of work. I know a lot of things—from the past couple of days—which came out during the hypnotic sessions, which he'd never have dreamed of telling me, or anyone else, consciously. And that comes under the heading of a professional confidence—even from you. And for that reason, I'm sending Kendricks along—and you're going to have to take the chance he'll recognize you. Isn't that Carthon down there?"

Carthon lay nestled under the outlying foothills of the Hellers, ancient and sprawling and squatty, and burned brown with the dust of five thousand years. Children ran out to stare at the 'copter as we landed near the city; few planes ever flew low enough to be seen, this near the Hellers.

Forth had sent his crew ahead and parked them in an abandoned huge place at the edge of the city which might once have been a warehouse or a ruined palace. Inside there were a couple of trucks, stripped down to framework and flatbed, like all machinery shipped through space from Terra. There were pack animals, dark shapes in the gloom. Crates were stacked up in an orderly untidiness, and at the far end a fire was burning and five or six men in Darkovan clothing—loose-sleeved shirts, tight-wrapped breeches, low boots—were squatting around it, talking. They got up as Forth and Kendricks and I walked toward them, and Forth greeted them clumsily in badly accented Darkovan, then switched to Terran Standard, letting one of the men translate for him.

Forth introduced me simply as "Jason", after the Darkovan custom, and I looked the men over, one by one. Back when I'd climbed for fun, I'd liked to pick my own men; but whoever had picked this crew must have known his business.

Three were mountain Darkovans, lean swart men enough alike to be brothers; I learned after a while that they actually were brothers, Hjalmar, Garin and Vardo. All three were well over six feet, and Hjalmar stood head and shoulders over his brothers, whom I never learned to tell apart. The fourth man, a redhead, was dressed rather better than the others and introduced as Lerrys Ridenow —the double name indicating high Darkovan aristocracy. He looked muscular and agile enough, but his hands were suspiciously well-kept for a mountain man, and I wondered how much experience he'd had.

The fifth man shook hands with me, speaking to Kendricks and Forth as if they were old friends. "Don't I know you from someplace, Jason?"

He looked Darkovan, and wore Darkovan clothes, but Forth had forewarned me, and attack seemed the best defense. "Aren't you Terran?"

"My father was," he said, and I understood; a situation not exactly uncommon, but ticklish on a planet like Darkover. I said carelessly, "I may have seen you around the HQ. I can't place you, though.''

"My name's Rafe Scott. I thought I knew most of the professional guides on Darkover, but I admit I don't get into the Hellers much," he confessed. "Which route are we going to take?"

I found myself drawn into the middle of the group of men, accepting one of the small, sweetish Darkovan cigarettes, looking over the plan somebody had scribbled down on the top of a packing case. I borrowed a pencil from Rafe and bent over the case, sketching out a rough map of the terrain I remembered so well from boyhood. I might be bewildered about blood fractions, but when it came to climbing I knew what I was doing. Rafe and Lerrys and the Darkovan brothers crowded behind me to look over the sketch, and Lerrys put a long fingernail on the route I'd indicated.

"Your elevation's pretty bad here," he said diffidently, "and on the 'Narr campaign the Trailmen attacked us here, and it was bad fighting along those ledges."

I looked at him with new respect; dainty hands or not, he evidently knew the country. Kendricks patted the blaster on his hip and said grimly, "But this isn't the 'Narr campaign. I'd like to see any Trailmen attack us while I have this."

"But you're not going to have it," said a voice behind us, a crisp authoritative voice. "Take off that gun, man!"

Kendricks and I whirled together to see the speaker, a tall young Darkovan, still standing in the shadows. The newcomer spoke to me directly:

"I'm told you are Terran, but that you understand the Trailmen. Surely you don't intend to carry fission or fusion weapons against them?"

And I suddenly realized that we were in Darkovan territory now, and that we must reckon with the Darkovan horror of guns or of any weapon which reaches beyond the arm's length of the man who wields it. A simple heat-gun, to the Darkovan ethical code, is as reprehensible as a super-cobalt planetbuster.

Kendricks protested, "We can't travel unarmed through Trailmen country! We're apt to meet hostile bands of the creatures—and they're nasty with those long knives they carry!"

The stranger said calmly "I've no objection to you, or anyone else, carrying a knife for self-defense."

"A *knife?*" Kendricks drew breath to roar. "Listen, you bug-eyed son of a—who do you think you are, anyway?"

The Darkovans muttered. The man in the shadows said, "Regis Hastur."

Kendricks stared pop-eyed. My own eyes could have popped, but I decided it was time for me to take charge, if I were ever going to. I rapped, "All right, this is my show. Buck, give me the gun."

He looked wrathfully at me for the space of seconds, while I wondered what I'd do if he didn't. Then, slowly, he unbuckled the straps and handed it to me, butt first.

I'd never realized how undressed a Spaceforce man looked without his blaster. I balanced it on my palm for a minute while Regis Hastur came out of the shadows. He was tall, and had the reddish hair and fair skin of Darkovan aristocracy, and on his face was some indefinable stamp—arrogance, perhaps, or the consciousness that the Hasturs had ruled this world for centuries long before the Terrans brought ships and trade and the universe to their doors. He was looking at me as if he approved of me, and that was one step worse than the former situation.

So, using the respectful Darkovan idiom of speaking to a superior (which he was) but keeping my voice hard, I said "There's just one leader on my trek, Lord Hastur. On this one, I'm it. If you want to discuss whether or not we carry guns, I suggest you discuss it with me in private

—and let me give the orders."

One of the Darkovans gasped. I knew I could have been mobbed. But with a mixed bag of men, I had to grab leadership quickly or be relegated to nowhere. I didn't give Regis Hastur a chance to answer that, either; I said, "Come back here. I want to talk to you anyway."

He came, and I remembered to breathe. I led the way to a fairly deserted corner of the immense place, faced him and demanded, "As for you—what are you doing here? You're not intending to cross the mountains with us?"

He met my scowl levelly. "I certainly am."

I groaned. "Why? You're the Regent's grandson. Important people don't take on this kind of dangerous work. If anything happens to you, it will be my responsibility!" I was going to have enough trouble, I was thinking, without shepherding along one of the most revered personages on the whole damned planet! I didn't want anyone around who had to be fawned on, or deferred to, or even listened to.

He frowned slightly, and I had the unpleasant impression that he knew what I was thinking. "In the first place, it will mean something to the Trailmen, won't it, to have a Hastur with you, suing for this favor?"

It certainly would. The Trailmen paid little enough heed to the ordinary humans, except for considering them fair game for plundering when they came uninvited into Trailmen country. But they, with all Darkover, revered the Hasturs, and it was a fine point of diplomacy. If the Darkovans sent their most important leader, they might listen to him.

"In the second place," Regis Hastur continued, "the Darkovans are my people, and it's my business to negotiate for them. In the third place, I know the Trailmen's dialect—not well, but I can speak it a little. And in the fourth, I've climbed mountains all my life. Purely as an amateur, but I can assure you I won't be in the way."

There was little enough I could say to that. He seemed to have covered every point—or every point but one, and he added, shrewdly, after a minute, "Don't worry; I'm perfectly willing to have you take charge. I won't claim—privilege."

I had to be satisfied with that.

Darkover is a civilized planet with a fairly high standard of living, but it is not a mechanized or a technological culture. The people don't do much mining, or build factories, and the few which were founded by Terran enterprise never were very successful; outside the Terran Trade City, machinery or modern transportation is almost unknown.

While the other men checked and loaded supplies and Rafe Scott went out to contact some friends of his and arrange for last-minute details, I sat down with Forth to memorize the medical details I must put so clearly to the Trailmen.

"If we could only have kept your medical knowledge!"

"Trouble is, being a doctor doesn't suit my personality," I said. I felt absurdly light-hearted. Where I sat, I could raise my head and study the panorama of blackish-green foothills which lay beyond Carthon, and search out the stone roadway, like a tiny white ribbon, which we could follow for the first stage of the trip. Forth evidently did not share my enthusiasm.

"You know, Jason, there is one real danger—"

"Do you think I care about danger? Or are you afraid I'll turn—foolhardy?"

"Not exactly. It's not a physical danger, Jason. It's an emotional—or rather an intellectual danger."

"Hell, don't you know any language but that psycho doubletalk?"

"Let me finish, Jason. Jay Allison may have been

repressed, overcontrolled, but you are seriously im-
pulsive. You lack a balance-wheel, if I could put it that
way. And if you run too many risks, your buried alter-ego
may come to the surface and take over in sheer self-pres-
ervation."

"In other words," I said, laughing loudly, "if I scare
that Allison stuffed-shirt, he may start stirring in his
grave?"

Forth coughed and smothered a laugh and said that
was one way of putting it. I clapped him reassuringly on
the shoulder and said "Forget it, sir. I promise to be god-
ly, sober and industrious—but is there any law against
enjoying what I'm doing?"

Somebody burst out of the warehouse-palace place,
and shouted at me. "Jason? The guide is here," and I
stood up, giving Forth a final grin. "Don't you worry. Jay
Allison's good riddance," I said, and went back to meet
the other guide they had chosen.

And I almost backed out when I saw the guide. For the
guide was a woman.

She was small for a Darkovan girl, and narrowly built,
the sort of body that could have been called boyish or
coltish but certainly not, at first glance, feminine. Close-
cut curls, blue-black and wispy, cast the faintest of shadows over a squarish sunburnt face, and her eyes were so
thickly rimmed with heavy dark lashes that I could not
guess their color. Her nose was snubbed and might have
looked whimsical and was instead oddly arrogant. Her
mouth was wide, and her chin round.

She held up her palm and said rather sullenly, "Kyla
Rainéach, free Amazon, licensed guide."

I acknowledged the gesture with a nod, scowling. The
guild of free Amazons entered virtually every field, but
that of mountain guide seemed somewhat bizarre even
for an Amazon. She seemed wiry and agile enough, her
body, under the heavy blanketlike clothing, almost as

lean of hip and flat of breast as my own; only the slender
long legs were unequivocally feminine.

The other men were checking and loading supplies; I
noted from the corner of my eye that Regis Hastur was
taking his turn heaving bundles with the rest. I sat down
on some still-undisturbed sacks, and motioned her to sit.

"You've had trail experience? We're going into the
Hellers through Dammerung, and that's rough going
even for professionals."

She said in a flat expressionless voice, "I was with the
Terran Mapping expedition to the South Polar ridge last
year."

"Ever been in the Hellers? If anything happened to
me, could you lead the expedition safely back to
Carthon?"

She looked down at her stubby fingers. "I'm sure I
could," she said finally, and started to rise. "Is that all?"

"One more thing—" I gestured to her to stay put.
"Kyla, you'll be one woman among eight men—"

The snubbed nose wrinkled up. "I don't expect you to
crawl into my blankets, if that's what you mean. It's not
in my contract—I hope!"

I felt my face burning. Damn the girl! "It's not in
mine, anyway," I snapped, "but I can't answer for seven
other men, most of them mountain roughnecks." Even as
I said it I wondered why I bothered; certainly a free Amazon could defend her own virtue, or not, if she wanted to,
without any help from me. I had to excuse myself by
adding, "In either case you'll be a disturbing element—
I don't want fights either!"

She made a little low-pitched sound of amusement.
"There's safety in numbers, and—are you familiar with
the physiological effect of high altitudes on men ac-
climated to low ones?" Suddenly she threw back her
head and the hidden sound became free and merry
laughter. "Jason, I'm a free Amazon, and that means—

no, I'm not neutered, though some of us are. But you
have my word, I won't create any trouble of any recognizably female variety." She stood up. "Now, if you
don't mind, I'd like to check the mountain equipment."

Her eyes were still laughing at me, but curiously I
didn't mind at all.

CHAPTER FOUR

WE STARTED that night, a curiously lopsided little caravan. The pack animals were loaded into one truck and didn't like it. We had another stripped-down truck which carried supplies. The ancient stone roads, rutted and gullied here and there with the flood-waters and silt of decades, had not been planned for any travel other than the feet of men or beasts. We passed tiny villages and isolated country estates, and a few of the solitary towers where the matrix mechanics worked alone with the secret sciences of Darkover, towers of unpolished stone which sometimes shone like blue beacons in the dark.

Kendricks drove the truck which carried the animals, and was amused by it. Rafe and I took turns driving the other truck, sharing the wide front seat with Regis Hastur and Kyla, while the other men found seats between crates and sacks in the back. Once, while Rafe was at the wheel, and the girl was dozing with her coat over her face to shut out the fierce sun, Regis asked me, "What are the trailcities like?"

I tried to tell him, but I've never been good at boiling things down into descriptions, and when he found I was not disposed to talk, he fell silent and I was free to drowse over what I knew of the Trailmen and their world.

Nature seems to have a sameness on all inhabited worlds, tending toward the economy and simplicity of the human form. The upright carriage, freeing the hands, the opposable thumb, the color-sensitivity of retinal rods and cones, the development of language and of lengthy parental nurture—these things seem to be indispensable to the growth of civilization, and in the end they spell *human*. Except for minor variations depending on climate or footstuffs, the inhabitant of Megaera or Darkover is indistinguishable from the Terran or Sirian; differences are mainly cultural, and sometimes an isolated culture will mutate in a strange direction or remain atavists, somewhere halfway to the summit of the ladder of evolution—which, at least on the known planets, still reckons *homo sapiens* as the most complex of nature's forms.

The Trailmen were a pausing-place which had proved tenacious. When the mainstream of evolution on Darkover left the trees to struggle for existence on the ground, a few remained behind. Evolution did not cease for them, but evolved *homo arborens:* nocturnal, nyetalopic humanoids who live out their lives in the extensive forests.

The truck bumped over the bad, rutted roads. The wind was chilly. The truck, a mere conveyance for hauling, had no such refinements of luxury as windows. I jolted awake—what nonsense had I been thinking? Vague ideas about evolution swirled in my brain like burst bubbles—the Trailmen? They were just the Trailmen, who could explain them? Jay Allison, maybe? Rafe turned his head and asked, "Where do we pull up for the night? It's getting dark, and we have all this gear to sort!" I roused myself, and took over the business of the expedition again.

But when the trucks had been parked and a tent

pitched and the pack animals unloaded and hobbled, and a start made at getting the gear together—when all this had been done I lay awake, listening to Kendricks' heavy snoring, but myself afraid to sleep. Dozing in the truck, an odd lapse of consciousness had come over me—myself yet not myself, drowsing over thoughts I did not recognize as my own. If I slept, who would I be when I woke?

We had made our camp in the bend of an enormous river, wide and shallow and unbridged—the river Kadarin, traditionally a point of no return for humans on Darkover. Beyond the river lay thick forests, and beyond the forests the slopes of the Hellers, rising upward and upward; and their every fold and every valley was filled to the brim with forest, and in the forests lived the Trailmen.

But through all this country was thickly populated with outlying colonies and nests, it would be no use to bargain with any of them; we must deal with the Old One of the North Nest, where I had spent so many of my boyhood years.

From time immemorial, the Trailmen—usually inoffensive—had kept strict boundaries marked between their lands and the lands of ground-dwelling men. They never came beyond the Kadarin. On the other hand, any human who ventured into their territory became, by that act, fair game for attack.

A few of the Darkovan mountain people had trade treaties with the Trailmen; they traded clothing, forged metals, small implements, in return for nuts, bark for dyestuffs and certain leaves and mosses for drugs. In return, the Trailmen permitted them to hunt in the forest lands without being molested. But other humans, venturing into Trailmen territory, ran the risk of merciless raiding; the Trailmen were not bloodthirsty, and did not kill for the sake of killing, but they attacked in packs of two or three dozen, and their prey would be stripped and plundered of everything portable.

Traveling through their country would be dangerous.

I sat in front of the tent, staring at the expanse of water, rippling pink in the sunrise. The pack animals cropped short grass behind the tent. The trucks were vast sphinxes, shrouded under tarpaulins glistening with early dew. Regis Hastur came out of the tent, rubbed his eyes and joined me at the water's edge.

"What do you think? Is it going to be a bad trip?"

"I wouldn't think so. I know the main trails and I can keep clear of them. It's only—" I hesitated, and Regis demanded, "What else?"

I said it, after a minute. "It's—well, it's you. If anything happens to you, we'll be held responsible to all Darkover."

He grinned. In the red sunlight he looked like a painting from some old legend. "Responsibility? You didn't strike me as the worrying type, Jason. What sort of duffer do you take me for? I know how to handle myself in the mountains, and I'm not afraid of the Trailmen, even if I don't know them as you do. Come on—shall I get breakfast or will you?"

I shrugged, busying myself near the fire. Somewhat to the surprise of the other Terrans—Kendricks and Rafe—Regis had done his share of the camp work at every halt; not ostentatiously either, but cheerfully and matter-of-factly. This surprised Rafe and Kendricks, who accepted the Terran custom of the higher echelons leaving such things to the buck privates. But in spite of their rigid caste distinctions, social differences of the Terran type simply don't exist on Darkover. Neither does gallantry, and only Kendricks objected when Kyla took on the job of seeing to the packloading and did her share of heaving boxes and crates.

After a while Regis joined me at the fire again. The three roughneck brothers had come out and were splashing noisily in the ford of the river. The rest were still sleeping. Regis asked, "Shall I roust them out?"

"No need. The Kadarin's fed by ocean tides and we'll have to wait for low water to cross. Nearly noon before we could get across without ruining half our gear."

Regis sniffed at the kettle. "Sounds good," he decided, and dunked his bowl in; sat down, balancing the food on his knee. I followed suit, and Regis demanded, "Tell me something about yourself, Jason. Where did you learn so much about the Hellers? Lerrys was on the 'Narr campaign, but you don't seem old enough for that."

"I'm older than I look," I said, "but I wasn't old enough for that." (During the brief civil war when Darkovans fought Trailmen in the passes of 'Narr, I had—as a boy of eleven—spied on the human invaders; but I didn't tell Regis that.) "I lived with them for eight years."

"*Sharra!* Was that you?" The Darkovan prince looked genuinely impressed. "No wonder you got this assignment! Jason, I envy you!"

I gave a short bark of laughter.

"No, I'm serious, Jason. As a boy I tried to get into the Terran space service. But my family finally convinced me that as a Hastur I had my work already cut out for me—that we Hasturs were committed to trying to keep Terra and Darkover on a peaceful basis. It puts me at a terrific disadvantage, you know. They all think I ought to be wearing cushions around my head in case I take a tumble."

I snapped, "Then why in hell did they let you come on a dangerous mission like this?"

The Hastur's eyes twinkled, but his face was completely deadpan and his voice grave. "I pointed out to my grandsire that I have been assiduous in my duty to the

Hasturs. I have five sons, three legitimate, born in the past two years."

I choked, spluttered and exploded into laughter as Regis got to his feet and went to rinse his bowl in the river.

The sun was high before we left the camp. While the others were packing up the last oddments, ready for the saddle, I gave Kyla the task of readying the rucksacks we'd carry after the trails got too bad even for the pack animals, and went to stand at the water's edge, checking the depth of the ford and glancing up at the smoke-hazed rifts between peak and peak.

The men were packing up the small tent we'd use in the forests, moving around with a good deal of horseplay and a certain brisk bustle. They were a good crew, I'd already discovered. Rafe and Lerrys and the three Dark-ovan brothers were tireless, cheerful, and mountain-hardened. Kendricks, obviously out of his element, could be implicitly relied on to follow orders, and I felt that I could fall back on him. Strange as it seemed, the very fact that he was a Terran was vaguely comforting, where I'd anticipated it would be a nuisance.

The girl Kyla was still something of an unknown quan-tity. She was too taut and quiet, working her share but seldom contributing a word—we were not yet in moun-tain country. So far she was quiet and touchy with me, although she seemed natural enough with the Dark-ovans, and I let her alone.

"Hi, Jason, get a move on," someone shouted, and I walked back toward the clearing, squinting in the sun. It hurt, and I touched my face gingerly, suddenly realizing what had happened. Yesterday, riding in the uncovered truck, and this morning, unused to the fierce sun of these latitudes, I had neglected to take the proper precautions against exposure and my face was reddening with sunburn. I walked toward Kyla, who was cinching a final load on one of the pack animals, which she did efficiently enough.

She didn't wait for me to ask, but sized up the situation with one amused glance at my face. "Sunburn? Put some of this on it." She produced a tube of white stuff; I twisted at the top inexpertly, and she took it from me, squeezed the stuff out in her palm and said, "Stand still and bend down you head."

She smeared the mixture across my forehead and cheeks. It felt cold and good. I started to thank her, then broke off as she burst out laughing. "What's the matter?"

"You should see yourself!" she gurgled.

I wasn't amused. No doubt I presented a grotesque appearance, and no doubt she had the right to laugh at it, but I scowled. It hurt. Intending to put things back on the proper footing, I demanded, "Did you make up the climbing loads?"

"All except bedding. I wasn't sure how much to allow," she said. "Jason, have you eyeshades for when you get on snow?" I nodded, and she instructed severely, "Don't forget them. Snowblindness—I give you my word—is even more unpleasant than sunburn—and *very* painful!"

"Damn it, girl, I'm not stupid!" I exploded.

She said, in her expressionless monotone again, "Then you *ought* to have known better than to get sunburnt. Here, put this in your pocket," she handed me the tube of sunburn cream. "Maybe I'd better check up on some of the others and make sure they haven't forgotten." She went off without a word, leaving me with an unpleasant feeling that she'd come off best, that she considered me an irresponsible scamp.

Forth had said almost the same thing.

I told the Darkovan brothers to urge the pack animals across the narrowest part of the ford, and gestured to

Lerrys and Kyla to ride one on either side of Kendricks, who might not be aware of the swirling, treacherous currents of a mountain river. Rafe could not urge his edgy horse into the water; he finally dismounted, took off his boots, and led the creature across the slippery rocks. I crossed last, riding close to Regis Hastur, alert for dangers and thinking resentfully that anyone so important to Darkover's policies should not be risked on such a mission. Why, if the Terran Legate had (unthinkably!) come with us, he would be surrounded by bodyguards, Secret Service men and dozens of precautions against accident, assassination or misadventure.

All that day we rode upward, encamping at the furthest point we could travel with pack animals or mounted. The next day's climb would enter the dangerous trails we must travel afoot. We pitched a comfortable camp, but I admit I slept badly. Kendricks and Lerrys and Rafe had blinding headaches from the sun and the thinness of the air; I was more used to these conditions, but I felt a sense of unpleasant pressure, and my ears rang. Regis arrogantly denied any discomfort, but he moaned and cried out continuously in his sleep until Lerrys kicked him, after which he was silent and, I feared, sleepless. Kyla seemed the least affected of any; probably she had been at higher altitudes more continuously than any of us. But there were dark circles beneath her eyes.

However, no one complained as we readied ourselves for the last long climb upward. If we were fortunate, we could cross Dammerung before nightfall; at the very least, we should bivouac tonight very near the pass. Our camp had been made at the last level spot; we partially hobbled the pack animals so they would not stray too far, and left ample food for them, and cached all but the most necessary of light trail gear. As we prepared to start upward on the steep, narrow track—hardly more than a rabbit-run—I glanced at Kyla and stated, "We'll work on rope from the first stretch. Starting now."

One of the Darkovan brothers stared at me with contempt. "Call yourself a mountain man, Jason? Why, my little daughter could scramble up *that* track without so much as a push on her behind!"

I set my chin and glared at him. "The rocks aren't easy, and some of these men aren't used to working on rope at all. We might as well get used to it, because when we start working along the ledges, I don't want anybody who doesn't know how."

They still didn't like it, but nobody protested further until I directed the huge Kendricks to the center of the second rope. He glared viciously at the light nylon line and demanded with some apprehension, "Hadn't I better go last until I know what I'm doing? Hemmed in between the two of you, I'm apt to do something damned dumb!"

Hjalmar roared with laughter and informed him that the center place on a three-man rope was always reserved for weaklings, novices and amateurs. I expected Kendricks' temper to flare up; the burly Spaceforce man and the Darkovan giant glared at one another, then Kendricks only shrugged and knotted the line through his belt. Kyla warned Kendricks and Lerrys about looking down from ledges, and we started.

The first stretch was almost too simple, a clear track winding higher and higher for a couple of miles. Pausing to rest for a moment, we could turn and see the entire valley outspread below us. Gradually the trail grew steeper, in spots pitched almost at a 50-degree angle, and was scattered with gravel, loose rock and shale, so that we placed our feet carefully, leaning forward to catch at handholds and steady ourselves against rocks. I tested each boulder carefully, since any weight placed against an unsteady rock might dislodge it on somebody below.

One of the Darkovan brothers—Vardo, I thought—was behind me, separated by ten or twelve feet of slack rope, and twice when his feet slipped on gravel he stumbled and gave me an unpleasant jerk. What he muttered was perfectly true; on slopes like this, where a fall wasn't dangerous anyhow, it was better to work unroped; then a slip bothered no one but the slipper. But I was finding out what I wanted to know—what kind of climbers I had to lead through the Hellers.

Along a cliff face the trail narrowed horizontally, leading across a foot-wide ledge overhanging a sheer drop of fifty feet and covered with loose shale and scrub plants. Nothing, of course, to an experienced climber—a foot-wide ledge might as well be a four-lane superhighway. Kendricks made a nervous joke about a tightrope walker, but when his turn came he picked his way securely, without losing balance. The amateurs—Lerrys Ridenow, Regis, Rafe—came across without hesitation, but I wondered how well they would have done at a less secure altitude; to a real mountaineer, a footpath is a footpath, whether in a meadow, above a two-foot drop, a thirty-foot ledge, or a sheer mountain face three miles above the first level spot.

After crossing the ledge, the going was harder. A steeper trail, in places nearly imperceptible, led between thick scrub and overhanging trees, closely clustered. In spots their twisted roots obscured the trail; in others the persistent growth had thrust aside rocks and dirt. We had to make our way through tangles of underbrush which would have been nothing to a Trailman, but which made our ground-accustomed bodies ache with the effort of getting over or through them; and once the track was totally blocked by a barricade of tangled dead brushwood, borne down on floodwater after a sudden thaw or cloudburst. We had to work painfully around it over a three-hundred-foot rockslide, which we could cross only one at a time, crab-fashion, leaning double to balance ourselves; and no one complained now about the rope.

Toward noon I had the first intimation that we were not alone on the slope.

At first it was no more than a glimpse of motion out of the corner of my eyes, the shadow of a shadow. The fourth time I saw it, I called softly to Kyla, "See anything?"

"I was beginning to think it was my eyes, or the altitude. I saw, Jason."

"Look for a spot where we can take a break," I directed. We climbed along a shallow edge, the faint imperceptible flutters in the brushwood climbing with us on either side. I muttered to the girl, "I'll be glad when we get clear of this. At least we'll be able to see what's coming after us!"

"If it comes to a fight," she said suprisingly, "I'd rather fight on gravel than ice."

Over a rise, there was a roaring sound. Kyla swung up and balanced on a rock-wedged tree root, cupped her mouth to her hands, and called, "Rapids!"

I pulled myself up to the edge of the drop and stood looking down into the narrow gully. Here the track we had been following was crossed and obscured by the deep, roaring rapids of a mountain stream.

Less than twenty feet across, it tumbled in an icy flood, almost a waterfall, pitching over the lip of a crag above us. It had sliced a ravine five feet deep in the mountainside, and came roaring down with a rushing noise that made my head vibrate. It looked formidable; anyone stepping into it would be knocked off his feet in seconds, and swept a thousand feet down the mountainside by the force of the current.

Rafe scrambled gingerly over the gullied lip of the channel it had cut, and bent carefully to scoop up water in his palm and drink. "Phew, it's colder than Zandru's ninth hell. Must come straight down from a glacier!"

It did. I remembered the trail and remembered the spot. Kendricks joined me at the water's edge, and asked, "How do we get across?"

"I'm not sure," I said, studying the racing white torrent. Overhead, about twenty feet from where we clustered on the slope, the thick branches of enormous trees overhung the rapids, their long roots partially bared, gnarled and twisted by recurrent floods; and between these trees swayed one of the queer swing-bridges of the Trailmen, hanging only about ten feet above the water.

Even I had never learned to navigate one of these swinging bridges without assistance; human arms are no longer suited to brachiation. I might have managed it once; but at present, except as a desperate final expedient, it was out of the question. Rafe or Lerrys, who were lightly built and acrobatic, could probably do it as a simple stunt on the level, in a field; on a steep and rocky mountainside, where a fall might mean being dashed a thousand feet down the torrent, I doubted it. The Trailmen's bridge was out—but what other choice was there?

I beckoned to Kendricks, he being the man I was the most inclined to trust with my life at the moment, and said, "It looks uncrossable, but I think two men could get across, if they were steady on their feet. The others can hold us on ropes, in case we do get knocked down. If we can get to the opposite bank, we can stretch a fixed rope from that snub of rock—" I pointed, "and the others can cross with that. The first men over will be the only ones to run any risk. Want to try?"

I liked it better that he didn't answer right away, but went to the edge of the gully and peered down the rocky chasm. Doubtless, if we were knocked down, all seven of the others could haul us up again; but not before we'd been badly smashed on the rocks. And once again I caught that elusive shadow of movement in the brushwood; if the Trailmen chose a moment when we were half-in, half-out of the rapids, we'd be ridiculously vulnerable to attack.

"We ought to be able to get a fixed rope easier than that," Hjalmar said, and took one of the spares from his rucksack. He coiled it, making a running loop on one end, and, standing precariously on the lip of the rapids, sent it spinning toward the outcrop of rock we had chosen as a fixed point. "If I can get it over—"

The rope fell short, and Hjalmar reeled it in and cast the loop again. He made three more unsuccessful tries before finally, with held breath, we watched the noose settle over the rocky snub. Gently, pulling the line taut, we watched it stretch above the rapids. The knot tightened, fastened. Hjalmar grinned and let out his breath.

"There," he said, and jerked hard on the rope, testing it with a long hard pull. The rocky outcrop broke, with a sharp *crack*, split, and toppled entire into the rapids, the sudden jerk almost pulling Hjalmar off his feet. The boulder rolled, with a great bouncing splash, faster and faster down the mountain, taking the rope with it.

We just stood and stared for a minute. Hjalmar swore horribly, in the unprintable filth of the mountain tongue, and his brothers joined in. "How the devil was I to know the *rock* would split off?"

"Better for it to split now than when we were depending on it," Kyla said stolidly. "I have a better idea." She was untying herself from the rope as she spoke, and knotting one of the spares through her belt. She handed the other end of the rope to Lerrys. "Hold on to this," she said, and slipped out of her blanket windbreak, standing shivering in a thin sweater. She unstrapped her boots and

tossed them to me. "Now boost me on your shoulders,
Hjalmar."

Too late, I guessed her intention and shouted, "No,
don't try—" But she had already clambered to an unsteady perch on the big Darkovan's shoulders and made
a flying grab for the lowest loop of the trailmen's bridge.
She hung there, swaying slightly and sickeningly, as the
loose lianas gave to her weight.

"Hjalmar—Lerrys—haul her down!"

"I'm lighter than any of you," Kyla called shrilly, "and
not hefty enough to be any use on the ropes!" Her voice
quavered somewhat as she added, "—and hang on to
that rope, Lerrys! If you lose it, I'll have done this for
nothing!"

She gripped the loop of vine and reached, with her
free hand, for the next loop. Now she was swinging out
over the edge of the boiling rapids. Tight-mouthed, I
gestured to the others to spread out slightly below—not
that anything would help her if she fell.

Hjalmar, watching as the woman gained the third
loop, which joggled horribly to her slight weight,
shouted suddenly, "Kyla, quick! The loop *beyond*—don't
touch the next one! It's frayed—rotted through!"

Kyla brought her left hand up to her right on the third
loop. She made a long reach, missed her grab, swung
again, and clung, breathing hard, to the safe fifth loop. I
watched, sick with dread. The damned girl should have
told me what she intended.

Kyla glanced down and we got a glimpse of her face,
glistening with the mixture of sunburn cream and sweat,
drawn with effort. Her tiny swaying figure hung twelve
feet above the white tumbling water, and if she lost her
grip, only a miracle could bring her out alive. She hung
there for a minute, jiggling slightly, then started a long
back-and-forward swing. On the third forward swing she
made a long leap and grabbed at the final loop.

It slipped through her fingers; she made a wild grab with the other hand, and the liana dipped sharply under her weight, raced through her fingers, and, with a sharp snap, broke in two. She gave a wild shriek as it parted, and twisted her body frantically in mid-air, landing asprawl half-in, half-out of the rapids, but on the further bank. She hauled her legs up on dry land and crouched there, drenched to the waist but safe.

The Darkovans were yelling in delight. I motioned to Lerrys to make his end of the rope fast around a hefty tree-root, and shouted, "Are you hurt?" She indicated in pantomime that the thundering of the water drowned words, and bent to secure her end of the rope. In sign language I gestured to her to make very sure of the knots; if anyone slipped, she hadn't the weight to hold us.

I hauled on the rope myself to test it, and it held fast. I slung her boots around my neck by their cords, then, gripping the fixed rope, Kendricks and I stepped into the water.

It was even icier than I expected, and my first step was nearly the last; the rush of the white water knocked me to my knees, and I floundered and would have measured my length except for my hands on the fixed rope. Buck Kendricks grabbed at me, letting go the rope to do it, and I swore at him, raging, while we got on our feet again and braced ourselves against the onrushing current. While we struggled in the pounding waters, I admitted to myself that we could never have crossed without the rope Kyla had risked her life to fix.

Shivering, we got across and hauled ourselves out. I signaled to the others to cross two at a time, and Kyla seized my elbow. "Jason—"

"Later, dammit!" I had to shout to make myself heard over the roaring water, as I held out a hand to help Rafe get his footing on the ledge.

"This—can't—wait," she yelled, cupping her hands

and shouting into my ear. I turned on her. *"What!"*

"There are—*Trailmen*—on the top level—of that bridge! I saw them! They cut the loop!"

Regis and Hjalmar came struggling across last; Regis, lighty-built, was swept off his feet and Hjalmar turned to grab him, but I shouted to him to keep clear—they were still roped together and if the ropes fouled we might drown someone. Lerrys and I leaped down and hauled Regis clear; he coughed, spitting icy water, drenched to the skin.

I motioned to Lerrys to leave the fixed rope, though I had little hope that it would be there when we returned, and looked quickly around, debating what to do. Regis and Rafe and I were wet clear through; the others were wet to well above the knee. At this altitude, this was dangerous, although we were not yet high enough to worry about frostbite. Trailmen or no Trailmen, we must run the lesser risk of finding a place where we could kindle a fire and dry out.

"Up there—there's a clearing," I said briefly, and hurried them along.

It was hard climbing now, on rock, and there were places where we had to scrabble for handholds, and flatten ourselves out against an almost sheer wall. The keen wind rose as we climbed higher, whining through the thick forest, soughing in the rocky outcrops, and biting through our soaked clothing with icy teeth. Kendricks was having hard going now, and I helped him as much as I could, but I was aching with cold. We gained the clearing, a small bare spot on a lesser peak, and I directed the two Darkovan brothers, who were the driest, to gather dry brushwood and get a fire going. It was hardly near enough to sunset to camp. But by the time we were dry enough to go on safely, it would be, so I gave orders to get the tent up, then rounded angrily on Kyla:

"See here, another time don't try any dangerous tricks unless you're ordered to!"

"Go easy on her," Regis Hastur interceded, "we'd never have crossed without the fixed rope. Good work, girl."

"You keep out of this!" I snapped. It was true, yet resentment boiled in me as Kyla's plain sullen face glowed under the praise from Hastur.

The fact was—I admitted it grudgingly—a light-weight like Kyla ran less risk on an acrobat's bridge than in that kind of roaring current. That did not lessen my annoyance; and Regis Hastur's interference, and the foolish grin on the girl's face, made me boil over.

I wanted to question her further about the sight of Trailmen on the bridge, but decided against it. We had been spared attack on the rapids, so it wasn't impossible that a group, not hostile, was simply watching our progress—maybe even aware that we were on a peaceful mission.

But I didn't believe it for a minute. If I knew anything about the Trailmen, it was this—one could not judge them by human standards at all. I tried to decide what I would have done, as a Trailman, but my brain wouldn't run that way at the moment.

The Darkovan brothers had built up the fire with a thoroughly reckless disregard of watching eyes. It seemed to me that the morale and fitness of the shivering crew was of more value at the moment than caution; and around the roaring fire, feeling my soaked clothes warming to the blaze and drinking boiling hot tea from a mug, it seemed that we were right. Optimism reappeared. Kyla, letting Hjalmar dress her hands which had been rubbed raw by the slipping lianas, made jokes with the men about her feat of acrobatics.

We had made camp on the summit of an outlying arm

of the main ridge of the Hellers, and the whole massive range lay before our eyes, turned to a million colors in the declining sun. Green and turquoise and rose, the mountains were even more beautiful than I remembered. The shoulder of the high slope we had just climbed had obscured the real mountain *massif* from our sight, and I saw Kendricks' eyes widen as he realized that this high summit we had just mastered was only the first step of the task which lay before us. The real ridge rose ahead, thickly forested on the lower slopes, then strewn with rock and granite like the landscape of an airless, deserted moon. And above the rock, there were straight walls capped with blinding snow and ice. Down one peak a glacier flowed, a waterfall, a cascade shockingly arrested in motion. I murmured the Trailmen's name for the mountain, aloud, and translated it for the others:

"The Wall around the World."

"Good name for it," Lerrys murmured, coming with his mug in his hand to look at the mountain. "Jason, the big peak there has never been climbed, has it?"

"I can't remember." My teeth were chattering and I went back toward the fire. Regis surveyed the distant glacier and murmured, "It doesn't look too bad. There could be a route along that western *arête*—Hjalmar, weren't you with the expedition that climbed and mapped High Kimbi?"

The giant nodded, rather proudly. "We got within a hundred feet of the top, then a snowstorm came up and we had to turn back. Some day we'll tackle the Wall around the World—it's been tried, but no one ever climbed the peak."

"No one ever will," Lerrys stated positively, "There's two hundred feet of sheer rock cliff. Prince Regis, you'd need wings to get up. And there's the avalanche ledge they call Hell's Alley—"

Kendricks broke in irritably, "I don't care whether it's

ever been climbed or ever will be climbed, we're not going
to climb it now!" He stared at me and added, "I hope!"

"We're not." I was glad of the interruption. If the
youngsters and amateurs wanted to amuse themselves
plotting hypothetical attacks on unclimbable sierras,
that was all very well, but it was, if nothing worse, a great
waste of time. I showed Kendricks a notch in the ridge,
thousands of feet lower than the peaks, and well
sheltered from the ice falls on either side.

"That's Dammerung; we're going through there. We
won't be on the mountain at all, and it's less than 22,000
feet high in the pass—although there are some bad
ledges and washes. We'll keep clear of the main tree-
roads if we can, and all the mapped Trailmen's villages,
but we may run into wandering bands—" abruptly I
made my decision and gestured them around me.

"From this point," I broke the news, "we're liable to
be attacked. Kyla, tell them what you saw."

She put down her mug. Her face was serious again, as
she related what she had seen on the bridge. "We're on
a peaceful mission, but they don't know that yet. The
thing to remember is that they do not wish to kill, only to
wound and rob. If we show fight—" she displayed a short
ugly knife, which she tucked matter-of-factly into her
shirt-front, "they will run away again."

Lerrys loosened a narrow dagger which, until this moment, I had thought purely ornamental. He said, "Mind
if I say something more, Jason? I remember from the
'Narr campaign—the Trailmen fight at close quarters,
and by human standards they fight dirty." He looked
around fiercely, his unshaven face glinting as he grinned.
"One more thing. I like elbow room. Do we have to stay
roped together when we start out again."

I thought it over. His enthusiasm for a fight made me
feel both annoyed and curiously delighted. "I won't
make anyone stay roped who thinks he'd be safer without

it," I said. "We'll decide that when the time comes, anyway. But personally—the Trailmen are used to running along narrow ledges, and we're not. Their first tactic would probably be to push us off, one by one. If we're roped, we can fend them off better." I dismissed the subject, adding, "Just now, the important thing is to dry out."

Kendricks remained at my side after the others had gathered around the fire, looking into the thick forest which sloped up to our campsite. He said, "This place looks as if it had been used for a camp before. Aren't we just as vulnerable to attack here as we would be anywhere else?"

He had hit on the one thing I hadn't wanted to talk about. This clearing was altogether too convenient. I only said, "At least there aren't so many ledges to push us off."

Kendricks muttered, "You've got the only blaster!"

"I left it at Carthon," I said truthfully. Then I laid down the law:

"Listen, Buck. If we kill a single Trailman, except in hand-to-hand fight in self-defense, we might as well pack up and go home. We're on a peaceful mission, and we're begging a favor. Even if we're attacked—we kill only as a last resort, and in hand-to-hand combat!"

"Damned primitive frontier planet—"

"Would you rather die of the Trailmen's disease?"

He said savagely, "We're apt to catch it anyway— here. You're immune, you don't care, you're safe! The rest of us are on a suicide mission—and damn it, when I die I want to take a few of those goddam monkeys with me!"

I bent my head, bit my lip and said nothing. Buck couldn't be blamed for the way he felt. After a moment, I pointed to the notch in the ridge again. "It's not so far. Once we get through Dammerung, it's easy going into the Trailmen's city. Beyond there, it's all civilized."

"Maybe *you* call it civilization," Kendricks said, and turned away.

"Come on, let's finish drying our feet."

And at that moment they hit us.

CHAPTER FIVE

KENDRICKS' YELL was the only warning I had before I was fighting away something scrabbling up my back. I whirled and ripped the creature away, and saw dimly that the clearing was filled to the rim with an explosion of furry white bodies. I cupped my hands and yelled, in the only Trailman dialect I knew, "Hold off! We come in peace!"

One of them yelled something unintelligible and plunged at me—another tribe! I saw a white-furred, chinless face, contorted in rage, a small ugly knife—a female! I ripped out my own knife, fending away a savage slash. Something tore white-hot across the knuckles of my hand; the fingers went limp and my knife fell, and the Trailman woman snatched it up and made off with her prize, swinging lithely upward into the treetops.

I searched quickly, gripped with my good hand at the bleeding knuckles, and found Regis Hastur struggling at the edge of a ledge with a pair of the creatures. The crazy thought ran through my mind that if they killed him all Darkover would rise and exterminate the Trailmen and it would all be my fault. Then Regis tore one hand free, and made a curious motion with his fingers.

54

It looked like an immense green spark a foot long, or like a fireball. It exploded in one creature's white face and she gave a wild howl of terror and anguish, scrabbled blindly at her eyes, and with a despairing shriek, ran for the shelter of the trees. The pack of Trailmen gave a long formless wail, and then they were gathering, flying, retreating into the shadows. Rafe yelled something obscene and then a bolt of bluish flame lanced toward the retreating pack. One of the humanoids fell without a cry, pitching senseless over the ledge.

I ran toward Rafe, struggling with him for the shocker he had drawn from its hiding place inside his shirt. "You blind damned fool!" I cursed him. "You may have ruined everything—"

"They'd have killed him without it," he retorted wrathfully. He had evidently failed to see how efficiently Regis defended himself. Rafe motioned toward the fleeing pack and sneered, "Why don't you go with your friends?"

With a grip I thought I had forgotten, I got my hand around Rafe's knuckles and squeezed. His hand went limp and I snatched the shocker and pitched it over the ledge.

"One word and I'll pitch you after it," I warned. "Who's hurt?"

Garin was blinking senselessly, half dazed by a blow; Regis' forehead had been gashed and dripped blood, and Hjalmar's thigh sliced in a clean cut. My own knuckles were laid bare and the hand was getting numb. It was a little while before anybody noticed Kyla, crouched over speechless with pain. She reeled and turned deathly white when we touched her; we stretched her out where she was, and got her shirt off, and Kendricks crowded up beside us to examine the wound.

"A clean cut," he said, but I didn't hear. Something

had turned over inside me, like a hand stirring up my
brain, and . . .

Jay Allison looked around with a gasp of sudden vertigo. He was not in Forth's office, but standing precariously near the edge of a cliff. He shut his eyes briefly,
wondering if he were having one of his worst nightmares,
and opened them on a familiar face.

Buck Kendricks was bone-white, his mouth widening
as he said hoarsely, "Jay! Doctor Allison—for God's
sake—"

A doctor's training creates reactions that are almost reflexes; Jay Allison recovered some degree of sanity as he
became aware that someone was stretched out in front of
him, half naked, and bleeding profusely. He motioned
away the crowding strangers and said in his bad Darkovan, "Let her alone, this is my work." He didn't know
enough words to curse them away, so he switched to Terran, speaking to Kendricks:

"Buck, get these people away, give the patient some
air. Where's my surgical case?" He bent and probed
briefly, realizing only now that the injured was a woman,
and young.

The wound was only a superficial laceration; whatever
sharp instrument had inflicted it, had turned on the
costal bone without penetrating lung tissue. It could
have been sutured, but Kendricks handed him only a
badly-filled first-aid kit; so Dr. Allison covered it tightly
with a plastic clipshield which would seal it from further
bleeding, and let it alone. By the time he had finished,
the strange girl had begun to stir. She said haltingly,
"Jason—?"

"Dr. Allison," he corrected tersely, surprised in a minor way—the major surprise had blurred lesser ones—
that she knew his name. Kendricks spoke swiftly to the
girl, in one of the Darkovan languages Jay didn't under-

stand, and then drew Jay aside, out of earshot. He said in a shaken voice, "Jay, I didn't know—I wouldn't have believed—you're *Doctor Allison?* Good God—Jason!"

And then he moved fast. "What's the matter? Oh, Christ, Jay, don't faint on me!"

Jay was aware that he didn't come out of it too bravely, but anyone who blamed him (he thought resentfully) should try it on for size; going to sleep in a comfortably closed-in office and waking up on a cliff at the outer edges of nowhere. His hand hurt; he saw that it was bleeding and flexed it experimentally, trying to determine that no tendons had been injured. He rapped, "How did this happen?"

"Sir, keep your voice down—or speak Darkovan!"

Jay blinked again. Kendricks was still the only familiar thing in a strangely vertiginous universe. The Spaceforce man said huskily, "Before God, Jay, I hadn't any idea—and I've known you how long? Eight, nine years?"

Jay said, "That idiot Forth!" and swore, the colorless profanity of an indoor man.

Somebody shouted, "Jason!" in an imperative voice, and Kendricks said shakily, "Jay, if they see you—you literally are not the same man!"

"Obviously not." Jay looked at the tent, one pole still unpitched. "Anyone in there?"

"Not yet." Kendricks almost shoved him inside. "I'll tell them—I'll tell them something." He took a radiant from his pocket, set it down and stared at Allison in the flickering light, and said something profane. "You'll—you'll be all right here?"

Jay nodded. It was all he could manage. He was keeping a tight hold on his nerves; if it went, he'd start to rave like a madman. A little time passed, there were strange noises outside, and then there was a polite cough and a man walked into the tent.

He was obviously a Darkovan aristocrat and looked vaguely familiar, though Jay had no conscious memory of seeing him before. Tall and slender, he possessed that perfect and exquisite masculine beauty sometimes seen among Darkovans, and he spoke to Jay familiarly but with surprising courtesy:

"I have told them you are not to be disturbed for a moment, that your hand is worse than we believed. A surgeon's hands are delicate things, Doctor Allison, and I hope that yours are not badly injured. Will you let me look?"

Jay Allison drew back his hand automatically, then, conscious of the churlishness of the gesture, let the stranger take it in his and look at the fingers. The man said, "It does not seem serious. I was sure it was something more than that." He raised grave eyes. "You don't even remember my name, do you, Dr. Allison?"

"You know who I am?"

"Dr. Forth didn't tell me. But we Hasturs are partly telepathic, Jason—forgive me—Doctor Allison. I have known from the first that you were possessed by a god or daemon."

"Superstitious rubbish," Jay snapped. "Typical of a Darkovan!"

"It is a convenient manner of speaking, no more," said the young Hastur, overlooking the rudeness. "I suppose I could learn your terminology, if I considered it worth the effort. I have had psi training, and I can tell the difference when half of a man's soul has driven out the other half. Perhaps I can restore you to yourself—"

"If you think I'd have some Darkovan freak meddling with my mind—" Jay began hotly, then stopped. Under Regis' grave eyes, he felt a surge of unfamiliar humility. This crew of men needed their leader, and obviously he, Jay Allison, wasn't the leader they needed. He covered his eyes with one hand.

Regis bent and put a hand on his shoulder, compassionately, but Jay twitched it off, and his voice, when he found it, was bitter and defensive and cold.

"All right. The work's the thing. I can't do it, Jason can. You're a parapsych. If you can switch me off—go right ahead!"

I stared at Regis, passing a hand across my forehead. "What happened?" I demanded, and in even swifter apprehension, "Where's Kyla? She was hurt—"

"Kyla's all right," Regis said, but I got up quickly to make sure. Kyla was outside, lying quite comfortably on a roll of blankets. She was propped up on her elbow drinking something hot, and there was a good smell of hot food in the air. I stared at Regis and demanded, "I didn't conk out, did I, from a little scratch like this?" I looked carelessly at my gashed hand.

"Wait—" Regis held me back, "don't go out just yet. Do you remember what happened, Doctor Allison?"

I stared in growing horror, my worst fear confirmed. Regis said quietly, "You—changed. Probably from the shock of seeing—" he stopped in mid-sentence, and I said, "The last thing I remember is seeing that Kyla was bleeding, when we got her clothes off. But—good Gods, a little blood wouldn't scare *me*, and Jay Allison's a surgeon, would it bring him roaring up like that?"

"I couldn't say." Regis looked as if he knew more than he was telling. "I don't believe that Dr. Allison—he's not much like you—was very concerned with Kyla. Are you?"

"Damn right I am. I want to make sure she's all right—" I stopped abruptly. "Regis—did they all see it?"

"Only Kendricks and I," Regis said, "and we will not speak of it."

I said, "Thanks," and felt his reassuring handclap. Damn it, demigod or prince, I *liked* Regis.

I went out and accepted some food from the kettle and sat down between Kyla and Kendricks to eat. I was shaken, weak with reaction. Furthermore, I realized that we couldn't stay here. It was too vulnerable to attack. So, in our present condition, were we. If we could push on hard enough to get near Dammerung Pass tonight, then tomorrow we could cross it early, before the sun warmed the snow and we had snowslides and slush to deal with. Beyond Dammerung, I knew the tribesmen and could speak their language.

I mentioned this, and Kendricks looked doubtfully at Kyla. "Can she climb?"

"Can she stay here?" I countered. But I went and sat beside her anyhow:

"How badly are you hurt? Do you think you can travel?"

She said fiercely, "Of course I can climb! I tell you, I'm no weak girl, I'm a free Amazon!" She flung off the blanket somebody had tucked around her legs. Her lips looked a little pinched, but the long stride was steady as she walked to the fire and demanded more soup.

We struck the camp in minutes. The Trailmen band of raiding females had snatched up almost everything portable, and there was no sense in striking and catching the tent; they'd return and hunt it out. If we came back with a Trailman escort, we wouldn't need it anyway. I ordered them to leave everything but the lightest gear, and examined each remaining rucksack. Rations for the night we would spend in the pass, our few remaining blankets, ropes, sunglasses. Everything else I ruthlessly ordered left behind.

It was harder going now. For one thing, the sun was lowering, and the evening wind was icy. Nearly every one of us had some hurt, slight in itself, which hindered us in climbing. Kyla was white and rigid, but did not spare herself; Kendricks was suffering from mountain

sickness at this altitude, and I gave him all the help I
could, but with my stiffening slashed hand I wasn't having too easy a time myself.

There was one expanse that was sheer rock-climbing,
flattened like bugs against a wall, scrabbling for handholds and footholds. I felt it a point of pride to lead, and
I led; but by the time we had climbed the thirty-foot
wall, and scrambled along a ledge to where we could pick
up the trail again, I was ready to give over. Crowding
together on the ledge, I changed places with the veteran
Lerrys, who was better than most professional climbers.

He muttered, "I thought you said this was a *trail!*"

I stretched my mouth in what was supposed to be a
grin and didn't quite make it. "For the Trailmen, this is
a super-highway. And no one else ever comes this way."

Now we climbed slowly over snow; once or twice we
had to flounder through drifts, and once a brief bitter
snowstorm blotted out sight for twenty minutes, while
we hugged each other on the ledge, clinging wildly
against wind and icy sleet.

We bivouacked that night in a crevasse blown almost
clean of snow, well above the tree-line, where only scrub-
by unkillable thornbushes clustered. We tore down some
of them and piled them up as a windbreak, and bedded
beneath it; but we all thought with aching regret of the
comfort of the camp gear we'd abandoned.

That night remains in my mind as one of the most
miserable in memory. Except for the slight ringing in my
ears, the height alone did not bother me, but the others
did not fare so well. Most of the men had blinding headaches, Kyla's slashed side must have given her considerable pain, and Kendricks had succumbed to
mountain-sickness in its most agonizing form: severe
cramps and vomiting. I was desperately uneasy about all
of them, but there was nothing I could do; the only cure
for mountain-sickness is oxygen or a lower altitude,

neither of which was practical.

In the windbreak we doubled up, sharing blankets and body warmth. I took a last look around the close space before crawling in beside Kendricks, and saw the girl bedding down slightly apart from the others. I started to say something, but Kendricks spoke first.

"Better crawl in with us, girl." He added, coldly but not unkindly, "You needn't worry about any funny stuff."

Kyla gave me just the flicker of a grin, and I realized she was including me on the Darkovan side of a joke against this big man who was so unaware of Darkovan etiquette. But her voice was cool and curt as she said, "I'm not worrying," and loosened her heavy coat slightly before creeping into the nest of blankets between us.

It was painfully cramped, and chilly in spite of the self-heating blankets; we crowded close together and Kyla's head rested on my shoulder. I felt her snuggle closely to me, half asleep, hunting for a warm place; and I found myself very much aware of her closeness, curiously grateful to her. An ordinary woman would have protested, if only as a matter of form, to sharing blankets with two strange men. I realized that if Kyla had refused to crawl in with us, she would have called attention to her sex much *more* than she did by matter-of-factly behaving as if she were male.

She shivered convulsively, and I whispered, "Side hurting? Are you cold?"

"A little. It's been a long time since I've been at these altitudes, too. What it really is—I can't get those women out of my head."

Kendricks coughed, moving uncomfortably. "I don't understand—those creatures who attacked us—all women—?"

I explained briefly. "Among the People of the Sky, as everywhere, more females are born than males. But the

Trailmen's lives are so balanced that they have no room
for extra females within the Nests—the cities. So when a
girl child of the Sky People reaches womanhood, the other women drive her out of the city with kicks and blows,
and she has to wander in the forest until some male
comes after her and claims her and brings her back as his
own. Then she can never be driven forth again, although
if she bears no children she can be forced to be a servant
to his other wives."

Kendricks made a little sound of disgust.

"You think it cruel," Kyla said with sudden passion,
"but in the forest they can live and find their own food;
they will not starve or die. Many of them prefer the forest
life to living in the Nests, and they will fight away any
male who comes near them. We who call ourselves human often make less provision for our spare women."

She was silent, sighing as if with pain. Kendricks made
no reply except for a non-committal grunt. I held myself
back by main force from touching Kyla, remembering
what she was, and finally said, "We'd better quit talking.
The others want to sleep, if we don't."

After a time I heard Kendricks snoring, and Kyla's
quiet even breaths. I wondered drowsily how Jay would
have felt about this situation—he who hated Darkover
and avoided contact with every other human being,
crowded between a Darkovan free Amazon and half a
dozen assorted roughnecks. I turned the thought off,
fearing it might somehow rearouse him in his brain.

But I had to think of something, anything to turn aside
this consciousness of the woman's head against my chest,
her warm breath coming and going against my bare
neck. Only by the severest possible act of will did I keep
myself from slipping my hand over her breasts, warm
and palpable though the thin sweater. I wondered why
Forth had called me undisciplined. I couldn't risk my
leadership by making advances to our contracted guide

—woman, Amazon or whatever.

Somehow the girl seemed to be the pivot point of all my thoughts. She was not part of the Terran HQ, she was not part of any world Jay Allison might have known. She belonged wholly to Jason, to *my* world. Between sleep and waking, I lost myself in a dream of skimming flight-wise along the tree-roads, chasing the distant form of a girl driven from the Nest that day with blows and curses. Somewhere in the leaves I would find her—and we would return to the city, her head garlanded with the red leaves of a chosen-one, and the same women who had stoned her forth would crowd about and welcome her when she returned. The fleeing woman looked over her shoulder with Kyla's eyes; and then the woman's form muted and Dr. Forth was standing between us in the tree-road, with the caduceus emblem on his coat stretched like a red staff between us. Kendricks in his Spaceforce uniform was threatening us with a blaster, and Regis Hastur was suddenly wearing a Space Service uniform too and saying, "Jay Allison, Jay Allison," as the tree-road splintered and cracked beneath our feet and we were tumbling down the waterfall and down and down and down . . .

"Wake up!" Kyla whispered, and dug an elbow into my side. I opened my eyes on crowded blackness, grasping at the vanishing nightmare. "What's the matter?"

"You were moaning. Touch of altitude sickness?"

I grunted, realized my arm was around her shoulder, and pulled it quickly away. After a while I slept again, fitfully.

Before light we crawled wearily out of the bivouac, cramped and stiff and not rested, but ready to get out of this and go on. The snow was hard, in the dim light, and the trail was not difficult here. After all the trouble on the lower slopes, I think even the amateurs had lost their desire for adventurous climbing; we were all just as well pleased that the actual crossing of Dammerung should be an anticlimax and uneventful.

The sun was just rising when we reached the pass, and we stood for a moment, gathered close together, in the narrow defile between the great summits to either side.

Hjalmar gave the peaks a wistful look.

"Wish we could climb them."

Regis grinned at him companionably. "Someday—and you have the word of a Hastur, you'll be along on that expedition." The big fellow's eyes glowed. Regis turned to me, and said warmly, "What about it, Jason? A bargain? Shall we all climb it together, next year?"

I started to grin back and then some bleak black devil surged up in me, raging. When this was over, I'd suddenly realized, I wouldn't be there. I wouldn't be anywhere. I was a surrogate, a substitute, a splinter of Jay Allison, and when it was over, Forth and his tactics would put me back into what they considered my rightful place— which was nowhere. I'd never climb a mountain except now, when we were racing against time and necessity. I set my mouth in an unaccustomed narrow line and said, "We'll talk about that when we get back—if we ever do. Now I suggest we get going. Some of us would like to get down to lower altitudes."

The trail down from Dammerung inside the ridge, unlike the outside trail, was clear and well-marked, and we wound down the slope, walking in easy single file. As the mist thinned and we left the snowline behind, we saw what looked like a great green carpet, interspersed with shining colors which were mere flickers below us. I pointed them out.

"The treetops of the North Forest—and the colors you see—are in the streets of the Trailcity."

An hour's walking brought us to the edge of the forest. We traveled swiftly now, forgetting our weariness, eager to reach the city before nightfall. It was quiet in the forest, almost ominously still. Over our heads somewhere, in the thick branches which in places shut out the sunlight completely, I knew that the tree-roads ran crisscross, and now and again I heard some rustle, a fragment of sound, a voice, a snatch of song.

"It's so dark down here," Rafe muttered, "anyone living in this forest would *have* to live in the treetops, or go totally blind!"

Kendricks whispered to me, "Are we being followed? Are they going to jump us?"

"I don't think so. What you hear are just the inhabitants of the city—going about their daily business up there."

"Queer business it must be," Regis said curiously, and as we walked along the mossy, needly forest floor, I told him something of the Trailmen's lives. I had lost my fear. If anyone came at us now, I could speak their language. I could identify myself, tell my business, name my foster parents. Some of my confidence evidently spread to the others.

But as we came into more and more familiar territory, I stopped abruptly and struck my hand against my forehead.

"I knew we had forgotten something!" I said roughly. "I've been away from here too long, that's all. Kyla."

"What about Kyla?"

The girl explained it herself, in her expressionless monotone. "I am an unattached female. Such women are not permitted in the Nests."

"That's easy then," Lerrys said. "She must belong to one of us." He didn't add a syllable. No one could have expected it; Darkovan aristocrats don't bring their women on trips like this, and their women are not like Kyla.

The three brothers broke into a spate of volunteering, and Rafe made an obscene suggestion. Kyla scowled obstinately, her mouth tight with what could have been embarrassment or rage. "If you believe I need your protection—!"

"Kyla," I said tersely, "is under *my* protection. She will be introduced as my woman—and treated as such."

Rafe twisted his mouth in an unfunny smile. "I see the leader keeps all the best for himself?"

My face must have done something I didn't know about, for Rafe backed slowly away. I forced myself to speak slowly. "Kyla is a guide, and indispensable. If anything happens to me, she is the only one who can lead you back. Therefore her safety is my personal affair. Understand?"

As we went along the trail, the vague green light disappeared. "We're right below the Trailcity," I whispered, and pointed upward. All around us the Hundred Trees rose, branchless pillars so immense that four men, hands joined, could not have circled one with their arms. They stretched upward for some three hundred feet, before stretching out their interweaving branches; above that, nothing was visible but blackness.

Yet the grove was not dark, but lighted with the startlingly brilliant phosphoresence of the fungi growing on the trunks, and trimmed into bizarre ornamental shapes. In cages of transparent fibre, glowing insects as large as a hand hummed softly.

As I watched, a Trailman, quite naked except for an ornate hat and a narrow binding around the loins, descended the trunk. He went from cage to cage, feeding the glowworms with bits of shining fungus from a basket on his arm.

I called to him in his own language, and he dropped the basket, with an exclamation, his spidery thin body braced to flee or to raise an alarm.

"But I belong to the Nest," I called to him, and gave him the names of my foster parents. He came toward me, gripping my forearm with warm long fingers in a gesture of greeting.

"Jason? Yes, I hear them speak of you," he said in his gentle twittering voice, "you are at home. But those others—?" He gestured nervously at the strange faces.

"My friends," I assured him, "and we come to beg the Old One for an audience. For tonight I seek shelter with my parents, if they will receive us."

He raised his head and called softly, and a slim child bounded down the trunk and took the basket. The Trailman said, "I am Carrho. Perhaps it would be better if I guided you to your foster parents, so you will not be challenged."

I breathed more freely. I did not personally recognize Carrho, but he looked pleasantly familiar. Guided by him, we climbed one by one up the dark stairway inside the trunk, and emerged into the bright square, shaded by the topmost leaves, into a delicate green twilight. I felt weary and successful.

Kendricks stepped gingerly on the swaying, jiggling floor of the square. It gave slightly at every step, and Kendricks swore morosely in a language that fortunately only Rafe and I understood. Curious Trailmen flocked to the street and twittered welcome and surprise.

Rafe and Kendricks betrayed considerable contempt when I greeted my foster parents affectionately. They were already old, and I was saddened to see it; their fur greying, their prehensile toes and fingers crooked with a rheumatic complaint of some sort, their reddish eyes bleared and rheumy. They welcomed me, and made arrangements for the others in my party to be housed in an abandoned house nearby. They had insisted that I must return to their roof, and Kyla, of course, had to stay with me.

"Couldn't we camp on the ground instead?" Kendricks asked, eying the flimsy shelter with distaste.

"It would offend our hosts," I said firmly. I saw nothing wrong with it. Roofed with woven bark, carpeted with moss which was planted on the floor, the place was abandoned, somewhat musty, but weathertight and seemed comfortable to me.

The first thing to be done was to dispatch a messenger to the Old One, begging the favor of an audience with him. That done, (by one of my foster brothers), we settled down to a meal of buds, honey, insects and birds' eggs; it tasted good to me, with the familiarity of food eaten in childhood, but among the others, only Kyla ate with appetite and Regis Hastur with interested curiosity.

After the demands of hospitality had been satisfied, my foster parents asked the names of my party, and I introduced them one by one. When I named Regis Hastur, it reduced them to brief silence, and then to an outcry; gently but firmly, they insisted that their home was unworthy to shelter the son of a Hastur, and that he must be fittingly entertained at the Royal Nest of the Old One.

There was no gracious way for Regis to protest, and when the messenger returned, he prepared to accompany him. But before leaving, he drew me aside:

"I don't much like leaving the rest of you—"

"You'll be safe enough."

"It's not that I'm worried about, Dr. Allison."

"Call me Jason," I corrected angrily. Regis said, with a little tightening of his mouth, "That's it. You'll have to be Dr. Allison tomorrow when you tell the Old One about your mission. But you have to be the Jason he knows, too."

"So—?"

"I wish I needn't leave here. I wish you were—going to stay with the men who know you only as Jason, instead of being alone—or only with Kyla."

There was something odd in his face, and I wondered at

it. Could he—a Hastur—be jealous of Kyla? Jealous of *me*? It had never occurred to me that he might be somehow attracted to Kyla. I tried to pass it off lightly.

"Kyla might divert me."

Regis said without emphasis. "Yet she brought Dr. Allison back once before." Then, surprisingly, he laughed. "Or maybe you're right. Maybe Kyla will—scare away Dr. Allison if he shows up."

CHAPTER SIX

THE COALS of the dying fire laid strange tints of color on Kyla's face and shoulders and the wispy waves of her dark hair. Now that we were alone, I felt constrained.

"Can't you sleep, Jason?"

I shook my head. "Better sleep while you can." I felt that this night of all nights I dared not close my eyes or when I woke I would have vanished into the Jay Allison I hated. For a moment I saw the room with his eyes; to him it would not seem cozy and clean, but—habituated to white sterile tile, Terran rooms and corridors—dirty and unsanitary as any beast's den.

Kyla said broodingly, "You're a strange man, Jason. What sort of man are you—in Terra's world?"

I laughed, but there was no mirth in it. Suddenly I had to tell her the whole truth:

"Kyla, the man you know as me doesn't exist. I was created for this one specific task. Once it's finished, so am I."

She started, her eyes widening. "I've heard tales of— of the Terrans and their sciences—that they make men who aren't real, men of metal—not bone and flesh—"

Before the dawning of that naïve horror I quickly held out my bandaged hand, took her fingers in mine and ran

71

them over it. "Is this metal? No, no, Kyla. But the man you know as Jason—I won't be he, I'll be someone different—" How could I explain a subsidiary personality to Kyla, when I didn't understand it myself?

She kept my fingers in hers softly and said, "I saw someone else—looking from your eyes at me once. A ghost."

I shook my head savagely. "To the Terrans, I'm the ghost!"

"Poor ghost," she whispered.

Her pity stung. I didn't want it.

"What I don't remember I can't regret. Probably I won't even remember you." But I lied. I knew that although I forgot everything else, unregretting because unremembered, I could not bear to lose this girl, that my ghost would walk restless forever if I forgot her. I looked across the fire at Kyla, cross-legged in the faint light—only a few coals in the brazier. She had removed her sexless outer clothing, and wore some clinging garment, as simple as a child's smock and curiously appealing. There was still a little ridge of bandage visible beneath it and a random memory, not mine, remarked in the back corners of my brain that with the cut improperly sutured there would be a visible scar. *Visible to whom?*

She reached out an appealing hand. "Jason! Jason—?"

My self-possession deserted me. I felt as if I stood, small and reeling, under a great empty echoing chamber which was Jay Allison's mind, and that the roof was about to fall in on me. Kyla's image flickered in and out of focus, first infinitely gentle and appealing, then—as if seen at the wrong end of a telescope—far away and sharply incised and as remote and undesirable as any bug underneath a lens.

Her hands closed on my shoulders. I put out a groping hand to push her away.

"Jason," she implored, "don't—go away from me like that! Talk to me, tell me!"

But her words reached me through emptiness—I knew important things might hang on tomorrow's meeting, Jason alone could come through that meeting, where the Terrans for some reason put him through this hell and damnation and torture—oh yes—the Trailmen's fever—

Jay Allison pushed the girl's hand away and scowled savagely, trying to collect his thoughts and concentrate them on what he must say and do, to convince the Trailmen of their duty toward the rest of the planet. As if they—not even humans—could have a sense of duty!

With an unaccustomed surge of emotion, he wished he were with the others. Kendricks, now. Jay knew, precisely, why Forth had sent the big reliable spaceman at his back. And that handsome, arrogant Darkovan—where was he? Jay looked at the girl in puzzlement; he didn't want to reveal that he wasn't quite sure of what he was saying or doing, or that he had little memory of what Jason had been up to.

He started to ask, "Where did the Hastur kid go?" before a vagrant logical thought told him that such an important guest would have been lodged with the Old One. Then a wave of despair hit him; Jay realized he did not even speak the Trailmen's language, that it had slipped from his thoughts completely.

"You—" he fished desperately for the girl's name, "Kyla. You don't speak the Trailmen's language, do you?"

"A few words. No more. Why?" She had withdrawn into a corner of the tiny room—still not far from him— and he wondered remotely what his damned alter ego had been up to. With Jason, there was no telling. Jay raised his eyes with a melancholy smile.

"Sit down, child. You needn't be frightened."

"I'm—I'm trying to understand—" the girl touched him again, evidently trying to conquer her terror. "It isn't easy—when you turn into someone else under my eyes—" Jay saw that she was shaking in real fright.

He said wearily, "I'm not going to—to turn into a bat and fly away. I'm just a poor devil of a doctor who's gotten himself into one unholy mess." There was no reason, he was thinking, to take out his own misery and despair by shouting at this poor kid. God knew what she'd been through with his irresponsible other self—Forth had admitted that that damned "Jason" personality was a blend of all the undesirable traits he'd fought to smother all his life. By an effort of will he kept himself from pulling away from her hand on his shoulder.

"Jason, don't—slip away like that! *Think!* Try to keep hold on *yourself!*"

Jay propped his head in his hands, trying to make sense of that. Certainly in the dim light she could not be too conscious of subtle changes of expression. She evidently thought she was talking to Jason. She didn't seem to be overly intelligent.

"Think about tomorrow, Jason. What are you going to say to him? Think about your parents—"

Jay Allison wondered what they would think when they found a stranger here. He felt like a stranger. Yet he must have come, tonight, into this house and spoken—he rummaged desperately in his mind for some fragments of the Trailmen's language. He had spoken it as a child. He must recall enough to speak to the woman who had been a kind foster mother to her alien son. He tried to form his lips to the unfamiliar shapes of words—

Jay covered his face with his hands again. Jason was the part of himself that rememberd the Trailmen. *That* was what he had to remember—Jason was not a hostile stranger, not an alien intruder in his body. Jason was a lost part of himself and at the moment a damn necessary part. If there were only some way to get back the Jason memories, skills, without losing *himself* . . . He said to the girl, "Let me think. Let me—" To his surprise and horror his voice broke into an alien tongue, "Let me alone, will you?"

Maybe, Jay thought, I could stay myself if *I* could remember the rest. Dr. Forth said Jason would remember the Trailmen with kindness, not dislike.

Jay searched his memory and found nothing but familiar frustration: years spent in an alien land apart from a human heritage, stranded and abandoned. *My father left me. He crashed the plane and I never saw him again and I hate him for leaving me* . . .

But his father had not abandoned him. He had crashed the plane trying to save them both. It was no one's fault—

Except my father's. For trying to fly over the Hellers into a country where no man belongs . . .

He hadn't belonged. And yet the Trailmen, whom he considered little better than roaming beasts, had taken the alien child into their city, their homes, their hearts. They had loved him. And he . . .

"And I loved them," I found myself saying half aloud, then realized that Kyla was gripping my arm, looking up imploringly into my face. I shook my head rather groggily. "What's the matter?"

"You frightened me," she said in a shaky little voice, and I suddenly knew what had happened. I tensed with savage rage against Jay Allison. He couldn't even give me the splinter of life I'd won for myself, but had to come sneaking out of my mind. How he must hate me! Not half as much as I hated him, damn him! Along with everything else, he'd scared Kyla half to death!

She was kneeling very close to me, and I realized that

there was one way to fight that cold austere fish of a Jay
Allison, send him shrieking down into hell again. He was
a man who hated everything except the cold world he'd
made his life. Kyla's face was lifted, soft and intent and
pleading, and suddenly I reached out and pulled her to
me and kissed her, hard.

"Could a ghost do this?" I demanded, "or this?"

She whispered, "No—oh, no," and her arms went up
to lock around my neck. As I pulled her down on the
sweet-smelling moss that carpeted the chamber, I felt the
dark ghost of my other self thin out, vanish and disappear.

Regis had been right. It had been the only way.

The Old One was not old at all; the title was purely
ceremonial. This one was young—not much older than I
—but he had poise and dignity and the same strange
indefinable quality I had recognized in Regis Hastur. It
was something, I supposed, that the Terran Empire had
lost in spreading from star to star—feeling of knowing
one's own place, a dignity that didn't demand recognition because it had never lacked it.

Like all Trailmen he had the chinless face and lobeless
ears, the heavy-haired body which looked slightly less
than human. He spoke very low—the Trailmen have
very acute hearing—and I had to strain my ears to listen,
and remember to keep my own voice down.

He stretched his hand to me, and I lowered my head
over it and murmured, "I make submission, Old One."

"Never mind that," he said in his gentle twittering
voice. "Sit down, my son. You are welcome here, but I
feel you have abused our trust in you. We dismissed you
to your own kind because we felt you would be happier
so. Did we show you anything but kindness, that after so
many years you return with armed men?"

The reproof in his red eyes was hardly an auspicious beginning. I said helplessly, "Old One, the men with me are not armed. A band of those-who-may-not-enter-cities attacked us, and we defended ourselves. I traveled with so many men only because I feared to travel the passes alone."

"But does that explain why you have returned at all?" The reason and reproach in his voice made sense.

Finally I said, "Old One, we come as supplicants. My people appeal to your people in the hope that you will be—" I started to say, *as human*, stopped and amended "—that you will deal as kindly with them as with me."

His face betrayed nothing. "What do you ask?"

I explained. I told it badly, stumbling, not knowing the technical terms, knowing they had no equivalents anyway in the Trailmen's language. He listened, asking a penetrating question now and again. When I mentioned the Terran Legate's offer to recognize the Trailmen as a separate and independent government, he frowned and rebuked me:

"We of the Sky People have no dealings with the Terrans, and care nothing for their recognition—or its lack."

For that I had no answer, and the Old One continued, kindly but indifferently, "We do not like to think that the fever which is a children's little sickness with us shall kill so many of your kind. But you cannot in all honesty blame us. You cannot say that we spread the disease; we never go beyond the mountains. Are we to blame that the winds change or the moons come together in the sky? When the time has come for men to die, they die." He stretched his hand in dismissal. "I will give your men safe-conduct to the river, Jason. Do not return."

Regis Hastur rose suddenly and faced him. "Will you hear me, Father?" He used the ceremonial title without

hesitation, and the Old One said in distress, "The son of
Hastur need never speak as a suppliant to the Sky People!"

"Nevertheless, hear me as a suppliant, Father," Regis
said quietly. "It is not the strangers and aliens of Terra
who are pleading. We have learned one thing from the
strangers of Terra, which you have not yet learned. I am
young and it is not fitting that I should teach you, but
you have said: 'Are we to blame that the moons come
together in the sky?' No. But we have learned from the
Terrans not to blame the moons in the sky for our own
ignorance of the ways of the Gods—by which I mean the
ways of sickness or poverty or misery."

"These are strange words for a Hastur," said the Old
One, displeased.

"These are strange times for a Hastur," said Regis
loudly. The Old One winced, and Regis moderated his
tone, but continued vehemently, "You blame the moons
in the sky. *I* say the moons are not to blame, nor the
winds, nor the Gods. The Gods send these things to man
to test their wits and to find if they have the will to master them!"

The Old One's forehead ridged vertically and he said
with stinging contempt, "Is this the breed of king which
men call Hastur now?"

"Man or God or Hastur, I am not too proud to plead
for my people," retorted Regis, flushing with anger.
"Never in all the history of Darkover has a Hastur stood
before one of you and begged—"

"—for the men from another world."

"—for all men on our world! Old One, I could sit and
keep state in the House of Hasturs, and even death could
not touch me until I grew weary of living! But I preferred
to learn new lives from new men. The Terrans have
something to teach even the Hasturs, and they can learn
a remedy against the Trailmen's fever." He looked round

at me, turning the discussion over to me again, and I said:

"I am no alien from another world, Old One. I have been a son in your house. Perhaps I was sent to teach you to fight destiny. I cannot believe you are indifferent to death."

Suddenly, hardly knowing what I was going to do until I found myself on my knees, I knelt and looked up into the quiet, stern, remote face of the nonhuman.

"My father," I said, "you took a dying man and a dying child from a burning plane. Even those of their own kind might have stripped their corpses and left them to die. You saved the child, fostered him and treated him as a son. When he reached an age to be unhappy with you, you let a dozen of your people risk their lives to take him to his own. You cannot ask me to believe that you are indifferent to the death of a million of my people, when the fate of one could stir your pity!"

There was a moment's silence. Finally the Old One said, "Indifferent—no. But helpless. My people die when they leave the mountains. The air is too rich for them. The food is wrong. The light blinds and tortures them. Can I send them to suffer and die, those people who call me father?"

And a memory, buried all my life, suddenly surfaced. I said urgently, "Father, listen. In the world I live in now, I am called a wise man. You need not believe me, but listen; I know your people, they are my people. I remember when I left you, more than a dozen of my foster parents' friends offered, knowing they risked death, to go with me. I was a child; I did not realize the sacrifice they made. But I watched them suffer, as we went lower in the mountains, and I resolved—I resolved . . ." I spoke with difficulty, forcing the words through a reluctant barricade, ". . . that since others had suffered so for me . . . I would spend my life in curing the sufferings of others.

Father, the Terrans call me a wise doctor, a man of healing. Among the Terrans I can see that my people, if they
will come to us and help us, have air they can breathe
and food which will suit them and that they are guarded
from the light. I don't ask you to send anyone, father. I
ask only—tell your sons what I have told you. If I know
your people—who are my people forever—hundreds of
them will offer to return with me. And you may witness
what your foster son has sworn here; if one of your sons
dies, your alien son will answer for it with his own life.

The words had poured from me in a flood. They were
not all mine; some unconscious thing had recalled in me
that Jay Allison had power to make these promises. For
the first time I began to see what force, what guilt, what
dedication working in Jay Allison had turned him aside
from me. I remained at the Old One's feet, kneeling, overcome, ashamed of the thing I had become. Jay Allison
was worth ten of me. Irresponsible, Forth had said. Lacking purpose, lacking balance. What right had I to despise
my sober self?

At last I felt the Old One touch my head lightly.

"Get up, my son," he said, "I will answer for my people. And forgive me for my doubts and my delays."

Neither Regis nor I spoke for a minute after we left the
audience room; then, almost as one, we turned to each
other. Regis spoke first, soberly.

"It was a fine thing you did, Jason. I didn't believe
he'd agree to it."

"It was your speech that did it," I denied. The sober
mood, the unaccustomed surge of emotion, was still on
me,—but it was giving way to a sudden upswing of ex-
altation. Damn it, I'd *done* it! Let Jay Allison try to
match *that*.

Regis still looked grave. "He'd have refused, but you
appealed to him as one of themselves. And yet it wasn't

quite that—it was something more—" Regis put a quick embarrassed arm around my shoulders and suddenly blurted out, "I think the Terran Medical played hell with your life, Jason! And even if it saves a million lives—it's hard to forgive them for that!"

CHAPTER SEVEN

LATE THE NEXT DAY the Old One called us in again, and told us that a hundred men had volunteered to return with us and act as blood donors and experimental subjects for research into the Trailmen's disease.

The trip over the mountains, so painfully accomplished, was easier in return. Our escort of a hundred Trailmen guaranteed us against attack, and they could choose the easiest paths.

Only as we undertook the long climb downward through the foothills did the Trailmen, unused to ground travel at any time, and suffering from the unaccustomed low altitude, begin to weaken. As we grew stronger, more and more of them faltered, and we traveled more and more slowly. Not even Kendricks could be callous about "inhuman animals" by the time we reached the point where we had left the pack horses. And it was Rafe Scott who came to me and said desperately, "Jason, these poor fellows will never make it to Carthon. Lerrys and I know this country. Let us go ahead, as fast as we can travel alone, and arrange at Carthon for transit—maybe we can get pressurized aircraft to fly them from here. We can send a message from Carthon, too, about accommodations for them at the Terran HQ."

I was surprised and a little guilty that I had not thought of this myself. I covered it with a mocking, "I thought you didn't give a damn about 'my friends'."

Rafe said doggedly, "I guess I was wrong about that. They're going through this out of a sense of duty, so they must be pretty different from the way I thought they were."

Regis, who had overheard Rafe's plan, now broke in quietly, "There's no need for you to travel ahead, Rafe. I can send a quicker message."

I had forgotten that Regis was a trained telepath. He added, "There are some space and distance limitations to such messages, but there is a regular relay net all over Darkover, and one of the relays is a girl who lives at the very edge of the Terran Zone. *If* you'll tell me what will give her access to the Terran HQ—" he flushed slightly and explained, "From what I know of the Terrans, she would not be very fortunate relaying the message if she merely walked to the gate and said she had a relayed telepathic message for someone, would she?"

I had to smile at the picture that conjured up in my mind. "I'm afraid not," I admitted. "Tell her to go to Dr. Forth, and give the message from Dr. Jason Allison."

Regis looked at me curiously—it was the first time I had spoken my own name in the hearing of the others. But he nodded, without comment. For the next hour or two he seemed somewhat more preoccupied than usual, but after a time he came to me and told me that the message had gone through. Some time later he relayed an answer; that airlift would be waiting for us, not at Carthon, but at a small village near the ford of the Kadarin where we had left our trucks.

When we camped that night there were a dozen practical problems needing attention: the time and exact place of crossing the ford, the reassurance to be given to terrified Trailmen who could face leaving their forests

but not crossing the final barricade of the river, the small
help in our power to be given the sick ones. But after
everything had been done that I could do, and after the
whole camp had quieted down, I sat before the low-burn-
ing fire and stared into it, deep in painful lassitude.
Tomorrow we would cross the river and a few hours later
we would be back in the Terran HQ. And then . . .

And then—and then nothing. I would vanish, I would
utterly cease to exist anywhere, except as a vagrant ghost
troubling Jay Allison's unquiet dreams. As he moved
through the cold round of his days, I would be no more
than a spent wind, a burst bubble, a thinned cloud.

The rose and saffron of the dying fire gave shape to my
dreams. Once more, as in the Trailcity that night, Kyla
slipped through firelight to my side, and I looked up at
her and suddenly I knew I could not bear it. I pulled her
to me and muttered, "Oh Kyla—Kyla, I won't even remember you!"

She pushed my hands away, kneeling upright, and said
urgently, "Jason, listen. We are close to Carthon, the
others can lead them the rest of the way. Why go back to
them at all? Slip away now and never go back! We
can—" she stopped, coloring fiercely, that sudden and
terrifying shyness overcoming her again, and at last she
said in a whisper, "Darkover is a wide world, Jason. Big
enough for us to hide in. I don't believe they would
search very far."

They wouldn't. I could leave word with Kendricks—
not with Regis, the telepath would see through me immediately—that I had ridden ahead to Carthon, with
Kyla. By the time they realized that I had fled, they
would be too concerned with getting the Trailmen safely
to the Terran Zone to spend much time looking for a
runaway. As Kyla said, the world was wide. And it was
my world. And I would not be alone in it.

"Kyla, Kyla," I said helplessly, and crushed her

against me, kissing her. She closed her eyes and I took a long, long look at her face. Not beautiful, no. But womanly and brave and all the other beautiful things. It was a farewell look, and I knew it, if she didn't.

After the briefest time, she pulled a little away, and her flat voice was gentler and more breathless than usual. "We'd better leave before the others waken." She saw that I did not move. "Jason—"

I could not look at her. Muffled behind my hands, I said, "No, Kyla. I—I promised the Old One to look after my people in the Terran World."

"You won't be *there* to look after them! You won't be *you!*"

I said bleakly, "I'll write a letter to remind myself. Jay Allison has a very strong sense of duty. He'll look after them for me. He won't like it, but he'll do it, with his last breath. He's a better man than I am, Kyla. You'd better forget about me," I said wearily. "I never existed."

That wasn't the end. Not nearly. She—begged, and I don't know why I put myself through the hell of stubborn refusal. But in the end she ran away, crying, and I threw myself down by the fire, cursing Forth, cursing my own folly, but most of all cursing Jay Allison, hating my other self with a blistering, sickening rage.

But before dawn I stirred in the light of the dying fire and Kyla's arms were around my neck in the darkness, her body pressed to mine, racked with convulsive crying.

"I can't convince you," she wept, "and I can't change you—and I wouldn't if I could. But while I can—while I can—I'll have you while you're you."

I crushed her to me. And for the moment my fear of tomorrow, my hate and bitterness against the men who had played with my life, were swept away in the sweetness of her mouth, warm and yielding, under mine. There in the light of the fading fire, desperate, knowing I would forget, I took her to me.

Whatever I might be tomorrow, tonight I was hers.

And I knew then how men feel when they love in the shadow of death—worse than death because I would live, a cold ghost of myself, through cold days and colder nights. It was fierce and savage and desperate; we were both trying to crowd a lifetime we could never have into a few stolen hours. But as I looked down at Kyla's wet face in the fading dawn, my bitterness had gone.

I might be swept away forever, a ghost, a nothing, blown away in the winds of one man's memory. But to that last fading spark of memory, I would be forever grateful, and in my limbo I would be grateful, if ghosts know gratitude, to those who had called me from my nowhere to know this: these days of struggle and the love of comrades, the clean wind of the mountains in my face again, a last adventure, the warm lips of a woman in my arms.

I had lived more, in my scant week of life, than Jay Allison would live in all his white and sterile years. I had had my lifetime. I didn't grudge him his, anymore.

Coming through the outskirts of the small village, next afternoon, the village where the airlift would meet us, we noted that the poorer quarter was almost deserted. Not a woman walked in the street, not a man lounged along the curbing, not a child played in the dusty squares.

Regis said bleakly, "It's begun," and dropped out of line to stand in the doorway of a silent dwelling. After a minute he beckoned to me, and I looked inside.

I wished I hadn't. The sight would haunt me while I lived. An old man, two young women and half a dozen children between four and fifteen years old lay inside. The old man, one of the children, and one of the young women were laid out neatly in clean death, shrouded, their faces covered with green branches after the Darkovan custom for the dead. The other young woman lay huddled near the fireplace, her coarse dress splattered with the filthy stuff she had vomited, dying. The children—even now I can't think of the children without retching. One, very small, had been in the woman's arms when she collapsed; it had squirmed free—for a little while. The others were in an indescribable condition, and the worst of it was that one of them was still moving, feebly, long past help. Regis turned blindly from the door and leaned against the wall, his shoulders heaving —not, as I first thought, in disgust, but in grief. Tears ran over his hands and spilled down, and when I took him by the arm to lead him away, he reeled and fell against me.

He said in a broken, blurred, choking voice, "Oh, Gods, Jason, those children, those children—if you ever had any doubts about what you're doing, any doubts about what you've done, think about that, think that you've saved a whole world from that, think that you've done something even the Hasturs couldn't do!"

My own throat tightened with something more than embarrassment. "Better wait till we know for sure whether the Terrans can carry through with it, and you'd better get to hell away from this doorway. I'm immune, but damn it, you're not." But, I had to take him and lead him away, like a child, from that house. He looked up into my face and said with burning sincerity, "I wonder if you believe I'd give my life, a dozen times over, to have done that?"

It was a curious, austere reward. But vaguely it comforted me. And then, as we rode into the village itself, I lost myself, or tried to lose myself, in reassuring the frightened Trailmen who had never seen a city on the ground, never seen or heard of an airplane. I avoided Kyla. I didn't want a final word, a farewell. We had had our farewells already.

Forth had done a marvelous job of preparing quarters

for the Trailmen, and after they were comfortably in-
stalled and reassured, I went down wearily and dressed in
Jay Allison's clothing. I looked out the window at the
distant mountains and a line from the book on mountaineering, which I had bought as a youngster in an alien
world, and Jay had kept as a stray fragment of personality, ran in violent conflict through my mind:

Something hidden—go and find it . . .
Something lost beyond the ranges . . .

I had just begun to live. Surely I deserved better than
this, to vanish when I had just discovered life. Did the
man who did not know how to live, deserve to live at all?
Jay Allison—that cold man who had never looked
beyond any ranges—why should I be lost in him?

Something lost beyond the ranges—nothing would be
lost but myself. I was beginning to loathe the overflown
sense of duty which had brought me back here. Now,
when it was too late, I was bitterly regretting—Kyla had
offered me life. Surely I would never see Kyla again.

Could I regret what I would never remember? I walked
into Forth's office as if I were going to my doom.
I *was*—

Forth greeted me warmly.

"Sit down and tell me all about it," he insisted. I
would rather not have spoken. Instead, compulsively, I
made it a full report—and curious flickers came in and
out of my consciousness as I spoke. By the time I realized
I was reacting to a post-hypnotic suggestion, that in fact
I was going under hypnosis again, it was too late and I
could only think that this was worse than death because
in a way I would be alive.

Jay Allison sat up and meticulously straightened his
cuff before tightening his mouth in what was meant for
a smile. "I assume, then, that the experiment was a success?"

"A complete success." Forth's voice was somewhat harsh and annoyed, but Jay was untroubled; he had known for years that most of his subordinates and superiors disliked him, and had long ago stopped worrying about it.

"The Trailmen agreed?"

"They agreed," Forth said, surprised. "You don't remember anything at all?"

"Scraps. Like a nightmare." Jay Allison looked down at the back of his hand, flexing the fingers cautiously against pain, touching the partially healed red slash. Forth followed the direction of his eyes and said, not unsympathetically, "Don't worry about your hand. I looked at it pretty carefully. You'll have total use of it."

Jay said rigidly, "It seems to have been a pretty severe risk to take. Did you ever stop to think what it would have meant to me, to lose the use of it."

"It seemed a justifiable risk, even if you had," Forth said dryly. "Jay, I've got the whole story on tape, just as you told it to me. You might not like having a blank spot in your memory. Want to hear what your alter ego did?"

Jay hesitated. Then he unfolded his long legs and stood up. "No, I don't think I care to know." He waited, arrested by a twinge of a sore muscle, and frowned.

What had happened, what would he never know, why did the random ache bring a pain deeper than the pain of a torn nerve? Forth was watching him, and Jay asked irritably, "What is it?"

"You're one hell of a cold fish, Jay."

"I don't understand you, sir."

"You wouldn't," Forth muttered. "Funny. I *liked* your subsidiary personality."

Jay's mouth contracted in a mirthless grin.

"You would," he said, and swung quickly around.

"Come on. If I'm going to work on that serum project I'd better inspect the volunteers and line up the blood donors and look over old whatshisname's papers."

But beyond the window the snowy ridges of the mountain, inscrutable, caught and held his eye; a riddle and a puzzle—

"Ridiculous," he said, and went to his work.

CHAPTER EIGHT

FOUR MONTHS LATER, Jay Allison and Randall Forth
stood together, watching the last of the disappearing
planes, carrying the volunteers back toward Carthon and
their mountains.

"I should have flown back to Carthon with them," Jay
said moodily. Forth watched the tall man stare at the
mountain; wondered what lay behind the contained
gestures and the brooding.

He said, "You've done enough, Jay. You've worked
like the devil. Thurmond, the Legate, sent down to say
you'd get an official commendation and a promotion for
your part. That's not even mentioning what you did in
the Trailmen's city." He put a hand on his colleague's
shoulder, but Jay shook it off impatiently.

All through the work of isolating and testing the blood
fraction, Jay had worked tirelessly and unsparingly;
scarcely sleeping, but brooding; silent, prone to fly into
sudden savage rages, but painstaking. He had overseen
the Trailmen with an almost fatherly solicitude—but
from a distance. He had left no stone unturned for their
comfort—but refused to see them in person except when
it was unavoidable.

Forth thought, we played a dangerous game. Jay Allison had made his own adjustment to life, and we disturbed that balance. Have we wrecked the man? He's expendable, but damn it, what a loss! He asked, "Well, why *didn't* you fly back to Carthon with them? Kendricks went along, you know. He expected you to go until the last minute."

Jay did not answer. He had avoided Kendricks, the only witness to his duality. In all his nightmare brooding, the avoidance of anyone who had known him as Jason became a mania. Once, meeting Rafe Scott on the lower floor of the HQ, he had turned frantically and plunged like a madman through halls and corridors, to avoid coming face to face with the man, finally running up four flights of stairs and taking shelter in his rooms, with the pounding heart and bursting veins of a hunted criminal. At last he said, "If you've called me down here to give me hell about not wanting to make another trip into the Hellers—!"

"No, no," Forth said equably, "there's a visitor coming. Regis Hastur sent word he wants to see you. In case you don't remember him, he was on Project Jason—"

"I remember," Jay said grimly. It was nearly his one clear memory—the nightmare of the ledge, his slashed hand, the naked body of the Darkovan woman,—and blurring these things, the too-handsome Darkovan aristocrat who had banished him for Jason again. "He's a better psychiatrist than you are, Forth. He changed me into Jason in the flicker of an eyelash, and it took you half a dozen hypnotic sessions."

"I've heard about the psi powers of the Hasturs," Forth said, "but I've never been lucky enough to meet one in person. Tell me about it. What did he do?"

Jay made a tight movement of exasperation, too controlled for a shrug. "Ask him, why don't you. Look, Forth, I don't much care to see him. I didn't do it for Darkover; I did it because it was my job. I'd prefer to forget the whole thing. Why don't you talk to him?"

"I rather had the idea that he wanted to see you personally. Jay, you did a tremendous thing, man! Damn it, why don't you strut a little. Be—be normal for once! Why, I'd be damned near bursting with pride if one of the Hasturs insisted on congratulating me personally!"

Jay's lip twitched, and his voice shook with controlled exasperation. "Maybe you would. I don't see it that way."

"Well, I'm afraid you'll have to. On Darkover nobody refuses when the Hasturs make a request—and certainly not a request as reasonable as this one." Forth sat down beside the desk. Jay struck the woodwork with a violent clenched fist and when he lowered his hand there was a tiny smear of blood along his knuckles. After a minute he walked to the couch and sat down, very straight and still, saying nothing. Neither of the men spoke again until Forth started at the sound of the buzzer, drew the mouthpiece toward him, and said, "Tell him we are honored—you know the routine for dignitaries, and send him up here."

Jay twisted his fingers together and ran his thumb, in a new gesture, over the ridge of scar tissue along the knuckles. Forth was aware of an entirely new quality in the silence, and started to speak to break it, but before he could do so, the office door slid open on its silent beam, and Regis Hastur stood there.

Forth rose courteously and Jay got to his feet like a mechanical doll jerked on strings. The young Darkovan ruler smiled engagingly at him.

"Don't bother, this visit is informal; that's the reason I came here rather than inviting you both to the Tower. Dr. Forth? It is a pleasure to meet you again, sir. I hope that our gratitude to you will soon take a more tangible form. There has not been a single death from the Trailmen's fever since you made the serum available."

Jay, motionless, saw bitterly that the old man had succumbed to the youngster's deliberate charm. The chubby, wrinkled old face seamed up in a pleased smile as
Forth said, "The gifts sent to the Trailmen in your name,
Lord Hastur, were greatly welcomed."

"Do you think that any of us will ever forget what they
have done?" Regis replied. He turned toward the window and smiled rather tentatively at the man who stood
there motionless since his first conventional gesture of
politeness.

"Dr. Allison, do you remember me at all?"

"I remember you," Jay Allison said sullenly.

His voice hung heavily in the room, its sound a
miasma in his ears. All his sleepless, nightmare-charged
brooding, all his bottled hate for Darkover and the memories he had tried to bury, erupted into overwrought bitterness against this too-ingratiating youngster who was a
demigod on this world and who had humiliated him, re-
pudiated him for the hated Jason. For Jay, Regis had suddenly become the symbol of a world that hated him,
forced him into a false mould.

A black and rushing wind seemed to blur the room. He
said hoarsely, "I remember you all right," and took one
savage, hurtling step.

The weight of the unexpected blow spun Regis
around, and the next moment Jay Allison, who had never
touched another human being except with the remote
hands of healing, closed steely, murderous hands around
Regis' throat. The world thinned out into a crimson rage.
There was shouting, and sudden noises, and a red-hot
explosion in his brain . . .

"You'd better drink this," Forth remarked, and I realized I was turning a paper cup in my hands. Forth sat
down, a little weakly, as I raised it to my lips and sipped.
Regis took his hand away from his throat and said huski-

ly, "I could use some of that, doctor."

I put the whisky down. "You'll do better with water until your throat muscles are healed," I said swiftly, and went to fill a throwaway cup for him, without thinking. Handing it to him, I stopped in sudden dismay and my hand shook, spilling a few drops. I said hoarsely, swallowing, "—but drink it, anyway."

Regis got a few drops down, painfully, and said, "My own fault. The moment I saw—Jay Allison—I knew he was a madman. I'd have stopped him sooner only he took me by surprise."

"But—you say *him* —I'm Jay Allison," I said, and then my knees went weak and I sat down. "What in hell is this? I'm not Jay—but I'm not Jason, either—"

I could remember my entire life, but the focus had shifted. I still felt the old love, the old nostalgia for the Trailmen; but I also knew, with a sure sense of identity, that I was Doctor Jason Allison, Jr., who had abandoned mountain climbing and become a specialist in Darkovan parasitology. Not Jay who had rejected the world; not Jason who had been rejected by it. But then who?

Regis said quietly, "I've seen you before—once. When you knelt to the Old One of the Trailmen." With a whimsical smile he said, "As an ignorant superstitious Darkovan, I'd say that you were a man who'd balanced his god and daemon for once."

I looked helplessly at the young Hastur. A few seconds ago my hands had been at his throat. Jay or Jason, maddened by self-hate and jealousy, could disclaim responsibility for the other's acts.

I couldn't.

Regis said, "We could take the easy way out, and arrange it so we'd never have to see each other again. Or we could do it the hard way." He extended his hand, and after a minute, I understood, and we shook hands briefly, like strangers who have just met. He added, "Your work with the Trailmen is finished, but we Hasturs committed ourselves to teach some of the Terrans our science— matrix mechanics. Dr. Allison—Jason—you know Darkover, and I think we could work with you. Further, you know something about slipping mental gears. I meant to ask: would you care to be one of them? You'd be ideal."

I looked out the window at the distant mountains. This work—this would be something which would satisfy both halves of myself. The irresistible force, the immovable object—and no ghosts wandering in my brain. "I'll do it," I told Regis. And then, deliberately, I turned my back on him and went up to the quarters, now deserted, which we had readied for the Trailmen. With my new doubled —or complete—memories, another ghost had roused up in my brain, and I remembered a woman who had appeared vaguely in Jay Allison's orbit, unnoticed, working with the Trailmen, tolerated because she could speak their language. I opened the door, searched briefly through the rooms, and shouted, "Kyla!" and she came. Running. Disheveled. Mine.

At the last moment, she drew back a little from my arms and whispered. "You're Jason—but you're something more. Different—"

"I don't know who I am," I said quietly, "but I'm me. Maybe for the first time. Want to help me find out just who that is?"

I put my arm around her, trying to find a path between memory and tomorrow. All my life, I had walked a strange road toward an unknown horizon. Now, reaching my horizon, I found it marked only the rim of an unknown country.

Kyla and I would explore it together.

THE WATERFALL

The Waterfall
by
Marion Zimmer Bradley

The lady Sybil-Mhari, fifteen years old and as frail as
a branch of willow, stood at the edge of an enclosed
courtyard, staring with pensive gray eyes into the valley,
flooded with the strange moonlight of the four moons. A
low wall of stone, barely knee-high, was the only thing
dividing the court where she stood from a steep, sheer
and hazardous cliff that dropped away sharply to a raging, foaming torrent of white water that fell, nearly a
thousand feet, into the valley. The muffled roar of water
beneath her, and the cold moon-flooded night, cut
through her with the dampness that rose from the waterfall far below, seemed to tremble hotly in her young
body, twisting a thick lump in her throat, a feeling that
was like hunger or thirst—or something else. . . . Something she could not even guess; a hunger, a loneliness,
for something she had never known.

Love? No. Her waiting-women chattered and
squealed of love continually, whispering together, giggling confidences of stolen kisses and furtive touches, of

seeking hands in the darkness, of courtly verses and
songs. And for a little while Sybil had believed it was,
indeed, love for which she hungered; but as confidences
had grown more definite, they had evoked neither excitement nor longing, but only a shudder of disgust. What—
she, Sybil-Mhari Aillard, *comynara*, the delicate and
queenly little sister of the Lord Ludovic, lonely and perfect as a single star, to surrender herself to these hungry
indecencies? She, born into the caste of Comyn, apart
and above, bearing—so the common folk said—the
blood of Gods, *she* to swoon in the arms of some clumsy
esquire, to lend herself to secret kissings, fumbling fingers, whispered words of love, in corridor or hall or
chapel? No. And no. The hunger that was in her was
surely for something other than this; it was as a burning
fire seeking fuel, and these huggings and clutchings were
damp and commonplace, smothering instead of feeding
the flame.

She looked down at the white water that coursed and
plunged and raced, throwing up silvery spray so far beneath her that the water seemed all one whiteness in the
moonlight, and suddenly imaged herself flying, falling
through that vast space, into the race and torrent;
whirled, battered, drowned—or would she, as some old
legends said that the Comyn folk could do, put forth sudden wings, fly wingless far above the world, wheeling on
hawkpinions, looking down from far above. . . . But that
was legend. Or dream. She hugged herself with thin bare
arms and clutched dizzily at the wall, almost hypnotized
by the tumult and sound of the distant waterfall. To fly,
borne on invisible wings, or the secret powers of the
Comyn, aloft, above everyone who sought to pin her
down and keep her earth-bound . . . but that was long
ago. Legend.

Now the Comyn held only the powers of the mind, and

even those she had been denied. The *leronis*, the great
sorceress of Hastur blood, had called Sybil to her but this
year, had made her look into the starstone, so that Sybil
felt she stood more naked than if the woman had
stripped from her the last garment, feeling the touch of
the *leronis* on her mind. Sybil had stood unflinching, not
daring to show fear; but inside her something cowered
and wept and could not raise its eyes, and at last the
leronis had sighed and put away the stone. "You have
laran, my child; you bear the Gift of our clan. And
yet . . ." the woman sighed again, and shook her head.
"There is a power in you, Sybil, that I do not understand;
and yet I had thought I knew all the Gifts of Comyn. You
are telepath—not greatly, but enough. You could be
trained in a Tower; could wield all the power of a *leronis*,
perhaps a Keeper. Yet something in me—something I
have come to trust—says . . . *no*."

Sybil had protested "Why, lady?" There was a sullen
anger in her. The women of the Towers wielded power
and force, they used the trained powers of the mind—all
other women of the Comyn were powerless, given in
marriage and forced to bear children for their clan, but
wielding no power of their own . . . and the *leronis*
would deny her this! Rage had surged in her, but she
made her voice sweet and docile as she had been taught,
and murmured, in the voice that her brother Ludovic,
lord of the clan, had said was like the gentle murmuring
of a green rainbird, "Why, lady? I am *comynara*, I have
laran, you yourself have said it . . . why?"

But the Hastur sorceress only shook her head, meeting
Sybil's eyes with a flash that told the girl that the older
woman knew, and did not fear, all of her hidden rage.
She said, "Because your mind is not the mind of a woman, Sybil; it holds something other than *laran*. I do not
know what it is, but I fear it; and I fear you; and I will not

have you in a Tower. If you are to master the craft of the starstones, if you are to wield all the ancient powers of the Comyn, I must know, absolutely, that you are to be trusted. So I say no."

And then Sybil had raised her eyes and glared at the woman and had thrust forth a power she did not know was in her, to seize the woman, to compel her will upon her—*I will have this power*. The woman had pushed her mind away easily, and had shaken her head with a sad laugh. "You see, my poor child? I do not fear you as you are now; but I fear what you might be, wielding the craft of the starstones." And she had gone away, taking with her Sybil's young foster-sister Rohana, to be brought to the Tower and trained in the craft of the starstones, and Sybil had been left here to loneliness, and hunger, and melancholy, and the aching need of something . . . something, she could not guess what it might be. . . .

After a long time, aware that she was cramped and chilled to the bone, she straightened and slowly turned away. Behind her lay the Comyn castle, a great and sprawling mass of stone and echoing silence; the empty courtyards gave resonant sighs as her silk-shod feet whispered on the flagstones, and even her own breathing seemed to stir an echoing murmur. The icy cold of the stones crept up her stiffened legs and throbbed in her breasts. From very far away Sybil heard a halt, a clash, a challenge, the echo of ringing steps and silence; the Guardsmen were making their nightly rounds. Hurrying her steps a little, she slipped shadowlike under an archway, sheltering against the chilly night breeze; then she started, catching her hands to her throat with a little squeak of surprise as a light, thrust abruptly forward, rayed harshly across her face.

Half blinded, she pressed her fingers over her eyes; then as her pupils slowly adjusted to the light, she lowered her hands to see a man's face above the crude flare of the lantern.

"Well, now! Look what I found!"

Sybil shrank back as the unfamiliar face spread into a wide grin. The voice was deep and harsh, almost hoarse, but it sounded good-natured. "What are you doing here, you?"

The spreading light was less painful to Sybil's eyes now. She could distinguish black leather straps on a green cloak; one of the Guardsmen who came from their homes, at Council season, to guard the Comyn lords and ladies. She had seen them from time to time; they bowed deeply as she passed, and lowered their eyes in humility when, as sometimes happened, she spoke some condescending word or gave some minor command. But this was one she had never seen before—and never before had one of them dared to address her uninvited, by so much as a word.

She said coldly, "Go about your business, fellow."

"Easy there, wench," the man chuckled, "My business is right here, see; finding out who goes in and out of this court. What's yours?"

Sybil's small white teeth clamped in her lip. It would be too humiliating to identify herself to this . . . this roughneck! She saw that he was a thickset man, with a heavy neck and burly broad shoulders, and his grin, through the untidily sprouting whiskers, showed very long, strong white teeth like a horse's!

"I live here," she said shortly.

The man laughed. "And so do a dozen other women, but I'll take your word for it. Come, give us a kiss, *chiya*, and I'll let you go." He bent and deliberately set the lantern on the ground, then deliberately stepped toward her, and Sybil—too frozen in astonishment to move—felt his rough hands on her bare arms. The hoarse, chuckling voice was very close to her ear.

"Who were you looking for, girl, won't I do instead?"

Paralyzed, a horrid sick emptiness clawing inside her belly, Sybil felt the rough arms around her waist, felt her feet leave the ground as he caught her up bodily against his chest, and the stubbled face scraped hard against her soft cheek. For a moment she hung limp, unable to move a muscle—this *couldn't* be happening! Then, in a convulsion of terror, she exploded like a frantic cat, arching backward, silently clawing at her captor. She opened her mouth to scream, but her dry throat would give voice only to a little whimper of terror.

"Take it easy, hell-cat!" the strange voice muttered in the half-dark. She felt rough and weathered fingers searching the silks and ribbons that confined her breast, and her voice came back in a choking scream.

"Put me down! How dare you? You'll be flayed alive for this!"

Something in her imperious command, even through the shrillness of hysteria, came through to the man, and he set her abruptly on her feet, snatching up the lantern. "Zandu's hells," he swore, "*Who are you?*"

She swayed as he released her, dizziness blurring her eyes, and caught for support at the rough stonework, steadying herself with a hand flattened against the wall. Her voice sounded high and strange in her own ears.

"I am Sybil-Mhari Aillard," she said hoarsely, "and the Lord Ludovic will have the skin stripped from your body in ribbons an inch wide!"

"*Domna!*" The man's voice was husky and disbelieving. He said protestingly, "But . . ." and he sagged and leaned back. A curious little stab, like a cramp in her belly, sharp but somehow not unpleasant, suddenly weakened Sybil's knees again as she contemplated his whitening face. He stared, gulped audibly once or twice.

After a moment he managed to collect himself some-what, the hoarse voice was puzzled and apologetic, but if Sybil had expected him to cringe—and she had—she was oddly disappointed.

"My lady, I must beg your forgiveness. I took you for a serving-girl—and what in the name of the Blessed Cassilda," he finished rationally, "are you doing, my lady, out here in the courtyard in the night air, in your smock like any wench from the kitchens?"

Sybil blinked, put oddly on the defensive. She started to say, I wanted to look at the waterfall, but then she realized she need not explain herself to a common Guardsman! The doings of a Comyn lady were no con-cern of his! He was holding the lantern close to her face, and his own features emerged more clearly—rough-cut and bronzed, an old scar seaming his cheek, but with twinkling eyes that even now looked good-humored. His breath was none too steady as he said "Well, my little lady, it's perfectly sure I'd be buzzard meat if you wanted to make trouble for me, but you wouldn't do a thing like that, would you? I meant no harm, you know, and after all, who'd expect the Lady Sybil-Mhari to be roaming about the courtyard after moonrise?" His smile was coaxing, almost intimate. "I can only say I'm sorry—or maybe I'm not," he finished suddenly. "If you'd not told me who you were, maybe I'd have wanted more than a kiss, and taken it too!"

Sybil swayed slightly, feeling—as she had felt when she looked into the starstone—the strange alien touch against her mind . . . *Desire* . . . *Fear* . . . His hot eyes were still fastened on her, searching through the untied ribbons at her bosom, but hesitant, somehow held back . . . *fear*. She could feel his fear . . . and the desire, burn-ing into her, burning *through* her . . . he dared not touch her now. . . .

She swayed slightly, and, this time without apology, he put his arms behind her shoulders, bent to support her light weight.

She whispered "I feel . . . faint. . . ." and let herself fall limp against him, her head dropping pliantly into the hollow of his shoulder; she could feel the slow pounding of his heart through his jerkin, she could feel . . . she buried her forehead still more closely into the heat of him. *There is a power in you,* the *leronis* had said. Now, feeling its surge, she knew what lay behind his fear and desire; her hands felt icy cold, and, shivering, she caught one of his warm ones and pressed it to her throat.

"I . . . I can't breathe," she whispered, making her voice soft, beguiling. She made sure, before releasing his hand, that he would not be able to let her go again. She closed her eyes, as he lifted her; hung suspended, it seemed, swaying between air and fire, and felt again the strange ecstatic sensation of hurling, tumbling, flying, falling—the waterfall roaring beneath.

When she opened her eyes, he had laid her down in a sheltered grass-plot opening from one of the courtyards and was kneeling beside her, his rough hands working, with deft blunt motions, on the ribbons imprisoning her breast. She breathed deeply and whispered "Now I feel better—I don't know what happened to me. . . ." But when he would have drawn his hands hesitantly away again, she captured and held them.

"No, no . . . don't let me go," she begged, feeling the cold, emptiness surge back again. She was frightened, sick with the fear she felt in him, and yet compelled by something more powerful still, something building. . . . She did not know what it was, was it only this? Then his arms were around her again, disbelieving, hungry, gentle, and his mouth forcing her lips apart.

It was strange, shaking and strange, the surge and

tremble that overwhelmed her. Never before had she
known any touch like this; the fumbling and sweatily respectful hand-kiss of her cousins, the cold fatherly hand
of the Lord of the Domain on her brow, the giggling
embrace of her girl-companions—nothing like this rough
hunger, so tender for all its fierceness. "My little lady,"
he whispered huskily, against her throat. "You don't
even know what it is you want, do you?"

No. But I will know, I will. . . . The memory spun in
her, there is a power in you, and I fear it . . . but could
it be only this, only this? She fastened her mouth to his,
biting savagely at his stiff lips, struggling furiously—not
in protest, but in eagerness, against the gentle pressure of
his hands. There was a writhing, a straining, a moment of
agony; she felt the dew damp on her back, icy cold
through the thin silk of her dress, his heavy rough hair-
iness drowning her silken breasts. She twisted and
fought, not with any desire to escape, but rather in the
same savage determination with which she fought to grip
an untamed horse with her thin thighs, the same grim
conflict with which she struggled to hood an unruly
falcon. She knew what was happening to him, she knew
what was happening to her, but it was not what she
thought, it was only a beginning, as she felt all his fear,
respect, hesitation, sink down and die beneath the growing urgency, need, hunger. . . .

She pushed away his hot kisses as the man's spent
breathing hissed past his parted teeth, and sat up, retying
her shoulder-ribbons with flying fingers. Was this the
final ineffable joy, the delight immeasurable, about
which the other maidens squealed and whispered? She
pushed his hand away when he would have assisted her,
her whole body flinching in revulsion. She felt bruised
and shaken, and she clenched her teeth tight to keep
them from chattering. She broke into his whispered

stream of endearments with a quick, shaken, "Take me back—they will be looking for me."

He raised her gently, as he might pick up a child who has stumbled, and she drew a deep breath, something . . . she hardly knew what . . . growing to swift birth inside her tight, throbbing breasts, her bruised and aching body. She forced herself to conceal her shaking, and to smile up at him, then leaned her head hard against his encircling arm and murmured with deliberate pathos, "You must take me back—I am almost a prisoner, you know."

He supported her faltering steps, half carrying her, whispering, "Yes, yes, my little silken bird, my little flower." He paused at the edge of the archway, retrieving his lantern from its hiding-place, and looked at her, saying hesitantly, "Little lady, you cannot return like this!"

In the crude light Sybil looked down at her crushed and torn ribbons, her crumpled and stained dress, tasting the blood on her lips with a slow satisfaction. She touched her tangled coppery curls with exploring fingers as he persuaded, "Come, little one, smooth your dress, let me fasten your sash. No one must see you like this!" There was fear in him again, and she could feel it like a taste in her mouth. Sybil tilted her head to one side, then heard the sound for which, without knowing it until this moment, she had been waiting. The clash of pikes, the ringing step and the challenge. She clenched her small fists, feeling her breath roughen and catch in her throat, smiling up at him.

"Must they not?" she murmured, then suddenly whirled, breaking away from him, and cried out imperiously, "Guard! Guard, to me!"

"What . . ." the man took a backward step; booted feet, running, echoed in harsh sequence on the flagstones and an explosion of lights burst in their faces; the face of a steel-capped Guard—*Blessed Cassilda be thanked! It's a Guard who knows me by sight!*—thrust through the archway and a startled voice gasped "Lady Sybil-Mhari!"

She pointed, with a dramatic gesture, feeling the frightening power surge up inside her. "Kill him!" she commanded, and heard her voice breaking on what she herself would have taken for a wild sob of shame and fright, if she had heard it from another throat. She could almost see herself reflected in the Guard's eyes, in his mind, swollen lips oozing a trace of bitten blood, the loosened ribbons falling to show her bruised breast, the skirt torn to show a hint of narrow thighs. The Guard spat out a cry of dismay and horror, shouting to his confederates; Sybil turned away, modestly mantling her face with her hair, as a second Guard appeared behind the first and his face echoed all the changes she had seen in the first. A tiny smile of contempt trembled on Sybil's lips, but she made it into a piteous grimace, widening her eyes as she looked down at the man in whose arms she had lain only a few minutes ago. She whispered pathetically "The Lord Ludovic must never know—my honor is in your hands—but how can it be? But if he were . . . somehow . . . to fall into the waterfall. . . ."

And now she saw the blanching of terror, the whitening of nostril and jaw, as the man's eyes sought hers in wild entreaty.

"Lady . . . little lady. . . ." he gasped helplessly, and his hoarse and husky voice, as when he had whispered endearments, sent a thrill of warmth through her.

There is a power in you . . . and I fear it . . . oh, she thought ecstatically, *if the Hastur sorceress could only know . . . she would have robbed me of this. . . .*

She watched the Guards seize the man, expertly pinion his arms; followed like a shadow, hugging herself with her thin arms, on the crest of rising excitement, as they hustled him rudely toward the cliff. He was shouting now, hoarse indecencies, until one of the Guards shoved a hand over his mouth. They struggled briefly at the wall, and suddenly Sybil felt a wild thrill surging through her body. It knifed hotly through her breasts, overwhelming as a kiss; stabbed fluid warmth all through her, gripped her thighs in a vise of pleasure. She gasped, her breath jolting out on the cresting heat of it, and cried aloud in unbearable delight as the man's figure tottered on the ledge, clawed wildly at the air, flailed and disappeared. Sybil sank down in the grass, breathing in heavy sobs, knowing now what was the true power, the joy of love—vaguely, in her overwhelming surge of emotion, she wondered what his name had been, how she could discover his name. She would remember it always in her prayers for the dead, the name of the one who had released the power within her, had brought her to fulfillment. She became aware that one of the Guards was bending solicitously over her. She was too spent to rise; she let him lift her, leaning heavily on his arm, swaying helplessly.

"Lady Sybil," he said gently, "Your honor, and your secret, are forever safe with me. I will conduct you safe to the women's quarters; see you only that your maids do not gossip, and this night's work shall never be known." He guided her tottering steps with reverent hands. "Poor little lady, if I had been at hand, that beast, that disgrace to the Guards and their honor, had never dared lay his hands on you . . ."

She lowered her long lashes. "What is your name? I would thank my . . . my preserver in my prayers, before I sleep."

"Reuel, my lady."

"Reuel. I shall . . . remember," she whispered. She would not make that mistake again. "You will not find me . . . ungrateful." Again the unendurable pleasures gusted up through her as she saw his thin swarthy face go foolish and soft with a sudden, incredible hope. She murmured, "I often walk in the courtyard here. Will you protect me?"

"With . . . with my very life, Lady." he stammered, and she looked at him and smiled. With him the terror need not strike till she had fed on the desire for a day or two, and the fear, and the hope . . . till she had fed herself full. Now that she knew her power, she could wait for her pleasure.

She smiled, with the drunken joy of a woman who has discovered true love, and ran lightly up the stairway toward her chamber.

THE SWORD OF
ALDONES

CHAPTER ONE

We were outstripping the night.

The *Southern Cross* had made planetfall on Darkover at midnight. There I had embarked on the Terran skyliner that was to take me halfway around a planet; only an hour had passed, but already the thin air was beginning to flush red with a hint of dawn. Under my feet the floor of the big plane tilted slightly as it began to fly aslant down the western ridge of the Hellers. Peak after peak fell away astern, cutting the sparse clouds that capped the snowline; and already my memory was looking for landmarks, although I knew we were too high.

After six years of knocking around half a dozen star-systems, I was going home again; but I felt nothing. Not homesick. Not excited. Not even resentful. I hadn't wanted to return to Darkover, but I hadn't even cared enough to refuse.

Six years ago I had left Darkover, intending never to return. The Regent's desperate message had followed me from Terra, to Samarra, to Vainwal. It costs plenty to send a personal message interspace, even over the Terran relay system, and old Hastur—Regent of the Comyn, Lord of the Seven Domains—hadn't wasted words in explaining. It had simply been a command. But I couldn't imagine why they wanted me back. They'd all been glad to see the last of me, when I went.

I turned from the paling light at the window, closing my eyes and pressing my good hand to my temple. The interstellar passage, as always, had been made under heavy sedation. Now the dope that the ship's medic had given me was beginning to wear off; fatigue cut down my barriers, letting in a teasing telepathic trickle of thought.

I could *feel* the covert stares of the other passengers; at my scarred face; at the arm that ended at the wrist in a folded sleeve; but mostly at *what,* and *who* I was. A telepath. A freak. An Alton—one of the Seven Families of the Comyn—that hereditary autarchy which has ruled Darkover since long before our sun faded to red.

And yet, not quite one of them. My father, Kennard Alton—every child on Darkover could repeat the story— had done a shocking, almost a shameful thing. He had married, taken in honorable *laran* marriage, a Terran woman, kin to the hated Empire people who have overrun the civilized Galaxy.

He had been powerful enough to brazen it out. They had needed my father in Comyn Council. After Old Hastur, he had been the most powerful man in the Comyn. He'd even managed to cram me down their throats. But they'd all been glad when I left Darkover. And now I had come home.

In the seat in front of me, two professorish-looking Earthmen, probably research workers on holiday from mapping and exploring, were debating the old chestnut of origins. One was stubbornly defending the theory of parallel evolutions; the other, the theory that some ancient planet—preferably Earth itself—colonized the whole Galaxy a million years ago. I concentrated on their conversation, trying to shut out awareness of the stares around me. Telepaths are never at ease in crowds.

The Dispersionist brought out all the old arguments for a lost age of star-travel, and the other man was arguing about the nonhuman races and the differing levels of culture on any single planet.

"Darkover, for instance," he argued. "A planet still in early feudal culture, trying to reconcile itself to the impact of the Terran Empire—"

I lost interest. It was amazing, how many Terrans still thought of Darkover as a feudal or barbarian planet. Simply because we retain, not resistance, but indifference to Terran imports of machinery and weapons because we prefer to ride horses and mules, as an ordinary thing, rather than spend our time in building roads. And because Darkover, bound by the ancient Compact, wants to take no chance of a return to the days of war and mass murder with coward's weapons. That is the law on all planets of the Darkovan League, and all civilized worlds outside. Who would kill, must come within reach of death. They could talk disparagingly of the code duello, and the feudal system. I'd heard it all, on Terra. But isn't it more civilized to kill your personal enemy at handgrips, with sword or knife, than to slay a thousand strangers at a safe distance?

The people of Darkover have held out, better than most, against the glamor of the Terran Empire. I've been on other planets, and I've seen what happened to most worlds when the Earthmen came in with the lure of a civilization that spans the stars. They don't subdue new worlds by force of arms. The Earthman can afford to sit back and wait until the native culture simply collapses under their impact. They wait till the planet begs to be taken into the Empire. And sooner or later the planet does—and becomes one more link in the vast, overcentralized monstrosity swallowing world after world.

It hadn't happened here, not yet.

A man near the front of the cabin rose and made his way toward me; without permission, he swung himself into the empty seat at my side.

"Comyn?" But it wasn't a question.

The man was tall and sparsely built; mountain Dark-ovan, Cahuenga from the Hellers. His stare dwelt, an instant past politeness, on the scars and the empty sleeve; then he nodded.

"I thought so," he said. "You were the boy who was mixed up in that Sharra business."

I felt the blood rise in my face. I had spent six years forgetting the Sharra rebellion—and Marjorie Scott. I would bear the scars forever. Who the hell was this man, to remind me?

"Whatever I was," I said curtly, "I am not, now, And I don't remember you."

"And you an Alton!" he mocked lightly.

"In spite of all scare stories," I said, "Altons don't go around casually reading minds. In the first place, it's hard work. In the second place, most people's minds are too full of muck. And in the third place," I added, "we just don't give a damn."

He laughed. "I didn't expect you to recognize me," he said. "You were drugged and delirious when I saw you last. I told your father that hand would have to come off eventually. I'm sorry I was right about it." He didn't sound sorry at all. "I'm Dyan Ardais."

Now I remembered him, after a fashion, a mountain lord from the far fastnesses of the Hellers. There had never been any love lost, even in the Comyn, between the Altons and the men of the Ardais.

"You travel alone? Where is your father, young Alton?"

"My father died on Vainwal," I said shortly.

His voice was a purr. "Then welcome, *Comyn* Alton!"

The ceremonial title was a shock as he spoke it. He glanced at the square of paling window.

"We're coming in to Thendara. Will you travel with me?"

"I expect to be met." I didn't, but I had no wish to prolong this chance acquaintance. Dyan bowed, unruffled. "We shall meet in Council," he said, and added, with lazy elegance, "Oh, and guard your belongings well, *Comyn* Alton. There are, doubtless, some who would like to recover the Sharra matrix."

He spun round and walked away and I sat slack, in shock. Damn! Had he picked my mind as I sat there? *How else had he known?* The dirty Cahuenga! Still doped with procalamin as I was, he could have gotten inside my telepathic barriers and out again before I knew it. *But would one of the Comyn stoop so far?*

I started after him, furiously; started to rise, and fell back with a jolt; we were losing altitude rapidly. The sign flashed to fasten seat belts; I fumbled at mine, my mind in turmoil.

He had forced memory on me—forced me to remember *why* I had left Darkover six years ago, scarred and broken and maimed for life. Wounds that had begun to heal, with time and silence, tore at me again. And he had spoken the name of Sharra.

A half-caste boy, a bastard, Comyn by special grace only because my father had no Darkovan sons, I had been easy prey for the rebels and malcontents swarming under the rallying cry of *Sharra*. Sharra—the legend called her a goddess turned daemon, bound in golden chains, called forth by fire. I had stood at those fires, using my telepath gifts to summon forth the powers of Sharra.

The Aldarans, the Comyn family exiled for dealing with the Terrans, had been at the center of the rebellion. I was a kinsman of Beltran, Lord of Aldaran.

Faces I had tried to forget marched relentlessly out to torment me. The man called Kadarin, rebel extraordinary, who persuaded me to join the rebels of Sharra. The Scotts; drunken Zeb Scott who had found the talisman matrix of Sharra, and his children. Little Rafe, who had followed me about, his hero; Thyra, with the face of a girl and the eyes of a wild beast. And Marjorie . . .

Marjorie! Time slid away. A frightened girl with soft brown hair and gold-flecked amber eyes stole to my side through the strange firelight. Laughing, she walked the streets of a city that was now smashed rubble, a garland of golden flowers in her hand. . . .

I slammed the memory shut. That wouldn't help. The thrum of the braking jets hurt my ears; out the window I could see the stubby towers of Thendara, rosy in the pink sunlight; a bright spot on the dark plains, patched with forests and low hills. We dipped lower and lower, and I saw lakes flash like silver mirrors; then the skyscraper peak of the Terran HQ building flashed past the window, the glare and whiteness of the spaceport struck my eyes, there was a jar and a bump, and we were down. I tore at my straps. Now for Dyan—

But I missed him. The airfield was a scrabble of humans from thirty planets, jabbering in a hundred languages, and as I pushed my way through the crowd, I ran with smashing force into a thin girl dressed in white.

She stumbled and fell, and I bent to help her to her feet. "Please forgive me," I said in Standard, "I should have been looking where I was going—" and then I got a good look at her.

"Linnell!" I cried out joyfully, "by all that's wonderful!" I caught her up clumsily, hugging her. "Did you come to meet me? But, little cousin, how you've grown!"

"I beg your pardon!" The girl's voice was dripping with ice. Suddenly aghast, I set her on her feet. She was speaking Darkovan now, but no Darkovan girl ever had such an accent. I stared at her, appalled.

"I'm sorry," I said at last, dumbfounded. "I thought—" but I kept on staring. She was a tall girl, very fair, with a soft heart-shaped face and soft dark brown hair and gentle gray eyes—but they were not gentle now; they were blazing with anger.

"Well?"

"I'm sorry," I repeated numbly, "I thought you were one of my cousins."

She gave a cool shrug, murmured something and moved away. I followed her with my eyes, still staring. The resemblance was fantastic. It wasn't just a superficial similarity of coloring and height; the girl was a mirror image of my cousin, Linnell Aillard. Even her voice sounded like Linnell's.

A light hand touched my shoulder and a gay girlish voice said "Shame, Lew! How you must have embarrassed poor Linnell! She brushed past me without even speaking! Have you been away so long that you have forgotten all your manners?"

"Dio Ridenow!" I said, startled.

The girl beside me was small and pert, with flaxen-gold hair fluttering about her shoulders, and her green-gray eyes were aslant with mischief. "I thought you were on Vainwal!" I said.

"And when you said good-bye to me there, you thought I would stay alone to cry my eyes out," she said saucily. "Not I! The space lanes are free to women as well as men, Lew Alton, and I, too, have a place in Comyn Council, when I choose to take it. Why should I stay there and sleep alone?" She giggled. "Oh, Lew, you should see your face! What's the matter?"

"It wasn't Linnell," I said, and Dio stared. "Who, then?" She looked around, but the girl who looked like Linnell had vanished into the crowds. "And where is my uncle? Have you quarreled with your father again, Lew?"

"No!" I said roughly. "He died on Vainwal!" Didn't *anyone* on Darkover know it yet? "Do you think anything less would bring me back here?"

I saw the mirth go out of Dio's face. "Oh, Lew! I'm sorry! I didn't know!"

She touched my arm again, but I shied away from her sympathy. Dio Ridenow was high explosive where I was concerned. On Vainwal, that had all been very well. But I knew, if she didn't, how quickly that old affair could flare up into passion again. I had troubles enough without woman trouble, too.

Once again I had failed to barricade my thoughts. Dio's fair face etched itself with crimson; and abruptly, catching her teeth in her lip, she turned and almost ran toward the spaceport barriers.

"Dio!" I called after her, but at that moment someone shouted my name.

And right there, I made my first mistake. I didn't go after her—don't ask me why. But someone called my name again.

"Lew! Lew Alton!"

And the next moment a slender, dark-haired boy in Terran clothing was smiling up at me.

"Lew! Welcome home!"

And I couldn't remember his name to save my life.

He looked familiar. He knew me, and I knew him. But I stood warily back, remembering how I had *recognized* Linnell. The youngster laughed.

"Don't you know me?"

"I've been away too long to be sure about anybody," I said. I reached for telepathic contact, but the drug was still fuzzing my brain; I sensed only the fringes of familiarity. I shook my head at the kid. He'd have been only a child when I left Darkover; he was still so young that I don't think he'd started shaving yet.

"Zandru's hells," I said, "you *couldn't* be Marius, could you?"

"Couldn't I?"

I still couldn't believe it. My brother Marius, the younger brother who had cost our Terran mother her life —could I possibly fail to recognize my own brother?

He was grinning up at me shyly, and I relaxed. "I'm sorry, Marius," I said. "You were so young, and you've changed so much. Well—"

"We can talk later," he said quickly. "You have to go through customs, and all, but I wanted to get to you first. What's the matter, Lew, you look funny. Sick?"

I leaned hard for a minute on his suddenly-steadying arm, until the vertigo passed. "Procalamin," I said ruefully, and at his blank look elucidated. "They shoot us full of it, on starships, so we can take the hyperdrive stresses without coming apart at the seams. It takes a while to wear off, and I'm allergic to the stuff anyhow."

I caught his sidewise glance and my face grew grimmer. "Do I look that bad? That's right, you haven't seen me, have you, since I lost my hand and got my face cut up. Well, get a good look."

His eyes slid away, and I tightened my arm around his shoulders.

"I don't mind you staring," I said more gently, "but damned if I want you sneaking a look at me when you think I won't notice, because I always do. See?"

He relaxed and studied me frankly for a minute, then grinned. "Not pretty, but you never were much of a beauty, as I remember. Let's go."

I looked past the skyscraper of the HQ, and the tall buildings of the Trade City. Beyond them rose the vast, splintered teeth of the mountains; and poised far above the plain, the loom of the Comyn Castle, topped by the tall spire of the Keeper's Tower.

"Are the Comyn already assembled in Thendara?"

Marius shook his head. I still couldn't get used to the notion that this was my brother. He didn't *feel* right. "No," he said, "they—we're meeting out in the Hidden City. Lew, did you bring any guns from Terra?"

"Hell, no. What would I want with guns? And they're contraband anyhow."

"Then you're not armed at all?"

I shook my head. "No. It's not allowed to carry side arms on most Empire planets and I've lost the habit. Why?"

He scowled. "I managed to get one last year," he said. "I paid four times what it was worth, and it has the contraband mark on it. I thought—wait, that's your name they're calling."

It was. I went slowly toward the low white customs building, Marius trailing after me. He shook his head at the officer on duty, and went on through. My luggage had been laid on the conveyer belt and the clerk glanced at me without much interest.

"Lewis Alton-Kennard-Montray-Alton? Landed at Port Chicago on the *Southern Cross?* Martix technician?"

I admitted all of it, and shoved the plastic chip which held my certification as a licensed matrix mechanic.

"We'll have to check this on the main banks," the Terran clerk said. "It will take an hour or two. We'll get in touch with you."

The clerk flicked his eyes over a printed form.

"Do-you-solemnly-affirm-that-to-the-best-of-your-knowledge-and-belief-you-have-not-in-your-possession-any-power-or-propulsion-weapons-guns-disintegrators-or-blasters-atomic-isotopes-narcotic-drugs-intoxicants-or-incendiaries?"

I sighed. He hefted my luggage under the clarifier; the screen stayed blank, as I'd known it would. The items named were all items of Terran manufacture; by solemn compact with the Hasturs, the Empire is committed not to let them be brought into the Darkovan Zone, or anywhere outside the Trade Cities. Such items, contraband on our planet, were treated before they were brought here with a small speck of radioactive substance, harmless but unremovable.

"Anything else to declare?"

"I have a pair of Earth-made binoculars, a Terran camera, and half a bottle of Vainwal *firi*," I told him.

"Let's see them."

He opened the cases, and I tensed. This was the moment I had been dreading.

I should have tried to bribe him. But that would have meant—if he happened to be honest—a fine and blacklisting. I couldn't risk that.

He glanced at the camera and binoculars. Terran lenses are a luxury item and usually highly taxed. "Ten *reis* duty," he said, and pushed the folds of clothing aside. "If the *fri* is less than ten ounces, there's no tax. What is this?"

I thought I'd bite through my tongue when his hand gripped it. It felt like a fist squeezing my heart. I said through a contracted throat, "Let it alone!"

"What in the—" he dragged it out. It was like a nail raking along a nerve. He started to unwrap the cloth. "Contraband weapon, huh? You—hell, it's a *sword!*"

I couldn't breathe. The blue crystals in the hilt winked up at me, and his hand gripping it was too vast an agony to be borne.

"It's a—an heirloom in my family."

He looked at me queerly. "Well, I'm not hurting it any. Just wanted to make sure it wasn't a contraband blaster, or something." He shoved the folds of silk around it again, and I remembered how to breathe. He picked up the half-empty bottle of the expensive Vainwal cordial and measured it with his eyes. "About seven ounces. Sign a statement that you're bringing it in for personal consumption and not for resale, and it's duty free."

I signed. He snapped the lock on the case, and I moved, with faltering steps, away from the customs barrier.

One hurdle past. And I'd managed to live through it—this time.

I rejoined Marius and went to hail a skycar.

CHAPTER TWO

The Sky Harbor Hotel was tawdry and expensive, and I didn't much like the place; but I wasn't apt to run into other Comyn there, and that was the main thing. So they showed us up to two of the square cubicles which Terrans call rooms.

I've gotten used to them on Terra and Vainwal, and they didn't bother me. But as I fastened the doors, I turned to Marius in sudden dismay.

"Zandru's hells, I'd forgotten! Does this bother you?"

I knew how doors, and walls, and locks, could affect a Darkovan. I'd known that terrible, suffocating claustrophobia all during my first years on Earth. More than anything else it sets Darkovan apart from Terran; Darkovan rooms had translucent walls, divided by thin panels or curtains or solid light barriers.

But Marius seemed quite at ease, sprawling idly on a piece of furniture so modernistic I couldn't tell whether it was a bed or a chair. I shrugged; I'd learned to tolerate claustrophobia, probably he had too.

I bathed, shaved, and wadded up, carelessly, most of the Terran clothing I'd worn on the starship. The things were comfortable, but I couldn't turn up in Comyn Council wearing them. I dressed in suede-leather breeches, low ankle-boots, and laced up the crimson jerkin deftly, making a little extra display of my one-handed skill because I was still too damned sensitive about it. The short cloak in the Alton colors concealed the hand that wasn't there. I felt as if I'd changed my skin.

Marius was roaming restlessly about the room. He still didn't feel familiar. I vaguely recognized his voice and manner, but there wasn't that sense of closeness usual between telepaths in a Comyn family. I wondered if he sensed it, too. Maybe it was the drugs.

I stretched out, shut my eyes and tried to doze, but even the quiet bothered me; after eight days in space, the thrumming of the drives an omnipresent nuisance under the veils of drug. Finally I sat up and hauled my smaller piece of luggage toward me.

"Do me a favor, Marius?"

"Sure."

"I'm still doped—can't concentrate. Can you open a matrix lock?"

"If it's a simple one."

It was; any nontelepath could have attuned his mind to the simple psychokinetic pattern broadcast by the matrix crystal which held the lock shut. "It's simple, but it's keyed to me. Touch my mind and I'll give it to you."

The request was not an uncommon one, within a telepath family. But the boy stared at me in something like panic. I looked back, amazed, then relaxed and grinned. After all, Marius hardly knew me. He'd been a small boy when I left, and I supposed, to him, I was the next thing to a complete stranger. "Oh, all right. Lock and I'll touch you."

I made a light telepathic contact with the surface of his thoughts, visualizing the pattern of the matrix lock. His mind was so totally barriered that he might have been a stranger, even a nontelepath. It embarrassed me; I felt naked and intrusive.

After all, I wasn't sure Marius was a telepath. Children don't show that talent to any extent before adolescence, and he'd been a child when I went away. In all else he had inherited Terran traits, why should he have this one Darkovan talent?

He laid the case, opened, on the bed. I lifted out a small square box and handed it to him.

"Not much of a present," I said, "but at least I remembered."

He opened the box, hesitantly, and looked at the binoculars that lay, shiny and alien, inside. But he handled them with a strange embarrassment, then laid them back in the box without comment. I felt mildly annoyed. I hadn't expected gratitude, especially, but he might have thanked me. He hadn't asked about father, either.

"The Terrans can't be beaten for lensed goods," he said, after a minute.

"They *can* grind lenses. And build spaceships. As far as I can tell, it's all they can do."

"And fight wars," he said, but I didn't take that up. "I'll show you the camera, too. I won't tell you what I paid for it, though—you'd think I was crazy."

I went through the cases, and Marius sat beside me, looking at things and asking diffident questions. He was obviously interested, but for some reason he seemed to be trying to conceal it. Why?

At last I drew out the long shape of the sword. And as I touched it, I felt the familiar mixture of revulsion and pleasure. . . .

All the time I'd been off Darkover, it had been dead. Dormant. Hidden between blade and hilt of the heirloom sword, the proximity of the strong matrix made me tremble. Off-world it was an inert crystal. Now it was *alive*, with a strange, living warmth.

Most matrices are harmless. Bits of metal, or crystal, or stone, which respond to the psychokinetic wave lenths of thought, transforming them into energy. In the ordinary matrix mechanic—and in spite of what the Terrans think, matrix mechanics is just a science, which anybody can learn—this psychokinetic ability is developed independent of telepathy. Though telepaths are better at it, especially on the higher levels.

But the Sharra matrix was keyed into the telepathic centers, and into the whole nervous system; body and brain.

It was dangerous to handle. Matrices of this kind were traditionally concealed in a weapon of some sort. Sharra's matrix was the most fearful weapon ever devised. It was reasonable to hide it in a sword. A lithium bomb would have been better. *Preferably one that would explode and destroy matrix and all . . . and me with it.*

Marius was gazing down at me, with a set, horror-stricken face. He was shaking.

"Sharra's matrix!" he whispered between stiff lips, "Why, Lew? Why?"

I turned on him, and demanded hoarsely, "How did you know—"

He had never been told. Our father had agreed to keep it from him. I got up, suspicion surging over me, but before I could complete the question, a burp from the intercom interrupted. Marius reached past me to grab it; listened, then held out the receiver and vacated his seat for me. "Official, Lew," he said in an undertone.

"Department three," said a crisp, bored voice, when I identified myself.

"Zandru!" I muttered. "Already? No—excuse me—go ahead."

"Official notification," said the bored voice. "A statement of intention to murder, in fair fight, has been filed with this office against Lewis Alton-Kennard-Montray-Alton. Declared murderer is identified as Robert Raymon Kadarin, address unregistered. Notification had been legally given; kindly accept and acknowledge the notice, or file a legally acceptable reason for refusal."

I swallowed hard. "Acknowledged," I said at last, and put down the receiver, sweating. The boy came and sat beside me. "What's wrong, Lew?"

My head hurt, and I rubbed it with my good hand.

"I just got an intent-to-murder."

"Hell," said Marius, "already? Who from?"

"Nobody you know." My scar twitched. Kadarin—leader of the rebels of Sharra; once my friend, now my sworn, implacable foe. He hadn't lost any time in inviting me to settle our old quarrel. I wondered if he even knew I'd lost my hand. Tardily it occurred to me—as if it were something happening to someone else—that this would have been a legally admissible reason for refusing. I tried to reassure the staring boy.

"Take it easy, Marius. I'm not afraid of Kadarin, in fair fight. He never was any good with a sword. He—"

"Kadarin!" he stammered. "But, but Bob promised—"

"*Bob!*" Abruptly my fingers bit his arm. "How do *you* know Kadarin?"

"I want to explain, Lew. I'm not—"

"You'll do a lot of explaining, brother," I said curtly. And then someone started to hammer purposefully on the door.

"Don't open it!" said Marius urgently.

But I crossed the room and threw back the bolt, and Dio Ridenow ran into the room.

Since I'd seen her on the spaceport she had changed into men's riding clothes, a little too big for her, and she looked like a belligerent child. She stopped, a step or two inside, and stood staring at the boy behind me.

"What—"

"You know my brother," I said impatiently.

But Dio stood frozen. "Your *brother?*" she gasped, at last. "Are you out of your mind? That's no more Marius

than—than I am!" I drew back incredulously, and Dio
stamped her foot in annoyance. "His eyes! Lew, you idiot, *look at his eyes!*"

My supposed brother made a quick lunge, taking me
off balance. He threw his whole weight against us. Dio
reeled, and I went down on one knee, fighting for balance. *Eyes.* Marius—now I remembered—had had the
eyes of our Terran mother. Dark brown. No Darkovan
has brown or black eyes. And this—this imposter who
was *not* Marius looked at me with eyes of a stranger,
gold-flecked amber. Only twice had I seen eyes like that.
Marjorie. And—

"Rafe Scott!"

Marjorie's brother! No wonder he had known me, no
wonder I had sensed his presence as familiar. I remembered him, too, only as a small boy!

He tried to push past me; I grabbed at him and we
swayed, struggling, in a bone-breaking clinch. "*Where's
my brother?*" I yelled. I twisted my foot behind his
ankle, and we crashed to the floor together.

He'd never said he was Marius, it flashed across my
mind in a split second. *He just hadn't denied it when I
thought so. . . .*

I got my knee across his chest and held him pinned
down. "What's the idea, Rafe? Talk!"

"Let me up, damn you! I can explain!"

I didn't doubt that a bit. How cleverly he had discovered that I was unarmed. But I should have known. I
should have trusted my instinct; he didn't *feel* like my
brother. He hadn't asked about father. He'd been embarrassed when I brought him a gift.

Dio said, "Lew, perhaps—" but before I could answer,
Rafe gave an unexpected twist and sent me sprawling.
Before I could scramble up, he thrust Dio un-
ceremoniously aside, and the door slammed behind him.

I got up, my breath coming hard, and Dio came to me.

"Are you hurt? Aren't you going to try and catch him?"

"No, to both questions." Until I found out why Rafe had tried this clumsy and daring imposture, there would be no point in finding him. And meanwhile, where was Marius?

"The situation," I remarked, not necessarily to Dio, "gets crazier every minute. Where do *you* come into it?"

She sat down on the bed and glared at me.

"Where do you think?"

For once I regretted that I could not read her mind. There was a reason why I couldn't—but I won't go into that now.

But Dio was trouble, in a pretty, small, blonde package. I was here on Darkover; I had to stay at least a while.

The social codes of Vainwal—where Dio, under the lax protection of her brother Lerrys, had spent the last two seasons—are considerably less rigid than the strict codes of Darkovan propriety. Her brother had had sense enough not to interfere.

But here on Darkover, Dio was *comynara*, and held *laran* rights in the vast Ridenow estates. And what was I? A half-caste of the hatred Terrans—entanglement with Dio would bring all the Ridenow down on my head, and there were a lot of them.

I would be grateful to Dio all my life. When Marjorie was torn from me, in the horror of that last night when Sharra had ravened in the hills across the river, something had been cut from me. Not clean like my hand, but rotting and festering inside. There had been no other women, no other love, nothing but a bleak black horror, until Dio. She had flung herself into my life, a pretty, passionate, willful girl, and she had gone unflinching into that horror, and somehow, after that, I had healed clean.

Love? Not as I knew the word. But understanding, and implicit trust. I would have trusted her with my reputation, my fortune, my sanity—my life.

But I trusted her brothers about as far as I could see through the hull of the *Southern Cross*. And I couldn't quarrel with them—not yet. I tried to make this clear to Dio without hurting her feelings, but it wasn't easy. She sat sulking and swinging her feet while I paced up and down like a trapped animal. Just having her here in my rooms could be dangerous if her family got wind of it—however innocent. And I knew if we were together very much it wouldn't be innocent. Dio's murmured "I understand," made me angry because I knew she did not really understand at all.

Her restless glance fell on the camouflage sword, lying across the bed. She frowned and picked it up.

Not pain, exactly, but a tension gripping me, a fist squeezing my nerves. I cried out, wordlessly, and Dio dropped it as if it burned her, staring open-mouthed.

"What's the matter?"

"I—can't explain." I stood regarding the thing for some minutes. "Before anything else, I'd better fix it so it's safe to handle. For the one who handles it and for me."

I rummaged my luggage for my matrix technician's kit. I had only a few lengths left of the special insulating cloth, but now I was back on Darkover, I could have more made for me. I wrapped the stuff around and over the juncture of hilt and blade until I could no longer feel the warmth and tingle of the matrix; frowned and held it away. I wasn't even sure if ordinary safeguards would work with this matrix.

I handed it to Dio. She bit her lip, but took it. It hurt, but manageably; a small nagging tension, no more. That much I could stand.

"Why ever did you leave a high-level matrix un-insulated?" Dio demanded, "and why did you let yourself be keyed into it that way?"

It was a very good question, especially the last. But I

ignored that one. "I didn't dare bring it through customs under insulation," I said soberly. "Earthmen know, now, what to look for. As long as it was just a sword, no one would look twice at it."

"Lew, I don't understand," she said helplessly.

"Don't try, darling," I said. "The less you know, the better for you. This isn't Vainwal, and I'm—not the man you knew there."

Her soft mouth was trembling, and in another minute I would have taken her in my arms; but at that moment someone banged on the door again.

And I had thought I'd have privacy here!

I stepped away from Dio. "That's probably your brothers," I said bitterly, "and I'll have another intent-to-murder filed on me."

I stepped toward the door. She caught my arm. "Wait," she said, urgently. "Take this."

I stared without comprehension at the thing she held out to me. It was a small propulsion pistol; one of the Terran-made powder weapons which do unbelievable havoc for their size and simplicity. I drew back my hand in refusal, but Dio thrust it into my pocket. "You don't have to *use* it," she said, "just carry it. *Please*, Lew."

The knock on the door was repeated, but Dio held me, saying, "*Please*," again, until at last, impatiently, I nodded. I went and opened the door a crack, standing in the opening so the girl could not be seen.

The boy in the hallway was stocky and dark, with heavy sullen features and amused dark eyes. He said, "Well, Lew?"

And then the presence of him was tangible to me. I can't explain exactly how, but I *knew*. All at once it was unbelievable that Rafe could have fooled me for a minute. Proof, if needed, that I'd been operating at minus capacity when I landed. I said huskily "Marius," and drew him inside.

He didn't say much, but his awkward grip of my hand was hard and intense. "Lew—father?"

"On Vainwal," I said. "There is a law. It is forbidden to transport bodies in space."

He swallowed and bent his head. "Under a sun I've never seen—" he whispered. I put my good arm round him, and after a minute he said thickly "At least you're here. You did come. They told me you wouldn't."

Touched, a little ashamed, I let him go. It had taken a command to bring me back, and I wasn't proud of that, now. I looked around, but Dio had gone. Evidently she had slipped out of the room by the other door. I was relieved; it saved explanations.

But in a way I was annoyed, too. Entirely too many people had been turning up and vanishing again. All the wrong people, for all the wrong reasons. Dyan Ardais—picking my mind on the skyliner. The girl on the spaceport, who looked like Linnell and wasn't. Rafe, passing himself off as my brother when he wasn't. Dio, turning up for no good reason, and disappearing again. And now Marius himself had turned up! Coincidence? Maybe, but confusing.

"Are you ready to leave?" Marius asked. "I've made all the arrangements, unless you've some reason for staying here."

"I've got to pick up my matrix certification at the Legation," I said. "Then we'll go." Maybe the sooner I got out of here, the better—or half of Darkover would be bursting in on me playing games!

"Lew," Marius asked abruptly, "do you have a gun?"

Rafe's question—and it grated on me. I was readjusting my thoughts, taking the fake Marius—Rafe—out of my thoughts and putting my brother where he belonged in them. I said curtly. "Yes," and let it go at that. "Will you come to the Legation with me?"

"I'll walk across the city with you." He looked around

the closed-in room and shuddered. "I couldn't *stay* in this beast-pit. You weren't going to sleep here tonight, were you?"

The Trade City had grown during my absence; it was larger than I remembered, dirtier, more crowded. Already it seemed more natural to call it the Trade City than by its Darkovan name, Thendara. Marius walked at my side, silent. At last he asked, "Lew, what's it like on Terra?"

He would ask that. Earth, home of the unknown forefathers he resembled so much. I had resented my Terran blood. Did he?

"It would take a lifetime to know Terra. I was only there for three years. I learned a lot of science and a little mathematics. Their technical schools are good. There was too much machinery, too much noise. I lived in the mountains; trying to live at sea level made me ill."

"You didn't like it there?"

"It was all right. They even fixed up a mechanical hand for me." I made a grim face. "There's the Legation."

Marius said, "You'd better give me that gun," then stared, in consternation, as I turned on him. "What's the matter, Lew?"

"Something very funny is going on," I said, "and I am getting suspicious of people who want me unarmed. Even you. Do you know a man called Robert Kadarin?"

When Marius looked blank, that dark face could be a masterpiece of obscurity, as unrevealing as a pudding. "I think I've heard the name. Why?"

"He filed an intent-to-murder on me," I said, and briefly drew the pistol out of my pocket. "I won't use this. Not on him. But I'm going to carry it."

"You'd better let me—" Marius stopped and shrugged. "I see. Forget I asked."

I rode the lift upward in the HQ building, past the barracks of Spaceforce, the census bureau, the vast floors of machines, records, traffic, all the business of the Empire. I walked down the corridors of the top floor, to a door that said: DAN LAWTON—Legate of Darkovan Affairs.

I'd met Lawton briefly before I left Darkover. His story was a little like mine; a Terran father, a mother from the Comyn. We were remotely related—I'd never figured out how. He was a big, rangy redhead who looked Darkovan and could have claimed a place in Comyn Council if he'd wanted it. He hadn't. He'd chosen the Empire, and was one of the top-ranking liaison men between Terran and Darkovan. No man can be honest who lives by Terra's codes; but he came closer than most.

We shook hands in the Terran fashion—a custom I hated—and I sat down. His smile was friendly, not over-hearty, and he didn't evade my eyes—and there are not many men who can, or will look a telepath square in the eyes.

He shoved the plastic chip across the table. "Here. I didn't need this; I just wanted a good excuse to talk to you, Alton."

I pocketed the certification, but I didn't answer.

"You've been on Terra, I hear. Like it?"

"The planet, yes. The people—no offense—no."

He laughed. "Don't apologize. I left, too. Only the dregs stay there. Anyone with any enterprise or intelligence goes out into the Empire. Alton, why did you never apply for Empire citizenship? Your mother was Terran—you had everything to gain by it, and nothing to lose."

"Why did you never accept a seat among the Hasturs?" I countered.

He nodded. "I see."

"Lawton, I don't fight Terra. I don't much like having the Empire here, but Darkover just *doesn't* fight by cities and nations and planets. If an Earthman were my enemy, I'd file an intent-to-murder, and kill him. If a dozen of them burned my house or stole my stud animals, I'd get my *com'ii* together and we'd kill *them*. But I can't feel anything at all about a few thousand people who have never done me either good or ill, just because they're *here*. It isn't our way. We do our hating by ones, not by millions."

"I can admire that psychology, but it puts you at a disadvantage against the Empire," Lawton said, and sighed. "Well, I won't keep you—unless there's something else I can do for you?"

"Maybe there is. Do you know a man who uses the name of Kadarin?"

The reaction was immediate. "Don't tell me he's in Thendara!"

"You know him?"

"I wish I didn't! No, I don't know him personally, I've never actually set eyes on him. But he pops up everywhere. He claims Darkovan citizenship when he's in the Terran Zone, and somehow manages to prove it; and I understand he claims to be a Terran, and prove it, outside."

"And?"

"And we can't deny him his Thirteen Days."

I chuckled. I had seen Terrans on Darkover baffled, before this, by the seemingly illogical catch-as-catch-can of the Thirteen Days. An exile, an outlaw, even a murderer, had an inalienable right—dating from time out of mind—to spend one day in Thendara, thirteen times a year, for the purpose of exercising his legal rights. During that time, provided he commits no overt offense, he enjoys absolute legal immunity.

"If he stayed one second over his limit, we'd grab him.

But he's careful. We aren't even able to hold him for spitting on the sidewalk. The only place he ever goes is the Spacemen's Orphanage. After which, seemingly, he vanishes into thin air."

"Well, you may be rid of him soon," I said. "Don't prosecute me when I kill him. He's filed intent-to-murder on me."

"If I could only be sure it wouldn't work the other way," Lawton smiled, as I rose to go.

But as I crossed the threshold, he called me abruptly back. The friendliness was gone; he strode toward me, wrathfully.

"You're carrying contraband. Hand it over!"

I handed the gun to him. There must, of course, have been a clarifier screen there. Lawton clicked the chambers; then he stared, frowned and handed it back to me.

"Here. Take it. I didn't realize."

He thrust it at me, impatiently. "Go on, take it! But get out of here before anyone else catches you. And give it back. If you need a permit, I'll try to get you one. But don't go around carrying contraband!" He pushed the gun back into my hand and virtually shoved me out of the office. I turned it over, baffled, as I walked toward the elevator. Then my eye fell on a small name plate: RAFAEL SCOTT.

And suddenly I knew I was not going to ask either Dio or Marius for an explanation.

CHAPTER THREE

"Very well, my lords. I will do as you wish!"

The woman's voice stopped me, cold, as I parted the curtains and stepped into the enclosure of the Altons, in the Council Hall of the Comyn.

We had come late to the Hidden City; so late that there had been no time to send word to Old Hastur, or even to make my presence known to Linnell who, as my nearest kinswoman and foster sister, would have been informed at once. Marius, who had never been accepted in Comyn Council, had parted from me outside the council hall, and gone to take his place in the lower hall among the lesser nobles and younger sons. I had climbed the stairs to the long gallery, intending to slip quietly through the curtains into the enclosure assigned to the Altons of the Comyn hierarchy.

I stood there, startled; for it was Callina Aillard who was speaking.

I had known her all my life, of course. She was my cousin, too; Linnell's half sister. But when I saw her last, six years ago—I shied away from the memory—she had been a girl, quiet, colorless. Now I saw that she was a woman, and beautiful.

She was standing, her head flung back, before the

High Seat; a slender woman with fair fragile features, in
a dark robe. Gems were braided into her long hair; gold
chains about her slender throat and a golden chain about
her waist, giving her somehow the look of a prisoner,
hung with fetters and yet defiant. Her voice rang out
again, clear and angry.

"When before this has a Keeper been subject to the
whims of the Council?"

So that was it!

Marius hadn't told me there was a new Keeper in
Comyn Council; and I hadn't thought to ask.

In fact, he hadn't told me much. I looked down now,
slipping into my seat behind the railings, at the Council
Hall of the Comyn.

It was a high, vaulted room, filled with shadows and
sunlight. In the lower hall, the lesser nobles were ranged;
along the dais, or gallery, where the Comyn, each family
in its own enclosure, ranged in a semi-circle. In the center, in the High Seat, old Dantan of Hastur, Regent of
the Comyn, was standing; behind him, in the shadows,
was a young man I could not see clearly. Beside him, I
recognized young Derik Elhalyn, Lord of the Comyn—
ruling under Hastur until he reached his majority next
year. Derik, lounging in a chair, looked bored.

I looked around, getting my bearings quickly. Dyan
Ardais glanced up, with an enigmatic grin, as if he
sensed my presence. Beyong him Dio Ridenow was
seated among her brothers; I saw my cousin Linnell, but
from where she sat I knew she could not see me.

But my eyes came back to Callina. A Keeper!

Not for years had there been a Keeper seated in Comyn Council. Old Ashara had kept to her tower during my
lifetime, during my father's lifetime. She must be unbelievably ancient now. During my childhood, for a short
time, there had been a frail flame-haired girl, veiled like
a shrouded star, before whom even the Hasturs showed

reverence. But when I was still a boy she had died or gone into seclusion, and since that day no young girls had been trained in the secrets of the master-screens. A few sub-keepers and matrix mechanics—I was one, when I cared to take my place among them—kept the relays working. It was hard to realize that my cousin Callina was the Keeper, holding in her frail hands all the incredible power of Ashara.

Yet I knew her courage. The thought roused painful memories. I didn't want to remember how and when I had last seen Callina.

Old Hastur spoke sternly.

"My lady, times have changed. In these days—"

"In these days they have changed indeed," she said, throwing back her head with a little silvery ringing of jewels, "when we have slavery on Darkover, and a Keeper can be sold like a shaol in the market place! No, hear me out! I tell you, we would do better to hand over all our secrets now to the accursed Terrans than to ally with the renegades out of Aldaran!

Her eyes searched and abruptly met mine in the shadows, and unexpectedly she raised her arm and pointed a slender finger at me.

"And there sits one who can prove what I say!"

But I was already on my feet. *Ally with Aldaran?* I heard my own voice, unbidden.

"You damned, incredible fools!"

Abrupt silence was followed by a sudden stir, a murmur of voices, and a growl; and in dismay I realized what I had done. I had jumped feet first into an affair I really knew nothing about. But the name Aldaran was enough. I looked straight at Old Hastur and defied him.

"Did I hear you say 'ally with Aldaran'? With that renegade clan whose name stinks all over Darkover? The men who sold our world to the Terrans." My voice cracked like a boy's.

Beside Hastur, young Derik Elhalyn rose to his feet. He made a sign to Hastur and spoke informally.

"Lew, you're forgetting yourself," he said, Then, leaning forward, the sunlight gleaming on his red-gold hair, he spoke to the whole council, with a charming smile.

"Look here! A Comyn Lord comes back to us, after six years, and we do nothing to welcome him, but let him creep in like a mouse coming to his hole! Welcome home, Lew Alton!"

I cut through the round of applause he was trying to start. "Never mind that," I said. "Lord Hastur—and you, my prince, consider this! Aldaran's men were Comyn, once, and held council voice here. Why were they exiled? Ask yourself that! Or has the old shame been turned into a bedtime tale for children? Who gave the Terrans a foothold on Darkover? Are we all mad here? Or did I hear someone say—*ally with Aldaran?*"

I turned here and there, searching the shadowed faces for a sign of comprehension anywhere. "Do we *want* the Terrans on our doorstep?"

Then, desperately, I made my last appeal. I raised the arm that ends in a pinned-down sleeve, and I knew my voice was shaking.

"Do we want *Sharra?*"

There was a short, ugly silence. Then they all began talking at once. They didn't want to hear about that. The voice of Dyan Ardais rose, clear and cheerful, over the rest.

"That's your hate speaking, Lew. Not your good sense. Friends, I think we can excuse Lew Alton for his words. He has reason for prejudice. But those days are gone; we must judge by today's facts, not yesterday's old grievances. Sit down, Lew. You've been away a long time. When you know more about this, maybe you'll change your mind. Listen to our side, anyway."

There was a general murmur of approval. Damn him!

Damn him, anyway! Shaking, I sat down. He had hinted —no, he had said right out—that I was to be pitied; a cripple with an old grudge, coming back and trying to take up the old feud where I left off. By skillfully focusing their unspoken feelings, he had given them a good reason to disregard what I said.

But the Aldarans had been at the center of the Sharra rebellion! Didn't they even know that?

Or didn't they want to know? The Sharra rebellion had only been a symbol, a symptom—like all civil wars—of internal troubles. The Aldarans were not the only ones on Darkover who were lured by the Terran Empire. The Comyn stood out, almost alone, against the magnet-like attraction of that star-spanning federation.

And I was an easy scapegoat for both sides. The Comyn conservatives distrusted me because I was half Terran, and the anti-Comyn faction distrusted me because my father, Kennard Alton, had been the staunchest leader of the Comyn. And they both feared what I knew of Sharra. In their minds I was still part of that terror which had flooded the countryside with leathered Terrans wearing blasters, instead of honest swords, and making the clean night rotten with the spew of their rockets. They had never forgotten or forgiven that. Why should they?

"Our grandfathers drove the Aldarans out of the Comyn," said Lerrys Ridenow, "but it's high time we forgot their superstitious nonsense."

From the shadows behind Old Hastur, a young and diffident voice spoke up. "Why not hear all of what Lew Alton has to say? He understands the *Terranan;* he's lived among them. And he's kin to Aldaran. Would he speak against his own kinsmen without good cause?"

"Let us, at least, discuss this among the Comyn!" Callina said, and finally Hastur nodded. He spoke the formula that dismissed the outsiders; there was some muttering among the men in the lower hall, but gradually they began to quiet down, to rise and depart by twos and threes.

My head was beginning to ache, as always in this hall. It was, of course, filled with the telepathic dampers which cut out mental interference—a necessary precaution when a large number of Comyn were gathered. One of them was located right over my head. They were supposed, by law, to be placed at random; but somehow they always turned up almost in the laps of the Altons.

Each family of the Comyn had its own particular gift, or telepathic talent; in the Altons, it was the hyperdeveloped telepathic nerve which could force rapport, undesired, or paralyze the minds of men, and the Comyn had always been a little afraid of the Altons. The Gifts are mostly recessive now, bred out by generations of intermarriage with nontelepaths, but the tradition remained, and the Altons always ended up with telepathic dampers in their laps. The continuous disrhythmic waves —half sonics, half energons—were a low-keyed annoyance.

The boy beside Hastur, who had spoken up for me, came down the long gallery toward me. By now I had guessed who he was; the old regent's grandson, Regis Hastur. As he passed Callina Aillard, she rose and, to my surprise, followed him.

"What is going to happen now?" I asked.

"Nothing, I hope." Regis smiled at me in a friendly way. He was one of those throwbacks, still born at times into old, Darkovan families, to the pure Comyn type; fairskinned, with the dark red hair of most Comyn, and eyes of almost metallic colorlessness. He was slightly built, and, like Callina, looked fragile; but it was the perfect tensile frailness of a dagger.

He said, "So you've been out into space and back. Welcome, Lew."

"It sounds like a welcome, doesn't it?" I said dryly.

"What's this about Aldaran? I came in only a few seconds before Callina pointed me out."

Regis moved his head toward the empty seats in the lower hall. "Politics," he said. "*They* want the Aldaran seated among the Comyn."

Callina interrupted. "And Beltran of Aldaran has submitted a request. He has had the insolence, the—the damned effrontery—to want to come into the Comyn by marriage! By marriage—to me!" She was white with rage.

I whistled in blank amazement. That *was* effrontery. Oh, yes, outsiders could marry into Comyn council. The man who marries a *comynara* holds all privileges of his consort. But the Keepers, those women trained to work among the master-screens, are bound by very ancient Darkovan custom to remain virgin while they hold their high office. The very offer was an insult; it should have meant bloody death for the man who spoke it. Wars have been fought on Darkover for a good deal less than that. And here they were calmly discussing it in council!

Regis gave me an ironical glance. "As my grandfather said, times have changed. The Comyn aren't anxious to have a Keeper in council again."

I thought about that. Thirty-four years without Ashara would not make the council very eager to slip back under a woman's hand.

Looking at the whole thing objectively, it made sense. As Hastur said, times had changed. Whether we liked it or not, they changed. The office of Keeper had once been a dangerous and sacred thing. Once, or so my father told me, all the technology of Darkover had been done through the matrix screens, operated by the linked minds of the Keepers. All the mining, all the travel, all energy-requiring transitions—even nuclear dispersions—had been done through the energon rings, each linked in mind with one of these young girls.

But changes in technology had made it unnecessary. There was no need for the Keepers to give up all human contact and live behind walls, guarding their powers in seclusion. Conversely, there was no need for them to be deferred to, near-worshipped.

Callina smiled wryly, guessing my thoughts. "That's true," she said, "and I'm not greedy for power. But," she met my eyes steadily, "you know why I'm against this alliance, Lew. I don't want to bring it out in council, because it's your affair really. I don't like to ask you this, but I must. Will you tell them about Sharra and the Aldarans?"

I bowed over her hand, unable to speak.

For the sake of my sanity, I tried never to think or to speak about what the Aldarans, and their horde of rebels, had done to me—or to Marjorie.

But now I must. I owed Callina a debt I could never pay. At the awful end, when I had fled with Marjorie— both of us wounded, and Marjorie dying—it had been Callina who opened the Hidden City to us. That night, when the swords of Darkover and the blasters of the Terrans had hounded us, alike, Callina had dared exposure to the radioactive site of the ancient starships, and risked a terrible death herself, to give Marjorie a bare chance of life. It had been too late for Marjorie; but I could never forget.

Just the same—to drag it all out before the Council again—I felt the sweat break out on my forehead.

Regis said quietly. "You're the only chance we have, Lew. They might listen to you."

I swallowed. At last I said, "I'll—try."

"Try to do what? Stay sober long enough to welcome us all?" Derik Elhalyn thrust his way gaily between Regis and Callina, and gripped my shoulders. "Lew, old fellow, I didn't know you were on Darkover at all, until you popped up like one of those toys your father used to make for us! Dyan said it, but I'll say it again—welcome home!" He stood back, waiting for me to return the clasp, then his eyes fell on my empty sleeve. He said quickly, trying to cover up the awkward moment, "I'm glad you're back. We had some good times once."

I nodded, upset by his confusion but glad of a pleasanter memory. "And we'll have more, I hope. Are the Elhalyn hawks still the finest in the mountains? Do you still climb the cliffs to take your own nestlings?"

"Yes, though I've not so much time now," Derik laughed. "Do you remember the day we climbed the north face of Nevarsin, hanging on by our eyebrows?" Once again he cut himself short, all too obviously remembering that I, at least, would never climb again. For my part, I was wondering what would happen to the Comyn when this scatterbrained lad assumed the place rightfully his. Old Hastur was a statesman and a diplomat. But Derik? For once I was glad of the telepathic dampers which kept them from following my thoughts.

Derik moved me toward the high seat, a hand on my shoulder. He said, "It was all arranged before your father died, you remember. But Linnell's refused even to talk about setting a day for the marriage, until you were home again! So I have two reasons for welcoming you back!"

I returned his affectionate grin. I wasn't wholly alone, after all. I had kinsmen, friends. That marriage had been in the air since Linnell put away her dolls, yet it waited for my consent. "I haven't even seen Linnell yet," I said. "Though I thought I had."

I wondered if Linnell knew she had a double in the Terran Zone. I'd have to tell her that; it would amuse her.

But Hastur was calling us all to order again, and I took a seat between Regis and Derik. I was shocked at the small number of those who could claim blood-right in the Comyn; counting men and women alike, there were not three dozen. Yet they looked like a hostile army when, at Hastur's signal, I rose to face them.

I began slowly, knowing I must plead my cause without heat.

"If I understand this, you want to ally with Aldaran, to restore the old Seventh Domain to the Comyn. You're counting on this alliance to make peace with his mountain lords, and choke off all the outbreaks of rioting and war on the border. To get the co-operation of the Aldarans, in keeping the out-laws and renegades and trailmen where they belong—on the other side of the Kadarin river. Maybe, even, to get us some Terran trade, and permits for machinery and planes, without making too many concessions to the Terrans themselves."

Lerrys Ridenow rose. "So far, you have been correctly informed," he drawled. "Can you tell us something new?"

"No." I turned, studying him. He was the only one of Dio's brothers worth the name of man, even when the term was used loosely. I'd known them, all three, on the pleasure moon off Vainwal. They were all delicate, effeminate, cat-graceful—and dangerous as so many tigers. They all tried to take the best of both worlds, a privilege which their great wealth, and the Comyn immunity from ordinary Darkovan laws, gave them. But Lerrys seemed to have the stuff of a man behind the languid, almost feminine mask, and he deserved an answer.

"No, but I can tell you something old. It won't work," I said. "Beltran of Aldaran, himself, is a decent sort of fellow. But he's tied himself up so tight with renegades and rebels and trailmen and half-breed spies, he couldn't make peace with us if he wanted to. And you want to bring him into the Comyn?" I spread my hands. "Certainly. Bring in Beltran of Aldaran. Bring in the man they call Kadarin, and Lawton from Thendara, and the Terran Co-ordinator from Port Chicago, while you're about it!"

Hastur frowned. "Who is this Kadarin?" he asked.

"Hell, I don't know. Supposed to be kin to Aldaran."

"Like you," Dyan murmured.

"Yes. Half Terran, maybe. Rabble-rouser on any world that will hold him. They deported him from at least two other planets before he came back here. And that man Beltran of Aldaran, that man you want to marry to a Keeper, made Castle Aldaran into a hidey-hole for all of Kadarin's damned ridge runners and renegades!"

"Kadarin isn't a man's name," Lerrys said.

"And I'm not so sure he's a man," I retorted. "The hills around Aldaran—you know what used to live back in those hills—all sorts of things you couldn't really call human. He looks human enough until you see his eyes." I stopped, turned inward on horror. Abruptly, remembering where I was, the wheels of my mind began to go round again.

"The name Kadarin is just defiance," I said. "In the hills across the river Kadarin, any bastard is called a son of the Kadarin. They say he never knew who or what his father was. When the Terrans hauled him in for questioning, he gave his name as Kadarin. That's all."

"Then he's working against the Terrans, too," Lerrys said.

"Maybe, maybe not. But he's tied up with Sharra—"

"And so were you," Dyan Ardais said softly. "But here you are."

My chair crashed over backwards. "Yes, damn you! Why else would I put myself through all this, if I didn't know what hell it is? You think the danger's all over? If I can *show* you where Sharra is still out of control—not ten miles from here—then will you call off this crazy alliance?"

Hastur looked troubled, motioning Dyan and Lerrys to silence. "Can you do that, Lew? You're an Alton, and a telepath. But you couldn't do anything like that alone. You'd need a mental focus—"

"He's counting on that," Dyan sneered. "It's a good safe bluff! He's the last living adult Alton!"

From the shadows a voice said, "Oh, no he isn't."

Marius got slowly to his feet, and I stared at my brother in amazement. I thought he had left with the others. Could he—or would he—dare that most fearful of the Comyn powers?

Dyan laughed aloud. "You? You—*Terran!*" The word was an insult as he spoke it.

I was not yet ready to crawl away beaten. "Shall we turn off the dampers—and prove it on *you*, Lord Ardais?"

That was a bluff. I hadn't the faintest idea whether Marius had the Alton Gift, or whether he would go down in a screaming frenzy when my mind ripped into his. But Dyan did not know either, and his face was white before he lowered his eyes.

"It's still a bluff," said Lerrys. "We all know that Sharra's matrix was destroyed. What bugbear is this you drag out to frighten us, Lew? We are not children, to shiver at shadows! Sharra! *That* for Sharra!" He snapped his fingers.

I flung caution to the winds. "Destroyed hell!" I raged, "It's in my rooms this minute!"

I heard the gasps that ran round the circle. "*You* have it?"

I nodded slowly. They wouldn't call me a liar again.

But then I caught a glimpse of Dyan's mocking eyes. And suddenly I realized I had not been clever at all.

CHAPTER FOUR

Marius leaned across his saddle as I laid the insulated sword across the pommel of my own.

"Going to unwrap it here?"

Around us the thin morning air was as expressionless as his face. Behind us the foothills rose; and I caught the thin pungent smell of slopes scorched by forest fire, drifting down from the Hellers. Further back in the clearing, the other Comyn waited.

My barriers were down, and I could feel the impact of their emotions. Hostility, curiosity, disbelief or contempt from the Ardais and Aillard and Ridenow men; interested sympathy, and disquiet, from the Hasturs and strangely, from Lerrys Ridenow.

I would have preferred to do this thing privately. The thought of a hostile audience unnerved me. Knowing that my brother's life depended on my own nerves and control didn't help, either. Suddenly, I shivered. If Marius died—and he very likely would—only these witnesses would stand between me and a charge of murder. We were gambling on something we couldn't possibly be sure about; and I was scared.

The Alton focus is not easy. Having both parties aware and willing doesn't make it easy, even for two mature telepaths; it just makes it possible.

What we intended was to link minds—not in ordinary telepathic contact; not even in the forced rapport which an Alton—or, sometimes, a Hastur—can impose on another mind. But complete, and *mutual* rapport; conscious and subconscious mind, telepathic and psychokinetic nerve systems, time-scanning and co-ordinating consciousness, energonic functions, so that in effect we would function as one hyperdeveloped brain in two bodies.

My father had done it with me—once, for about thirty seconds—with my full awareness that it would probably kill me. He had known; it was the only thing that would prove to them that I was a true Alton. It had forced the Comyn to accept me. I had been trained for days, and safeguarded by every bit of his skill. Marius was taking it on almost unprepared.

I seemed to be seeing my brother for the first time. The difference in our ages, his freakish face and alien eyes, had made him a stranger; the knowledge that he might die beneath my mind, a few minutes from now, made him seem somehow less real; shadowy, like someone in a long dream. I made my voice rough.

"Want to back down, Marius? There's still time."

He looked amused again. "Jealous? Want to keep the *laran* privilege all to yourself?" he asked softly. "Don't want any more Altons in the Comyn, huh?"

I put the question point blank. "*Do* you have the Alton Gift, Marius?"

He shrugged. "I haven't the least notion. I've never tried to find out. What with one thing and another, I was given to understand that it would be unwarrantable insolence on my part."

I felt cold. That sentence outlined my brother's life. I'd have to remember that. There was a chance that what I gave him would *not* be death, but full Comyn status as an Alton. If he thought it was worth a gamble, what right had I to deny him? My father had gambled with me, and won. I lowered my head, and started to strip the insulating cloth from the sword.

"Is it a real sword?" Derik Elhalyn asked, guiding his horse toward us.

I shook my head, giving the hilt a hard twist. It came off in my hand and I removed the silk-wrapped thing inside. A familiar hand crushed down on my chest.

"No," I said, "the sword's camouflage. You can look at it." I thrust the pieces, hilt and blade, at him, but he backed away convulsively.

I saw the men hide unkind grins. But it wasn't funny —that Derik, Lord of the Comyn, was a coward. Hastur took the pieces and fitted them neatly together.

"The platinum and sapphires in this thing would buy a good sized city," he said, "but Lew's got the dangerous part."

I stripped the matrix, feeling the familiar live warmth between my hands. It was egg-shaped and not quite egg-sized, a hunk of dull metal laced with little ribbons of shinier metal, and starred with a pattern of blue winking eyes. "The pattern of sapphires in the sword hilt—sensitized carbon—matches the pattern of the matrix. They've altered my nerve reactions some way, to respond to it—" I stopped, my throat dry. What idiocy of self-flagellation had made me bring the thing back to Darkover? I was walking back, on my own feet, into the corner of hell that Kadarin had opened for me.

"Just what are you going to do?" Derik asked.

"I tried to put it into words he'd understand. "All over the Hellers, there are certain spots which are activated— magnetized, somehow, to respond to the—the vibrations that key in Sharra. They can be used to draw on the power of Sharra."

Nobody asked the question I feared. *What is Sharra?*

I would have had to say, I didn't know. I knew what it could *do*, but I didn't know what it was. Folklore says a goddess turned demon. I don't want to theorize about Sharra. I wanted to stay away from it.

And that was the one thing I couldn't do.

Hastur took pity on me. "Once a certain locus has been put into key with the Sharra matrix, and the Sharra forces—as was done, years ago—a residue of power remains, and that spot can be drawn on. Lew has kept the matrix all these years, hoping for a chance to find these spots, through the original activator, and de-activate them. Once all the activated sites are released, the matrix can be monitored and then destroyed. But even an Alton telepath can't do that sort of work without a focus. One body can't handle that kind of vibration alone."

"And I'm the focus, if I live that long," Marius said impatiently. "Can we get on with it?"

I gave him one quick look; then, without further preliminary, made contact with his mind.

There is no way to describe the first shock of rapport. The acceleration of a jet, the hurt of a punch in the solar plexus, the shock of diving headfirst into liquid oxygen, might approximate it if you could live through all three at once. I felt Marius physically slump in his saddle under the impact of it, and felt every defense of his mind concentrated to blocking me away. The human mind wasn't built for this. Blind instinct locked his barriers against me; a normal mind would die under the thrust needed to shatter that kind of resistance.

It was just as bald as that. If he had inherited the Alton Gift, he wouldn't die. If he hadn't, it would kill him.

Inwardly I was concentrated on Marius, in agonized concentration, but outwardly every detail around us was cut sharp and clear on my senses, as it etched there in acid; the cold sweat running down my body, the pity in the old Regent's eyes, the faces of the men around us. I heard Lerrys moaning, "Stop them! Stop them! It's killing them both!"

There was an instant of agony so great I thought I would scream aloud, the tension of a bow drawn back—and back—and bent to the very point where it must snap, where even the snap and break of death would be relief unspeakable.

Regis Hastur moved like a thrown spear; he tore the sword hilt from Hastur's hands and forced the matching pattern of gleaming stones into Marius' clenched fists. I saw, and felt, the agony dissolve in my brother's face, then the web of focused thought spread, gleamed, and wove together. Marius' mind firmed, held, a tangible rock of strength, against my own.

Alton! Terran blood in his veins—but true Alton, and my brother!

My sigh of relief caught almost into a sob. There was no need of words, but I spoke anyhow. "All right, brother?"

"Fine," he said, and stared at the sword hilt in his hands. "How the hell did I get hold of this thing?"

I handed him the Sharra matrix. I tensed in the familiar, breathless anticipation of anguish as his hands closed around it; but there was nothing but the familiar sense of rapport. I let my breath go.

"That's that," I said. "Well, Hastur?"

He made a brief, grave bow to Marius; a formal sign of recognition. Then he said quietly, "You're in charge."

I looked around at the mounted men. "Some of the activated spots are near here," I said, "and the sooner we break them up, the sooner we're safe. But—" I paused. I'd been so intent on the horror that possessed me, I hadn't thought to ask for a larger escort of mounted men. Besides the Hasturs, Dyan, Derik and the Ridenow brothers, there were only a scant half dozen guardsmen.

I said, "Sometimes the trailmen come this close to the Hidden City—"

"Not since the 'Narr Campaign," said Lerrys languidly. His unspoken thought was clear. *You and your friends of Sharra stirred them up against us. Then you cleared out, but we did the fighting!*

"Just the same—" I looked up at the thick branches. Was it safe to ride so far with so few? Some of the trailmen, far in the Hellers, are peaceful arboreal humanoids, no more harmful than so many monkeys. But those who have overflowed from the country around Aldaran, where every sort of human and half-human gathered, are a mixed breed—and dangerous.

Finally I shrugged. "I'm not afraid if you're not."

Dyan jeered. "You and your brother made a boast, Alton. Are you afraid someone will ask you to fulfil it?"

Nothing, I knew, would have suited him better than for Marius to break under my mind, and die.

I raised my eyes at Marius in question. He nodded, and we rode into the shadow of the trees.

For hours we rode under hanging branches, my mind in acute subliminal concentration on the power spots we could sense through the live crystal. My body and mind were aching with uncomfortable awareness; I wasn't used to this kind of prolonged mental strain any more— and what was more, I hadn't been on a horse since I left Darkover. They talk about the power of mind over matter. It doesn't work that way. A sore backside is just as effective an inhibitor of concentration as anything I know about.

The red sun had begun to swing downward when I reined in beside Hastur. "Listen," I said, low, "we're being decoyed. I was fairly sure no one else on Darkover knew I had the matrix, but someone must. Someone's taking power from the activated spots and drawing us."

He regarded me gravely. "Is that all?"

"I don't—"

He beckoned to Regis; the boy rode up and said,
"We're being followed, Lew. I thought so before; now
I'm sure of it. I've been in trailman country before this."

I glanced up at the thick branches, meeting overhead.
Above there, I knew, old tree-roads wound in an endless
labyrinth; but in these latitudes, I believed, they had
been long deserted.

"We're in no shape to meet an armed attack," the Regent said. He looked uneasily at Regis and Derik, and I
followed his thought—my barriers were all down now.

*The whole power of the Comyn is here. One attack,
now, could wipe us out. Why did I let them all come,
unguarded?* And then, a thought he could not conceal,
Are these Altons leading us into a trap?

I gave him a bleak smile. "I don't blame you," I said.
"As it happens, I'm not. But if anyone were around who
really knew how to handle the Sharra power—I don't really—I'd be just a pawn. I might do just that."

The Regent did not question me. He turned in his saddle. "We'll turn back here."

"What's the matter?" Corus Ridenow sneered. "Have
the Altons turned coward?"

By unlucky chance Marius was riding next him; he
leaned over abruptly and his flat hand smacked across
Corus' face. The Ridenow reared back, and his hand
swept down and flicked the knife loose from his boot—

And in that instant it happened!

Corus stopped dead, as if turned to stone, knife still
raised. Then, horribly loud in the paralyzed silence,
Marius screamed. I have never heard such agony from a
human throat. The full strength of the Source flooded us
both. God or demon, force, machine or elemental—it
was Sharra, and it was hell, and hearing a second outraged shout of protest, I did not even realize that I, too,
had cried out.

And in that moment wild yells rang around us, and on

every side men dropped from the trees into the road. A hand seized my bridle—and I knew just who had led us into the trap.

The man in the road was tall and lean; a shock of pale hair stood awry over a weathered gaunt face and steel gray eyes that glared at mine; he looked older, more dangerous than I remembered him. *Kadarin!*

My horse reared, almost flinging me into the road. Around me yells coalesced into a brawling melee; the clash of iron, the stamping and neighing of panicked horses. Kadarin bellowed, in the gutteral jargon of the trailmen, "Away from the Altons! I want them!"

He was jerking my horse's bridle this way and that maneuvering to keep the animal's body between us. I swung to one side, almost lying along the horse's back, and felt the crack of a bullet past my ear. I yelled "Coward!" and jerked at the reins, wheeling the horse abruptly. The impact knocked him sprawling. He was up again in a second, but in that second I was clear of the saddle and my sword was out—for what that was worth.

At one time I had been a fine swordsman, and Kadarin had never learned to handle one. Terrans never do. He carried one and he used it when he had to; it was the only way, in the mountains.

But I had learned to fight when I had two hands and I was wearing only a light dress-sword. Idiot that I was! I'd smelled danger, the air had been rotten with it—and I hadn't even worn a serviceable weapon!

Marius was fighting at my back with one of the non-human trailmen, a lean crouched thing in rags with a long evil knife. The pattern of his strokes beat through our linked minds, and I cut the contact roughly; I had enough trouble with one fight. My steel clashed against Kadarin's.

He'd improved. In a matter of seconds he had me off balance, unable to attack, able only to keep up, somehow, a hard defense. Yet there was a kind of pleasure in it, even though my breath came short and blood dripped down my face with the sweat; he was here, and this time there was no man—or woman—to pull us apart.

But a defensive fight is doomed to lose. My mind worked, fast and desperately. Kadarin had one weakness; his temper. He would go into a flaming rage, and for a few minutes, that keen judgment of his went, and he was a berserk animal. If I could make him lose his temper for half a second, his acquired skill at swordplay would go with it. It was a dirty way to fight. But I wasn't in any shape to be fastidious.

"Son of the River!" I shouted at him in the Caheunga dialect, which has nuances of filth unsurpassed in any other language. "Sandal-wearer! You can't hide behind your little sister's petticoats *this* time!"

There was no change in the fast, slashingly awkward— but deadly—sword strokes. I hadn't really hoped there would be.

But for half a second he dropped the barriers around his mind.

And then he was my prisoner.

His mind gripped in the unique, locked-on paralysis of an Alton Telepath. And his body rigid—paralyzed. I reached out, taking his sword from the stiff fingers. I lost consciousness of the battle round us. We might have been alone on the forest road, Kadarin and I—and my hate. In a minute I would kill him.

But I waited a second too long. I was exhausted already from the struggle with Marius; a flicker of faltering pressure, and Kadarin, alert, leaped free with a savage cry. He outweighed me by half; the impact knocked me full-length to the ground, and the next minute something crashed and struck my head and I plunged miles into darkness.

A million years later, Old Hastur's face swam out of

nowhere into focus before my aching eyes. "Lie still, Lew. You've been shot. They're gone."

I struggled to raise myself; subsided to the hands that forced me gently back. Through a swollen eye I counted the faces that swung around me in the red, murky sunset. Very far away, I heard Lerrys' voice, harsh and muted, mourning, "Poor boy."

I was bruised and in pain, but there was a worse ache, a great gaping emptiness torn loose, that made me deathly alone.

They didn't have to tell me that Marius was dead.

CHAPTER FIVE

I had a concussion. Kadarin's second bullet had knocked loose a splinter of bone; and Marius' death had been a shattering shock to the cells of my brain. The neuronic and synaptic links so recently made had all been torn apart again when he died, and for days my life—and sanity—hung in the balance.

I remember only shattering light and cold and shock, jolting movement, the pungency of drugs. Without any apparent sense of transition, one day I opened my eyes and found myself in my old rooms in the Comyn Castle in Thendara, and Linnell Aillard was sitting beside me.

She was very like Callina, only taller, darker, somehow gentler, with a sweet and childish face—although she was not really much younger than I. I suppose she was pretty. Not that it mattered. In every man's life there are a few women who simply don't register on his libido. Linnell was never a woman to me; she was my cousin. I lay contentedly watching her for some minutes, until she sensed my look and smiled.

"I thought you'd know me this time. Head ache?"

It did. I felt awkwardly at the ache, discovered bandages. Linnell caught my hand gently away.

"How long have I been here?"

"Here in Thendara? Only two days. You've been unconscious for days and days, though."

"And—Marius?"

Her eyes filled with tears. "He is buried at the Hidden City. The Regent gave him full Comyn honors, Lew."

I freed my hand gently from hers and lay for a long time staring at the pattern of light on the translucent walls. Finally I asked, "The council?"

"They rushed it through, before we came here to Thendara. The marriage ceremony will be Festival Night."

Life went on, I was thinking. "Yours to Derik?"

"Oh, no." She smiled, shyly. "There's no hurry about *that*. Callina's, to Beltran of Aldaran."

I sat bolt upright, disregarding knifing pain. "Do you mean they're still going through with that alliance? You're joking, Linnell! Or is everyone mad?"

She shook her head, looking troubled. "I think that's why they rushed it through; they were afraid you'd recover, and try to block them again. Derik and the Hasturs wanted to wait for you; the others overruled them."

I didn't doubt that a bit. There was nothing the Comyn wanted less than a capable Alton in council. I threw back the covers. "I want to see Callina!"

"I'll ask her to come to you; you needn't get up."

I vetoed that. These rooms had been assigned to the Altons, during council season, for generations; they were probably well-monitored with telepathic traps and dampers. The Comyn had never trusted the male adult Altons too much. I wanted to see Callina somewhere else.

Her servants told me where to find her. I swung back an innocent-looking panel of curtain and a flood of searing light literally exploded in my face. Swearing, I flung my hands over my tormented eyes; the closed lids dripped red and yellow after-images, and a surprised

voice spoke my name. The lights died down and
Callina's face swam into focus.

"I am sorry. Can you see now? I must protect myself,
you know, when I work."

"Don't bother apologizing." A Keeper among the
matrix screens is vulnerable in ways ordinary people
know nothing about. "I should have had more sense than
to come in like that."

She smiled and held the curtain aside for me to pass
through. "Yes. They told me you were a matrix worker."

And as she let the curtain fall, I suddenly became conscious of the subtle *wrongness* in her beauty.

One can tell everything about a woman by the way she
walks. The very step of a wanton is suggestive. Innocence
proclaims itself in carefree romping. Callina was young
and lovely; but she did not move like a beautiful woman.
There was something both very young and very old
about her movements, as if the gawkiest stage of
adolescence and the staid dignity of great old age had
met, with no intermediary stage in her.

She let the curtains close, and the sense of strangeness
vanished. I looked around the patterned walls, feeling
the soothing effect of the even, diffused sonics. I had had
an old, small matrix laboratory in the old wing, but nothing like this.

There was the regular monitor system, flashing with
tiny star-like glimmers, one for every licensed matrix on
every level in this section of Darkover. There was a spe-
cially modulated telepathic damper which filtered out
telepathic overtones without confusing or inhibiting ordinary thought. And there was an immense panel with a
molten-glass shimmer whose uses I could only guess; it
might have been one of the almost legendary psychokinetic transmitters. Curiously prosaic, an ordinary screw
driver and some glittering scraps of insulating cloth lay
on a table.

She said, "You know, of course, that they got away with the Sharra matrix?"

"If I'd had the brains of a mule," I said violently, "I'd have tossed it into a converter somewhere on Terra, and been well rid of it—and Darkover well rid of it too!"

"That *would* have put things out of control forever; at best, Sharra was only dormant while the matrix was off-world. Destroying the matrix would have ended any hope of putting the activated sites out of action. Sharra isn't on the master banks, you know. It's an illegal matrix —unmonitored. We can't monitor it until all the loose sites, and the free energy, is located and controlled. What was the pattern?"

I let her tune out the dampers, and tried to project the pattern on a monitor screen; but only blurs swirled against the crystal surface. She was contrite; "I shouldn't have let you try that, so soon after a head injury! Come out of here and rest!"

In a smaller room, whose open sky-wall looked down into the valley, I relaxed in a soft chair, while Callina watched me, aloof and reflective. I asked finally, "Callina, if you knew the pattern, could you duplicate the matrix and monitor the focal sites with the dupli-cate?"

She didn't even have to think it over. "No. I can dupli-cate a first or second level matrix like this—" She touched the tiny crystals that held her blue dress togeth-er over her breast. "And I might be able to construct a matrix lattice of complexity *equal* to the Sharra one— although I wouldn't care to try it alone. But two identical matrices of fourth level or higher can't exist simultane-ously, in one universe and in time, without space distor-tion."

"Cherillys' Law," I recalled. "A matrix is the only unique thing in spacetime, and thus existing without any equilibrium point has the power to shift energy."

She nodded. "Any attempt to make an exact molecular duplicate of a matrix like the one commanding Sharra— is it ninth level or tenth?—would warp half the planet right out of spacetime."

"I was afraid of that," I said, "but I told myself only a Keeper would really know."

"Keeper!" She gave a short, wry little laugh.

At last she said, "Linnell told you, I suppose? Lew, it isn't just the alliance that bothers me. If they're determined to put me out of the way, make sure I won't seize council power—well, they will. I can't stand against them all, Lew. If they think the alliance will help the Comyn, who am I to argue? Hastur is no fool. They could be right. I don't know anything about politics. If I weren't a Keeper, they wouldn't even have asked my consent as a formality; they would say marry, and I would marry! I suppose one husband is as good as another," she said, and again I had the curious impression of extreme and naïve youth, superimposed on the beautiful woman who sat watching me. She spoke of her own marriage as a passive little girl, married by proxy to a doll, might speak. Yet she was a beautiful and desirable woman. It was uncanny!

"It's the rest of it," she went on after a minute. "I can't believe ordinary trailmen would know enough to attack you, just then, and steal the Sharra matrix. Who set them on?"

I stared. "Didn't Hastur tell you who set them on?"

"I don't think he knew."

"Trailmen," I said with angry emphasis, "would steal weapons, food, clothing—jewelry, perhaps—they would never dare to touch a matrix! And that matrix—why am I still alive, then?" I demanded. "Callina, I was keyed *into* that thing, body and brain! Even when it was insulated, if any out-of-phase person so much as laid a hand on it, it *hurt!* There are three people on the planet who could handle it, without killing me! Didn't they tell you it was Kadarin himself?"

Her face went white. "I don't think Hastur would know Kadarin by sight," she said. "But how did Kadarin know you had the matrix?"

I did not want to think Rafe Scott would have betrayed me to Kadarin. The fires of Sharra had singed him, too. I'd rather believe that Kadarin could still read my mind, even from a distance. Suddenly, my loss hit me with overwhelming pain. Now I was absolutely alone.

"Don't grieve," Callina said softly. But I knew; to her, Marius had been only an alien, a half-caste, despised for his difference. How could I explain to Callina? We had been in total rapport, Marius and I, for perhaps three hours, with all that implies. I had known Marius as I knew myself; his strengths and weaknesses, his desires and dreams, hopes and disappointments. Years of living together could have told me no more. Until the moment of rapport I had never known a brother and until his dying mind ripped from mine I had never known loneliness. But there was no way to explain this to her.

Finally she asked, "Lew, how did you first get yourself involved with—" She started to say, *with Sharra*, looked at my twisting face and didn't. "With Kadarin? I never knew?"

"I don't want to talk about it," I said curtly. *Again and again—must those old wounds be torn?*

"I know it's not easy," she said. "It's not easy for me to be handed over to Aldaran." She did not look at me again. She took a cigarette from a crystal dish, and sparked it alight with the jewel in her ring. I reached for one and fumbled it; she raised her head and frankly stared, and I looked at her defiantly.

"Men smoke on some planets."

"I don't believe it!"

"They do." Still defiant, I took one, remembered I had no light, and reached clumsily for her hand, raising her ring to light it. "*And* no one laughs. Or considers them effeminate. It is an accepted custom which causes no curiosity. And I learned to like it. Do you think you can endure the sight, Callina *comynara?*" We looked at each other in a blaze of hostility which had nothing to do with the small and silly argument over the cigarette.

Her lip curled. "One would expect it of the *Terranan,*" she said scornfully. "Please yourself."

I was still holding her hand and the ring. I let them go, drawing in a deep breath of the thin sweetish smoke. "You asked me a question," I said, staring at the distant snowcapped peaks. "I'll try to answer.

"Kadarin was Aldaran's foster brother, I've heard. No one knows who, or what, his parents were. Some say he's the son of a Terran renegade, Zeb Scott, by one of the nonhuman *chieri,* back in the hills. Whatever he is, or isn't, he has the mind of a clever man. He learned some matrix mechanics—don't ask me how. He worked a while in Terran intelligence, got deported from two or three worlds, finally settled in the Hellers. Some of the Terrans back there have Darkovan, even nonhuman blood. He started organizing the rebels, the malcontents. Then he found me."

I got up and walked away from her. "You know what my life had been. Here—a bastard, an alien. Among the Terrans—a telepath, a freak. Kadarin, at least, made me feel that I belonged somewhere."

Not even to myself did I want to admit that once I had liked the man. I sighed.

"I spoke about a renegade, Zeb Scott."

The flood of memory rushed on, resistless, only a few bald words escaping to fill in years of adventure and the long search. "Zeb Scott died drunk, raving, in a

wineshop in Carthon, babbling about the blue sword
with the power of a hundred demons. We guessed that it
was Sharra.

"The Aldarans, centuries ago—so the legend ran—had
summoned Sharra to this world; but the power had been
sealed off again, and the Aldarans exiled for their crime.
Only after that had the Aldarans played traitor to Darkover, and sold the Terrans a foothold on our world.

"Kadarin went after the Sharra sword, found it, and
experimented with the power. He needed a telepath. I
was right at hand, and too young, too damned reckless to
know what I was doing. And there were the Scotts. Rafe
was just a child then. But there were the girls; Thyra, and
Marjorie—"

I quit there. It was no use. There was no way, no way
at all to tell her about Marjorie. I flung my cigarette
savagely from the window and watched it spinning away
on a little eddy of wind.

Callina said softly, when I had almost forgotten her,
"What was he trying to do?"

This was safe ground. "Why does any traitor steal or
betray? The Terrans have been trying for centuries to
beg, borrow or steal some secrets of matrix mechanics.
The Comyn were incorruptible, but Kadarin knew the
Terrans would pay well. Experimenting with the power,
he activated some of the focal points, showed them what
he could do. But at the end he betrayed the Terrans too,
and opened up a—a hole in space, a Gate between
worlds, to take on all that power—"

My voice cracked like a boy's. "Damn him! Damn him
waking and sleeping, living and dead, here and here after!" I fought suddenly back to self-control and said quietly. "He got what he wanted. But Marjorie and I were
at the poles of power, and—"

I shook my head. What more could I say? The
monstrous terror that had flamed and ravened between

worlds, the hellfire. Marjorie, confident and unafraid at the pole of power, suddenly crumpling in agony, under the backlash of that awful thing—

"I broke out of the matrix lock, and somehow managed to slam the Gate again. But Marjorie was already—"

I broke there, unable to say another word, and slumped into a chair, hiding my face on my arm. Callina came swiftly to me, kneeling, her arms around my bent shoulders. "I know, Lew. I know."

I jerked away from her touch. "You *know!* Thank your Gods you *don't* know!" I said savagely. Then, gripped in the fist of memory, I let my head fall forward on her breast. She did know. She had tried to save us both. Marjorie had died in her arms. "Yes," I muttered, "you know the rest."

My head was throbbing, and I could feel the echoing throb-throb of her heart through the soft silk of her dress. Her hair was like the dust of flowers against my face. I raised my good hand to clasp her soft fingers in mine.

She threw back her head and looked at me.

"We're alone with this, Lew. Hastur's bound by Compact to obey the council. Derik's an imbecile, and Regis is only a boy. The Ridenow, the Ardais—they want anything that will keep them in power; they'd sell out to Sharra themselves if they thought they could do it safely! You're powerless alone. And I—" her mouth worked, but no sound came.

Finally she said, "I'm a Keeper, and I could hold all the power of Ashara if I would. Ashara would give me strength enough to rule the whole council if I would let her, but I—I won't be a puppet, Lew. I don't want to be only her pawn! I won't! The council pulling me one way, Ashara the other. Beltran couldn't be worse!"

We were clinging together like children frightened by the darkness. She was soft in my arms. I tightened my clasp on her; then her half-breathed protest went lax in the middle of a kiss. She made no resistance when I lifted her to her feet and drew back her head beneath my own.

Outside the last red trace of the sun dropped behind Nevarsin Peak and the stars began to wink in the denuded sky.

CHAPTER SIX

At the height of Comyn power, centuries ago, the Crystal Chamber must have seemed small for all those who could claim blood-right in the hierarchy. An even blue light spilled diffused radiance over the glass walls; green, scarlet, golden flashes struck through. At noon it was like dwelling in a rainbow's heart; at night it seemed to hang high and alone, buffeted on the winds of space.

Here I had first been presented to the Comyn, a boy of five, too big-boned and dark for a true Comyn child; young as I had been, I remembered the debates, and old Duvic Elhalyn shouting, "Kennard Alton, you waste our time and insult this holy place bringing your half-caste bastard into Council."

And I could see in memory my father turning savagely to lift me high above them, in full sight of the Comyn. "*Look* at the boy, and eat those words!" And the old Lord had eaten them. No one ever defied my father twice. Much good his raging had done. Half-caste I was, bastard I remained, alien I was and would be; as much as that small boy who had sat for hours, fidgeting through the long ceremonials he did not understand, arm aching from the touch of the matrix that had set its pattern in the flesh to seal his *Comyn*. I glanced impassively at my wrist. I still had the mark. About three inches above where they had had to take off my hand.

"What are you brooding about?" Derik demanded.

"Sorry. Did you ask me something? I was thinking about my first council. There were more of us then."

Derik laughed. "Then it's high time you began raising sons to follow you, laggard!"

The thought was not unpleasant. My own estates, fertile green valleys in the uplands around Daillon, were waiting for me. I glanced at Callina; she sat beside Linnell, the two snuggled together in a great chair that would have held half a dozen girls their size. Derik went over to them and stood talking to Linnell. She looked happy, and the prince's shallow handsome face seemed lighted from within. Not really stupid, Derik; only dull. Not good enough for Linnell. But she loved him.

Dio Ridenow caught my eyes, then lowered her own with a resentful flush. Dyan Ardais came through the prism door, and I frowned suspiciously. Dyan, and Dyan alone, had known I had the Sharra matrix. Marius, while I was away, had been nothing more than a lonely boy, despised by the Comyn for his alien blood, powerless. I, alone, was powerless and maimed. But together we formed a powerful threat to his ambition.

Kadarin's attempt on my life was a personal feud, and he had fairly filed his intentions. The trailmen would always steal. But would they risk killing an Alton, even by accident? Reprisals for such things were swift and terrible—or had been when the Comyn was worthy of the name. With swift decision, I reached out and made contact with Dyan's mind. He scowled and raised his head, locking barriers against me; and I did not take up the challenge. Not yet.

Hastur was calling us to order. This was a formality, of course; a gesture toward appeasing those who had been absent or ill. Ostensibly, since this closing ceremony of Comyn could not be held unless everyone who held *laran* rights in the Comyn were present, no member could complain that he had no chance to be heard. In theory I could keep them there as long as I chose—I, or any dissatisfied member—simply by refusing my assent to close the session. But in fact, any triviality, and small time-consuming matter, would be brought up and argued at length; anything to keep me from getting a chance to speak. Until time, or weariness, brought the session to an end and silence me on those issues forever. Once the council was closed, I was bound by Comyn law and many oaths to contest the issues no further. I'd seen the blocking technique used before.

The triviality was not long in coming. Lerrys Ridenow arose and glared belligerently around the room, and Hastur stretched his baton to Lerrys, ignoring me.

"Comyn, I have a personal complaint—"

I saw Dio's hands knot into small fists. Would Lerrys really drag that affair out in Comyn council, or demand satisfaction from me at this late date and on another planet? But Lerrys did not look at me, but at Derik.

"My lords, in these days when the Comyn and the other powers of Darkover drift apart, our young ruler should take a consort outside of council, and bring in some strong alliance. Linnell Aillard, too, could give marriage-right to some strong and loyal man."

I stared. Dio and I had escaped public censure—but this was almost as bad. Linnell was white with shock, and Callina broke in angrily, rising to her feet, "Linnell is *my* ward! This is no matter for council meddling!"

Dyan caught up the phrase maliciously. "Meddling? Does a Comyn Keeper question the will of the council?"

"Not where I am concerned," Callina retorted, standing straight and defiant. "But for Linnell, yes!"

I knew this was only a point of delay, but I could not look at Linnell's small stricken face and keep silent. "Idiots!" I said harshly. "Yes, you too, Lord Regent! You very cleverly rushed the council through while I was out of my head—"

"From his utter disregard of council manners," drawled Lerrys in languid rebuke, "Lew Alton is still out of his head."

"Then more of you should have your wits addled like that," I retorted, turning on him. "This council is a farce, and now it is turning into a brawl! Here we sit like gaffers in the market square, haggling over marriages! Can a burst dam be mended with toothpicks?"

They were all listening to me, but I stopped, a familiar fist squeezing my throat. *What was this?*

Callina's face seemed to waver in the rainbow shimmer or was it my eyes? But she caught up my words.

"Oh, we are so safe, my lords, we have so much time for this nonsense! While the Terrans lure the people away, and make a reeking, filthy Trade City out of our Thendara, we sit wrangling among ourselves, letting our young lords and ladies enjoy themselves on other planets—" her glance rested coldly on Dio Ridenow— "while we sit in the Crystal Chamber making marriages. And Sharra's matrix in Kadarin's hands! You had a demonstration, the other day, of our Comyn powers and what did you do? You let Marius Alton be killed, and Lew hurt. Those two you should have guarded above all the others! Which of you can answer for the life of Marius? Which of you would dare take his place?"

Before anyone could answer, I jumped in again.

"The Terrans have left us a little power to rule, and we play with our corner of the planet like little children squabbling over their playgrounds! The people used to hate the Terrans! Now they hate us instead! A leader could jump up from anywhere, or nowhere, and strike fire to all this tinder! While I was on Earth, I heard someone call Darkover the weak link in the Terran Empire. We could be the link to snap the chain of conquest! Are we doing it?"

Abruptly I stopped, out of breath, aware, first, that Callina and I were in telepathic contact—in spite of the dampers—and, second, that even this faint surface contact was exhausting me completely. I sent a desperate command; *Break it! Get out!* What was the girl doing? I couldn't hold that kind of rapport under a damper! She clung, uncomprehending, and I lashed out with a quick telepathic surge, to knock her out of rapport. I was already so limp I could hardly stand up. I caught at the edge of the railing and let myself slide back into my seat, but I could not loose the merciless grip on my mind. *Was* it Callina?

The room was very quiet. I saw Dio's face taut and pale. Lerrys choked, "What's wrong with the dampers?"

Hastur stood up, leaning over the long table, and started to speak, then looked up. His mouth dropped open.

Callina froze, motionless.

The floor dipped under my feet and would not stay still. And above us there was a little shimmering, a distortion of the air.

Dio screamed.

"The—the death sign," someone faltered, and voices died in deadly stillness.

I stared at the sign that flared like letters of living fire in the air, and I felt my blood freeze and the strength

running out of me like water. Twisted space writhed and
flared, and the inside me was howling and gibbering,
reduced to primal panic. *From time out of mind, before
Darkover's sun faded to a dying ember, that sign
meant doom and death, bodies and minds seared to
ruin.*

"Sorceress! She-devil!" It was Dyan's voice exploding
in curses; he took three quick strides toward Callina,
caught her by the shoulders, and wrenched her away
from her place before the High Seat; flung her, with all
the strength in his lean body, out into the room.

And young Regis, through some uncanny sensing,
leaped up and caught Callina's reeling body as she fell.
The sight broke the static horror that held me; I whirled
to face Dyan. At last I had reason! The man who dared to
touch a Keeper had forfeited immunity. Annihilating
fury swept from me, taking Dyan unaware. The Alton
Gift, even unfocused, can be a vicious thing. His mind
lay, in seconds, stripped before mine. I rained vicious
mental slaps on it. It was immensely satisfying. I had
been holding this in check ever since he picked my mind
on the skyliner. He writhed, crumpled and fell, gasping
in loud desperate hoarse half-sobs.

The pattern of fire flamed and died and was gone.
Space in the room was quiet, normal again.

Callina stood leaning on Regis, pallid and shaken. I
still stood over Dyan; his defenses were slashed away,
and it would have been easy to snap the thread of his life.
But Derik threw himself forward, flinging restraining
arms around me.

"What are you about, you madman?"

There is something in a touch which can lay the mind
bare. And what I touched then, shook my world. Derik
was a weakling; I had always known that; but this—this
tumbling, impassable confusion? I drew away, unable to

endure even a second of it, letting my savage attack on Dyan relax.

Hastur's voice, harsh, and sombre, commanded, "In the name of Aldones! Let us have peace here, at least!"

Dyan stumbled to his feet and backed away. I could not move, though I had no will left to defy Hastur. The Regent looked gravely at Callina.

"A serious occasion, Callina *comynara*."

"Serious truly. But only for me?" She freed herself from Regis' protecting arm. "Oh, I see. You blame me for the—the manifestation?"

"Who else?" Dio cried shrilly. "So innocent, so innocent she looks, but she and Ashara—she and Ashara—"

Callina turned terrible eyes on her.

"Can all your life be told in open council then, Dio Ridenow *comynara?* You sought Ashara once."

Dio's eyes sought mine. Then, with the quick desperate move of one deserted, she threw herself into the arms of her brother Lerrys and burrowed her bright head in his shoulder.

Callina faced them all with aloof dignity. "I need not defend myself from your silly panic, Dio." she said. "But you, Dyan Ardais, I ask no courtesies of you, but you touch me again at your life's risk. Let everyone hear, and let him beware of a finger's weight laid on me; I am Keeper. *And no man lives to maul me three times.*"

She turned toward the door. And until the curtains had folded down softly behind her, there was silence.

Then Dyan laughed, low and ugly. "In six years you have not changed, Lew Alton. Still you have a passion for witches. You stand here defending our sorceress, even as you once threw away all your Comyn honor for that mountain hellion of Kadarin's, trying to lure a Comyn lord to her bed—"

But that was all he got to say. "Zandru's hells!" I

shouted, "she was my wife and you keep your filthy tongue from her name!" I smashed my flat hand, hard, across that sneering mouth. He yelped and staggered back, then his hand swept like lightning into his shirt—

And Regis was on him like lightning, seizing the small deadly thing he raised to his lips. The boy flung it to the floor in disgust. "A poison-pipe—in the Crystal Chamber! And you spoke of honor, Dyan Ardais?"

The two Hasturs held Dyan back between them. One of the Ridenow brothers had a restraining hand on my arm, but he didn't need it.

I'd had all I could stand.

I turned my back on them all and left.

I'd have strangled if I'd stayed there another minute.

Not knowing or caring where my steps led, I went up and up toward the height of the Comyn Castle. I found bitter relief in climbing flight after flight of stairs; head bent and aching, but a need for physical action driving me on.

Why the hell hadn't I stayed on Terra?

That damnable sign! Half the Comyn would take it for a supernatural apparition, a warning of danger. It meant danger, all right, but there was nothing supernatural about it. It was pure mechanics, and it scared me more than any ghostly visitation.

It was a trap-matrix; one of the old, illegal ones, which worked directly on the mind and emotions, rousing racial memories, atavistic fears—all the horrors of the freed subconscious of the individual and the race, throwing man back to the primal, reasonless beast.

Who would build a pattern like that?

I could have, but I hadn't. Callina? No Keeper alive would blaspheme her office that way. Lerrys? He might think it a perverted joke, but I didn't think he had the training. Dyan? No, it had scared him. Dio, Regis, Derik?

Now we were getting silly; I'd be accusing Old Hastur, or my little Linnell, next!

Dyan, now. I couldn't even have the relief of killing him in fair fight.

Even with one hand, I wasn't afraid to fight him. Not a man Dyan's age. I don't read my antagonist's mind, like a telepath in a bad scare-story, to figure out his sword strokes. That sort of stuff takes intent, motionless concentration. Nobody—not the legendary Son of Aldones—could fight a duel that way.

But now I could fight him before a hundred witnesses, and they'd still cry murder. After today and what they'd seen me do to Kadarin. I couldn't do that to anyone else. Kadarin and I had once been in rapport through Sharra, and we had—however little we liked it—a foothold in each other's minds.

By Dyan didn't know that.

Dyan didn't know this either, but he'd had his revenge already.

Six years of knocking around the Empire had cured me, as far as cure was possible. I am not, now, the shattered youngster who had fled Darkover years ago. I am not the young idealist who found, in Kadarin, a hope of reconciling his two warring selves, or saw in a girl with amber eyes everything he wanted in this world or next.

Or I thought I wasn't. But the first knock on my shell had cracked it wide open. What now?

I was standing on a high balcony, jutting out over the walls of the Comyn Castle. Below, the land lay spread like a map, daubed in burnt sienna and red and dusty gold and ochre. Around me rose the iridescent castle walls, which gave back the dropping light of the red sun, setting in blood and fire. *The bloody sun.* That is what the Terrans call the sun of Darkover. A just name—for them, and for us.

And far above me soared the high spire of the Keeper's Tower, arrogantly aloof from castle or city. I looked up at it, apprehensively. I did not think that Ashara, ancient though she must be, would remain aloof from a holocaust in the Comyn.

Someone spoke my name and I turned, seeing Regis Hastur in the archway.

"I've got a message for you," he said. "I'm not going to give it, though."

I smiled grimly. "Don't, then. What is it?"

"My grandfather sent me to call you back. As a matter of fact, I wanted an excuse to get out myself."

"I suppose I ought to thank you for pulling that blow-pipe away from Dyan. Right now, I'm inclined to think you'd have saved us all trouble if you'd let him use it."

"Are you going to fight him?"

"How can I? You know what they say about the Altons."

The youngster joined me at the railing. "Want me to fight him as your proxy? That's legal, too."

I tried to hide how much the offer had touched me. "Thanks. But you'd better keep out of this business."

"It's too late for that. I'm in it already. Waist-deep."

I asked, on impulse, "Did you know Marius well?"

"I wish now, that I could say yes." His face held a queer sort of shame. "Unfortunately—no, I never did."

"Did anybody?"

"I don't think so. Although he and Lerrys were friends, in a way." Regis traced an idle pattern in the dust, with his bootheel. After a minute he rubbed his toe over it and said, "I spent a few days in the Ridenow *forst* before coming to council, and—" he paused. "This is difficult— I heard it by chance, and the only honorable thing I could do, was to pledge not to repeat it. But the boy is dead now, and I think you have a right to know."

I said nothing. I had no right to insist that a Hastur violate his word. I waited for him to decide. At last he said, "It was Lerrys who suggested the alliance with Aldaran, and Marius himself went to Castle Aldaran as ambassador. Do you think Beltran would have had the insolence to *offer* marriage to a Keeper, unsolicited?"

I should have realized that. Someone must have told Beltran that such an offer would meet with serious consideration. But was Regis breaking his pledge, just to tell me my brother had been pawn-hand in a mildly treasonable intrigue?

"Can't you *see?*" Regis demanded. "Why *Callina?* Why a Keeper? Why not Dio, or Linnell, or my sister Javanne, or any of the other *comynara?* Beltran wouldn't care. In fact, he'd probably have an ordinary girl, provided she could give him *laran* rights in council. No. Listen, you know the law—that a Keeper must remain a virgin, or she loses her power to work in the screens?"

"That's nonsense," I said.

"Nonsense or not, they believe it. The point is, this marriage launches two ships on one track. Beltran allied to them, and Callina out of the council's way by good, fair, safe, legal means."

"It begins to fit together," I said. "Dyan and all." There *was*, after all, something Dyan wanted less than a capable, adult male Alton in council; a Comyn Keeper might be even more of a threat to him. "But that marriage will take place only over my dead body."

He knew immediately what I meant. "Then marry her yourself, *now*, Lew! Do it illegally, if you have to, in the Terran Zone."

I grinned ironically and held out my mutilated arm. I could not marry, by Darkovan law, while Kadarin lived. An unsettled blood-feud takes precedence over every other human obligation. But by Terran law we could marry.

I shook my head, heavily. "She'd never consent."

"If only Marius had lived!" Regis said, and I was moved by the sincerity of his words; the first honest regret I had heard from anyone, though they had all expressed formal condolences. I liked it better that he did not pretend to any personal sorrow, but simply said, "The Comyn needed him so. Lew, could you use any other telepath—me, for instance—for a focus like that?"

"I don't know," I said. "I don't think so. I'd rather not try. You're a Hastur, and it probably wouldn't kill you, but it wouldn't be fun." My voice suddenly turned hard. "Now tell me what you really came here to tell me!"

"The death sign," he blurted, then his face crumpled in panic. "I didn't mean that, I didn't—"

I could have had his confidence if I had waited. Instead I did something that still shames me. I caught one of his wrists with my good hand, and with a quick twist, a trick hold I'd learned on Vialles, forced him against the railing. He started to leap at me, then I caught his thought.

I can't fight a man who has only one hand.

That hardened my rage; and in that instant of black wrath I lashed out and forced rapport on him; I drew into his mind roughly, with a casual swift searching that took what it wanted, then withdrew.

Stark white, shaking, Regis slumped against the railing; and I, the taste of triumph bitter on my tongue, turned my back on him. To justify my own self-contempt, I made my voice hard. "So you built the sign! You—a Hastur!"

Regis swung around, shaking with wrath. "I'd smash your face for that, if you weren't—why the hell did you *do* that?"

I said harshly, "I found out what I wanted to know."

He muttered, "You did."

Then, his eyes blazing but his voice unsteady, he said,

"That's what scared me. That's why I came to you. You're an Alton, I thought you'd know. At the council, something hit me. I—I don't know anything about matrix machanics, surely you must know that now? I don't know how I did it, or why. I just bridged the gap and threw the sign. I thought I could tell you—ask you—" His voice broke, on the ragged edge of hysteria; I heard him swear, chokingly, like a child trying not to cry. He was shaking all over.

At last he said, "All right. I'm still scared. And I could kill you for what you did. But there's no one else to ask for help." He swallowed. "What you did, you did openly. I can stand that. What I can't stand is not knowing what I might do next."

Shamed and unnerved, I walked away from him. Regis, who had tried to befriend me, had received the same treatment I'd given my worst enemy. I couldn't face him.

After a minute he followed me. "Lew. I said, we'll have to forget it. We can't afford to fight. Did it occur to you? We're both in the same fix, we're both doing things we'd never do in our right mind."

He knew, and I knew, it wasn't the same; but it made me able to look round and face him.

"Why did I do it, Lew? How, why?"

"Steady," I said. "Don't lose your head. We're all scared. I'm scared, too. But there must be a reason," I paused, trying to muster my memory of the Comyn Gifts. They are mostly recessive now, bred out by intermarriage with outsiders, but Regis was physically atavistic, a throwback to the pure Comyn type; he might also be a mental throwback. "The Hastur Gift, whatever that is, is latent in you," I said. "Perhaps, unconsciously, you knew the council should be broken up, and took that drastic way of doing it." I added, diffidently, "If what had happened—hadn't happened, I'd offer to go into your mind and sift it. But—well, I don't think you'd trust me now."

"Probably not. I'm sorry."

"Don't be," I said roughly. "I don't even trust myself, after that. But Ashara or Callina, for that matter, either of the Keepers, could deep-probe and find out for you."

"Ashara—" He looked up thoughtfully toward the Keeper's Tower. "I don't know. Maybe."

We leaned across the railing, looking down into the valley, dulled now and darkened by the falling night. A baritone thunder suddenly shook the castle, and a silver dart sped bullet-like across the sky, trailing a comet's tail of crimson, and was lost.

"Mail-rocket," I said, "from the Terran Zone."

"Terra and Darkover," said a voice behind us, "the irresistible force, and the immovable object."

Old Hastur came out on the balcony. "I know, I know," he said, "you young Altons don't like being ordered around here and there. Frankly, I don't enjoy doing it; I'm too old." He smiled at Regis. "I sent you out to keep you from jumping into the mess along with Lew. But I wish you'd managed to keep your temper, Lew Alton!"

"*My* temper!" The unfairness of that left me speechless.

"I know. You had provocation. But if you had controlled your righteous wrath—" he spoke the words with a flavor of sour irony— "Dyan would have been clearly in the wrong. As it is—well, you broke Comyn immunity first, and that's serious. Dyan swears he'll write a writ of exile on you."

I said, almost indulgently, "He can't. The law requires at least one *laran* heir from every Domain or why did you go to such trouble to have me recalled? I am the last living Alton, and childless. Even Dyan can't break up the Comyn that way."

Hastur scowled. "So you think you can break all our laws—being irreplaceable? Think again, Lew. Dyan swears he's found a child of yours."

"Mine? It's a stinking, sneaking lie," I said angrily. "I've lived off-world for six years. And I'm a matrix mech. You know what *that* means. And it's common knowledge I've lived celibate." Mentally I absolved myself for the single exception. If Dio had borne my child, after that summer on Vainwal, I would have known. Known? I'd have been murdered for it!

The Regent looked at me skeptically. "Yes, yes, I know. But before that? You weren't too young to be physically capable of fathering a child, were you? The child *is* an Alton, Lew."

Regis said slowly, "Your father wasn't exactly a recluse. And I suppose—how old was Marius? He might have fathered a chance-child somewhere."

I thought it over. It seemed unlikely that I should have a son. Not impossible, certainly, remembering certain adventures of my early manhood, but improbable. On the other hand, no Darkovan woman would dare swear me, or my dead kinsmen, father to her child unless she were sure past all human doubts. It takes more courage than most women have, to lie about a telepath.

"And suppose I call Dyan's bluff? To produce this alleged child, prove his paternity, set him up where I am now, write his writ of exile and be damned to him? I never wanted to come back anyhow. Suppose I say go right ahead?"

"Then," said Hastur, gravely, "we'd be right back where we started." He laid his lined old hand on my arm. "Lew, I fought to have you recalled, because your father was my friend and because we Hasturs were pretty desperately outnumbered in council. I thought the Comyn needed you. Downstairs just now, when you were raking them out for their squabbles—*like children in a playground*, you said—I had high hopes. Don't make a fool of me by breaking the peace at every turn!"

I bent my head, feeling grieved and unhappy. "I'll try," I said at last, bleakly, "but by the sword of Aldones, I wish you'd left me out in space."

CHAPTER SEVEN

After the Hasturs left me, I went back to my rooms and thought over what I'd learned.

I had walked into Dyan's trap and it had snapped shut on me. I had Hastur to thank if I hadn't been already exiled. All along—I could see now—they had been goading me into open defiance. Then there was this child of mine, or my father's or Marius', a docile puppet; not a grown man with power in his own hands.

And Callina. That idea that a Keeper must be a virgin —superstitious drivel, but there must be some grain of scientific truth behind it, as with all other fables and Comyn-traditions.

The superstitious could believe what they liked. But out of my own experience I knew this; any telepath working among the monitor screens will discover that his nervous and physical reflexes are all keyed into the matrix patterns. A matrix technician undergoes some prolonged periods of celibacy—strictly involuntary. This impotence is nature's safeguard. A matrix mech who upsets his nerve reactions, or through physical or emotional excesses, upsets his endocrine balance, pays for it. He can overload his nervous system to the point where he will short-circuit and blow out like a fuse; nervous depletion, exhaustion and usually death.

A woman does not have the physical safeguard of impotence. The Keepers have always been severely cloistered. Once a girl has been aroused, once that first sensual response is awakened, so disastrously physical in its effect on nerves and brain, there is no way to determine the limit of safety. For a woman the picture is black or white. Absolute chastity, or giving up her work in the screens.

I, too, must be careful; I exposed Callina to a terrible danger.

I turned around to see old Andres scowling at me; a squat ugly Terran, fierce and surly; but I knew him too well to be deceived by his fierce looks.

I never knew how a Terran ex-spaceman had won his way into my father's confidence, but Andres Ramirez had been part of our home since I could remember. He'd taught me to ride, made toys for Marius, spanked us when we punched each other's heads or raced at too breakneck a pace, and told us endless lying tales which gave no hint about his true history. I never knew whether he could not return to Terra, or whether he would not; but twenty years dropped from my age as he growled, "What are you standing there sulking about?"

"Not sulking, damn you! Thinking!"

The old fellow snorted. "Young Ridenow is waiting to see you. You keep fine company these days!"

In the other room Lerrys stood waiting for me, tense, seemingly uneasy; his attitude made my nerves jump, but with a curt semblance of politeness, I motioned him to a seat. "If you came as Dyan's proxy, tell him not to bother. The fight's off. Hastur said so."

Lerrys sat down. "Well, no. As a matter of fact, I had a proposition for you. Has it occurred to you, now that your father's gone, you and I and Dyan are the strength of the Comyn?"

"You keep good company," I said dryly.

"Let's do without the insults. There's no reason we should fight among ourselves, there's enough for us all. You're half Terran; I suppose you have some Terran common sense. You know how the Terran Empire will handle this, don't you? They'll deal with anyone who's in a position to give orders. Why shouldn't you, and I, and Dyan, make the terms for Darkover?"

"Treason," I said slowly. "You're speaking as if the Comyn were already out of the way."

"It's bound to fall apart in a generation or two," Lerrys said quietly. "Your father, and Hastur, have been holding it together by pure force of personality for the last dozen years. You've seen Derik. Do you think he can take Hastur's place?"

I didn't. "Nevertheless," I said, "I am Comyn, and I'm vowed to stand behind Derik while he lives."

"And hold off disaster one more generation, at any cost?" Lerrys asked. "Isn't it better to make some arrangement now, rather than waiting for the big smash, and letting things lapse into anarchy for years before we can get them squared away again?"

He leaned his chin on his hands, regarding me intently. "The Terrans can do a lot for Darkover and so can you. Listen to me, Lew. Every man has his price. I saw the way you looked at Callina today. I wouldn't touch that she-devil's fingers, let alone take her to bed, but I suppose it's a matter of taste. I thought for a while it was Dio you wanted. But you'd fit perfectly well into our plans. You'd be better than Beltran. You're educated on Terra, but you look Darkovan. You're Comyn—one of the old aristocracy. The people would accept you. You could rule the planet!"

"Under the Terrans?"

"Someone will. And if you don't—well, you're unpopular because of the Sharra rebellion. And you're

Comyn. The *Terranan* make a habit of disposing of hereditary monarchies, unless they collaborate. Terra wouldn't care whether you lived or died."

Lerrys was probably right. In these days of toppling empires, no man is overburdened with loyalties. The Comyn would come crashing down eventually; why shouldn't I salvage something from the ruins?

Lerrys said, "Then you'll consider it?"

I didn't answer. A sudden intuition made me look up, and see that he had gone gray-white, his narrow fine features pinched and pale. That *bothered* me. The Ridenow are supersensitives. In the distant past of the Comyn, when Darkover dealt with nonhumans, the Ridenow Gift had been bred into their family and they were used to detect strange presences, or give warning of unhealthy psychic or telepathic atmospheres.

He said with a strange intensity, "There are worse things than Terra, Lew. Better to make Darkover a Terran colony, even, than to face Sharra, or anything like that, from our own people."

"Erlik defend us from either!"

"The choice might be up to you, in the end."

"Hell, Lerrys, I'm not that important!"

"You may not know it," he said, "but you may be the key to everything."

Suddenly it seemed I was looking, not at one man, but at two. My brother's friend, intent on trying to get me to come over to their faction—and some deeper thing, using Lerrys for its own purpose. I was seriously debating whether I ought to turn on a damper, before he could work some mental trick on me. But I didn't more fast enough.

A flood of pure malevolence suddenly surged out of him. I jumped up, and with a terrible effort, managed to shut it out of my consciousness. Then I leaped at Lerrys, gripped him with one hand and angrily thrust my mind against his.

It wasn't Lerrys!

I met perfect, locked defense—and Lerrys alone could never have barred me from his mind. I was using a force harder than I had used on Dyan—and the Ridenow are especially vulnerable to telepathic assault. And while it did not touch whatever was using Lerrys, it tortured *him*. He writhed a moment, slumped; suddenly, frenized into convulsions by the thing that held him, he twisted in frantic resistance. With the strength of a maniac or a berserker, he flung off my one-handed grip. And from somewhere, he found strength, too, to slam down a final defense against the assault I was using on him. Gritting my teeth in despair, I let my telepathic touch break loose. If that possessing mind should suddenly withdraw, leaving Lerrys to stand the assault alone, Lerrys would be dead or raving mad before I could get out.

Lerrys lay still, sobbing in air, for a moment. Then he sprang upright. I tensed for a renewed attack, but instead he said, quite unexpectedly, "Don't look so startled! Does it surprise you to know you're important to Darkover? Think over what I said, Lew. Your brother was a man of sense, you might have some of it too. I imagine you'll decide I'm right." Smiling in a friendly way, he held out his hand. Almost numbed, I touched his fingers, wary against some further trick.

His mind was blank, innocent of any guile, the alien gone. *He didn't even know what he had done.*

"What's the matter? You look a bit off color," he said. "I'd put on a damper, if I were you, and get some rest. You still need it, I'd say; that blow on the head was nothing to laugh at." He bowed and went out, and I sank on a couch, wondering if the blow had, indeed, damaged my reason. *Must I be alert to attack from everyone? Or was I stark raving mad?*

A battle like that is never easy, and I was shaking in very nerve. Andres, coming through the curtains, stopped and stared in consternation.

"Get me a drink."

He started his routine protest about drinking on an empty stomach; looked at me again, stopped in mid-grumble and went. More than once I've suspected him of being more telepathic than he'll admit. When he came back it was no Darkovan cordial, but the strong Terran liquor that is sold contraband in Thendara.

I could not close my hand on the glass; to my tremendous shame, I had to lean back and let Andres hold it to my mouth. I hated the fiery stuff; but after I had swallowed a little my head cleared and I could sit up and take the glass without shaking.

"And stop trying to baby me!" I yelled at Andres, who was hovering around as if he thought I'd explode into fragments. But his familiar grumbling had a soothing effect; he'd grumbled just like this when I'd taken a tumble off my pony and broken a couple of ribs on the way down.

Just the same, I waved away his various suggestions of food and bed, and went out.

The sky was murky with traces of a storm; I could see rain squalls coming down across Nevarsin. Bad weather for the Terrans, with their dependence on planes and rockets and the shifty upper atmosphere. Our mountain-bred beasts could endure storms, blizzards, and rain. Why would a sensible people put their trust in a tricky element like the air?

I crossed the courtyard, standing at the edge of the steep embankment where the cliff fell away; a thousand feet below me, the city of Thendara lay sprawled. I leaned on the low stone wall. If one wished to attack the Terrans, one need only choose a stormy night of rain or sleet, so that their planes and rockets were laid up to meet them on equal terms.

Behind that, the ridge of the mountains were a darker line against the dark sky, and far away, on the high slopes, I saw a gleam of fire. Some hunter's fire, perhaps; yet the glimmer reminded me that somewhere, a strange white smoke spiraled up through fires that were not ordinary flame, and an incredible tenth-level matrix twisted space around itself.

When once a man has stood at the fires of Sharra, the strange flames call to him, play on his nerves as a heavy hand sweeps harpstrings. But I knew that unless I stilled their harpings I would break completely; so I fought against the maddening live warmth that pulsed somewhere in me, reminding me of things I loathed and feared with all my heart—yet in some strange, shameful way, longed for; loved; desired.

Where could I go to still that harping?

Only to Callina.

CHAPTER EIGHT

The Aillard rooms were spacious and brilliant; shimmering walls diffused delicate colors over Callina, who knelt on the floor, playing with a little striped beast from the rainforests. It leaped on her shoulder, purring, and flickering two-toed claws in and out of her silk sleeves.

Linnell was seated near her, a harp laid flat across her knees, and Regis standing beside Linnell; but they all sensed my presence at once. Linnell put the harp aside and Callina rose hastily, putting the kitten-thing on the floor and pulling at her skirts; but I went to her and took her in my arms. She would never know how precious she had made herself to me by that glimpse of a self less guarded, less aloof. I held her a moment, then the old frustration slipped back, thrusting like an unsheathed sword between us. *Careful.*

She evaded me by speaking of Linnell. "Poor child. I'm afraid she and Derik have quarreled. She loves him—"

"It's who *you* love that interests me!" I interrupted.

She said, "I am Keeper—and *comynara!*"

"*Comynara!*" I suppose I sounded as bitter as I felt. "The Comyn would write your death warrant as soon as your marriage, if it would serve any cause!"

"If it would serve any cause, I would write my own,"

she said steadily. My arms strained about her.

"Are you going to let them *sell* you?" I flung the words at her like a curse. "What do we owe the Comyn? They've played hell with our lives since we were born!"

"Lew, I don't think you understand. I was mad, to let you think we could ever belong to each other. We can't. Not ever." Her hands went out, blindly, to push me away. "I can marry Beltran—and still keep my power to aid you, and the Comyn—because—because only because I do *not* love him. Do you understand?"

I did. I let her go and stood back, looking at her in consternation. Matrix work, for a man, has its frustrating aspects. But I had never stopped to think—more accurately I had never cared a damn—what particular refinements of hellishness it might have for a woman. But before I could break out with the outrage I felt, she turned to Regis.

"Ashara has sent for us. Are you coming?"

"Not now," he said. Regis had changed, in only a few hours; he seemed older, hardened somehow. He smiled in the old easy way, but I was not wholly comfortable in his presence. It hurt to realize that Regis was keeping himself barriered from me, but in a way it was a relief.

A servant folded Callina in a wrap like a gray shadow. As we went out, and down the staircase, Linnell stood between the panels of curtain, watching us, smiling. The colored lights, spilling over her pale dress, made her a rainbow statuette in a golden aureole; suddenly, for an instant, vague unrest crystallized and fell together into one of those flashes of prevision which touch a telepath in moments of stress.

Linnell was doomed!

"Lew, what's the matter?"

I blinked. Already the certainty, that sick instant when my mind had slid off the time-track, was fading. The confusion, the sense of tragedy, remained. When I looked up again, the curtains had dropped shut and Linnell was gone.

Outside, a thin fine rain was falling. The lights had faded in the old city, dark in the lee of the cliff below; but further out, in the Terran Zone, a neon glare of wet orange and red and green streaked the night sky with garish colors. I looked over the low wall.

"I would like to be down there tonight," I said wearily. "Or anywhere away from this hell's castle."

"Even in the Terran Zone?"

"Even in the Terran Zone."

"Why aren't you, then? No one keeps you here, if that is where you would rather be."

I turned to Callina. Her cobweb cloak spun out winglike on the wind; her hair blew, like a fine spray, about her face. I turned my back on the distant lights and pulled her close. A moment she held herself away from me, then suddenly she clung wildly, her lips frantic under mine, her arms gripping me with desperate dread. When we pulled apart, she was shaking like a young leaf.

"What now, Lew? What now?"

I gestured violently at the glare of neon. "The Terran Zone. Confront the Comyn with an accomplished fact, and let them find themselves another pawn to play with."

Slowly, the spark faded in her eyes. Turning her back on the city, she pointed at the distant ridge of the mountains, and again the illusion came; *thin white smoke, strange fire . . .*

"Sharra's fires burn there, still, Lew. You are no freer than I."

I put my arm around her, returning by slow degrees to sane acceptance. The rain was icy cold on our faces; we turned and went silently toward the dark mass of the tower.

The wind, broken in its sweep by the angles of the

castle, flung little spits and slashes of rain at us. We passed through walled courts and pillared passages, and finally stopped before a dark arch. Callina drew me forward, and a shaft began to rise.

Ashara's Tower—so the story goes—was built for the first Keeper when Thendara was no more than a row of mud huts huddled under Nevarsin peak. It belongs to the strange days before our world writhed in earthquakes and cast off her four spinning moons. The smell of centuries hung between the musty walls with the shadows that slipped past, flitting into darkness. We rose and rose. At last the shaft halted and we stood before a carven door of glass. Not a curtain or panel of light. A door.

We stepped into blueness. Uncanny lights so mirrored and prismed the room that it seemed to have no dimension; to be at once immense and confined. The shimmer of blue glistened in the air, and under our feet; it was just like swimming in blue waters or in the fire of a blue jewel.

"Come here," said a low voice, clear as winter water running under ice. "I am waiting for you."

Then and only then could my eyes focus enough in the frosty dayshine, to make out a great throne of carven glass; and the figure of a woman, seated on the throne. A straight tiny figure, almost as small as a child, in robes which so absorbed and mirrored the light that she appeared transparent.

"Ashara," I whispered, and bent my head before the Sorceress of the Comyn.

Her pale features, innocent of wrinkles as Callina's own, seemed almost fleshlessly pure. But they were old for all that, so old that even wrinkles had been smoothed away by the hand of time. The eyes, long and large, were colorless too, although in a normal light they might have been blue. There was a faint, indefinite resemblance between the two Keepers, nevertheless; as if Ashara were a stylized portrait of Callina, or Callina an embryo Ashara, not yet what Ashara was but one day to become so.

And I began to believe that she was immortal indeed, as they whispered; that she had lived on Darkover since before the coming of the Sons of Light.

She said softly, "so you have been beyond the stars, Lew Alton?"

It would not be fair to say the voice was unkind. It was not human enough for that. It only sounded as if the effort of conversing with actual, living persons, was too much for her; as if our life disturbed the cool crystalline peace that should always reign here. Callina, accustomed to this—or so I suppose—answered gently.

"You see all things, Mother. You know what we have seen."

A flicker of life crossed the ancient face. "No, not even I can see all things. And you refused my only chance to aid you, Callina. You know I have no power now, outside this place." Her voice had more vitality now, as if she were wakening to our living presence.

Callina's head bowed low. "Yet aid me with your wisdom, Ashara," she whispered. The ancient sorceress smiled remotely.

"Tell me," she said.

We sat together on a carven glass bench at Ashara's feet, and told her of the events of the last few days. I asked her at last, "Can *you* duplicate the Sharra matrix?"

"Even I cannot alter the laws of matter and energy," she said. "Yet, I wish you knew less Terran science, Lew."

"Why?"

"Because, knowing, you look for explanations. Your mind would be steadier if you could call them Gods, demons, sacred talismans, as the Comyn did long ago. Sharra—a demon? No more than Aldones is a God," she

said, and smiled. "Yet they are living entities of a kind.
Nor are they good or evil, though they may seem so in
their contacts with men. What says the old legend?"

Callina whispered, "Sharra was bound in chains, by
the Son of Hastur, who was the Son of Aldones, who was
the Son of Light . . ."

"Ritual," I said impatiently. "Superstition!"

The still old face turned to me. "You think so? What
do you know of the Sword of Aldones?"

I swallowed. "It is—the weapon against Sharra," I
said. "I suppose it's a matrix, and, like the Sharra one, it's
set in a sword for camouflage."

It was a hypothetical discussion anyhow, and I said so.
The Sword of Aldones was in the *rhu fead*, the holy place
of the Comyn, and might as well have been in another
Galaxy.

There are things like that on Darkover. They can't be
destroyed; but they are so powerful, and so deadly dangerous, even the Comyn, or the Keepers, can't be trusted
with them.

The *rhu fead* was so keyed and so activated by
matrices that no one can enter it but the Comyn who
have been sealed into council. It is physically impossible
for an outsider to get inside without stripping his mind
bare. By the time he got through the forcelayer, he
would be an imbecile without enough directive power to
know why he had come.

But inside—the Comyn of a thousand years ago had
put them out of our own reach. They are guarded in the
opposite fashion. No Comyn can touch them. An outsider could have picked them up freely, but no Comyn
can come near the force-field surrounding them.

I said, "Every unscrupulous Comyn for three hundred
generations has been trying to figure that one out."

"But none of them have had a Keeper on their side,"
Callina said. She looked at Ashara. "A Terran?"

"Perhaps," Ashara said. "At least, an outsider. Not a Terran born on Darkover, with a mind adjusted to the forces here, but a real alien. Such a one would pass where we never could. His mind would be locked off and sealed against those forces, because he wouldn't even know they were there."

"Fine," I said. "All I have to do is go some fifty light years, and bring one back, without telling him anything about this planet, or what we want him for, and hope he has enough telepathic talent to co-operate with us."

Ashara's colorless eyes held a flicker of scorn. "You are a matrix technician. What about the screen?"

Abruptly, I remembered the strange, shimmering screen I had seen in Callina's matrix laboratory. So it was one of the legendary psychokinetic transmitters, then? Vaguely, I began to see what they were aiming at. *To transmit matter, animate or inanimate, instantaneously through space—*

"That hasn't been done for hundreds of years!"

"I know what Callina can do," Ashara said with her strange smile. "Now. You and Callina touched minds, at the council—"

"Surface contact. It exhausted us both."

Ashara nodded. "Because all your energy—and hers—went into *maintaining* the contact. But I could put the two of you into focus as you and Marius were linked."

I whistled soundlessly. That was drastic; normally only the Altons can endure that deep focus.

"The Altons—and the Keepers."

I looked dubiously at Callina, but her eyes were averted. I understood; that sort of rapport is the ultimate intimacy. I wasn't any too eager myself. I had my own private hell that would not bear the light of day; could I open it for Callina's clear seeing?

Callina's hand twitched in a shuddering denial.

"No!"

The refusal hurt. If I could steel myself to this, why should she refuse?

"I will not!" There was anger in her voice, but terror, too. "I am mine—I belong to myself—No one, no one, least of all you, shall violate that!"

I was not sure whether she spoke to me or to Ashara, but I tried to calm her with tenderness. "Callina, do this for me? We can't be lovers yet, but you can belong to me this way—"

I needed her so, why did she go rigid in my arms as if my touch were shameful? She sobbed wildly, stormily. "I can't, I won't, I can't! I thought I could, but I cannot!" She faced Ashara at last, her face white, burning. "You made me so—I'd give my life if I had never seen you, I'd die to be free of you, but you made me so, and I cannot change!"

"Callina—"

"No!" Her voice vibrated with passionate refusal. "You don't know everything! You wouldn't want it, either, if you knew!"

"Enough!" Ashara's voice was a cold bell, recalling us to the silence in the tower; it seemed that even the flame in Callina's eyes died. "Be it so, then; I cannot force it. I will do what I can."

She rose from the glass throne. Her tiny, blue-ice form hardly reached to Callina's shoulder. She looked up and met my eyes for the first time; and that icy, compelling stare swallowed me . . .

The room vanished. For a moment I looked on blank emptiness, like the starless chasms past the rim of the universe; a shadow among shadows, I drifted in tingling mist. Then a stream of force pulsed in me; deep in my brain a spark, a core waked to life, charging me with power that stung through my whole being. I could feel myself as a network of live nerves, a sort of lacework of living force.

Then, suddenly, a face sketched itself on my mind.

I cannot describe that face, although I know, now, what it was. I saw it three times, but there are no human words to describe it. It was beautiful beyond imagining; and it was terrible beyond all conception. It was not even evil. But it was damnable and damnèd. Only a fraction of a second it swam in my eyes, then it burned out in the darkness. But in that instant, I looked straight in at the gates of hell.

I struggled back to reality. I was in Ashara's blue-ice tower room again. Again? Had I left it? I felt giddy and confused, disoriented; but Callina threw herself at me, and the convulsive pressure of her arms, the damp fragrance of her hair and her wet face against mine, brought me back to sanity.

Over her shoulder I saw that the carven throne was empty. "Where is Ashara?" I asked numbly.

Callina straightened, her sobs vanishing without trace. Her face held a sudden, uncanny stillness. "You had better not ask me," she murmured. "You would never believe the answer."

I frowned. I could only guess at the bond between the Keepers. Had we seen Ashara at all, or only her semblance? Had Callina seen that face?

Outdoors the lights had faded; we walked through the rainy courtyard and the echoing passages without once speaking. In Callina's matrix laboratory it was warm; I pulled off my cloak, letting the heat soak into my chilled body and aching arm, while Callina busied herself adjusting the telepathic dampers. I crossed the room to the immense screen I had seen the day before, and stared, frowning, into its cloudy depths. *Transmitter*.

At its side, cradled in the silk shock-absorber, was the largest matrix I had ever seen. An ordinary matrix mechanic operates the first six levels. A telepath can manip-

ulate the seventh and eigth. Sharra was ninth or tenth—
I had never been sure—and demanded at least three
linked minds, one of them a telepath. I could not even
guess at the level of this one.

Sorcery? Unknown laws of science? They were one.
But the freak Gift born in my blood, a spark in my nerves
—I was Comyn, and for such things as this the Comyn
had been bred.

To explain the screen fully would be impossible outside the Comyn. It captured images. It was a duplicator;
a trap for a desired pattern. An automatic assembly of a
set of predetermined requisites—no, I can't explain and
I won't try.

But with my telepathic force, augmented by the
matrix, I could search, without space limitation, for such
a mind as we wanted. Of all the billions of human and
nonhuman minds in the million worlds in spacetime,
somewhere was one exactly suited to our purpose, having
a certain awareness—and a certain *lack* of awareness.

With the screen, we could attune that mind's vibration
to *this* sector in spacetime; here, now, between the poles
of the screen. Then, space annihilated by the matrix, we
could shift the energons of mind and body and bring
them here. My brain played with words like hyperspace
and dimension-travel and matter-transmitter, but those
were only words.

I dropped into the chair below the screen, bending to
calibrate the controls to my own cerebral pattern. I fid-
dled fussily with the dial, not looking up. "You'll have to
cut out the monitor screen, Callina."

She crossed the room and touched a series of studs; the
bank of lights winked out, shunting every matrix on
Darkover out of this monitor. "There's a bypass relay
through the Arilinn tower," she explained.

A grill crackled and sent out a tiny staccato signal.
Callina listened a moment then said, "Yes, I know,

Maruca. But we have cut out the main circuits. You'll have to hold the energons in Arilinn tonight."

She waited; then rapped out, "Put up a third-level barrier around Thendara! That is a command from Comyn; acknowledge and comply!" She turned away, sighing.

"That girl is the *noisiest* telepath on the planet," she said. "I wish any other Keeper had been at Arilinn tonight. There are a few who can cut through a third-level barrier, but if I asked for a fourth—" she sighed. I understood; a fourth-level barrier would have alerted every telepath on the planet to the fact that something was going on in the Comyn Castle.

We'd chance it. She took her place before the matrix, and I blanked my mind against the screen. I shut out sense impressions, reaching to adjust the psychokinetic waves into the pattern we wanted. What sort of alien would suit us? But without volition on my part, a pattern laid itself down.

I saw, in the instant before my optic nerve overloaded and went out, the dim symbols of a pattern in the matrix; then I went blind and deaf in that instant of overload that is always terrifying.

Gradually, without external senses, I found orientation in the screen. My mind, extended to astronomical proportions, swept incredible distances; traversed, in fractional seconds, whole parsecs and galaxies of subjective spacetime. There came vague touches of consciousness, fragments of thought, emotions that floated like shadows —the flotsam of the mental universe.

Then, before I felt contact, I *saw* the white-hot flare in the screen. Somewhere another mind had fitted into the pattern. We had cast it out through time and space, like a net, and when we met a mind that fitted, it had been snared.

I swung out, bodiless, divided into a billion subjective

fragments, extended over a vast gulf of spacetime. If anything happened, I would never get back into my body, but would float in the spacetime curve forever.

With infinite caution, I poured myself into the alien mind. There was a short but terrible struggle; it was embedded, enlaced in mine. The word was a holocaust of molten-glass fire and color. The air writhed with cold flames, and the glow on the screen was a shadow and then a clearing darkness and then an image, captive in my mind, and then—

Light tore at my eyes. A ripping shock slammed through my brain, the floor seemed to rock and the walls to crash together and apart, and Callina was flung, reeling, against me as the energons seared the air and my brain.

Half stunned, but conscious, I looked up at Callina. The alien mind was torn free of mine. The screen was blank.

And in a crumpled heap on the floor, at the base of the screen, where she had fallen, lay a slender, dark-haired girl.

CHAPTER NINE

Unsteadily, Callina knelt beside the crumpled form. I followed slowly, and bent over beside her.

"She isn't dead?"

"Of course not." Callina looked up. "But that was terrible, even for us. What do you think it was like for her? She's in shock."

The girl was lying on her side, one arm across her face. Soft brown hair, falling forward, hid her features. I brushed it lightly back—then stopped, my hand still touching her cheek, in dazed bewilderment.

"It's Linnell," Callina choked. "Linnell!"

Lying on the cold floor was the girl in the spaceport; the girl I had seen in my first confused moments in Thendara.

For a moment, even knowing as I did what had happened, I thought my mind would give way. The transition had taken its toll of me, too. Every nerve in my body ached.

"What have we done?" Callina moaned. "*What have we done?*"

I held her tight. Of course, I thought; of course. Linnell was near; she was close to both of us; we had both been talking, and thinking of Linnell tonight. And yet . . .

"You know Cherrillys' two point law?" I tried to put it

into simple words. "Everything, everywhere, except a matrix exists in one *exact* duplicate. This chair, my cloak, the screwdriver on your table, the public fountain in Port Chicago—everything in the universe exists in *one* exact molecular duplicate. Nothing is unique except a matrix; but there are no *three* things alike in the universe."

"Then this is—Linnell's twin?"

"More than that. Only once in a million years or so would duplicates also be twins. This is her *real* twin. Same fingerprints. Same retinal eye patterns. Same beta-graphs and blood type. She won't be much like Linnell in personality, probably, because the duplicates of Linnell's environment are scattered all over the galaxy. But in flesh and blood, they're identical. Even her chromosomes are identical with Linnell's.

I took up the girl's wrist and turned it over. The curious matrix mark of the Comyn was duplicated there. "Birthmark," I said, "but the effect is identical in her flesh. See?"

I stood up. Callina stared and stared. "Can she live in this environment, then?"

"Why not? If she's Linnell's duplicate, she breathes oxygen in the same ratio we do, and her internal organs are adjusted to about the same gravity."

"Can you carry her? She'll get another bad shock if she wakes up in this place!" Callina indicated the matrix equipment.

I grinned humorlessly. "She'll get one anyway." But I managed to scoop her up, one-armed. She was frail and light, like Linnell. Callina held curtains aside for me, showed me where to lay her. I covered the girl, for it was cold, and Callina murmured, "I wonder where she comes from?"

"She was born on a world with gravity about the same as Darkover, which narrows it considerably. Vialles, Wolf, even Terra. Or, of course, some planet we never heard of." Her speech had impressed me as Terran; but

I hadn't told Callina about the episode on the spaceport, and didn't intend to. "Let's leave her to sleep off the shock, and get some sleep ourselves."

Callina stood in the door with me, her hands locked on mine. She looked haggard and worn, but lovely to me after the shared danger, shared weariness. I bent and kissed her.

"Callina," I whispered. It was half a question, but she freed her hand gently and I did not press her. She was right. We were both desperately exhausted. It would have been raving insanity. I put her gently away and went out without looking back. It was raining hard, but until the wet red morning rose sunlessly over Thendara I paced the courtyard, restless, and the drops on my face were not all rain.

Toward dawn I fought back to self-control, and went back to the Keeper's Tower. I was afraid that without Callina at my side I would not find a way into the blue-ice room, or that Ashara had vanished into some inaccessible place. But she was there; and such was the illusion of the frosty light, or of my tired eyes, that she seemed younger, less guarded; like a strange, icy, inhuman Callina. My brain almost refused to think clearly, but I finally managed to formulate my plea.

"You can see—time. Tell me. The child Dyan calls mine—"

"It is yours," Ashara said.

"Who—"

"I know. You've been celibate, except for Diotima Ridenow Comyn, since your Marjorie died." She looked right through my astonished stare. "No, I didn't read your mind, I thought the Ridenow girl might be suitable to train as I—as I trained Callina. She was not. I'm not concerned with your moralities or Diotima's; it's a matter of physical nerve alignments." She went on, passionlessly, "Hastur would not accept the bare word of those who brought the child; so he brought her to my keeping for search. She is here in the Tower. You may see her. She is yours. Come with me."

To my surprise—I don't know why, but somehow I had felt that Ashara *could* not leave her strange blue-ice room—she led me through another of the bewildering blue doors and into a plain circular room. One of the furry nonhuman mutes—the servants of the Keeper's Tower—scurried away on noiseless padded feet.

In the cool normal light Ashara's flickering figure was colorless, almost invisible. I wondered; was it the sorceress herself, or merely a projection she wanted me to see? The toom was simply furnished, and on a narrow white cot at the center, a little girl lay fast asleep. Pale reddish-gold hair lay scattered on the pillow.

I went slowly to the child, and looked down. She was very small; five or six, maybe younger. And as I looked down I knew they had told the truth. In ways impossible to explain, except to a telepath and an Alton, I knew; this was my own child, born of my own seed. The tiny triangular face bore not the slightest resemblance to my own; but my blood knew. Not my father's. Not my brother's. My own. My flesh.

"Who was her mother?" I asked softly.

"You'll be happier all your life if I never tell you."

"I can take it! Some light woman of Carthon or Daillon?"

"No."

The child murmured, stirred and opened her eyes. I took one step toward her—then turned, in an agony of appeal, on Ashara. Those eyes, those eyes, gold-flecked amber . . . "Marjorie," I said hoarsely, painfully, "Marjorie died, she *died* . . ."

"She is not Marjorie Scott's daughter." Ashara's voice was clear, cool, pitiless. "Her mother was Thyra Scott."

"Thyra?" I fought an insane impulse to laugh.

"Thyra? That's impossible! I never—I wouldn't have touched that she-devil's fingertips, much less—"

"Nevertheless, this is your child. And Thyra's. The details are not clear to me. There is a time—I am not sure. They may have had you drugged, hypnotized. Perhaps I could find out. It would not be easy, even for me. That part of your mind is a closed and sealed room. It does not matter."

I shut my teeth on a black, sickening rage. *Thyra!* That red hellion, so like and so unlike Marjorie, perfect foil for Kadarin! What had they done? How—

"It does not matter. It is your child."

Resentfully, accepting the fact, I glowered at the little girl. She sat up, tense as a scared small animal, and it wrenched at me with sudden hurt. *I had seen Marjorie look like that. Small, scared. Lost and lonesome.*

I said, as gently as I could, "Don't be afraid of me, *chiya.* I'm not a very pretty sight, but I don't eat little girls."

The little girl smiled. The small pointed face was suddenly charming; a tiny gnome's grin marred by a dimple. There were twin gaps in the straight little teeth.

"They said you were my father."

I turned, but Ashara was gone, leaving me alone with my unexpected daughter. I sat down uneasily on the edge of the cot. "So it would seem. How do they call you, *chiya?*"

"Marja," she said shyly. "I mean *Marguerhia*—" she lisped the name, Marjorie's name, in the odd old-world dialect still heard in the mountain sometimes. "Marguerhia Kadarin, but I just be Marja." She knelt upright, looking me over. "Where is your other hand?"

I laughed uneasily. I wasn't used to children. "It was hurt, and they had to take it off."

Her amber eyes were enormous. She snuggled against my knee, and I put my arm around her, still trying to get it clear in my mind.

Thyra's child. Thyra Scott had been Kadarin's wife—if you could call it that. But everyone knew he was rumored to be half-brother to the Scotts, Zeb Scott's child by one of the half-human mountain things. Back in the Hellers, half-brothers and sisters sometimes married; and it was not uncommon for such a marriage to adopt the child of one by someone else, thus avoiding the worst consequences of too much inbreeding. I scowled, trying to penetrate the gray murk which surrounded part of the Sharra affair in my mind. I had never probed that partial amnesia; I had felt, instinctively, that madness might lie there.

Perhaps I had been drugged with aphrosone. I knew how that worked. The one drugged lives a life outwardly normal, but he himself knows nothing of what he does, losing continuity of thought between each breath. Memory is retained in symbolic dreams; a psychiatrist, hearing what was dreamed during the time spent under aphrosone, can unravel the symbols and tell the victim what really happened. I had never wanted to know. I didn't now.

"Where were you brought up, Marja?"

"In a big house with a lot of other little girls and boys," she said. "*They're* orphans. I'm not. I'm something else. Matron says it's a wicked word I must never, *never* say, but I'll whisper it to you."

"Don't." I winced slightly; I could guess.

And Lawton, in the Trade City, had told me; *Kadarin never goes anywhere—except to the spaceman's orphanage.*

Marja put her head sleepily on my shoulder. I started to lay her down. Then I felt a curious stir and realized, abruptly, that the child had reached out and made contact with my mind!

The thought was staggering. Amazed, I stared at the

tiny girl. Impossible! Children do *not* have telepathic power—even Alton children! Never!

Never? I couldn't say that; obviously, Marja *did* have it. I caught my arms around her; but I broke the contact gently, not knowing how much she could endure.

But one thing I *did* know. Whoever had the legal right of it, this little girl was *mine!* And no one and nothing was going to keep her from me. Marjorie was dead; but Marja lived, whoever her parents, with Marjorie's face sketched in her features, the child Marjorie would have borne me if she had lived, and the rest was better forgotten. And if anyone—Hastur, Dyan, and Kadarin himself—thought they could keep my daughter from me, they were welcome to try!

Dawn was paling outside the tower, and abruptly I was conscious of exhaustion. I had had quite a night. I laid Marja down in the cot; drew up the warm covers under her chin. She looked up at me wistfully, without a word.

On an impulse I bent and hugged her. "Sleep well, little daughter," I said, and went very softly out of the room.

CHAPTER TEN

The next day, Beltran of Aldaran, with his mountain escort, came to the Comyn Castle.

I had not wanted to be present at the ceremonies which welcomed him; but Hastur insisted and I finally agreed. I'd have to meet Beltran sometime. It had better be among strangers where we could both be impersonal.

He greeted me with some constraint; we had once been friends, but the past lay between us, with its grim shadow of blood. I was grateful for the set phrases of custom; I could mouth them without examining them for a hostility I dared not show.

Beltran presented me, ceremoniously, to some of his escort. A few of them remembered me from years ago; but I looked away as I met a dark familiar face.

"You remember Rafael Scott," Beltran of Aldaran said.

I did.

There is no such word as endless, or the ceremonies would still be going on. However, at last Beltran and his people were handed over to servants, to be shown to rooms, fed and permitted to recuperate for the further formalities of the evening. As we dispersed, Rafe Scott

followed me from the hall, and I turned to him brusque-
ly.

"Listen, you," I said, "you're here under Beltran's
safe-conduct, and I can't lay a hand on you. But I warn
you—"

"What the hell's the *matter?*" he demanded. "Didn't
Marius explain? Where *is* Marius, anyhow?"

I looked at him, bitterly. This time I would not be
taken in by the confiding manner that had gulled me
before, when I was sick from space and too trusting to
doubt him.

He laid rough hands on me. "Where's Marius, damn
you?"

It got to him through the touch. He let me go and fell
back. "Dead! Oh, no—*no!*" He covered his face with his
hands, and this time I could not doubt his sincerity. That
momentary shock of rapport had at least convinced us
that we were telling the truth to each other.

His voice was not steady when he spoke. "He was my
friend, Lew. The best friend I had. May I die in Sharra's
fire if I had a hand in it."

"Can you blame me for doubting you? You were the
only one who knew I had the Sharra matrix, and they
killed him to get it."

He said evenly, "Believe what you like, but I haven't
seen Kadarin twice in the last year." His face was wrung
with grief. "Didn't Marius ever get a chance to explain it
to you? Damn it, if I wanted to hurt him would I have
loaned him my pistol? He gave it to the Ridenow boy—
Lerrys—because he was afraid to take it into the Terran
Zone. Like I said, it has the contraband mark on it. I have
a permit but he didn't. When you thought I was Marius,
I pretended—I thought, if I could only get a chance to
keep the two of you apart, until you understood what was
going to happen—"

I could not disbelieve his sincerity. After a moment I

put my hand on his shoulder. Had we been Darkovan men, we would have embraced and wept; but we both have the reserve of our Terran blood. I said baldly, at last, "You *have* seen Kadarin?"

"A few times, with Thyra. I've tried to keep out of his way." Rafe looked at me, oddly. "Oh, I see. They've told you about her baby."

"And mine," I said grimly. "I imagine I was drugged with aphrosone. Why did she do it?"

"I don't know," Rafe said. "Thyra never tells anyone anything. There's an odd streak in Thyra—almost inhuman. She's very strange with the baby, too. In the end Bob had to put the kid in the spaceman's orphanage. He didn't want to. He loved the kid."

"And knew she was mine?" It didn't make sense, any of it. Least of all that a child of mine had grown up to call Kadarin father, to bear his name, to love him.

"Of course he knew. How could he help it? I think he made Thyra do it," Rafe said. "He's had Marja home a dozen times, but he couldn't keep her. Thyra—"

But before he could go on, we were interrupted by a palace servant with a message from Callina.

"We'll talk again," Rafe said, as I took my leave. And I was not sure whether it was a promise or a threat.

Callina looked tired and harried.

"The girl's awake," she greeted me. "She was hysterical when she came to; I gave her a sedative, and she's calmed down a little. Lew, what are we going to do now?"

"I won't know until I see her," I said emptily.

The girl had been moved to a spacious room in the Aillard apartments. When we came in, she was lying across a bed, her face buried in the covers; but it was a tearless and defiant face she raised to me.

She was still Linnell's double. She looked more so, having been decently dressed in Darkovan clothing, which I supposed—correctly—to be Linnell's own.

"Please tell me the truth," she said steadily. "Where am I? Oh—" she cried out, and hid her face. "The man with one hand who kissed me in the spaceport, back on Darkover!"

Callina stood apart, a figure of dignified disdain, leaving me to squirm alone. "That was a—a mistake," I said, lamely. "Allow me to introduce myself. Lew Alton-Comyn z'par servu. And you?"

"That's the first sensible thing anyone has said." Although she spoke the language badly, I was amazed at the luck that gave us someone who could speak it at all. "Kathie Marshall."

"Terranan?"

"Terran, yes. Are you Darkovan? What's all this?"

"I suppose we do owe you an explanation," I said, and broke off, staring with what I suppose must have been a very stupid expression. "But I'm damned if I know how to explain it!"

"You have nothing to fear. We brought you here because we need your help—"

"But why me? Where's here? And what makes you think I'd help you, even if I could—after you've kidnaped me?"

It was, I supposed, a fair question.

Callina said, "Shall we bring Linnell here, and let her see? You were brought here, Kathie, because you are twinned in mind with my sister Linnell. We had to take the chance that you would be willing to help us, but there will be no compulsion involved. And no one will hurt you."

As Callina moved toward her, Kathie sprang up and backed away. "Twinned minds? That's—that's ridiculous! Where am I?"

"In the Comyn Castle in Thendara."

"Thendara? But that's—that's on Darkover! I—I left

Darkover *weeks* ago. I arrived on Samarra just last night. No," she said, "no, I'm dreaming. I saw you on Darkover and I'm *dreaming* about you!" She went to the window and I saw her white hands clench on the fold of curtain. "A—a *red* sun—Darkover—oh, I have dreams like this when I can't wake up. I can't wake up—" She was so deathly white that I thought she would faint. Callina came and put an arm around her, and this time Kathie did not pull away.

"Try to believe us, my child," Callina said. "You are on Darkover. Have you heard anything of matrix mechanics? We brought you here like that." It was a grossly inaccurate description, but it calmed her somehow.

"Who are you, then?"

"Callina Aillard, Keeper of the Comyn."

"I've heard about the Keepers," Kathie said shakily. "Look, you—you *can't* take a Terran citizen, and—and pull her halfway across the Galaxy; my father's going to tear the planet apart looking for me—" Her voice broke and she covered her face with her hands. She was only a child. From the child came the scared wail. "I'm afraid! I—I want to go home!"

Gently, as she might have spoken to Linnell herself, Callina murmured, "Poor child! Don't be frightened!"

There was something else I had to do. Kathie must keep her immunity, and unawareness, of Darkovan forces. I knew one way to do that. Yet I hated doing it; I must make myself vulnerable. In effect, I meant to put a barrier around her mind; built into the barrier would be a sort of bypass circuit, so that any attempt to make telepathic contact with Kathie, or dominate her mind, would be immediately shunted from her open mind to my guarded one.

There was no sense in explaining to Kathie what I meant to do. While she clung to Callina, I reached out as gently as I could and made contact with her.

It was an instant of screaming pain in every nerve. Then it blanked out, and Kathie was sobbing convulsively. "What did you *do?* Oh, I felt you—but no, that's crazy. What are you?"

"Why couldn't you wait till she understood?" Callina demanded. But I stood looking at them somberly, without answering. I had done what I had to do, and I had done it *now*, because I wanted Kathie safely barriered before anyone saw her and guessed. And, above all, before Callina confronted her with Linnell. That moment of prevision last night had left me desperately uneasy. Why, of all the patterns in the world, why Linnell?

What happened when a pair of exact duplicates met? I couldn't remember ever hearing.

It hurt to see her cry; she was so like Linnell, and Linnell's tears had always upset me. Callina looked up helplessly, trying to soothe the weeping girl. "You had better go away for now," she said, and as Kathie's sobs broke out afresh, "Go *away!* I'll handle this!"

I shrugged, suddenly angry. "As you please," I said, and turned my back on them. Why couldn't she trust me?

And that moment, when I left Callina in anger, was the moment when I snapped the trap shut on us all.

CHAPTER ELEVEN

Once in every journey of Darkover around its sun, the Comyn, city folk, mountain lords, off-world consuls and ambassadors and Terrans from the Trade City, mingled together in carnival with a great outward show of cordiality. Centuries ago, this festival had merely brought Comyn and commoner together. Now it involved everyone of any importance on the planet; and the festival opened with the display of dancing in the great lower halls of the Comyn Castle.

Centuries of tradition made this a masked affair; in compliance with custom, I wore a narrow half-mask, but had made no further attempt at disguise. I stood at one end of the long hall, talking indifferently and listening with half an ear to a couple of youngsters in the Terran space service, and as soon as I decently could, I got away and stood staring out at the four miniature moons that had nearly floated into conjunction over the peak.

Behind me the great hall blazed with colors and costumes that reflected every corner of Darkover and almost every known form of human or half-human life throughout the Terran Empire. Derik glittered in the golden robes of an Arturian sun-priest; Rafe Scott had assumed the mask, whip and clawed gloves of a *kifırgh* duelist.

In the corner reserved, by tradition, for young girls, Linnell's spangled mask was a travesty of disguise, and her eyes were glowing with happy consciousness of all the eyes on her. As *comynara*, she was known to everyone on Darkover; but she rarely saw anyone outside the narrow circle of her cousins and the few selected companions permitted to a girl of the Comyn hierarchy. Now, masked, she could speak to, or even dance with perfect strangers, and the excitement of it was almost too much for her.

Beside her, also masked, I recognized Kathie. I didn't know why she was here, but I saw no harm in it. She was safely barricaded by the bypass circuit I had built into her mind; and there was, probably, no better way of proving that she was not a prisoner, but an honored guest. From her resemblance to Linnell, they'd only think her some noblewoman of the Aillard clan.

Linnell laughed up at me as I joined them:

"Lew, I am teaching your cousin from Terra some of our dances! Imagine, she didn't know them."

My cousin. I suppose that was Callina's idea. Anyway, it explained her badly accented Darkovan. Kathie said gently, "I wasn't taught to dance, Linnell."

"Not taught to *dance*? But what did you learn, then?" Linnell asked incredulously. "Don't they dance on Terra, Lew?"

"Dancing," I said dryly, "is an integral part of all human cultures. It is a group activity passed down from the group movements of birds and anthropoids, and also a social channeling of mating behavior. Among such quasi-human races as the *chieri* it becomes an ecstatic behavior pattern akin to drunkenness. Men dance on Terra, on Megaera, on Vainwal, and in fact, from one end of the civilized Galaxy to the other, as far as I know. For further information, lectures on anthropology are given in the city; I'm not in the mood."

I turned to Kathie in what I hoped was properly cousinly fashion; "Suppose we do it instead?"

I added to Kathie, as we danced, "Of course you wouldn't know that dancing is a major study with children here. Linnell and I both learned as soon as we could walk. I had only the public instruction, but Linnell has been studying ever since." I glanced affectionately back at Linnell. "I went to a dance or two on Terra. Do you think our Darkovan ones are so different?"

I was studying the Terran girl rather closely. Why would a duplicate of Linnell have the qualities we needed for the work in hand? Kathie, I realized, had guts and brains and tact; it took them, to come here after the shock she had had, and play the part tacitly assigned to her. And Kathie had another rare quality. She seemed unconscious that my left arm, circling her waist, was unlike anyone else's. I've danced with girls on Terra. It's not common.

With seeming irrelevance, Kathie said. "How *sweet* Linnell is! It's as if she were really my twin; I loved her, the minute I saw her. But I'm afraid of Callina. It's not that she's unkind—no one could have been kinder! But she doesn't seem quite human. Please, let's not dance? On Terra I'm supposed to be a good dancer, but here I feel like a stumbling elephant."

"You probably weren't taught as intensively." That, to me, was the oddest thing about Terra—the casualness with which they regarded this one talent which distinguishes man from four-footed kind. Women who could not dance! How could they have true beauty?

I just happened to be watching the great central curtains when they parted and Callina Aillard entered the hall. And for me, the music stopped.

I have seen the black night of interstellar space flecked by single stars. Callina was like that, in a scrap torn from the midnight sky, her dark hair netted with pale constellations.

"How beautiful she is," Kathie whispered. "What does the dress represent? I've never seen one just like it."

"I don't know," I said. But I lied. I did not know why any girl on the eve of her marriage—even an unwilling marriage—should assume the traditional costume of *la damnee;* Naotalba, daughter of doom, bride of the daemon Zandru. What would happen when Beltran caught the significance of the costume? A more direct insult would have been hard to devise—unless she had come in the dress of the public hangman!

I excused myself quickly from Kathie and went toward Callina. She had agreed to the wishes of the Comyn; she had no right to embarrass her family like this, at such a late date.

But by the time I reached her, she was already getting that lecture from old Hastur; I caught the tail of it.

"Behaving like a naughty, willful child!"

"Grandfather," said Callina, in that quiet, controlled voice, "I will neither look nor act a lie. This dress pleases me. It is perfectly suited to the way I have been treated by the Comyn all my life." Her laugh was musical and unexpectedly bitter. "Beltran of Aldaran would endure more insults than this—for *laran* rights in council! You will see." She turned away from the old man.

"Dance with me, Lew?"

It was no request but a command; as such I obeyed, but I was upset and didn't care if she knew it. It was shameful, to spoil Linnell's first dance like this!

"I am sorry about Linnell," Callina said. "But the dress pleases my mood. And it is becoming, is it not?"

It was. "You're too damned beautiful," I said hoarsely. "Callina, Callina, you're *not* going through with this— this crazy farce! I drew her to a recess and bent to kiss her, savagely crushing my mouth on hers. For a moment she was passive, startled; then went rigid, bending back and pushing me frantically away. "No! Don't!"

I let my arms drop and stood looking at her, slow fury heating my face. "That's not the way you acted last night!"

She was almost weeping. "Can't you spare me this?"

"Did you ever think there were things you might have spared me? Farewell, Callina *comynara;* I wish Beltran joy of his bride." I felt her catch at my sleeve, but I shook her off and strode away.

I skirted the floor, grimly quiet. A nagging unease, half telepathic, beat on me. Aldaran was dancing with Callina now; viciously I hoped he'd try to kiss her. Lerrys, Dyan? They were in costume, unrecognizable. Half the Terran colony could be here, too, and I'd never know.

Rafe Scott was chatting with Derik in a corner; Derik looked flushed, and his voice, when he turned and greeted me, was thick and unsteady. "Eve'n, Lew."

"Derik, have you seen Regis Hastur? What's his costume?"

"Do' know," Derik said thickly. "I'm Derik, tha's all I know. Have 'nough trouble rememberin' that. You try it some time."

"A fine spectacle," I muttered. "Derik, I wish you would remember who you are! Get out and sober up, won't you? Do you realize what a show you are giving the Terrans?"

"I think—forget y'self," he mumbled. "Not your affair wha' I do—ain' drunk anyhow."

"Linnell should be very proud of you!" I snapped.

"Li'l girl's mad at me." He forgot his anger and spoke in a tone of intimate self-pity. "Won't even dansh—"

"Who would?" I muttered, standing on both feet so I would not kick him. I resolved to hunt up Hastur again; he had authority I didn't, and influence with Derik. It was bad enough to have a Regency in such times. But when the heir presumptive makes a public idiot of himself before half a planet!

I scanned the riot of costumes, looking for Hastur. One

in particular caught my eye; I had seen such harlequins in old books on Terra. Parti-colored, a lean beaked cap over a masked face, gaunt and somehow horrible. Not in itself, for the costume was only grotesque, but there was a sort of atmosphere, the man himself—I scowled, angry at myself. Was I imagining things already?"

"No. I don't like him either," said Regis quietly at my side. "And I don't like the atmosphere of this room—or this night." He paused. "I went to grandfather today, and demanded *laran*."

I gripped his hand, without a word. Every Comyn comes to that, soon or late.

"Things are different," he said slowly. "Maybe *I'm* different. I know what the Hastur Gift is, and why it's recessive in so many generations. I wish it was as recessive in me as in grandfather."

I didn't have to answer. He would heal. But now that new strength, that added dimension—whatever it was— was a raw wound in his brain.

He said, "You remember about the Hastur and Alton Gifts? How tight can you barrier your mind? Hell could break loose, you know."

"In a crowd like this, my barriers aren't worth too much," I said. I knew what he meant, though. The Hastur and Alton Gifts were mutually antagonistic, the two like poles of a magnet which cannot be made to touch. I didn't know what the Hastur Gift was; but from time immemorial in the Comyn, Hastur and Alton could work together only with infinite precaution—even in the matrix screens. Regis, a latent Hastur, his Gift dormant, I could join in rapport; could even force it on him un-desired. A developed Hastur, which he had suddenly be-come, could knock my mind from his with the fury of lightning. Regis and I could read each other's minds if we wanted to—ordinary telepathy isn't affected—but we could probably never link in rapport again.

Reluctantly I found myself wondering. I had forced contact on Regis; had he taken this step to protect himself from another such attempt? Didn't he trust me?

But before I could ask him the dome lights were switched off. Immediately the room was flooded with a streaming, silvery moonlight; there was a soft "A—ah!" from the thronged guests as, through the clearing dome, the four moons, blazing now in full conjunction, lighted the floor like daylight. Suddenly, I felt a light touch, and looked down to see Dio Ridenow standing beside me.

Her dress—a molded tabard of some stuff that gleamed, green and blue and silver, in the shifting moonlight—was so breathtakingly fitted to her body that it might as well have been sprayed on; and her fair hair, the color of the moonlight, rippled like water with the glint of jewels. She tossed her head, with a little silvery chiming of tiny bells.

"Well? Am I beautiful enough for you?"

I tried to sidestep the provocative tone, the green witchfire in her saucy eyes. "I must say it is an improvement over your riding breeches," I said dryly.

She giggled and tucked her hand through my arm; a hard, light little hand. "Dance with me, Lew? A *secain?*" Without waiting for my answer, she tapped the rhythm-pattern on the light-panel, and after a moment the steady, characteristic beat of the *secain* throbbed into the invisible music.

The *secain* is no formal promenade. Last year Dio and I had outraged the dowagers and the dandies, even on the pleasure-world of Vainwal, by dancing it there. I didn't want to dance it here. The floor was almost cleared now; most of the Thendara women are too prim for this wild and ancient mountain dance.

Still, I owed Dio something.

For a Darkovan girl, Dio was not a particularly expert dancer. But she was warm and vibrant; she smiled teasingly up at me, and, resenting that smile which took so much for granted, I whirled her till another girl would have screamed for mercy. But as she came upright she laughed at me; as always, she was scornful of my strength. She was like spring-steel tempered to my touch.

In the last figure of the dance I caught her tighter than the pattern of the dance demanded. This we had come to know well, this sense of being in key, body and mind, a closer touch than any physical intimacy. The beat of the *secain* throbbed in my blood, and as the music pulsed and pounded to climax, my senses pounded and pulsed, and as the final explosive drum-and-cymbal chord quivered and rang, I kissed her—hard.

The silence was anticlimax. Dio slid from my arms, and under the softening music we passed out under the open sky.

"I've been wondering—" teasingly, Dio lowered her voice, "when Hastur told you about your child—did you wonder about me?"

I frowned, displeased. That came too close for comfort. She laughed, but the laugh was sharp and mirthless.

"Thanks. I wasn't, if that helps any. Lew—do you really want that girl Callina?"

This I would not discuss with Dio.

"Why? Do you care?"

"Not much." But it didn't sound convincing. "But I think you're a fool. After all, she's not a woman—"

Now I was really shocked. This was not like Dio. I said, angrily, "As much as yourself!"

"That's almost funny, as yourself!"

"That's almost funny, coming from you!"

I threatened, "Dio, if you make a scene, I will find it a pleasure to break your neck."

"I know you will!" She was laughing again, but this time it was high and hysterical. "That's what I love about you! Your solution for all problems! Kill someone! Break a neck or two! But one thing I know, for sure: Callina's finished, and Ashara's going to lose her pawn!"

"What the devil are you talking about?"

She was still laughing that wildly hysterical laughter, "You'll see. It could have been you, you know, you could have saved them all that trouble! You and your crazy scruples! You cheated yourself, and especially Callina! Or, should I say, you played Ashara's game—"

I caught her wrist with the trick hold I'd used on Regis and wrenched her abruptly around. My fingers crushed on her wrist till she writhed. "You brute, you're breaking my arm! Damn it, Lew, you're not funny, you're *hurting* me!"

"You ought to be hurt," I said savagely. "You ought to be beaten! *What are they going to do to Callina?* Tell me, or I swear, Dio, I've never used the Gift on a woman before, but I'll tear it out of you if I have to!"

"You couldn't!" We were facing each other now in a blaze of fury that obliterated everything outside. "Remember?"

"Damn you!" The truth made me savage. Dio alone of all people was completely and perfectly protected against my Gift, forever—because of what had been between us on Vainwal. It had to be that way.

There are things no telepath, no man, can control. That—touching—in intimacy, is one of them. And Dio was one of the hypersensitive Ridenow. To safeguard her sanity, I had given her certain defenses against me. I could never take more from her, telepathically, than she wanted to give. More was impossible. I could remove that barrier—*if I wanted to kill her*. No other way.

I swore, impotently. Suddenly Dio flung her arms around my neck, eyes burning at me like green flames. "You blind fool," she choked, "you can't see what's before your very eyes, and you'll go blundering in again and spoil it all! Can't you trust me?"

She was very close, and the contact was dizzying. Realizing what she was doing, I thrust her suddenly and roughly away. "That won't get you anywhere."

Her face hardened. "Very well. There is a rumor current—and believed—that only a virgin may hold Callina's particular powers. There is, shall I say, a certain faction which holds to the belief that we would all be better off if Callina were—let's say—made suddenly powerless. And since your conduct is above reproach, there is *one* way to remedy the situation—"

I stared at her, dimly beginning to realize what she meant. But that was horrible! And was there any man on Darkover who would dare— "Dio, if this is your idea of a filthy joke—"

"A joke, but it's on Ashara," she said. Suddenly she grew quiet and deadly serious. "Lew, trust me. I can't explain, but you've got to keep out of it. Callina isn't what you think, not at all. She isn't—"

I brought my hand back and slapped her, hard. The blow sent her reeling. "You've had that coming for a year," I grated.

Suddenly Regis was close beside me; in an instant he had caught the overflowing of my thought, and his face paled. "Callina!"

Dio stood holding her cheek where I had slapped her, staring open-mouthed; but she threw herself forward on me now. "Wait," she begged, "Wait, you don't understand—"

I thrust her aside, swearing. Regis kept pace with me. Finally he breathed, "But who would dare? A Keeper, remember—actually to lay hands on her?"

I stopped. "Dyan," I said at last, quietly. "What did she say, in council? No man lives to maul me *three* times. If that were the first—"

We were in light surface contact. Abruptly I stopped him; he looked at me grimly and the touch of his mind fell from mine as clasped hands loosen.

"I thought so," I said. "When we touch, all the strength drains out of us both. They've smuggled some trap-matrix in there, eighth or ninth level, the kind that picks up vital energy—" My jaw fell. "Sharra!"

"Lew, are we *feeding* that damned thing?"

"We'll hope not," I said. "Can you touch Callina?"

I felt Regis, almost instinctively, grope for contact again; quickly, I barricaded myself. "Don't ever do that!" I commanded. The fumbling touch was raw agony; yet endure it I must, danger or no, at least once more. "Regis, when I say the word, link with me—for about a thousandth of a second. But whatever you do, don't freeze into rapport with me! If you do, we'll both burn out. Remember, you're Hastur and I'm Alton!"

He swallowed, convulsively. "You'd better do the linking. I can't control it yet."

For the barest instant, then, we contacted, in a scanning that sifted the whole diameter of the crowd. It was not a hundredth of a second, but even that flung us apart in a shock of blinding pain. A full tenth of a second would have burned out every spark of vital energy in our bodies. To whoever controlled the hidden matrix, it must have flamed like a star-ship on a radar screen.

But I knew what I wanted. Somewhere in the castle, a trap-matrix—not Sharra this time—was focused, with obscene intensity, on the weakest link in the Comyn: Derik Elhalyn.

And I had thought him only drunk!

The thick, inarticulate speech; the irritable confusion of brain, the fumbling limbs—all symptoms of a mind under an unmonitored matrix. And whoever set it, had a mind both perverted and sadistic—that this complex revenge on Callina should be carried out by Linnell's lover!

I reached for Callina, but only emptiness greeted my

seeking mind. It is a horrifying thing to feel only an empty place in the fluid mechanism of space, where once there was a living mind. Could even death blank her away so completely?

Regis turned a strained, heartbroken face to me.

"Lew, if he's touched her—"

"Easy. Derik doesn't know, he never will know what he's doing, you know. Listen; I need your help. I'm going straight into Derik's mind and try to lift the matrix trap." For the first time in my life I was grateful for the Alton Gift, which could force rapport—and which could go into a matrix without the half-dozen monitors and dampers an ordinary matrix mech would need. "Those things are plain hell, Regis. Now, when I get it lifted, you try to break it up. But don't you touch me—or Derik—or you'll kill all three of us."

It was a desperate chance. No sane person will go into a mind controlled by a trap-matrix; it is walking into a blind alley which may be filled with monsters ready to spring. And I would have to drop all my barriers, and trust the untried strength of a newly-*laran* Hastur who could kill me with a random touch.

Every instinct screamed *no;* but I reached out and focused on Derik.

And knew, at once, I had touched that thing before; when I tried to probe Lerrys.

Derik, like a man who feels the sting of a knife through an incomplete anesthetic, twisted to escape; but this time I held fast, grimly, forcing my focused strength as a wedge between mind and the trick matrix that held it in submission.

Behind me, as a man may look at mirrored light he dares not face, I sensed Regis; he had seized on that alien force, and he was tearing it to bits; destroying each strand of force as I lifted that telepathic web, thread by thread, out of the nerves of Derik's brain.

But now it was being forced on me, too. As a man at a screen may watch two starships battle, so the holder of this unholy matrix was watching the three-way duel, perhaps ready with a new weapon. Necessity and the need for haste made me careless how I tortured Derik; but I knew, too, if Derik were himself, he would thank me for this.

As I forced down barrier after barrier, something fought me, a grotesque parody of the real Derik; but I won. I felt it flicker, vanish like a trace of smoke, burnt away. The compulsion was gone, the trap-matrix destroyed—and Derik, at least, was clean.

I withdrew.

Regis leaned against a pillar, his face dead white. I asked, "Could you tell who was controlling it?"

"Not a trace. When the matrix shattered, I felt Callina, but then—" Regis frowned, "she blanked again and all I felt was *Ashara!* Why Ashara?"

I didn't know. But if Ashara were aroused and aware, at least she would protect Callina.

We had given ourselves away, Regis and I; we had lost vital strength; but for the moment, perhaps, we were safe. My main worry now was for Regis. I was mature, trained in the use of these powers, and I knew the limits of my own endurance. He didn't. Unless he learned caution, the next step would be nerve depletion and collapse.

I tried to warn him, but he shrugged it off. "Don't worry about me. Who's that with Linnell?"

I turned to see if he meant Kathie or the man in harlequin costume who had so disturbed me. Beside them was another masked figure, a man in a cowled robe which hid his face and body completely. But something about him reminded me, suddenly and horribly, of the hell in Derik's mind. Another victim—or the controller? I had to fight myself to keep from running across the room and pitching him bodily away from Linnell.

I went toward them, slowly. Linnell asked, "Lew, where have you been?"

"Outside, watching the eclipse," I said briefly.

Linnell glanced up at me, timidly, troubled.

"What is it, *chiya?*" The childish pet name still came easily.

"Lew, who is Kathie, really? When I'm near her, I feel terribly strange. It's not just because she *looks* so like me, it's as if she *were* me. And then I feel—I don't know—as if I had to come close to her, touch her, embrace her. It's a kind of pain! I can't keep away from her! But if I do touch her, I want to pull away and scream—" Linnell was twisting her hands nervously, ready to burst into hysterical tears or laughter. I didn't know what to say. Linnell wasn't a girl to fret over trifles; if it affected her like this, it was no minor whim.

Kathie had been dancing with Rafe Scott. As she came back, she smiled at Linnell; and almost without discernible volition, Linnell began to move in her direction. Was Kathie working some malicious trick on my little cousin? But no. Kathie had no awareness of Darkovan powers. I knew that. And nothing could get through that block I'd put on her.

Linnell touched Kathie's hand, almost shyly; in immediate response, Kathie put an arm around Linnell's waist, and they walked for a minute like that, enlaced. Then, with a sudden lithe movement Linnell drew herself free and came and caught at me.

"There's Callina," I said.

The Keeper, aloof in her starry draperies, threaded her way through the maze of dancers. "Where have you been, Callina?" Linnell demanded. She looked at her sister's strange costume with sorrowful puzzlement, but she did not comment; and Callina made no attempt to justify or explain herself.

"Yes," I demanded, with an intent look at Callina, shading the words telepathically, "where *have* you been?"

She seemed unaware of either overtone, and her careless words were devoid of any hidden message that I could read. "Talking with Derik. He drew me apart to hear some long confused drunken tale of his, but he never did get it told. I don't envy you, darling," she added, smiling at her sister. "Fortunately all the wine conquered him at last—may he never be defeated by a worse enemy." She shrugged daintily. "Hastur is signaling to me. Beltran is there. I suppose it's time for the ceremony."

"Callina—" Linnell almost sobbed, but the woman moved away from her outstretched hands. "Don't pity me, Linné," she said, "I won't have it." And I could tell what she meant was, "I can't bear it."

I don't know what I might have said or done, but she drew herself away; her eyes brooded, blue ice like Ashara's, past me into silence. Bitterly helpless, I watched her shrouded form move through the bright crowd.

I should have guessed everything then, when she left us without a touch, silent and remote as Ashara's self, making a lonely island of her tragedy and cutting us all away from her. I listened, numbed, as Hastur made the formal announcement and locked the doubled marriage bracelets upon the arms of the pair. Callina was Beltran's consort from the moment Hastur released her hand.

I glanced round at Regis and suddenly, appalled, sucked in air; the boy had turned ashen gray. I slid an arm around him and half-carried him to the archway. He drew a sobbing breath as the cold air reached his face, and muttered, "Thanks. Guess you were right." And abruptly he doubled up and collapsed on the floor. His lax hand was clammy and his breathing was shallow. I looked around for help. Dio was crossing the floor, on Lerrys arm—

Lerrys stopped dead in his tracks. He stared around wildly for a moment, his face convulsed; stiffened and clutched at Dio.

That was the first shock-wave. Then hell broke loose. Suddenly the room was a distorted nightmare, warped out of all perspective, and Dio's scream died in shivering air that would not carry sound. Then she was struggling in the grip of something that shook her like a kitten. She took one faltering step—

Then I saw two men standing together, the only calm figures in the distorted air. The harlequin and the horrible cowled man. Only now the cowl was flung back, and it was Dyan's cruel thin-lipped face that glared bleakly at Dio. She moved, fighting, another step, another; slid to the floor and lay there without moving.

I fought the paralysis of the warped space that held us in frozen stasis. Then harlequin and cowl turned—and caught Linnell between them.

They did not physically touch her. But she was in their grip as if they had bound her hand and foot. I think she screamed, but the very idea of sound had died. Linnell writhed, caught by some invisible force; a dark, flickering halo suddenly sprang up around them; Linnell sagged, held up hideously balanced on empty air; then fell, striking the floor with a crushing impact. I sobbed soundless curses; I could not move.

Kathie flung herself down by Linnell. I think she was the only person capable of free motion in the entire hall. As she caught Linnell in her arms, I saw for a moment that the tortured face had gone smooth and free of horror; a moment Linnell lay quiet, soothed, then she struggled in a bone-wrenching spasm and slackened—a loose, limp, small thing with her head lolling on her twin's breast.

And above them harlequin and cowled shadow swelled, took on height and power. For a moment, seeing clearly outside space, Kadarin's gaunt features blazed through the harlequin mask. Then the faces swam together, coalesced—and for a moment the beautiful, damnable face I had seen in Ashara's tower reeled before my eyes; then the shadows closed down.

Only seconds later the lights blazed back; but the world had changed. I heard Kathie's scream, and heard the crowd milling and crying out as I elbowed and thrust my way savagely to Linnell.

She was lying, a tumbled, pathetic heap, across Kathie's knees. Behind her, only blackened and charred panels of wall and flooring showed where distortion and warp had faded to normal, and Kadarin and Dyan were gone—melted away, evaporated, not there.

I knelt beside Linnell. She was dead, of course. I knew that, even before I laid my hand to the stilled breasts. Callina thrust Kathie aside, and I stood back, giving my place to Hastur, and put an arm around Callina; but though she leaned heavily on me, she took no notice of my presence.

Around me I heard the stir of the crowd, sounds of command and entreaty, and that horrible curiosity of a crowd when tragedy strikes. Hastur said something, and the crowds began to thin out and clear away. I thought, *this is the first time in forty generations that Festival Night has been interrupted.*

Callina had not shed a tear. She was leaning on my arm, so numbed with shock that there was not even grief in her eyes; simply, she looked dazed. My main worry was now for her; to get her away from the inquisitive remnant of the crowd. It was strange I did not once think of Beltran, though the marriage bracelet about her arm lay cold against my wrist.

Her lips moved.

"So that was what Ashara intended . . ." she whispered.

With a long, deep sigh, she went limp on my arm.

CHAPTER TWELVE

The thin red sunlight of another dusk was filtering
through the walls of my room when I woke; I lay still,
wondering if the whole thing had been a delirious nightmare born of concussion. Then Andres came in, and the
drawn face of the old Terran, grief deep in its ugliness,
convinced me; it was all too real. I remembered nothing
after Callina's collapse, but that wasn't surprising. I had
been warned, after the head-wound, not to exert myself;
instead I'd been throwing myself into battle with some of
the strongest forces on Darkover.

"Regis Hastur is here," Andres said. I tried to sit up;
he pressed me flat with strong hands. "You young idiot,
don't you know when you're done in? You'll be lucky to
be on your feet again in a week!" Then his real feelings
burst through the gruffness. "Boy, I've lost two of you!
Don't send yourself after Marius and Linnell!"

I yielded and lay quiet. Regis came in, and Andres
turned to go—then abruptly went to the window and
jerked the curtains shut, cutting the lurid sunlight.

"The bloody sun!" he said, and it sounded like a curse.
Then he went away.

Regis asked me gently, "How are you feeling?"

"How do you think?" My jaw set. "I have some killing to do."

"Less than you think, maybe." The boy's face was grim. "Two of the Ridenow brothers are dead. Lerrys will live, I think, but he won't be good for much, not for months."

I had expected that. The Ridenow were hypersensitive even to ordinary telepathic assault; he would probably lie in a semicoma for months. He was fortunate to have survived at all. "Dio?"

"Stunned, but she's all right. Zandru's hells, Lew, if I'd only been stronger—"

I quieted him with a gesture. "Don't blame yourself. It's incredible that you're not completely burnt out; the Hasturs must be hardier than I ever thought. Callina?"

"Dazed. They took her to the Keeper's Tower."

"Tell me the rest. All at once, don't dribble out the bad news!"

"This may not be bad. Beltran's gone; he left the castle that night, as if all Zandru's scorpions were chasing after him. That leaves Callina free."

I felt sourly amused. Beltran could have stepped in, with the Comyn in disorder and shock, and seized the reins of power as Callina's consort. That had, no doubt, been the idea. But in Beltran of Aldaran—superstitious, Cahuenga of the Hellers—they had relied on the weakest of tools, and it had broken in their hand.

"This is bad. There are Terrans here, and they've put an embargo on the castle. And—" he stopped, but he was keeping something back.

"Derik—is he dead too?"

Regis shut his eyes. "I wish he was," he whispered, "*I wish he was.*"

I understood. Under terrible need, we had cut into Derik's mind. We could not have foreseen that greater forces would be loosed so soon after. Corus and Auster

Ridenow were the fortunate ones; their bodies had died when their minds were stripped bare.

Derik Elhalyn lived. Hopelessly, permanently insane.

Outside I heard a strange voice, a Terran, protesting, "How the devil does one knock when there's no door?" Then the curtains parted and four men came into the room.

Two were strangers, in the uniform of Terran Space-force. One was Dan Lawton, Legate from Thendara.

The fourth was Rafe Scott, and he was wearing the uniform of the Terran service.

Regis rose and faced them angrily. "Lew Alton has been hurt! He's in no shape to be—interrogated—as you questioned my grandfather!"

"What do you want here?" I demanded.

"Only the answers to a few questions," said Lawton politely. "Young Hastur, we warned you before; stay in your own quarters. Kendricks, take the Hastur kid back to his grandfather, and see that he stays there."

The bigger of the Terrans put a hand on Regis' shoulder. "Come along, sonny," he said kindly.

Regis twisted away. "Hands off!" His hand, flashing to his boot, whipped out a narrow skean. He faced them across the naked steel, saying with soft, cold fury, "I will go when the *vai Dom* Alton bids me—unless you think you can carry me out."

I said, "I prefer him to stay. And you won't get any-where with violence in the Comyn Castle, Lawton."

He almost smiled. "I know," he said. "Perhaps I wanted them to see that. Captain Scott told me—"

Captain Scott.

"Traitor!" said Regis, and spat.

Lawton ignored that, looking down at me.

"Your mother was a Terran—"

"Black shame to me that I must admit it—yes!"

"Look," Lawton said quietly, "I don't like this any

more than you do. I'm here on business; let me do it and get out. Your mother was—"

"Elaine Aldaran Montray."

"Then you are kin to— How well do you know Beltran of Aldaran?"

"I spent a year or so in the Hellers, mostly as his guest. Why?"

He countered with another question, this time to Rafe. "Exactly what relation are you two, anyhow?"

"On the Aldaran side, it's too complicated to explain," said Rafe, "Distant cousins. But he married my sister Marjorie. You could say—brother-in-law."

"No spy for Terra can claim kin here!" I sat up, my head exploding painfully, but too much at a disadvantage flat on my back. "The Comyn will look after the law in this zone. You go and attend to your affairs in the Terran Zone! Since that was your choice!"

"That is exactly what we're doing," Lawton said. "Lerrys was working for us, so his brothers are our business; and they're dead."

"And Marius," said Rafe. "You never had a chance to hear it, Lew; but Marius had been working for Terra—"

I flung the lie into his face. "My brother never took a copper from Terra, and you know it! Lie to *them*, but don't try to lie to an Alton about his brother!"

"The plain truth will do," Lawton said. "You are right so far; your brother was not in our pay, nor a spy. But he worked for us, and he had applied for Empire citizenship. I sponsored him myself. He had as good a right to it as you, though you never chose to claim it. Even by your standards, that is no spy." Lawton paused. "He was probably the only man on Darkover working to bring about an honest alliance. The rest were out to line their pockets. How come this is news to you? You're a telepath."

I sighed. "If I had a *sekal* for every time I've explained

that, I could buy and sell the Terran Zone," I said. "Telepathic contact is used to project conscious thoughts. Quicker than words, no semantic barriers—and no one but another telepath can listen in. But it takes deliberate effort; one to send, the other to receive. Then, even when I'm not trying, I get a sort of—well—leakage. I can feel; right now you're confused, and sore as hell about something. I don't know what and I'm not trying to find out; telepaths learn not to be curious. I've been in rapport with my brother. I know everything he knew. But I don't remember—and I don't want to remember."

Suddenly, from Lawton's complete calm, I knew he had simply been trying to goad me; to make me lose my temper and drop my barriers. He was half Comyn; for all I knew, he might be a telepath himself. He'd been trying to find something out, and whatever it was, he'd probably found it.

"I'll tell you why I'm here," Lawton said abruptly. "Usually we let city-states govern themselves, until the government collapses. It usually does, within a generation after the Empire comes. When we meet real tyranny, we depose it; planets like Darkover, we simply wait for them to fall apart. And they do."

"I heard it all on Terra. *Make the universe safe for democracy—and then for Terran Trade!*"

"Maybe," Lawton said, imperturbably. "While you rule peaceably, you can rule till the planet crumbles. But there's been disorder lately. Riots. Raiding. Smuggling. And too much telepathic dirty-work. Marius died after you had forced rapport on him."

Regis said. "Who told you those lies. I saw him die with a knife in his heart."

"Marius wasn't a citizen yet, so I can only ask questions about his death, not punish it," he said. "But there's another report that you're holding a Terran girl here, prisoner."

My heart pounded suddenly. *Kathie*. Had Callina and I rashly exposed this last secret of Darkovan science?

"The daughter of the Terran Legate on Samarra—Kathie Marshall. She was scheduled to leave Darkover on the *Southern Cross*, days ago; I thought she had gone. But she's missing, and someone saw her here."

Regis said indifferently, "There were a great many Terrans here Festival Night. Some one must have seen—" he raised his voice. "Andres? Bring the *comynara* here; she is with Dio Ridenow."

His eyes held an intensity whose meaning escaped me; I started to open my mind, but sensed his instant prohibition. Lawton and Rafe would both know it, if we were exchanging telepathic messages, even if they couldn't read what they were about.

Regis said, "I would not, of course, know anything about Miss—is it Marshall? But I know who you saw. The resemblance has caused us some amusement, and a little embarrassment. Since, of course, no *comynara* could possibly be permitted to behave in public as your *Terranis* do."

Inward I raged and worried. What now? Why must they drag the name of the dead into this? After an eternity, I heard light, familiar footsteps, and Kathie Marshall came into the room.

She wore Darkovan dress; a ruffled gown that hung loose from her slender shoulders, her unbound hair dusted with metallic fragments. Bangles tinkled on her ankles and slender wrists.

"Kathie?" said Lawton.

Kathie raised a pretty, uncomprehending face. "*Chi'zei?*"

"Linnell, my dear," Regis drawled, "I have spoken of the foolish resemblance to some *Terranis*; I wished them to see at first hand."

I was praying that none of them knew Kathie well. The

difference was so haunting that it struck me with passionate grief; a ghost, a mockery.

Kathie put a hand down to touch my face. It was not a Terran gesture. She walked and moved like a Darkovan. "Yes, Regis, I remember," she said, and I had all I could do to keep back a cry of astonishment. For Kathie was speaking the complicated, liquid-syllabled pure mountain Darkovan—not with her own harsh Terran accent but with soft quick fluency. "But should you have so many strangers around you when you are hurt? To tell you some fantastic story about the Terrans?"

It wasn't Linnell's intonation. But the face remained, she was speaking Darkovan, and speaking it with an accent as good as my own or Dio's.

Lawton shook his head. "Fantastic," he muttered, "There certainly is a resemblance! But I happen to know Kathie couldn't speak the language anything like that!"

The big Terran broke in. "Dan, I tell you, I *saw*—"

"You were mistaken." Lawton was still looking intently at Kathie, but she did not move. Another false note. It is rudeness unspeakable to stare at an unmasked young girl on Darkover; men have been killed for it. Lawton knew it. Linnell would have been dying of confusion. But as that thought crossed my mind, Kathie blushed and ran out of the room.

"I'm trying to *tell* you," Kendricks said, "I was on spaceport duty when the Marshall girl left. I checked the passenger list after they were all drugged and tied-in. She certainly didn't get off after that, and it's been reported from Samarra by relay, so how could she be here? The fastest ship made takes seventeen days hyperdrive, between there and here."

Lawton muttered. "I guess we've made prime fools of ourselves. Alton, before I go, can you tell me how the Ridenow brothers died?"

Regis said, "I tried to explain—"

"But it didn't make sense. You said someone had a trap-matrix out. I know a little about matrices, but that's a new one on me."

No Terran can really grasp that concept, but tried. "It's a sort of mechanical telepath that conjures up horrifying images from race-memory and superstition. The person who sets one can control the minds and emotions of others. The Ridenow are sensitives—disturbed mental atmospheres affect them physically. This one was so badly disturbed that it short-circuited all the neural patterns. They died of cerebral hemorrhage."

It was a grossly over-simplified explanation, but Lawton at least seemed to understand. "Yes, I've heard of things like that," he said, and I surprised a strange, bitter look on his face. Then, to my surprise, he bowed.

"Thank you for your co-operation," he said. "There will be other matters to discuss when you are recovered."

Rafe Scott lingered when the others had gone.

"Look, if I could talk to you by yourself, Lew," he said, glowering at Regis.

Regis only said with angry contempt, "Get out of here, you filthy Terran half-caste!" He put his hand in the middle of Rafe's back, giving him a sharp push—more offensive than a blow.

Rafe turned around and hit him.

Regis' fist slammed into Rafe's chin. The Terran boy lowered his head, rushed in and clinched, and they swayed back and forth in a struggling, furious grip. All Regis' contempt, all the humiliation Rafe had suffered at the hands of the Comyn, exploded; they slammed at each other, the room filled with their pummeling violence. I lay there forgotten by both, yet somehow more a part of the fight than they were themselves. I felt, half deliriously, that the two halves of myself were slugging it out; the Darkovan Lew, the Terran. Rafe, once almost a brother—Regis, my best friend in the Comyn—both were myself and I was fighting myself, and each blow struck was in my own quarrel.

Andres settled it abruptly by collaring both the angry young men and jerking them violently through the curtains. "If you've got to fight," he growled, "do it outside!"

There was the brief sound of a scuffle, then Regis' voice, clear and scathing. "I should dirty my hands!"

Somehow, being part of their contention, these words were strangely meaningful; as if my own inward struggle had been somehow resolved.

After a while Andres came in, keeping up a steady monotoned grumble that was vaguely soothing. His hands were gentle as he looked at the half-healed wound at the back of my head; he ignored my profane protests that I was perfectly capable of taking care of myself, grinned when I swore at him, until finally I broke into rueful laughter that hurt my head, and let him do what he would. He washed my face as if I were a fretful child, would have fed me with a spoon if he'd thought for a minute that I'd allow it—I didn't—and finally dug out a pack of contraband cigarettes smuggled in from the Terran Zone. But when I had finally chased the old fussbudget off to rest, I could elude thought no longer.

Time had healed, a little, my grief for Marjorie. My father's death, bitterly as I regretted it, was more the Comyn's loss than mine. We had been close, especially toward the end, but I had resented the thing that made me half-caste. Much as I missed him, his death had set me at ease with my own blood. And the murder of Marius was a nightmare thing, mercifully unreal.

But Linnell's death was a grief from which I have never been free; that night my own pain was only an obligato to the torture of my nerves.

What had killed Linnell? No one had touched her, except Kathie. She was not, like Dio, a sensitive.

And then I understood.

I had killed Linnell.

All evening, intuitively, Linnell had been striving for contact with her duplicate. Their instinct had been better than my science. I—pitiful, damned, blind imbecile—I had blocked them away from one another. When the horror of Sharra had been loosed, Linnell had instinctively reached for the safety of contact with her duplicate. What had I said to Marius? *One body can't take it* . . .

And the bypass circuit in Kathie's mind had thrown Linnell into contact with me—and through me, into that deadly matrix in Kadarin's hands. Years ago, Sharra had been given a foothold in my brain. And force flows toward the weaker pole. It had all rushed into the unprotected Linnell, overloading her young nerves and immature body.

She had gone out like a burnt match.

Havoc had indeed raged in the Comyn. Linnell, the Ridenows, Derik, Dio. I smiled, grimly. The defenses I'd given Dio had probably saved her from the fate of her brothers. And after her malice—

Blinding light broke suddenly on me. There wasn't a scrap of malice in Dio. In her own way, the perverse little imp had been *warning* me.

A narrow chink of moonlight lay in a cold streak across my face; in the shadows there was a stir, a step and a whisper. "Lew, are you asleep?"

The dim light picked out a gleam of silvery hair, and Dio, like a pale ghost, looked down at me. She turned and slid the curtains back, letting the light flood the room and the moons peer over her shoulder.

The chill radiance cooled my hot face. I found no words to question her. I even thought, incuriously, that I might have fallen asleep and be dreaming she was here. I could see the shadow of the bruise lying on her cheek, and murmured, "I'm sorry I hurt you."

She only smiled, half-bewildered. Her voice was as dreamy as the unreal light when she bent down to me.

"Lew, your face is so hot—"

"And yours is so cool," I whispered. I touched the bruise with my good hand, wanting to kiss it. Her face was in shadow, very grave and still. Suddenly, forcefully, Callina came into my mind. Not the aloof Keeper, but the proud and passionate woman defying the council, refusing before Ashara to bare her mind to my touch—

Dio, too, had feared that. Could any woman endure that intimacy, that bond that was deeper than any physical touch? Callina, remote, precious, untouchable—and Dio, who had been everything to me that a woman can be to a man. Or almost everything. And why was I thinking of Callina, with Dio beside me? She seemed to be forcing the thought on me; so strongly, I was almost constrained to speak the name aloud. Her pallid face seemed to flicker, to be Callina's own, so dreamishly that I could not believe I was awake.

"Why are you here?"

Dio said, very simply, "I always know when you are in pain or suffering."

She drew my head to her breast. I lay there with my eyes closed. Her body was warm and cool at once and the scent of her was at once fresh and familiar, the mysterious salty smell of tears mingling with the honey and musk of her hair.

"Don't go away."

"No. Never."

"I love you," I whispered. "I love you."

For a moment Callina's sobs deepened—Callina? *Callina?* She was almost a physical presence between us; rather the two women blended and were one. To which one had I whispered my love? I did not know. But the soft arms around me were real.

I held her close, knowing with a sort of sick certainty

that—as a woman—I had nothing for her now. The telepath's personal hell, just as painful as ever.

But it didn't seem to matter. And suddenly I knew that the Dio I had loved on Vainwal, passionate and superficial and hoydenish, was not the real girl at all. This was the real one. I was not the man she had known there, either.

I could not have spoken if I had tried. There was shame, and a proffered apology, in my kiss; but she gave it back as it was given, gently, without passion.

We fell asleep like little children, clasped in each other's arms.

CHAPTER THIRTEEN

When I woke, I was alone. For several minutes, in the morning sunlight, I wondered if the whole bizarre episode had been a dream; then, as the curtains parted and Dio came in, a grim smile turned up my mouth. In a dream, I would surely have possessed her.

"I've brought you another visitor," she said. I began to protest; I didn't want to see anyone. But she pulled the curtains aside—and Marja ran into the room.

She stopped, staring—then ran and flung herself on me with a smothering hug.

I loosened her, staring at Dio. "Gently, *chiya*, gently, you'll have me on the floor. Dio, how—"

"I learned about her when Hastur first brought her here," Dio said. "But Ashara's Tower is no place for her now. Take care of him, Marja *mea*," she added, and before I could ask any more questions, she went away again.

Andres reported that there were Terrans still guarding the castle corridors, but no one came near us all day. I resigned myself to inaction, and spent the day playing with Marja and making a few hazy plans. She would not be taken from me again! Andres seemed puzzled, but there was no way to explain without speaking of Marjorie and Thyra, and even to Andres, I could not do that. I told him, simply, that she was my daughter; he gave me a knowing look and, to my relief, left it at that.

I tried to ask Marja a few careful questions, but the answers were vague and meaningless; all one could expect from so young a child. Toward nightfall, since no one had come to reclaim her, I told Andres to put her to bed in a sleeping-cubicle near my own, and when she had fallen asleep I left her there and called Andres.

"How many Terrans are in the castle?"

"Ten, maybe fifteen. Not Spaceforce—even Lawton wouldn't have that much insolence. They're in plain clothes, and they behave themselves."

I nodded. "None of them would know me by sight, I suppose. Hunt me up a suit of Terran clothes."

He gave me a bleak grin. "No use trying to stop you, I suppose. I'll look after the little lass, then. And, I don't have to be a telepath to know what you're thinking, *via dom*. I've lived with your family half my life. If that don't answer your question, what would?"

There were many doors to the Alton suites, and the Terrans couldn't guard them all. In the hallways no one paid the slightest attention to me. They were looking after a Darkovan man with one hand; a man in Terran clothing, one hand stuck in a pocket, roused not the slightest curiosity.

I hesitated outside the Hastur apartments, wanting to take counsel with the old Regent; then, regretfully, passed. If he knew our plan, he might forbid me, and a thousand oaths bound me to obey him. Better not chance it.

I found Callina in her own rooms, seated before Linnell's harp; her head was buried in her arms and I thought she was crying; then with sudden suspicion, I grabbed her and jerked her head up.

She came up stiffly, resisting; her eyes, blank and dead, stared at me without recognition. "Callina!" I shouted, but I might as well have whispered. I dragged her bodily to her feet. Her eyes were fixed in a lifeless, blue-ice stare. "Wake up!" I shouted, and shook her hard. But I had to put her in a chair and slap her before the spark of life suddenly blazed in her eyes and her head went up.

"What do you think you are doing? Let me go!"

"Callina, you were in trance—"

"Oh, no! No!" She threw herself on me, pressing herself to me in desperate appeal. I caught the words, "Ashara" and "—send—her—out," but they meant nothing, and I held her away. I dared not touch her until this was over. Gradually, she calmed. "I'm sorry, Lew. I'm—me again."

"But who are you?" I said at hazard, "Dio? Ashara?"

She smiled, a sorrowful smile. "If you don't know, who does?"

I dared not show tenderness. "We've got to act tonight, Callina, while the Terrans think I'm still too weak to do anything. Where is Kathie?"

Her face twisted. "It's like Linnell's ghost—"

I dreaded it, too, but I said nothing, and finally Callina sighed. "Shall I go to her?"

"Let me," I said. I walked through two cubicles, finally found the one where we had taken Kathie. She was lying on a couch, almost naked, scanning a set of tiles, but she heard my step and started violently, catching a sort of veil around her. "Get *out!*" she squeaked. "Oh—it's you again!"

"Kathie, I haven't the slightest designs on you, except to ask you to dress and come with us. Can you ride?"

"Yes. Why?" She paused. "I think I know why. Something strange happened to me, I think, when Linnell was killed."

I couldn't discuss that. I reached to the dressing panel, rummaged among the forcebars and racks, finally pulled out some garments. I recognized them, with a stab of pain; Linnell's perfume hung about them; but there was nothing else I could do. I threw the armful in her lap. "Put these on," I said, and sank down to wait, but her angry stare made me recall, suddenly, the Terran taboos. I rose, actually reddening. How could Terran women be so immodest out of doors and so prudish within? "I forgot. Call me when you are ready."

A queer sound made me turn back. She was staring helplessly at the clothes.

"I've no idea how to get into these things!"

"After what you were just *thinking* at me," I said, "I'm certainly not going to offer to help you."

It was her turn to blush. "Besides—how can I ride in skirts?"

"Zandru, girl," I exploded, genuinely shocked now. "What else?"

"I've ridden all my life, but I never tried it in a skirt, and I'm not going to start. If you want me to ride anywhere, you can certainly get me some decent clothes."

"These clothes are perfectly decent."

"Damn it, get me some *indecent* ones then," she blazed. I laughed. I had to.

"I'll see what I can do, Kathie."

Fortunately, I knew where Dio slept, and no one stopped me. I parted the curtains and looked in. She was asleep, but sat up quickly, blinking. "Are things starting again?"

They had never stopped, we had simply been flung out of them. I explained what I wanted; she giggled, then the laughter broke off. "I know it isn't really funny, Lew. I just can't help it. All right, then. I think my things will fit Kathie."

"And can you find Regis, and tell him to slip out and find horses for us?"

She nodded. "I can come and go pretty much as I please. Most of the Terrans know me. Lerrys—" she stopped, biting her lip. There was nothing I could say, I'd hated her brothers and she knew it. Dio was as alone, now, as I was.

Seeing Dio made me remember something else. I slipped back to my rooms and got Rafe's pistol. There were still bullets in the chamber. I still abhorred these coward's weapons—but tonight I might be fighting men without honor or conscience.

When I went back to Kathie's rooms, Dio and Callina were already there, and the Terran girl had been dressed in the sleeveless tunic and close-fitting breeches which Dio had worn for riding on Vainwal. Callina, more conventionally dressed, looked on with mild disfavor.

"Fine, but how are we going to get out?"

I laughed. I was not Kennard Alton's son for nothing. The Altons, aeons ago, had designed the Comyn castle, and their knowledge was handed down, son to son. "Don't you know your own rooms, Callina?" I went into the central room of the suite, and stepped into certain imprints of the flooring. I cautioned them to stand back, then frowned; my father had told me of this doorway, but had never bothered to teach me the pattern; nor did I have a sounder to test the matrix lock. I tried two or three of the standard patterns, but they did not respond; then turned to Callina.

"Can you sound a fourth-level without equipment?"

Her face took on concentrated seriousness; after a minute a section of flooring dropped out of sight, revealing deep, dusty stairs that led away downward.

"Stay close to me," I warned, motioning them ahead. "I've never been down here before." Behind us the square of light revolved, spun—and we were in darkness.

"I wish that old great-grandfather of mine had provided a light! It's dark as Zandru's pockets!"

Callina raised her hand—and the tips began to glow. Light spread—sparkled—radiated from those twelve

slender fingertips! "Don't touch me," she warned softly.
The passage was long and dark, with steep steps, and in
spite of the ghost-light, dark and dangerous. Once
Kathie slipped on the strangely slippery surfaces, and fell
jarringly a step or two before I could catch her; and twice
my outstretched hand broke sticky invisible webs. There
was no rail and I found it hard to balance, but Callina
picked her way securely and delicately, never stumbling,
as if the way were perfectly well known to her.

Down, and down. Finally a door slid back and we
stood in the semilight of Thendara under three waning
moons. I looked around. We were in a disorderly section
of the city, where the Terrans probably never came twice
in fifteen years. Down the dark street was a place where
horses were shod and swords and tools mended; here
Regis was to meet me, if my message had reached him.

It had. He was there, standing in the shadow of several
horses, in the deserted street.

"Lew, take me with you? Leave the women here."

"We need Kathie. And someone has to stay here, Regis. This is our only chance. If we don't make it, you'll
have to make what terms you can. I think, as a last resort,
you might be able to trust Lawton." I stopped, then
shrugged, without finishing what I had started to
say. There was no point in farewells and we made
none.

Out through the streets of Thendara; into the open
country. We passed a few houses and deserted farm-
steads; they grew wider apart and finally ceased. No one
rode this path now; on the Forbidden Road, radioactivity
was still virulent, in spots, from the Years of Desolation.
The road itself was safe now, but the fear lingered; too
many men, in past days, had died. Hairless, toothless,
their blood turned to water, because they had taken this
path. The Comyn had fostered that fear, with tricks and
traps; and now it was useful, because we could ride un-
seen. Only Dyan knew those tricks and traps as well as I.

We skirted the site of the ancient spaceships, their huge bulk still glowing feebly with the poisonous radiance. Then we were on the Forbidden Road itself; the canyon, nature's own roadway, which stretches from the highest point in the Hellers down to the Sea of Dalereuth a thousand miles away. Just wide enough for six horses to ride abreast, thirty feet below the surface of the plain, and nearly a thousand miles long, the Forbidden Road runs all across the continent as if some giant or some God, in the lost years, had reached out and scratched the molten land with a titan fingernail, cutting across mountains, foot-hills, plains.

Legend had it the Forbidden Road was the track where the Gods walked, ages ago, when they spread their terror on the land and the children of the Comyn were born with their minds awry with the strange Comyn Gifts. A barren land, seared of growth, the track of something that had marred the land to freakishness, creating the Comyn. Mutation? The children of Gods? I did not know or care.

Two of the moons had set, leaving a single pallid face on the horizon, when we turned aside from the Road and saw the *rhu fead*, a white, dim, gleaming pile, rising above the thinly gleaming shore of the lake of Hali. We reined in our horses near the brink. Mist curled up whitely along the shore, where the sparse pink grass thinned out on the rocks. I kicked a pebble loose and it dropped into the glimmering cloud-waves, sinking without a splash, slowly, visible for a long time. Kathie stared at the strangely-surfaced lake.

"That isn't water, is it?"

I shook my head. No living being, save those of Comyn blood, had ever set foot on the shores of Hali.

She said confusedly, "But I've been here before—"

"No. You have some of my memories, that's all." I patted her wrist clumsily, as if she were Linnell. "Don't be afraid."

Twin pillars rose white, a rainbow mist sparkling like a veil between them. I frowned at the trembling rainbow. "Even blocked, it would strip your mind. I'll have to do what I did before; hold your mind completely under mine." She shuddered, and I warned tonelessly, "I must. The veil is a force-field attuned to the Comyn brain. It won't hurt us but it would kill you."

She glanced at Callina. "Why not you?"

Callina shook her head. "It has something to do with polarity. I'm a Keeper. If I tried to submerge your mind for more than a second or two, it would destroy you—permanently." A curious horror showed in her mind. "Ashara showed me—once."

I picked Kathie up bodily. When she protested, I scowled. "You fainted once, and went into hysterics the second time I touched you," I reminded her grimly. "If you do that again, inside the Veil, I want to make sure you'll get out the other side."

This time, however, she was barriered against me, by my own bypass circuit. It was easy to damp out the alien brainwaves. We got through the shimmering, blinding rainbow, with blurred eyes; I set her down and withdrew as gently as I could.

The *rhu fead* stretched bare before us, dim and cool. There were doors and long passages, filled with chilly curls of mist. Kathie made a sudden turn into one passage and began to walk forward into the dimness.

"Lew, I know! How do I know where to go?"

The passage angled into an open space of white stone and curtained crimson. A dais, set back into the wall and paneled in iridescent webs, held a blue crystal coffer. I set my foot on the first step—

I could not pass. This was the inner barrier; the barrier no Comyn could penetrate. I leaned on an invisible wall; Callina, curious, put out her hands and saw them jerk back of themselves. Kathie asked, "Are you still blocking my mind?"

"A little."

"Then don't. That bit of *you* is what holds me back."

I nodded and withdrew the blocking circuit. Kathie smiled at me, less like Linnell than she had ever looked; then walked through the invisible barrier.

She disappeared into a blue of darkening cloud. A blaze of fire seared up; I wanted to shout at her not to be afraid, it was only an illusion—but even my voice could not pass the barrier reared against the Comyn. A dim silhouette, she vanished; the flames swallowed her. Then a wild glare swept up to the roof and a burst of thunder rolled and rocked the floor.

Kathie darted back to us; and in her hand she held a sheathed sword.

CHAPTER FOURTEEN

So the Sword of Aldones was a real sword, after all; long and gleaming and deadly, and of so fine a temper that it made my own look like a child's leaden toy. In the hilt, through a thin layer of insulating silk, winking jewels gleamed blue.

It might have been a duplicate of the Sharra sword, but that now seemed an inferior forgery of the glorious thing I held.

This was not a concealment for a hidden matrix; rather it *was* a matrix. It seemed to have a life of its own. A tingle of power, not unpleasant, flowed up my arm. I gripped the hilt and drew it a little way—

"No," Callina said warningly, and gripped my hand. A moment, stubborn, I resisted; then slid it back into the sheath.

"That's that," I said harshly. "Let's get out of here."

Dawn was breaking over the lake when we came out, and the wet sunlight glinted, ominously, on steel. Kathie cried out, in terror, as three men stepped toward us.

Three men? No; two—and a woman. Kadarin, Dyan— and between them, slim and vital as a dark flame, Thyra Scott smiled up at me, her mocking mouth daring me to speak or strike. I caught the dagger from my belt. Thyra stood steady, her naked throat upturned to the steel.

My hand tilted and the knife fell from it.

"Get out of my way, witch."

Her low key laughter raised a million ghosts, but her voice was steel. "What have you done with my daughter?"

"My daughter," I said. "She's safe. But you can't have her."

Dyan took a step, but Kadarin took his elbow and hauled him back. "Wait, you."

Thyra said, "We will bargain. Give me what the Keeper holds, and you go free."

"We will anyhow," I said.

Kadarin drew his sword. I should have known; it was the one bearing the Sharra matrix. "Will you?" he asked softly. "Better hand it over. I intend to kill you, but you couldn't give me a fair fight, not now." His eyes swept, with gentle contempt, from my bandaged head to my feet. "Don't try."

"I suppose you have Trailmen in hiding with your usual odds of twenty to one?"

Kadarin nodded. "They won't touch you. You're for me. But the women—"

"Go to hell," I snarled, flashing the sword from the sheath, I flung myself at Kadarin. The touch of the hilt poured that stream of overflowing life through me; the blood beat so hard in my temples that I was faint with it. Kadarin whipped up the Sharra sword. The swords touched—

The Sword of Aldones blazed blue fire! Like a living thing it leaped from my hand and clattered down, coruscating blue fire from hilt to point. The two swords lay crossed on the ground, streams of wild blue flame cascading about them. Kadarin was reeling.

I picked myself up. We stood back, neither daring to approach the fallen blades.

But Kathie darted between us and caught up both swords. To her, I think, they were only swords. She held one in either hand, carefully. The blue flames died.

"That won't help," Kadarin said, and added grimly, "Don't be a self-sacrificing fool. Give me the Sharra matrix and go. We couldn't take the Sword of Aldones, maybe. But we can take the Sharra one, and we will. You could kill me, kill Dyan, kill Thyra—but you can't kill them all!"

Of course there was no choice. I had the women to guard. "Give it to him, Kathie," I said at last. This was only a draw. The real fight would come later.

"Give it up? Now?"

"I'm no hero," I said savagely, "and you've never seen the Trailmen fight." I took Sharra's matrix from her hand. Dyan stepped forward, but Kadarin elbowed him away. "Not you!"

It was fortunate we had Kadarin to deal with. When we fought, it would be to death—but it would be fair. "We can go. His word's good."

But Thyra flung herself forward, the knife bright in her hand. I twisted, just too late; she drove the knife into my side.

I got my arm up and knocked her hard, stunningly, across the face; then I sat down, hard, my hand to the numb slash. Blood dripped through my fingers. I heard Kadarin cry out like a berserker; dimly saw him shaking Thyra with maniac strength, back and forth, and finally he cast her to the ground, where she lay moaning. *She had violated his word.*

And then I blacked out.

There was a roaring sound around me. I was lying with my head in Kathie's lap.

"Lie still. They're taking us to Thendara in a rocket-car."

"Keep him quiet, Kathie."

I reached for Callina's hand, but it was the cool brittle fingertips of Ashara that were fetters on my wrist, her cold eyes in the grayness. I jolted awake; something had touched my mind. Marja! I reached for her, but where she had been was only an empty place in the world—

I shook my brain free of delirium for a minute. Of course I could not touch Marja. Not in pain like this. I would not want to let her share this now.

But a man's mind is so alone, shut up inside the bones of the skull.

I sank into the gray night again.

I was walking. . . .
There was an arm beneath my shoulders, and Kadarin's voice said, "Easy! He can walk. It's just a scratch, the knife turned on the ribs."

My eyes wouldn't focus. I heard someone say sharply, "Good God! come in here, and sit down."

The dizziness cleared. I was standing in the Terran HQ, a rolling view of the spaceport lying far below me, and straight before me, at a big glass-topped desk, Dan Lawton was standing, looking at me with surprise and concern. Kadarin's arm was still holding me upright. I pulled away; from somewhere out of my range of vision, Regis Hastur got up, came to me, took me firmly by the shoulders and put me into a chair.

"Who in the hell are you?"

Kadarin bowed, ever so slightly.

"Robert Raymond Kadarin, *z'par servu*. And you?"

Behind us, a door opened and Kathie's voice said anxiously, "Is he really—oh, hello, Dan."

The Terran Legate shook his head. "In a minute," he said to nobody in particular, "I shall begin to gibber. Hello, Kathie. It *is* you?"

She looked dubiously at me. "May I tell him?"

"Wait, wait. One thing at a time. I'll go nuts, if I have

to unravel anything more just now. Kadarin. I've wanted to set eyes on you for quite a while. You know you've finally stepped over the line?"

"I claim immunity," Kadarin said harshly. "Lew Alton would have died at Hali. I had given him safe-conduct, and his life has been formally claimed; it is mine to dispose of as I will. I brought him here of my own free will, when I could have preserved my own immunity by staying away and letting him die. I claim immunity."

Lawton groaned. But Kadarin had the legal right of it. "All right. But no telepathic tricks."

He smiled bitterly. "I couldn't, if I would. Dyan Ardais ran off with the Sharra matrix. I'm as helpless as Lew, here!"

Rafe Scott came suddenly into the office. The boy's face took on a stunned look as he saw me, and Regis, and Kadarin, and Kathie; but he spoke to Lawton.

"Why have you locked Thyra up downstairs?"

"Do you know that woman?" Lawton demanded sharply.

"She's his sister," Kadarin said, while Rafe was still sputtering.

"Damn it!" Lawton exploded, "every troublemaker on the planet is related to you one way or another, Rafe! She tried to murder Lew Alton, that's all. When we brought her in, all of a sudden we had a screeching maniac on our hands, so I had the doctor give her a shot, and dumped her in a cell to cool off."

Rafe came to me, his voice urgent. "Lew, why would Thyra—"

"Let him alone, you!" Regis shoved Rafe roughly away. I gripped Regis' arm. "Don't start another fight," I implored. "Don't! Don't!"

A moment he resisted, then shrugged, and sat on the arm of my chair, glaring at Rafe. "Wasn't Callina with you?"

"The medical officer kept her too," Kathie said. "She was dizzy—sick. She kept falling asleep."

Trance again? I sat upright, feeling lightheaded. "I've got to get to her!"

"You can't do anything now," Regis said.

"What are you doing here?"

Lawton answered for him. "I sent, last night, for the Regent, and we've been talking most of the night."

Regis said quietly, "We're finished, Lew. The Comyn will have to make terms. Even Grandfather realizes that. And if Sharra gets out of hand—"

The sword of Aldones was lying across Lawton's desk. Kadarin came and stood over it. "I let Sharra loose," he said, "It was an experiment that misfired, that's all. But our damned idiot hero here made matters worse by taking the Sharra matrix off-world, and for six years, all those activated spots just ran wild. And now Dyan has it!" He turned restlessly, a prowling animal.

"I knew Alton wouldn't deal with me on any terms. So I tried to find someone in the Comyn, anyone who would steal the thing back for me. Just so I could monitor those sites, and then destroy the matrix. But after all that work—" his shoulders sagged. "I walked from the trap to the cookpot, when I tried to deal with Dyan Ardais!"

"Did he kill Marius to get it?" Regis asked.

"I imagine so. I'm not sure, but I'm not very wise in the accomplices I choose, am I? That—" he pointed at the Sword of Aldones, "is a last resort. It will put Sharra out, permanently, but it's murder. Anyone who's ever been keyed into the Sharra matrix—"

Lawton said, "I'll keep it for the time being."

Kadarin laughed, a harsh animal sound. "Just try! Now that it's been crossed with Sharra's, even I—" he reached for the sword, then his hands contracted visibly, and he drew back with an audible gasp. Shaking his fingers, agonized, he glanced at Rafe and said, "You try."

"Not if I know it!" Rafe backed away.

Lawton was no coward. He reached over and took the hilt firmly. Then, in a shower of blue sparks, he went flying across the room. He crashed into the wall, fell, and picked himself up, dazed, rubbing his head. "Good lord!"

"My turn." I reached for the Sword, which had fallen to the floor. I managed to lift it to the desk, but finally, trembling, had to let it fall. "I can touch it," I said, feeling the hot, unbearable tingling, "but I can't hang on to it."

"No one man can," Regis said. "But I'll keep it for the moment." Easily, he picked it up and belted it at his waist. "I am Hastur," he said quietly.

Then the Hastur Gift is the living matrix!

Regis nodded. The matrix had found its support and focus, the monitoring balance, in the brain and nerves of the Hastur who bore it. No one else could handle that sword—or even hold it without danger.

Sharra was only a dreadful and lethal copy of this.

"Yes," Kadarin said quietly. "I guessed. That was why your hand never healed, Lew. The wound itself was not so bad, but you'd handled the matrix, and human flesh and blood won't take it. I never did, without at least one other telepath in rapport—"

Suddenly, down the corridor, Thyra began to scream.

Kadarin jumped out of his chair. I sat bolt upright. That something which had set Thyra to mad shrieking had jolted in me, too; black emptiness, loss, tearing—

"Marja!" I almost sobbed the name.

Kadarin whirled to face me; I have never seen such a look on a human face, before or since. "Quick! Where is she?"

"What's the matter?" Lawton demanded.

Kadarin moved his lips, but no sound came. Finally he said, "Dyan Ardais has the matrix—"

I finished. "He doesn't dare use it alone. He saw me—what happened to my hand. He'll need a telepath, and Marja's an Alton—"

"Dirty, treacherous—". Kadarin's voice was thick with fear, but not for himself. My mind was open, and for a minute, seeing Kadarin, my hate receded. Regis turned, unbelted the Sword of Aldones, and put it into Kathie's hands. "Keep this," he said, "you're still immune. Don't be afraid; no Darkovan alive can take it from you, or harm you while you hold it." He turned to me, and without a word, knowing what he wanted, I gave him Rafe's pistol.

"What are you—"

Regis said tersely, cutting Lawton short, "This is a Comyn affair, and with the best will in the world, you could only hinder, not help. Rafe, come with me."

Kadarin said harshly, "You fool, it's for Marja! Go with him!"

They went. The rhythmic, hysterical shrieks never stopped. Kadarin stood still, as if holding himself in check with his whole body; then suddenly broke free. "I'm going," he shouted at Lawton over his shoulder, and slammed out of the room. Lawton grabbed my arm.

"No, you don't! Have sense, man! You can hardly stand on your feet!" He forced me into the chair again. "What set them off? Who or what is Marja?"

The screaming stopped, abruptly, as if a switch had been flipped, leaving a silence that was somehow frightening. Lawton swore and stamped out of the room, leaving me lying in the chair, swearing with helpless rage, unable to rise. I heard shouts and voices ringing in the corridors, and wondered what had happened now, and then Dio stormed into the room.

"And they left you here!" she raged. "What did that red-headed bitch do to you? And they've doped Callina —oh, Lew, Lew, your shirt's all blood—" She knelt by me, her face as white as her dress. Lawton came stamping back and stood over me, his face furious.

"Gone! That Thyra woman is *gone*—out of a sheet-steel cell, with guards all over the place! When that happens, with a Comyn matrix mechanic in the building—" He caught sight of Dio and his scowl deepened. "I know you, you're that sister of Lerrys. What are you doing here?"

"At the moment," she blazed, "trying to see what's wrong with Lew—which nobody else is bothering about!"

"I'm all right," I muttered, angry at the solicitude which weakened me. But I let her take me down to the Medical Floor where a little fat man in a white coat grumbled about a damned uncivilized planet where he spent his time patching up knife wounds. He did me up in plastic shields which hurt like hell, burned me with ultra-light of some kind and made me swallow something red and sticky which burnt my mouth and made my head swim, but it took the pain away; and when the dizziness stopped, I could think clearly again.

"Where's Callina Aillard?"

"In there," Dr. Forth said. "Asleep. She was faint and sick, so I gave her a shot of hypnal and had a nurse put her to bed in the women's infirmary."

"Any chance she could be in shock-trance?"

He put the things he'd used under the light-machine. "I wouldn't know. She saw you stabbed, didn't she? Some women react that way."

I damned the man for a fool. Darkovan women don't faint at a little blood. What was he doing here, if he couldn't diagnose matrix-shock? And if he had drugged Callina, there wasn't a chance I could bring her out of it. Not until all the drug wore off.

"It might be best," Dio said quietly. "Before she wakes, I want to tell you all about Callina. Not now."

Lawton, in his office, was setting the mechanism of search into action. Time crawled by; I waited. Once his puzzlement exploded into frustrated questions. "Damn it, I still haven't figured out how the Marshall girl got here from Samarra. And I'm still trying to get it all straight—the way you, and Rafe, and this Thyra woman, and Kadarin, are all brothers and sisters or cousins or whatever. And now this Thyra person vanishes into thin air! Did you witch her out of there someway?"

"I did not." Thyra could lie in a cell forever, for all I cared.

As the narcotic slowly wore off, I felt pain in my side again, but deeper down was that horrible sense of something torn away—I was afraid to know what it was.

The bloody sun of Darkover had reached its height and begun to angle sharply downward when I heard dragging footsteps and Regis and Rafe and Kadarin came in.

Regis had changed shockingly in a few hours. There was blood on his face, and blood on his sleeve, but it went deeper than his first serious fight. The last trace of the boy had burnt away and it was a man, and a Hastur, who looked at me in despair.

"You're hurt!" Lawton exclaimed, with the horror of a Terran for personally inflicted wounds.

"Not much. Cut my shirt up, mostly. I fought with Dyan."

"Dead?" I asked.

"No, damn it!"

Lawton demanded "Kadarin! Where's that woman of yours?"

Kadarin's gaunt face contracted in fear. "Thyra? Isn't she here with you? Zandru's hells, how can I tell her—" He covered his face with his hands. Suddenly he came to me. All the rest of the people in the office might as well have been on another planet for all the regard he gave them, and he looked into my eyes with an intensity that burned years away; back to the days when we had been friends, not sworn foes.

My voice came through dry lips.

"Bob, what is it? What's happened?"

His face twisted. "Dyan! Zandru send him scorpion whips! Naotalba twist his feet off in hell forever! He's taken her into Sharra—my little *Marguerhta*." His voice broke. The words burned at me like acid. Dyan, with the Sharra matrix. Marja, a child but an Alton—a telepath. And the blankness where she had been, the sense of something torn away.

Then she was dead.

Marjorie. Marius. Linnell.

Now Marja.

Lawton did not press us for details. He must have known we were all touching our last reserves of strength. I found myself sitting and asking questions as if anything could matter now. "Andres?"

"Dyan left him for dead, but he may pull through."

It was savage comfort to know that Andres had defended her like that. "Ashara?"

Dio stood up, her mouth pinched tight. I think we had all forgotten she was there. "Regis! Keep them! I am going to the Tower!"

I cried, "What for?" but she was already gone.

Lawton said grimly, "The first thing is to have Dyan picked up. If he has the little girl—"

Kadarin broke in. "You can't! There's no way to take the Sharra matrix away from him now. I've had the thing in my own hands often enough to know! Dyan could get it away from Marius only because he didn't know how to guard himself. No man living—" Kadarin started upright. "Lawton! all of you! Bear witness! His life is mine, when, how and as I can kill him, fair fight or unfair, his life is—"

"Mine!" I cut through his words. "Marja was mine! And whoever kills him, owes me a life—"

"You pair of maniacs!" Lawton said, "let's catch him first, before you start fighting for the privilege of killing him!"

With a gesture that was animal in its ferocity, Kadarin said, "If he frees Sharra, don't trust *me!* I'm the master-seal, and I'll be right *in* it!"

Regis turned to me. "Well, Lew, it will have to be you. You've touched Sharra, but you're sealed to the Comyn too. If we could hold you in rapport from *here*, you could go into the Sharra matrix—"

I cracked, then. "No!" I shouted. "No!" They could all die before they'd force me into that; why should I care now if Sharra ravaged Darkover? What had I left to lose? I grabbed the pistol out of Rafe's belt, and snapped off the safety. "I'll blow out my own brains first!"

Regis' hand caught mine in a bone-crushing grip. We struggled briefly, crazily, but he had two hands; the recoil of the gun knocked me back and the bullet fired harmlessly through the window, in a burst of shattering glass. Regis shook my cramped fingers from the butt.

"You're insane!" he said. He tossed the pistol to Rafe. "Here. This was yours originally, wasn't it? Take it. It's been around a lot lately. One lunatic is enough!"

Lawton swore, kicking at the glass on the floor. "I ought to throw you all in the clink. Rafe, go get somebody to clean this mess up, and take Alton downstairs. He's off his head again."

I dragged to my feet, but I had to hold the chair. "I'm a prisoner?"

"Hell, no! But you walk out of here now, you'll pass out on the sidewalk! Man, use your head! Go on down to the infirmary! We'll let you know when we need you!"

Quite suddenly the rage dissolved, leaving me empty and numb. Kadarin unfolded his long legs and came to me. "Truce, Lew," he said quietly. "Marja was mine, too. We can't do much now. You're worn out. Maybe later we can figure out some way to get me out of that hellish thing before Dyan burns us all to hell-and-gone." His eyes met mine; there was no hate left in them. Mine, too, had burnt away. I stumbled and let myself lean wearily on his arm. "Truce," I said.

So it was Kadarin who took me down to Medical and into the hospital wing. I sat down on the cot in the cubicle, my emotions burned out but my nerves jumping and my telepathic barriers nonexistent. I bent to pull off my boots.

"Need any help?"

I asked him, straight, "You think Dyan will let Sharra loose?"

"I'm damn sure he'll try."

It felt unreal. For six years my main compulsion had been to kill Kadarin. I had pictured it to myself a thousand times, and here we were, talking, quietly and rationally and from the same side. It felt unpleasant, but somehow sensible. I suppose it was the Terran way of doing things.

"Want me to get you something from the Medic?"

"No." I added, grudgingly, "No, thanks."

Then I looked up, squarely at him. I knew he would never stoop to lie about it. "Bob, was it by your order that Marjorie was—forced into the Sharra fire, that last time? Was it your way of revenging yourself on me? When you knew—" I swallowed, "that it would kill her?"

"Why would I kill *her*—to revenge myself on *you*?" He flung the question at me with a passionate sincerity I could not doubt; the same agonized question that had been tormenting me for six years.

"Lew, I knew Sharra as no living man has ever known. There was no danger, not for either of the girls, while I was in control. You know I loved Thyra, yet I managed to keep her safe." His face was bitter, agonized. "There aren't ten men alive who can determine the limits of safety for a woman they've had, but I did it for Thyra! Marjorie—"

His dark face was ravaged by such misery that I almost pitied him; his barriers were down too, and the violence of his grief was like a burning in me. He would never be free of all that grief, that guilt. "Marjorie—Margie was just a child, I thought. She never told me! I swear I never knew you had been her lover! I swear it!"

I rolled over and buried my face, unable to endure it, but Kadarin went on his voice heavy with pain. "So she went into it—and you know what happened. Any woman would have died coming from the arms of a lover to the pole of such power, and I've hated you for that—"

His voice suddenly softened into deep compassion.

"But it never occurred to me that you couldn't know. Hell, you were just a kid yourself. A pair of babies, you and Marjorie, and I never even warned you. Zandru's hells, Lew, talk about revenge, you had yours—!"

Abruptly he was calm; dead calm. He said without inflection, "I claimed your life once. I give it back to you."

I looked up at him, equally numbed. He had claimed my life; a solemn obligation, irrevocable in Darkovan law, while we both lived. Had another killed me, he would have been legally obligated to track down and kill my murderer. But Darkovan law was collapsing around us. We stood in the smashing rubble. I did not know my own voice when I said, "I'll take it from you."

Gravely, unsmiling, we shook hands.

"Tell me this," I said wearily. "Why was Thyra's child mine?"

There was irony in his gaunt face. "I thought you'd have that all figured out. I hoped for a telepath son, with the Alton Gift."

Damned, insolent—

He said evenly, "Thyra never forgave me. I was so pleased with Marja that she was jealous, she refused to have the child where I could see her—" Suddenly his face twisted again. "It will kill Thyra! I swore Marja should not be used as a pawn, and I couldn't even keep her safe. Thyra has pretended so long to hate the child. Gods! Great Gods! Everything I love, everyone I love, I hurt or kill!" I flinched with the anguish of his despair. Abruptly he turned and went out, slamming the door so violently that the walls trembled.

CHAPTER FIFTEEN

I must have slept.

I opened my eyes at last in the bare infirmary cubicle to see Callina kneeling beside me. Her soft eyes were filled with tears; she seized my hand, but did not speak. I wanted to catch her in my arms and crush her to me; but Kadarin's words still held me, compelled with horror. For her very life, I dared not touch her.

But it would be harder than ever. I sensed, without knowing how, that some inner reserve in Callina was gone. There was no longer that chill, that conscious and wary aloofness.

"We've gone through it all for nothing, Callina," I said. "Marius and Linnell are gone, we've let the Comyn have our lives to play with, and what have we got?"

"There may still be something to save. Darkover—"

"The hell with Darkover! Let the Terrans have it and welcome!"

Callina passed her hand briefly across my eyes. I saw, in a blur, the horrifying face I had seen once before. It vanished; I saw Dyan, and Kadarin.

"The Sword of Aldones will cancel out Sharra," she said. "Kadarin was helping them to make plans, when he —vanished. He just wasn't there! Like Thyra."

That meant Sharra was free. I looked helplessly at the girl. "I've tried," I told her, "but I can't even touch the Sword of Aldones. Regis can, but he can't use it alone. No one man can."

Her fingers closed blindly on my good hand. "Ashara said you could use me for a focus—"

I shook my head. I couldn't hurt Callina that way. I would literally have to tear our two minds to pieces and rebuild them into one. I'd been through it myself, I could take it. But Callina!

Her voice was soft and resolute. "It's—well, it's you. And I want to."

Her bravery shamed me. Whatever happened, no woman should outdo me in courage. Suddenly, tenderly, I gave her arm a little shake. "All right, girl," I said, "we'll try it. But think about it. I want you to be sure."

"I'm sure now," she said.

It was strange to see her there; lovely Callina, all the beauty and mystery of the *comynari*, star-like and remote, there in that bare white cubicle. The note of grotesquerie in these surroundings, the tumbled cot where I had slept, made it all seem more, not less strange.

She laughed, nervously; her hand in mine felt cold and fragile. Physical contact can lay the mind bare. I would have liked to hold her in my arms for this, but I did not dare. I had learned with Dio how such contact can break down barriers, but I forced the thought back. I felt curiously shy; I did not want to touch Callina's mind with another woman in the forefront of my thoughts.

I reached for contact.

For a moment there was a frighteningly familiar resistance; like Dio, every defense of her mind went up to bar me away. This time I made it a rough shock-wave;

her hand tore loose from mine and she slumped down, her arms over her head as if by this desperate hiding she could arrest the soul-stripping contact. She did not resist actively, but her passive, trembling terror was worse. It was worse than anything I had ever had to do.

A tense moment of shock, and then Callina, white and shaking, snapped the rapport, sobbing wildly. I let it break, and drew her into my arms, and gradually the weeping quieted. "I—I tried so hard—"

"I know." She had made every effort to endure the unbearable. Perhaps no woman can endure that absolute rapport with a man. If I had kept on, forced the resistance —it hadn't killed Marius, and Callina was Keeper, a *comynara*—but I simply was not capable of torturing a woman like that. It was worse than rape.

There was an alternative. It was drastic, but I was desperate. "Could *you* make the rapport?" I asked her. I said it easily, but inside, I was shaking. It put me wholly at her mercy, although a Keeper, she was not trained in handling that particular kind of focus.

Could I endure the forcible breaking of all my barriers? I had closed off those old areas, years ago, to save my sanity. I dropped that line of thought. I had to endure it, simply because I was stronger than she.

Her touch was uncertain, fumbling, raw—an agony. It was desperately hard to keep from flinging her out of my brain; but with grim self-command, I endured it, lowering each barrier as she touched it. *How had she come to be Keeper, if she was as clumsy a telepath as this?* The bridge was stronger now, but she had not made the decisive move that would snap identity and bring it to completion and I dared not move.

But it was so close to complete that I grew tense with the unbearable need to have it done, even if it killed us both. Force flows toward the weaker pole. I, who had chosen the passive part, was overloaded to the limit of endurance. I could neither see nor hear her now. If I made a move to end the torture, I could burn us both out. But if this did not end soon, I must risk it, even to the release of death.

Then the shock, the numbing flare of contact—

Regis!

Unbelievably, for a single unendurable moment, we—I—it—*fused* into an impossible *triple* rapport. The load of emotion was terrible, breaking down every barrier in each brain, and our three minds went into one great glare of force, too vast and too searingly painful to comprehend.

Groping for sanity, I forced the rapport apart. We were three separate people again. Then, as blinding physical pain forced itself on me, Regis was incredibly there in the room with us, and he caught me as I pitched forward in a dead faint.

"Damn it, this is getting to be a habit," I said shakily. I was lying on the bed again, Regis and Callina looking down at me anxiously. Regis pressed my hand as I sat up. "You've been doing all the hard work," he said.

"What happened?"

"Don't *you* know? How did I get here, anyway?" He swallowed convulsively and turned to Callina. Although we were deep in rapport, our conscious thoughts had dropped apart and I could not tell what they were thinking. But *three!* Even the Altons could link only two, and that with infinite danger! THREE!

Regis said, "What happened to us? I only know that something exploded in me—then it broke up, and I thought you were dead, Lew. I couldn't think of anything but to get to you and Dio. I didn't even know where you were, I was frantic, then all of a sudden, I was *here*, and you pitched off the bed, and I grabbed you," he finished blankly.

"Callina and I had tried to link minds in focus—"

"Callina?" Regis stared. Callina suddenly stood on tip-toe and put her lips lightly against his. "Regis," she said softly, "we aren't resentful. We can—make room for you."

Regis put his arms around the girl and held her. "Doesn't he know? Not even now?"

"I've always been barricaded," she said.

Regis let her go, turning abruptly to me, "Now that we're aware, and guarded, let's set up contact again and see what this thing is, and what kind of power we have with it. As far as I know, this is something pretty new, and almost unique."

Callina reached out and made the linkage; this time there was no hesitation or fumbling, and I glanced at her with a surge of possessive pride. Regis, rather red about the ears, looked round.

If you two are going to think things like that at each other, his thought twisted humorously into ours, *I'd better drop out!*

Then the circle of contact was complete. Yet, strangely, the personal barriers were back, intact. We could work as one, at the deep levels, but identity remained inviolate, and privacy. We were three separate personalities; only for the first fusion was there that searing down of emotions, of barricades.

Yet there was a sympathy, a togetherness that was extremely pleasant. It was as if all my life I had been getting along with a third of my brain.

Three telepaths, though not in rapport, had been needed to handle the Sharra matrix. This deep linkage, made through the living matrix of Aldones, was our weapon. Regis was the sword blade. Mine was the strength behind the sword; the Alton Gift, that hyper-developed psychokinetic nerve, was the hand to direct that striking force. And Callina, locked between hand

and blade, was the sword hilt; the necessary insulation.

Yes, there was symbolism in concealing these things in a sword. Regis and I, Hastur and Alton—sword and hand —could never join power to strength without exhaustion, nerve depletion and death—unless Callina were between us. The explanation swam up from somewhere in our linked minds. Comyn race-memory, perhaps, for they were not conscious memories. And Regis himself was the focus, the energy-source, the matrix if you will, through which, by means of the talisman sword, we could tap the energy-source and power of Aldones. Son of Hastur who was the son of Light—we stood close to what my race called a God.

My acquired knowledge knew this was a rational thing, science, mechanical and explainable; but there was a residue I could not explain. The *feel* of an actual living entity behind the Sword obsessed me.

I had felt the daemon-touch of Sharra. This was not evil—and somehow, that frightened me more. Infinite good is as terrifying as infinite evil.

But I was still physically weak, and Regis (*Guard your strength, Lew, you will need it soon!*) dissolved the linkage. I almost regretted it; a man's mind is a fearfully lonely place. Yet I could not have borne much more.

Regis touched Callina's arm. "Don't wait too long," he warned, and went away.

I feared that she, too, would withdraw; but, still tentative, she remained in contact, an immeasurable comfort. Her fingers laced in mine; closer yet was the delicate caress of her thoughts, and as I lay there, my face resting against her knees, I felt again a familiar, cool sweetness. The women tangled again in my thoughts, like the prism facets of a jewel.

How long the interval lasted I have no idea, but with a suddenness terrific in its impact, we both felt Regis, a

desperate clamor in our minds, and knew that he had
unsheathed the Sword.

And even as that warning rang out, space reeled, and
we were flung together into the great courtyard of the
Comyn Castle. Before us Regis stood, braced and erect,
and in his hand the Sword of Aldones—live, shimmering
blue from hilt to point. I caught my breath, and Callina
cried out, a strange wordless cry; then she reached out,
drew our three hands together on the sword-hilt and we
were ONE.

Through my suddenly-extended senses, I made out, at
the far end of the court, a wavering black mist through
which pulsed strange flame. Sharra's fires! Hell-fires! I
sensed, rather than saw, the other triad there:

Kadarin, Thyra, and Dyan Ardais.

The sight maddened me. For an instant I was one person again, and I leaped at Dyan, pulling out of the
linkage. But as I touched him the blue lightning exploded, and we were flung apart; for Kadarin faced Regis, the Sharra sword naked in his hands.

But this time the swords did not short-circuit in flames.
I was aware of a luminous mist that surged from the
Sword of Aldones; wrapped Regis in a rainbow aurora,
glowed like a cape around Callina's shoulders, folded me
in lucent brilliance. It licked out at the darkness that was
Sharra. And in that dark center, like figures of smoke,
Kadarin and Dyan and Thyra pulsed with the beating
heart of the Thing they had evoked.

Darkness, comet-shot with the lightning that flared
from the matrix-swords, crossing and recrossing. It was
not Regis and Kadarin fighting with identically forged
swords. It was not even matrix warring against space-
twisting matrix, or linked minds against linked minds.
No. Something tangible and alive and intelligent fought
behind them. Regis and Kadarin were only the poles of

their power. The real forces were not warring in this
world at all, or the planet would have been torn from its
orbit and sent reeling through the dark night of space
forever.

But enough projected here to be dangerous. Kadarin,
beaten back, snatched hastily at his belt; with a quick,
deadly flick, his knife flashed, and I was so much a part
of Regis that for a moment I did not know whether it had
struck him or myself. Only the deadly searing pain in my
heart, and I felt, not saw, the Sword of Aldones drop from
a limp hand. Regis slipped to the paving-stones. But he
was still part of the linkage; as Kadarin drew himself upright, I lunged to grip the Sword of Aldones. Using it—
only as a sword now—I drove the point through
Kadarin's heart. He fell without a cry. Sharra's matrix-
sword clattered on the pavement. I wrenched the Sword
of Aldones free. It was over.

The luminous haze coiled up; the black mist pulsed
and weakened, linkages broken. Then, abruptly, I leaped
back for Regis was incredibly on his feet again. He
caught the Sword of Aldones from my hand. There was
a stain of blood on his shirt, but he seemed unwounded;
untouched. The three-fold linkage snapped together
again. Behind us, Callina stood, blazing at Thyra with a
strange terrible intense stare. Thyra, too, stood locked,
intent, motionless. None of us had uttered a single sound
since the cry that had announced our coming.

A slim, girlish form burst suddenly from an opened
door and ran madly, as if compelled, toward Dyan.
Kathie! A few inches short of where he stood, she
stopped, digging in her heels in panic terror; but Dyan
caught her about the waist with one arm and snatched up
the Sharra-sword. Kathie screamed. She had been immune; but now, my block withdrawn from her mind, her
blindness to Darkovan forces was withdrawn. *Linnell's*

duplicate—with Linnell's powers. Dyan forced her savagely into the Sharra triad. Kathie and Dyan and Thyra seemed almost to coalesce, to flow together.

The Sword of Aldones stirred like a live thing. Then Callina flung up her free arm and with all the concentrated force of a Comyn Keeper, wrenched Thyra out of the Sharra triad. It was only telepathic contact; not our deeply-molded rapport. I saw the lightning blast over Dyan, beat at him, and Callina's cry rang in my brain.

"Now, Lew! Now!"

Desperately, a bare chance, I forced a wedge between Dyan and his pawn. Kadarin had been taken so far into Sharra that he could not withdraw. Hate Dyan as he would and did, they were sealed together. But Thyra might be still vulnerable. I sent, frantically, one thought to Thyra.

Marja! Marja is dead! Dyan killed her!

Thyra moved like a striking snake. She wrenched the Sharra matrix from Dyan's hand; and with all the fury and rage and concentrated power of a mind trained by Kadarin, turned on him. And all the concentrated force of my Alton Gift struck through her as I, once sealed to Sharra, turned that full force-flow on Dyan.

And I saw Dyan crumple, shrivel and fall to the pavement, his mind thinned and gone. Stone dead.

The black mist pulsed like a heartbeat. It was trying to draw me into it! For a moment Regis and Kathie were flung out of the triads and for a moment it was threefold; Thyra, in Sharra; Callina, in Aldones; and I, pole of power, caught between them in that terrible struggle.

But our threefold linkage was stronger, the link broke and I was free of Thyra—and Sharra. In the storms of living light Callina and I moved close, Callina's hand insulating Regis' hand from mine on sword hilt, her mind guarding us one from the other. If Regis and I had directly touched minds, if we had even physically touched hands, the power would have seared us to cinders.

The pulsing black mist swept back, gathering itself for fresh assault, coagulating around Thyra and the dead men.

And Kadarin rose!

He was dead. He must have been dead. Yet horribly, with the galvanic movements of a strung puppet, he rose. I saw the blackness shake itself as three hands met on Sharra's hilt. Fire-colors gleamed in its depth, and there was a tall shining in the black mist, and that swept on us. The three shadows twisted like smoke. Then, through the darkness, the face looked out. The face I had seen on the black night when terror walked in the Comyn and Linnell died.

But this time I knew what it was.

Long before Ashara, the Keeper, a further Keeper—a woman, born a Hastur, with the living matrix inherent in body and brain—had forged a matrix which should duplicate the powers of the Sword of Aldones. Two identical matrices cannot exist in one space and one time; and Sharra, Keeper of the Hasturs, had thrust herself outside *this* world.

Yet the matrix, not the living matrix of her brain, but the talisman matrix of the Sharra sword, remained here; and gave her a foothold in this world, through which she could be summoned when telepaths of certain skill should call her forth. Changed as she was, she still had power. And they called her daemon, Goddess.

But Sharra had been bound once, by the Son of Hastur. So ran the legend Ashara had repeated. Now another Son of Hastur, braced to endure the force by a rapport of three Comyn minds, held the Aldones matrix, intent on forcing her back again.

And under that power, space twisted and opened

worlds reeled; Kathie was thrust back first, through the interlocking universes, to her own place from which we had snatched her. And in one thing, at least, the balance was restored.

Now Thyra and Kadarin, alone, together, held that focus of Sharra's power. They called me to them! I, once sealed to Sharra, wavered and bent like a candle in the wind toward that monstrous thing I had helped, years ago, to summon. I caught desperately at Callina to steady my hold.

Callina faltered. The strength of Aldones' power ceased; again the confusion, while lightnings danced at the heart of the black flame where the Face of Sharra stared out horribly and beautifully between the reeling worlds.

Callina was—GONE!

Only Ashara's cold, only Ashara's icy nothingness, thinned against the eternities of space. I felt the triad of Aldones dissolve. Despairing, I felt myself drawn toward the ravenous maw of Sharra. . . .

Then, between a breath and a breath, there was a sharp shattering, as if a crystal broke under a cruel touch, and Callina was there again; I felt her strength, freed, cool and delicate, locking me to Regis again. Held steady. The blue lightning surged up, and our tripled brain was forged, suddenly, and welded, into a Cup. And into the Cup of Power flowed a force and a glory.

Regis seemed to grow taller, to take on height and majesty and the cloak of blue light lapped his limbs.

And clothed in his cloak of living light Aldones came!

Like a white spark I could see the Sharra matrix, blazing out through the metal of the sword that held it. Pointing straight at the coruscating light that circled Regis like a diadem.

Once, I think, Kadarin might have held Sharra's power completely, and conquered. Nerves and body and brain —it was hardly sure at the last which was man, which matrix. But Kadarin was human; and at the end, when his sustaining hate of me had faded, I think there was something in him which broke and played traitor; which made him will for self-destruction; which broke Sharra and made the Thing vulnerable.

Two identical matrices cannot exist in one space. While separate brains controlled them, they were non-identical enough to remain, though the stress-conditions put the ground of battle in a little place outside space and time. But Sharra's instrument had broken first. I knew, because for a moment everything that was weak or evil in me fought with Sharra, and for a moment, at the end, I was one with Kadarin and Thyra again, back in the old days. All the immense strength and courage of Kadarin, all Thyra's beauty, generosity, grace, before the alien horror strangled her womanhood, these fought for Sharra too.

Then the face dimmed to a wraith; Kadarin and Thyra, two tiny, separating ghosts, were flung into each other's arms, and for a moment I saw them clinging together, silhouetted against the dissolving mist and fires. Then they were swept away, as Sharra's ghost-face vanished into some reeling hell of darkness, and with it went Thyra and Kadarin, somewhere, somewhere. . . .

Aldones! Lord of the Singing Light! Is there mercy for them, too?

Then that, too, was gone, and I, Lew Alton, was kneeling in the damp dawnlit courtyard, arms around Callina, before a shaking, trembling boy holding a sword from which all the lights had faded. And there was no sign of Kadarin or of Thyra or Kathie. Dyan lay dead, a blackened corpse, on the scorched pavingstones. And in his hand the Sharra sword lay broken, a few shattered pieces of metal. There was no matrix now in the hilt of the sword. The hilt, blackened with fire, was dull and grayed, and the jewels lay scattered on the stones. The first rays of the red sun touched the castle turrets, and seemed to tremble for a moment in the heart of the jewels.

They shimmered, evaporated like bright spots of blue dew—and were gone. The sword of Sharra was broken—and the power of Sharra was broken in this world, forever.

Regis still held the Sword of Aldones. He was white, and trembling as if with deadly cold. Then, slowly, he sheathed the Sword. A flowing peace seemed to radiate from him, enlacing us in its net. The Sharra matrix had made Kadarin, who was not a bad man or a weak one, into a friend. The Sword of Aldones had made Regis—what?

"Regis—" My lips were stiff on the sound of his name, "What are you?"

"Hastur," he said gravely.

But the legend said Sharra was bound in chains by the son of Hastur, who was the son of Aldones, who was the son of Light.

He turned away and walked toward the archway. His face was the face of a God, at that moment, yet something less—and more. Supreme content . . . and awful loneliness. Then that, too, dimmed out, and it was only a grave young man's face, the face of one doomed to walk forever with the memory of an hour's godhead—and be forevermore denied it.

The rising sun touched his hair, snow white.

He disappeared through the arched door.

And I saw Dio Ridenow walking from the Keeper's Tower, slowly, dazed, like a woman in a dream. *Now when it was over*—but I had no thoughts for Dio, for Callina had risen, and drew me to my feet.

And for the first time without fear, I took Callina in my arms, crushing my mouth to hers.

And all desire died as I looked into the cold eyes of Ashara.

I should have known, all along.

CHAPTER SIXTEEN

Only a moment and it was Callina again, clinging to me, crying; but I had seen, and I knew. My arm fell and I stared in horror as she turned away, desolately. "Sharra," I heard her whisper, "Sharra . . . Then it was no use, no use for me, and I cannot live. . . ."

"Not by treachery, Ashara!" Dio faced the sorceress, steadily, "Not by damning another as you doomed Callina! You failed, because Lew was too human, and because Callina was not human enough! You failed, you failed!"

Stricken, madness rocking my brain, I came to where the frail figure cowered before Dio. Callina, Ashara—I could not tell. They blended; were one. Reason swam away; I took Callina blindly in my arms and the form and the face shifted and changed and were now Callina and now Ashara and now Callina again; then a look of peace and my arms were empty, and a whisper faded and died and was still.

"Dio!" I sobbed the name and went to her arms like a hurt child, "Dio, Dio, have I gone mad?"

There were tears on Dio's face. "I tried so many times to tell you. Ashara was not real, had not been real for generations. Didn't you wonder why her Tower room seemed so immense? It was not in the Tower at all, the blue door was a matrix, a—a gateway to somewhere else.

She was only a—a thought-form by now. She lived *in* the matrix, and whenever she left it, to take place in Comyn Council, she went in the body of one of the Keepers. Her power was so immense, and they were so frail, that for many generations she effaced them altogether; she only seemed ageless. She was born an Alton, Lew; she set her focus not in the minds, but in the living bodies of the Keepers. But her power was fading. Now she could not project her own form upon their bodies; she could only control their minds. And even that power was waning. She would have done anything for a new source of power . . ."

Dio gasped, then pulled herself together a little.

"I was to be Keeper—I could sense it, a little, how horrible it was, what she wanted. I begged Lerrys to take me away to Vainwal. Why do you think I threw myself at you? I came to love you, but at first, I only wanted to be unfit for her!" Even her hands burned on mine.

"So it was Callina. But—sometimes Ashara had to withdraw, or Callina would have burnt out. Then Callina was normal, or else she was in trance. When I knew that Regis would have to use the Sword, I—went to the Tower, and smashed one of the crystals. That trapped Ashara for a little while. I had been trained a little, when they thought I was to be the Keeper, and I knew what to do, but I couldn't do it in my own body, because—" Again her cheeks flooded with color. "Callina, at least, was a virgin. Callina was in trance, and the Terrans had drugged her. So I went to Regis, and he used his Gift, and—and switched *me* into Callina's body. It was I who linked with you and Regis."

"No," I gasped, "No, it was Callina, Callina—"

Dio pressed herself to me, her arms around my neck. "No, my darling, no, Callina could not have linked in focus with you. She had not enough independent mind left. Lew, remember—you had never touched my mind, you gave me a barrier against you. And I knew that when it broke, we'd all be too overloaded to know whether I was Callina, or Dio, or someone else. And after that, the barriers were up again. But—darling—see?"

Suddenly she reached for me and went into complete rapport again. The familiar solace, sweetness, the cool and delicate warmth! "Callina!" I breathed.

No. This is the part of me you never knew . . .

Even now the rapport was too intimate to hold for long.

"In the old days, Lew—before you left Darkover—Callina was a lovely girl, sweet and generous and brave. You know that. She risked her life for you. But Lew, the real Callina died when Ashara took her. Days ago. She was already only a shell of herself, but oh, Lew, the bravery, the wonderful bravery of that poor, poor girl!" Dio was sobbing like a child. "Lew, she loved you. She refused rapport with you—before Ashara—because she knew it would have given Ashara a foothold in *your* brain and body, too. With her last spark of will, she saved you from that and it was the last thing she ever did. It was her death—her real death. You thought Ashara disappeared? No; she had only overshadowed Callina. You thought Callina acted strangely on Festival Night? No. She was only—"

"Don't, don't tell me more!" I begged.

"Only one thing more." She touched the still-discolored bruise on her cheek. "Why do you think I didn't try to stop Dyan—warn Callina against Derik? Lew, it was a desperate chance, but if they'd succeeded, it would have played into our hands. If a man—any man—had taken Callina, even in rape, so soon after Ashara had taken over her body, it would have caused enough disruption to drive Ashara out. It might have killed Callina, but there was a bare chance that it would have *freed* her, instead. Ashara would have had to withdraw, not for a few minutes, but permanently."

"Don't!" I implored, sick with horror.

"I tried to save Callina myself—" Dio broke off. "Oh, Lew, didn't it mean anything that Callina came to you that night, and slept in your arms? Callina was in trance, and I—I knew Ashara could drive me out of her body any minute, but I knew you wanted Callina, and I hoped—"

"Oh, Dio!" In spite of my horror, I began weakly to laugh; the first step of the long healing. "Dio, my darling love, *don't you ever look in a mirror?* By the time you reached my rooms, it *was* you again—in your own body! And Callina would have known I could not—" Suddenly, violently, I caught her to me, kissing the flaxen hair and the wet face. "Darling, darling, I'm going to have to explain a lot of things to you about matrices and the men who work with them!"

Crying and laughing at once, she raised her eyes. "But if it was me, me myself—then—Lew, you love me?"

Over her head my eyes blurred. *Callina!*

Her gray-green eyes, shorn forever of mischief, met mine tenderly. "I'm not Callina any more," she said gravely, "but I'm not Ashara either. I think you're cured, Lew. If not, I too am damned."

I kissed her, and it was an exorcism for the past and an oath for the future. But I shut my eyes to the rising sun over her shoulder, knowing that forever I would walk with doubt, and face the sun with troubled eyes.

Abruptly the dawn was shattered with a burst of noise; Rafe and Regis ran into the courtyard.

"Lew," Rafe shouted harshly. "Come quickly! They've found Marja, alive!"

I let Dio go. Regis said, breathlessly, "Dyan had her under the matrix, and it blanked her like death; so he hid her the one place on Darkover where we would never look. When the matrix smashed, she went into shock, but there's a bare chance—"

Rafe grabbed my arm. "We've got a rocket-car."

We all crowded in, Rafe driving. The jets roared and we jerked back wildly as it screamed through a long curve and rammed back along the roadway not meant for these Terran inventions, horses and people fleeing in panic as we raced through the streets of Thendara.

Regis shouted, "When she collapsed, they called the Medical service at the HQ, and Lawton—"

Lawton, I thought, must be raving crazy by now, with first Thyra, then Kadarin, then Callina—Callina? and me disappearing. But I could not worry about him now. We roared into the Terran Zone. The streets were wider here, and the jets screamed as we slammed around corners still lighted with the neons of the night. We swept, in a wild slipstream of noise, into open country, and only minutes later we shrilled to a bone-shaking stop.

The sign read: THE READE ORPHANAGE FOR THE CHILDREN OF SPACEMEN

Rafe banged on the door and a tall woman, prim-faced, in Terran garments, looked out at us. Rafe demanded, "Where is Marguerhia Kadarin?"

"Captain Scott? How did you know? Your niece is very ill; we were going to send for her guardian. Where is he?"

"You can't," I cut in. "He's dead. The child's in shock. I'm a matrix tech, lady; let me in."

Her eyes narrowed with suspicion and dislike at my crumpled Terran clothing, put on days ago to ride to the *rhu fead;* bloodstained; my unshaven face, my mutilated arm. "I'm afraid I must say—no visitors."

Another female voice interrupted. "Miss Tabor, can you keep the hallway quiet? Remember we have a very sick child—" She broke off, looking at the four of us. Only Rafe was presentable. "Who are these people?"

"I'm Marja's father," I begged. "Believe me, every second we stand here, we're losing what little chance—"

Suddenly, with almost a prayer of thanks, I remembered the Terran cert card I had stuck into the pocket of this suit; the day I came to Darkover. I dived into the pocket. "Here. This will identify me."

She barely glanced at the plastic chip. "Come along," she said, and led me along the hallway. "We had to take her out of the dormitory. The other girls were frightened."

The room was small and clean and full of sunlight. Marja was lying in a high-sided crib, and Dr. Forth, from the Terran HQ, raised his head as I walked in.

"You? Did you say you know about this sort of thing?"

"I hope so," I said tonelessly and bent over her. My heart stopped. It was like looking at a dead child, one who has slept and slept and died sleeping. She lay slack on one side, her small hands limp and open, her mouth loose, breathing shallow and just audible. A single vein beat blue in her temple.

I frowned, making a tentative effort to touch her mind. No use. She was deep in trance; her mind was simply not in her body at all, and now even her body was failing.

No man can work among matrices without knowing all about shock-trance and how to cure it—if a cure is still possible. "Have you tried—" I named off a list of common restoratives, even though I knew that a child so young might not respond to treatment at all. It was almost unheard-of for a child to have any telepathic ability. I had never heard of a precedent for this.

And if it were to be much longer, she might better not return at all, for she would be too changed.

The sun had crept high and was burning through the glass. I straightened finally, sweat dripping down my face, and said wearily, "Where are Regis and Dio—the boy and girl who came with me? Get them."

They came in, softly, and stopped, appalled, looking down at the limp Marja. I said, despairingly. "It's a last resort. We were in rapport with a matrix almost identical to Sharra." When Sharra smashed, and the Gate was shut, everyone sealed to Sharra was flung into that world —except me. I had been held to this world by a power stronger still. There was a chance we could still reach Marja with a triple touch. Her body was here, and that was a powerful tie. I had fathered that body, and that was another. But she could not force her way back alone.

"Regis. Can you hold me if I go out after her?"

His eyes held momentary dread, but he did not hesitate. Dio stretched a hand to both of us and for the last time that threefold consciousness locked between us; an extension of myself which went outward, farther and farther, through spaceless, timeless distance.

Shadows flickered, cold and malign. Then something stirred there and fluttered, something twitched drowsily away from my touch; something dreaming, happy, unwilling to wake—

Swiftly, with a harsh roughness that made Dio sob aloud, I smashed the fourfold rapport and caught Marja in my arms, with the feverish relief after deathly despair.

"Marja!" I heard my own voice, husky, broken, "Marja, precious, wake up!"

She stirred in my arms. Then her lashes fluttered and she smiled, sleepy and sweet, up at me.

"*Chi' z'voyin qui?*" she murmured drowsily.

I don't know what I said. I don't know what I did. I suppose I behaved like any man half crazy with relief. I know I hugged her till she whimpered; then I sat down, cradling her in my lap.

She pouted, "Why is ev'body looking at me?" And, as I tried to speak through my choked throat, she complained pettishly, "I'm *hungry!*"

In sudden, weak reaction, I realized I hadn't eaten for two days. I felt an almost insane relief at the chance to end this whole thing on a note of the most ridiculous anticlimax.

"I'm hungry too, *chiya*," I said weakly. "Let's all go

and find you something to eat."

"And that," said Dio, lifting Marja easily by her little nightgown, "is the first sensible thing you've said since you came back to Darkover. Let's all go and eat. Matron, will you find this child some clothes?"

Two hours later, washed and fed and clothed, we made a respectable group around Lawton's desk in the HQ. He waved a spaceform at me.

"This just came over the relay," he said, and read it aloud. "Abandon leads on Darkover. Katharine Marshall discovered on Samarra, slight amnesia, unharmed. Haig Marshall."

"Allowing for the time lags in the relay," he said grimly, "she turned up on Samarra about half an hour after I talked to her here. Times, I'm tempted to throw up this job and turn spacehand." He looked at Regis' white hair; at Dio; at Marja, sitting in my lap. "You owe me an explanation, Lew Alton."

I looked back, gravely. I liked Dan Lawton. Like myself, he was a child to two worlds; but he, too, had chosen his path, and it was mine. "Perhaps I owe you that," I said, "but it is a debt I fear you will never collect."

He shrugged, tossing the spacegram into a basket. "So I'll always have something coming. We've got to talk, anyway. Darkover's years of grace are over."

I nodded in slow agreement. The Comyn had won against Sharra, but it had lost, too.

"I got word from GHW; I'm to start setting up a provisional government here, under Hastur—the Regent, not the kid. Hastur's sound, and honest, and the people trust him."

I agreed. The Hasturs had been the strength of the Comyn for generations; Darkover would be better off without the rest of us.

"You, young Regis, will probably come after him. By the time you're your grandfather's age, the people will be psychologically ready to choose their own rulers. Lew Alton—"

"Count me out," I said shortly.

"You have your choice. Exile—or staying and helping to keep things in order."

Regis turned to me, earnestly. "Lew, the people need Darkovan leaders, too. Someone who'll work wholly on their side. Lawton will do the best he can, but he's been Terra's man, all his life."

I looked sorrowfully at the young Hastur. Perhaps that was where he belonged. Ruler, even a figurehead; working for Darkover, stemming the tides of Terra as best one man could. Perhaps I belonged at his side.

"Won't you help me, Lew? We can do so much together!"

He was right. But all my life I had walked between two worlds, accused by each of belonging to the other. Neither would ever trust me.

"If you go, it's for good," Lawton warned. "Your estates will be confiscated. And you won't be allowed to come back. We don't want any more Kadarins!"

The words hurt, with their truth. That was the flaw in the Comyn. Misguided patriotism, self-sufficiency, the lack of some steadying balance—perhaps just the inability to see good in an enemy.

But I was Comyn. I had not asked to be born so, but I could not change. I looked away from the entreaty in Regis' eyes. "No," I said, "we'll go. I only want three things. Can I have 'em?"

"Depends," said Lawton. "I hope so."

I took Dio's hand. "To be married by our own people before we go," I said quietly, "and to straighten out the adoption papers on Marja. She's mine. But there are some mixed—"

He put out a hand to stop me. "Good God, let's not get tangled up in those weird family relationships again! Yes,

I'll arrange it, unless—" he glanced at Rafe, but Rafe shook his head, a little regretfully.

"What could I do with a kid? It would just be the orphanage again."

Lawton nodded. "What else?"

"A passport to clear space for four people." Four; Andres would not care to see the Terrans take over, I thought, even though it was the only right and logical way to end the story of the Comyn.

Regis asked, "Where will you go?"

I looked at the steady courage in Dio's eyes. I knew where I wanted to go and what I wanted to do, but could I ask it of Dio? Undecided, I looked at her. After all, I had lands and an heritage on Terra, which I could claim, and live there at ease.

Marja wriggled on my lap, clambered down and ran to Dio. She laid her mop of curls on Dio's shoulder, and Dio put both arms around her, and suddenly I made up my mind.

Halfway across the Galaxy there were pioneer worlds, where the name of Terra was a vague echo and Darkover a name unknown. There went all those who could find no place outside the stylized universe of today.

If the Empire ever came so far, it would not be in our lifetime.

I went to Marja and Dio and circled them both with my arms.

"The farther, the better," I said.

Lawton glanced at me. For a moment I thought he would protest. Then he changed his mind, smiled in his friendly, reserved way, and rose. Regret and farewell were in the gesture.

"I'll arrange that, too," he said.

Three days later we were in space.

Darkover! Bloody sun! What has become of you?

My world is fair, but at sunset there are times when I remember the towers of Thendara, and the mountains I have known. An exile may be happy, but he is an exile, no less. Darkover, farewell! You are Darkover—no more!

DARKOVER RETROSPECTIVE

A DARKOVER RETROSPECTIVE

by
Marion Zimmer Bradley

(Some portions of this Retrospective were adapted from an article entitled "My Life on Darkover," published in the amateur magazine *Fantasiae*, edited by Ian Miles Slater, c/o The Fantasy Association, Box 24560, Los Angeles CA 90024, in Vol 2 #11, #12, and Vol 3 #1. Copyright 1974 by The Fantasy Association and used by permission of Ian Miles Slater.)

There are times when I have referred to the Darkover books as "the series that just growed" . . . like Topsy. Most of my problem with the Darkover series is that I never thought of it as a series at all until the fifth, or was it the sixth or seventh, book. I wrote each new book about Darkover with a certain surprise to find myself doing this again, and a firm resolve that next time I would get busy and write an original novel about a new and original world. I was always astonished and a little chagrined to discover myself back on Darkover again, with yet more to say about the world of the bloody sun.

A good part of the credit for encouraging the Darkover

series to continue must go to Donald A. Wollheim, who, I am convinced, has done more to encourage fantasy and science-fantasy in this country during the lean years before "adult fantasy" became respectable, than any other single person. There were some years when I was doing the starving-writer bit, with a sick husband and two very small children to support, and now and then, having exhausted all other resources (because I didn't want to abuse his kindness), I would go to Don and ask him, with as much persuasion as I thought proper, if he would buy another book from me. On a surprising number of these occasions he actually suggested another Darkover book, and when I protested, rather diffidently, that I thought people must be getting awfully tired of them by now, he encouraged me to continue. But I never actually thought of them as a series. In the first place, I do not really like series books. The essence of a "series" to me is that the characters and background remain static, for the benefit of the reader who wants a safe, predictable reading experience just like the one he had last year. In the second place, I am simply not up to the kind of planning and long-range forethought that a "series" demands of its creator. My mind just does not work that way.

I am, for instance, incapable of thinking out anything of the nature of Robert A. Heinlein's "Future History" series. I have another friend, Jacqueline Lichtenberg, who thinks *only* in terms of series . . . or should I say, serieses. I have never heard her speak of a "new novel" —only of a new novel in one of her established series, or occasionally of a "new series." She has currently published two novels and, I think, two short stories in her major series, and told me once that she had it planned for about two thousand years into the future, and that she really thought of it as a single eight-million-word novel, with all the books in the series, written and unwritten, as

episodes in a vast hyper-novel. For her, she said, no single episode may ever be allowed to interfere or conflict
with anything in the vast Master Plan.

Personally, I think that's *horrible*. I love Jacqueline's
books . . . but how any person can be willing to lock
herself into a pattern that might last for *years*. . . . I think
I'd rather go to prison right away and be done with it.
How can I know what I am going to be doing, or thinking, or wanting to write, even two years from now, let
alone ten?

("It's a good thing," the Scotsman said, "that we don't
all like the same thing. Think what an oatmeal shortage
there would be!")

I have a group of friendly but outraged fans who seem
to enjoy picking holes in the Darkover books for the most
minor inconsistencies. Oh, they enjoy the books, but
when I ask them why they READ the Darkover books, if
the inconsistencies bother them so much, they say "But
I *love* Darkover! The books are great! But—" (wistfully)
"they'd be so much BETTER if the author would just take
the trouble to make them a little more consistent. . . ."

There's another problem I have. The fan who comes
up to me, shiny-eyed, and eager, and says "I'm really
anxious to read the Darkover books, but I've promised
myself I won't read them until I have them *all*. Will you
please tell me which one I ought to read first?"

As if it were a school assignment and he would be pun-
ished for reading them in the "wrong" order!

Admittedly the inconsistencies are many. Some are minor, and they occurred simply because I have a very
faulty memory with a self-correcting mechanism. If I per-
petrate anything in a Darkover book which I think could
be altered for the better, I simply write it in the next book
the way I think it ought to have been all along. The system of nomenclature for the lords of the Domains, the
seven Great Families of the Comyn, is like that. I was

dissatisfied, in retrospect, with some of the forms of address I had invented for the lords and ladies of the Domains when I was young (I started writing the books
when I was VERY young) and, not wishing to be bound by
a juvenile concept, I simply allowed the forms of address
to evolve in each book until now I have something that
makes sense to me. I can't imagine why readers should be
bothered by this kind of thing. If they are, they can go
back to the earlier books, mark out with a pencil the offending inconsistent forms, and write in the ones that
suit them better; after all, they own the books.

Then there are the *major* inconsistencies, and I admit
that some of them are whoppers. About the worst one
comes in the second, or maybe the first book of the series,
depending on whether you are talking about order of
writing or order of publication.

In the first *published* Darkover story, *The Planet
Savers*, which was written for a magazine (*Amazing
Stories*, I think) the four moons of Darkover were referred to as reaching a major conjunction every forty-
eight years, and that forty-eight-year cycle was supposed
to co-ordinate with a vector which spread an epidemic on
Darkover, repeatedly decimating the human population.
In the novel on the flip side of that in the original Ace
Double, *The Sword of Aldones*, the four moons are
spoken of as reaching a conjunction and multiple eclipse
configuration every year at Midsummer-Festival.

That, of course, is no way to write a series. But when
I wrote *The Planet Savers*, I hadn't the slightest idea that
The Sword of Aldones, or any other Darkover story,
would ever be published; I was cannibalizing some un-
published stories in my masses of juvenilia, to write some
hopefully salable commercial novelettes. I did the same
thing with the novelette *Birds of Prey*, which I sold to
Venture science fiction sometime in the fifties, and
which Don Wollheim picked up as half an Ace Double

under the title of *The Door Through Space;* this is why the typical Dry-Town culture with some Darkovan names, appears on a planet called Wolf, complete with the Terran Empire background structure. This has caused questions ever since as to whether *The Door Through Space* is part of the Darkover series; the answer, of course, is both yes and no. Anyway, I have been trying to ignore these three stories ever since. The Darkover series, if it is a series, and I suppose I have to bow to the majority opinion, (though I prefer to call it a Human Comedy) began with *The Bloody Sun,* and that will be discussed in due time.

I never wanted, or intended, to write a series. The first hint I ever had that it was considered a series was years later, when Don changed the title of *Summer of the Ghost Wind* to the title under which it appeared in print. *Darkover Landfall.* He said that the Darkover series was a known series and a popular one, and "I want the fans to be able to identify it; also, the distributors ask for your Darkover books and say they can always sell them."

I was, to put it mildly, startled and shocked. But I realized that I'd have to take it seriously. I had always thought that the special interest in the Darkover books was limited to a little circle of my family or close friends, and I wrote each new Darkover book rather guiltily, as if I were succumbing to two temptations; first, laziness, the lack of ambition to create a new background, and second, the desire to write for my friends instead of aiming the book at a vast, faceless, impersonal "general audience."

But one thing I was very definite about. I wasn't going to make a "series" out of it, with one book beginning where the last one had left off, predictable plots and similar characters and situations. All along, I told myself, I would never be guilty of the arrogance of assuming that the reader had read the previous book, or, in fact, any single one of the previous books. Every book was to be

absolutely complete in itself, without the need for the
reader to refer back to any previous book.

To that stricture I still cling. Nor will I ever succumb
to the temptation to leave a book half-finished, so that
the reader has to wait, chewing his fingernails, for the
next book to come out. I still remember the outrage and
fury I felt at the end of one of the Roger Zelazny
"Amber" books—I think it was *The Guns of Avalon*—
where the heroes follow a mysterious girl all the way
through the book for an explanation of her mysterious
doings. As I approached the end I thought with relief
"Oh, boy, only a few pages left, now it will HAVE to be
explained. . ." and then, just as they caught up with the
mystery girl, she popped into the pattern and disappeared . . . presumably to reappear in the next book! I
have forgotten everything about that book except the
outrage and frustration I felt at the end. How DARE the
author torture his readers this way? Is he just trying
to insure a good sale for the next book? I resolved, then
and there that I would not read the next book. It wasn't
fair.

At the same time I re-resolved that I would never do
that to any reader of mine! When my reader buys a book,
I swore, he or she will get a COMPLETE NOVEL . . . not a
chunk of one with a cliff-hanger at the end. It reminded
me of one of the Edgar Rice Burroughs "John Carter of
Mars" series, where at the very end of the book the heroine—was that Dejah Thoris? I've never been a Burroughs
fan—was stolen away and popped into some kind of
giant wheel with cubicles which moved at a fixed rate, so
that the one in which she was imprisoned (hopefully in
suspended animation) would not reappear for a whole
year. John Carter and his sidekick were left staring at the
giant wheel until the next book . . . no more frustrated
than *I* was!

So these are the ground rules for the Darkover books,
series or not; every one is complete in itself, and I do not

assume that the reader has read, or will ever read, any other book in the series. Also, that whenever consistency from book to book threatens to impair the artistic unity of any single book as a unit in itself, inter-book consistency will be relentlessly sacrified. Every game has its rules. These are the rules of the universe I call Darkover.

But there are people who not only regard the Darkover books as a series, but like them that way. And I am, every now and then, completely bemused by the phenomenon called "Darkover fandom." Grateful, certainly. But puzzled.

I used to say that I never wanted or expected to be a writer. As a kid, I cherished dreams of becoming an opera singer, and began serious study; at the same time I knew that the chances of succeeding anywhere near the top in the performing arts were minimal; so I conscientiously trained for a job at which I could earn my living, attending a teacher's college despite my distaste for the whole business. (Somewhere along the way I became a drop-out from three teacher's colleges, but that's neither here nor there.) Poor health in my middle teens caused me to give up all thought of singing professionally. But all during my teens, whether my health was good or bad, all the time I was studying voice and singing in choirs and auditioning for solo parts, I was WRITING. Obsessively. Compulsively. I never stopped. And so I suppose that behind all the thoughts and daydreams of singing, the knowledge that I wanted to be a writer was slowly surfacing. Or rather, I never wanted to "be a writer" at all. I just couldn't stop writing, no matter what else I did or didn't do. It never even *occurred* to me to stop.

Well, in my middle teens, about the time I was adjusting to the absolute knowledge that I would never sing *Norma* at the Metropolitan Opera, I discovered the science fiction pulp magazines and science fiction fandom. Immediately I plunged over my head into the world of

MARION ZIMMER BRADLEY

fanzines and amateur fan publishing. About the same time I started to write fantasy novels with a framework of science fiction.

"I'd always written voluminously. I believe my mother has a handful of poems I wrote before I was school age. When I was about eleven I started writing "historical" novels, scribbling them down in longhand in those black-and-white mottled notebooks with COMPOSITIONS printed on the front. I remember dong one about Bonnie Prince Charlie, and one about Roman Britain, and an ambitious project called *Ten Tales of the Ancients*, which had a short story about a girl in ancient Rome, and one in ancient Greece, and one from an Arabian-nights kind of world, and then I ran out of ancient civilizations and gave up. But, although I had read a great many fantasy novels, Rider Haggard, and Talbot Mundy, Robert W. Chambers, and Sax Rohmer, it never occurred to me to write fantasy until I discovered the science-fictional fantasy style of the novels of Moore and Kuttner. Suddenly all my novelistic energy exploded into a combination of Kuttner-style fantasy and Graustarkian romance; in the next two or three years I wrote two or three novels, and started or planned several others, all in a kind of imaginary country/parallel universe which I named Al-Merdin. Most of these fantasies were concerned with the doings of a ruling caste of telepaths which I named Seveners—who later became the Comyn. Gradually, all of these narrowed down to a hugely sprawling novel which I called *The King and the Sword*. It took me about three years to get it into anything resembling recognizable shape, mostly because I had no notion of how to plot a story; I just started writing the adventures of my characters and wrote on and on, without anything one could call a plot structure. During this time I married and dropped out of college, but the book went on and on. It was full of echoes of all the fantasies

I liked best: A. Merritt, Kuttner and Moore, Brackett and Hamilton, with a liberal splash of Graustark, the Prisoner of Zenda, Zorro, and the lost races of H. Rider Haggard. During this time I also managed to read a few books on writing and began to get some foggy notion of what a plot was, and that a book should optimally have a beginning, a middle and an end. I would lay down my novel from time to time and try writing, and plotting, short stories and novelettes, and the experience carried over. One of these novelettes—the only one which actually sold, and I wish it hadn't—was later called *Falcons of Narabedla*, which was a really shameless pastiche of a Kuttner story. It isn't a Darkover story either, and I wrote the whole thing before my nineteenth birthday. The only excuse I have for the pastiche quality of this one is that when I was a teen-ager I honestly didn't know any better.

There are some survivals from *The King and the Sword* even in the most recent of the Darkover novels. The seven families of telepaths, each with its own distinctive Gift, has survived into the Comyn. In those days, the Hasturs, the Elhalyn, the Serrais, the Ardais and the exiled Aldarans were much as they are now. The Altons were then known as the Leyniers, and the Marceau of Valeron became the Aillards because, after seeing the title of *Skylark of Valeron* (a book I have never read) I feared that E.E. Smith, whom I admired for his "Lensman" stories, might think I had copied it from him. Actually I suppose we both got it from the same place—the Valerii family of Imperial Rome.

Well, Sam Merwin of *Startling Stories* read chapters and outline of *The King and the Sword* (I knew enough by now to make an outline, though, I suppose, not a very coherent one) and rejected it with a few sharp and valuable comments. So I decided it was far too complicated to make a good book as it was, and started out with a much simpler episode, central to the story (cutting out begin-

ning and end) dealing with the confrontation of the twin
magical talismans or "matrixes" of Sharra and Aldones. I
think it was in this version that I changed the name of
Gwynn Leynier to Lew Alton, and located the whole
thing on an imaginary planet with a red sun (shades, I
suppose, of Jack Vance's *The Dying Earth*, which I
adored) called Darkover. Instead of a fantasy parallel
world, I laid the whole thing against a Galactic Empire of
the kind now familiar to me from the enormous sprawling Edmond Hamilton novels such as *The Star of Life*, or
the E. E. Smith "Lensmen" stories. So that instead of a
Ruritanian exile in faraway mountains, my scarred hero
had returned from exile on alien worlds, other planets. I
cut the whole thing down drastically, and actually managed to finish it. It was still about 500 manuscript pages
long. This one was rejected too, as being much too long
and discursive. This original version has long since been
destroyed and I haven't the faintest idea how I managed
to get all that wordage into it. I remember that there
were a couple of duels, and Lew Alton had a couple of
other romantic encounters somewhere in the book, but
the rest has mercifully vanished from my memory. (I
can't of course vouch for my subconscious.)

So I stuck the whole thing into a drawer and forgot
about it while I tried to learn my craft. I wrote a few
novels, none of which got published, and a few novelettes, some of which were pretty damn good, or at least
I thought so, anyhow they managed to get into the magazines. And then Ray Palmer, who had long since left the
old Ziff-Davis *Amazing* to publish some flying-saucer
magazines, and try to get his obsession published (a mon-
umental monstrosity which he may have written himself,
or merely discovered, rejoicing in the fearful
title/concept of *Tarzan on Mars*) revived a fantasy magazine which he called *Other Worlds*, and actually
bought *Falcons of Narabedla*. He published it in May,

1957; I didn't get paid for it, but at that time I was pleased to have it in print. Emboldened, I submitted *The Sword of Aldones* to him, and he accepted that too. From time to time during the next three or four years he would put out an advertising flyer about all the wonderful things he was going to do with *Other Worlds*, including *Tarzan on Mars*, and mentioning *The Sword of Aldones*, too, I paid about as much attention to this as I did—excuse me, Harlan—to the things Harlan Ellison said about what he was going to do with his fanzines. Namely, that it would be wonderful if he ever got around to it, but I wasn't going to hold my breath waiting. Anyway, by that time I had grown up enough to have a certain contempt for the stupid thing, and that contempt carried over to an editor who would actually consider printing it.

(Note that this is NOT the version of *The Sword of Aldones* which appeared from Ace Books in 1961 or thereabouts.)

Anyway, by this time I had outgrown, or thought I had outgrown, fantasy-adventure; I was interested in writing science fiction, and I did, having several short stories and novelettes printed in the lesser pulps. I hit *F & SF* twice in those years, and one of Damon Knight's magazines once, and the rest were minor sales to minor magazines which lasted, sometimes, long enough actually to print the stories they bought! Then I managed to do a lead novel for *Amazing Stories*, which was no longer the lead-selling magazine in the field, as it had been for years, but had not yet dropped to the depths of the Sol Cohen/Ted White days, either; it was still a completely respectable and professional magazine, with Cele Goldsmith at the helm. This novel was *Seven from the Stars*, which brought me, not money alone, but an agent, and a long and mutually profitable relationship with Ace Books. Next, I wrote, and managed to sell, an early ver-

sion of *The Door Through Space*, published by Venture
as *Birds of Prey*; and for this one I cannibalized that
drawerful of "Terran Empire/Darkover" stuff, which by
now I considered hopelessly juvenile. There were times,
in fact, when I actually considered throwing away the
whole file of it; in fact, the complete manuscript of a
novel called *The Dark Flower* actually *did* get thrown
out, by mistake, in the course of the peripatetic wander-
ings of the Bradley family in the wake of the Atchison,
Topeka and Santa Fe Railroad in West Texas. Portions of
this novel were rewritten, from memory, years later, as
part of *The Heritage of Hastur*.

In rewriting an expanded version of *Birds of Prey* for
the paperback market, I also found myself cannibalizing
some of the fantasy-science fiction elements of the "Terran Empire/Darkover" background I had created for
The Sword of Aldones. I might very well have laid this
story on Darkover, but I decided not to; I remembered
reading somewhere that the star Wolf 354 had a visible
planet, so I named the planet Wolf, and the hero, Race
Cargill, became a far-too-blatant imitation of Northwest
Smith; the whole thing read like a bad imitation Leigh
Brackett, up to and including the pseudo-Chandler
dialogue. Leigh, bless her, never held this against me. I
also revived the character of Evarin, the Toymaker, from
Falcons of Narabedla which had been read by—perhaps
—as many as a thousand readers in Palmer's *Other
Worlds*.

However, the villain/hero of *The Door Through
Space* was borrowed directly from *The Sword of
Aldones* as it was then; he was Rakhal Darriell, bastard
son of the same father as Thyra and Marjorie . . . also
known as Kadarin. And the hero, Race Cargill, had the
terrible facial scars and the murderous hatred which
characterized Gwynn Leynier/Lew Alton in *Sword*. In

short, *The Door Through Space* was a kind of replay of the old *The King and the Sword*—a replay of the basic situation—but the difference was that I was beginning to learn how to plot, and how to tell a story.

It became a fairly straightforward adventure story, using the catmen, the two deadly rivals, and a sort of *Planet Stories*-type plot with some slush about matter-transmitters. I regard it as my first wholly successful piece of commercial fiction. As I say, it came out like bad imitation Leigh Brackett, but it was the first time I'd managed to plot a solid adventure story, and I was proud of it.

During those years, while I was going mad with loneliness in West Texas, my then agent, Forry Ackerman, had loaned me a series of books and magazines, and to amuse me, he had included some fairly risqué stuff, very mild sado-masochistic fetish stuff; bondage, torture, etc; not quite pornographic, but very definitely from the sexual underground. Since this kind of thing amused him, I wrote some of it into *The Door Through Space*—it seemed to go well with the tough-guy dialogue—and that was where the chained women of the Dry Towns had their origin.

I have since heard that this kind of thing by female writers is almost unheard-of. Believe me, I have no ambition to be known as science fiction's own Marquise de Sade! Well, Forry sold the expanded, novel-length version to a German publisher, still under the title *Raubvogel der Sterne (The Falcon from the Stars)*. When I changed agents in 1960 or thereabout I had to re-translate this into English, probably improving it enormously in the process. Don Wollheim bought it, and displayed some interest in publishing another novel by me.

And that was the real beginning of what can now be called DARKOVER.

II

Shortly after I sold *Seven from the Stars* to Cele Goldsmith at *Amazing Stories*—I have long forgotten the precise date—Cele indicated that she would be receptive to another book-length novel (as book-lengths were in the magazines of that day). About that time I was reading *The Three Faces of Eve*, and was fascinated by the concept of multiple personality. When I read Clifford Simak's *Good Night, Mr. James*, the two ideas seemed to blend and fuse into a single concept. The Simak story, for those who haven't been fortunate enough to read it, is about a man who has an identical android duplicate of himself constructed to perform a special task—killing a dangerous monster—the duplicate being able to function with all the special skills of the original, but without risking the original. The android—today it would probably have been called a clone—was an identical duplicate of the man, and the story was concerned with his attempts to escape destruction, kill the original and take his place.

About that time, in an early issue of *Galaxy*, Wyman Guin's *Beyond Bedlam* had hypothesized that every individual had two alternate personalities, "hypoalter" and "hyperalter," who were, in this society, allowed equal access to consciousness in the body. In my new story, then, I postulated that a person might have suitable skills for a given task—but find that his ordinary personality was unfitted for it. Suppose that person had a buried alternate personality, and suppose that hypnotic and other techniques could draw forth that buried personality, to emerge when needed for a special task?

So that a deeply repressed Terran Medic, Jay Allison, discovered himself in the personality of his repressed alternate who calls himself Jason. (My original title for *The Planet Savers* was *Project Jason*.) I resurrected Darkover for this story; as I said above, I had by now lost hope that

Ray Palmer would ever print the silly thing, and I felt that I would just as soon leave it decently buried.

But the planet I had invented for *The Sword of Aldones* struck me as a good locale for this story, so I built an enormous spaceport at Thendara, and borrowed a fairly minor character, Regis Hastur, for a representative of the Hastur nobility. I didn't feel, at this length, that I could justify explaining the entire Comyn nobility, or the Seven Domains, so I mentioned only the Hasturs. A combination of a misprint and an attempt to be clever endowed Regis with five sons, three legitimate—which has led to many fans asking me who he married—whereas the original in my manuscript read that he had five sons, three legitimat*ed*—meaning that he had given them recognized status as *nedestro* Comyn sons; bastards, from casual love affairs.

I also, alas, for the purposes of this story, needing something to justify a cyclic fever, invented the fairly-unlikely mechanism of the forty-eight-year eclipse cycle. When I wrote it, I had not the foggiest notion that some day there would be thirteen Darkover novels. I was just hoping I could do well enough with this assignment that there would be *one!*

And people have been dragging it up ever since.

About the time Scott Meredith sold *The Planet Savers* to Ace for a reprint (I still think that *The Planet Savers* is the most horrible title ever foisted on a helpless novel by a cruel editor. . . .) Don Wollheim wrote to me, saying that he intended to buy *The Planet Savers,* and asking if I had another novel to back it up with. How different my life would have been if I had obeyed my first impulse and sent Don the short novel which had been on the cover of *F & SF* in 1954, *The Climbing Wave!* Instead, I remembered the novel which was mouldering away in Ray Palmer's custody. His magazine had not had a single issue for more than two years. I decided that this was the moment of decision. *The Sword of Aldones* might be a bad novel—I didn't know then quite HOW bad a novel that version was—but I didn't think it was quite bad enough to rot away in Ray Palmer's files for the next twenty years!

So I wrote to Ray with an ultimatum. I demanded that he publish it, or pay for it, or else return it to me. At that point I didn't much care which he did; but I wanted him to do *something*. And what he did was to return it to me.

Well, I sat down and re-read the thing. It was even more awful than I remembered; it was completely hopeless. But I had grown a lot in the last three or four years, and now I could see just WHY it was hopeless. So I sat down to run it through the typewriter and try to tighten it up into something Don Wollheim could publish.

First I strengthened the conflict between Terran Empire and Darkovan, making this the basic conflict of the book—the clash of cultures. This was ultimately to become the theme of all the early Darkover novels. And because I had already used, in *The Door Through Space*, the theme of the terribly scarred and disfigured man, but Lew's personality seemed to me essentially that of a maimed man, "with one cruel stroke of the typewriter I lopped off his hand," as I once wrote flippantly in a fanzine. I consolidated three (yes, *three*) villains to make the figure of Dyan Ardais, which is why the Dyan of *Sword* seems to be so completely devoid of the slightest redeeming qualities—he had to portray the dastardly deeds of three separate and distinct villains! (I was to resurrect the Dyan of the original in *Heritage*, making him a complex man, with his own concept of honor.)

And I made what I now consider the greatest mistake I ever made in all the Darkover books; I killed Callina Aillard at the end of that book because a friend of mine identified very heavily with Dio Ridenow and wanted *her* to have Lew.

I ran the whole thing through the typewriter in ten days and sent it off to Don Wollheim.

And he bought it.

Nothing in my whole career has ever astonished me as much as the enthusiasm with which this book was received—enough to give it a push for the Hugo. *Sword* actually reached the voting finals and came in, I believe, second. I still don't understand it. In the preface to the Gregg Press edition, Dick Lupoff commented that the book is hampered by a juvenile concept, and he's certainly right; I can't forget that the first draft of this book was written when I was about fifteen years old, and the many rewritings were not enough to eliminate some of the major flaws. Even now, to me, the Darkover books still suffer from the need to maintain at least a basic consistency with that juvenile concept. When I finally decided to ignore—completely—absolutely EVERYTHING I had established in *The Sword of Aldones*, (except for Marjorie's death and the concept of Thyra's child) only then did *Heritage of Hastur* become a good, mature novel.

And yet *The Sword of Aldones*, I suppose, has its virtues. To me, it is the hastily written, badly plotted, overemotional, and much too rambling quickie I turned out in a rush for Don Wollheim; and yet it must have *something*, judging by the number of battered and dog-eared copies, read almost to disintegration, which are still shoved into my face to autograph at conventions. Lengthy introspection turns up some things to like about the book. It has immediacy; absurd as the plot elements may be, the people who keep turning up and giving Lew Alton guns or taking them away again, the pointless way in which the women shift bodies and identities, the action is so fast that nobody *notices* that it's all busy-work without meaning. The first-person narrative probably adds to this. I said, once, commenting on people who identified very strongly with the hero of *Sword*, "Well, yes, I guess the thing is that you believe it while it's happening. You have to. There's the poor guy bleeding all over the page."

But mostly I don't much like this one. I'm rather bemusedly grateful to my fans who like it, but when it is criticized, even very severely criticized, about all I can do is to hang my head and say "Uh huh. Uh huh. I was a lot younger when I wrote it. It's a juvenile." And when people tell me how much they like it, even—as some people do—rave about it, I'm completely at a loss for words. I can't insult them by saying I think them very foolish for liking it. Maybe it hit something in them, something which I was feeling when I wrote it and they just happened to tune into when they read it. But I find it very difficult to understand.

III

And then I went back to writing hackwork for a living. Confessions. Magazine stories. During much of the early sixties, I was writing mildly risqué novels for Monarch books, on contract from Scott Meredith; I suspect Scott had a contract to supply Monarch with a set number of these junky things per month and farmed them out to any writer who was hungry enough, and facile enough, to turn them out by the yard. I wrote these things under a variety of pen names, to put myself through college— I was still hedging my bets, not sure that all my markets wouldn't dry up under me, so that I'd have to teach for a living. I didn't want to teach, but without a college diploma, the alternative was slinging hash in a greasy spoon somewhere. All the time my first marriage was slowly disintegrating, I was writing these things, and turning out yard-goods romances and confessions. I got to where I could turn out a two hundred page novel in three months and never miss a deadline.

In the winter of 1962-63, Donald A. Wollheim, making a trip to Dallas to see some Western writers, came a couple of hundred miles to Abilene to see me (at the time I thought it a tremendous compliment and was flattered and excited), and asked if I had anything else on hand that he might use.

I had used, as an epigraph to *The Sword of Aldones*, a cryptic phrase which had struck my imagination in Franz Werfel's *Star of the Unborn:* "The stranger who comes home does not make himself at home, but makes home strange." The epigraph had been cut from the printed version, but I was still mulling over the phrase, and so I had written a two-or-three-chapter sketch about an exile returning to Darkover; I typed *The Bloody Sun* at the head of the fragments, and gave them to Don with a brief outline of the plot. I never had much hope for it, but that summer, on a visit to my mother, I paid a brief visit to the old Ace offices and spent a few minutes with Wollheim. While he was telling me about some of the books he was going to publish in the next year, he said in passing "And we have something by you—we're going to buy it of course—" and immediately went on to other things.

I don't think any other moment in my writing career has ever held so much excitement and delight for me as that one. "We're going to buy it—*of course.*" OF COURSE! Something happened to me at that moment. I had always been thinking of my writing as a sort of small skill, which I managed to sell because I had no other talents, as long as I confined myself strictly to hackwork and formula stuff. Painstaking, skilled craftsmanship, for which I could claim no credit, since I felt this sort of thing could be turned out by the ream by any high-school graduate who could write a literate English sentence. In that moment, when Wollheim said that to me, my whole self-image changed. I suddenly saw myself, not as a potential schoolteacher patiently turning out skilled hackwork to finance her education, but as a writer, and the writing itself as my real work, a knack or talent or skill which was itself, and could be, and should be, a genuine lifework for which I should have no need to apologize. Suddenly, instead of saying hesitantly "I write, because it's the only thing I know how to do, and it's better than working as a waitress somewhere," I realized that the writing in itself *was* a respectable career, a vocation, not just a little hobby I could justify by selling enough to pay my husband back for spending so much on paper and typewriter ribbons and stamps.

Instead, that day—and from that day forth—I have said, I am a writer, a serious working professional, accepted as such. If I put my mind to it, there is no reason I cannot earn a decent living at it, and no reason I should feel compelled to do anything else. I have mastered my craft; now I can make it an art and a profession as well.

Maybe this is why *The Bloody Sun* has always been, and in a sense still is, my favorite of all my own books. Perhaps because, in this book, I tried to measure, consciously, my powers as a writer, a storyteller, an entertainer.

But the actual writing was a nightmare. My marriage, long shaky, and more nominal than anything else, suddenly and abruptly collapsed in a messy divorce. I was carrying the final semester of work on a Bachelor's degree. I had three hackwork-novel contracts which I had to honor to pay the rent. The doctor put me on tranquilizers to try and ease the stress attendant on the disruption of my marriage. And in the middle of the whole thing, I developed a horrifying "writer's block"—the inability to sit down and write a single sentence. I would write a paragraph or two, laboriously, and then stare at the page and realize I hadn't the faintest idea of what ought to come next. I would stare at the paragraph I had just written, cry a little, go away and iron a shirt, then painfully figure out what happened next and try to figure out a way to put it into words. It was a nightmare. It lasted three weeks. It went away just as suddenly as it had come, but even that, in retrospect, was a boon; when the book appeared in print, even I could not distinguish the parts I had ground out with agonizing slowness and deliberation, feeling that every sentence was lifeless and dreadful, from the parts that had come in great flashing fast pagefuls as rapidly as I could type them out. And so I learned to trust my subconscious, to try and keep it in mind that I was a professional, a trained craftsman, and that I could not turn out anything very far below my current standard of competence.

The Bloody Sun was another first for me; it marked perhaps the first serious approach to sex in my books. Taniquel, in the original version of this book, written in 1963, is the first woman in science fiction to have an independent and autonomous sex life not dependent on some man in the story. Not the first such character written by a woman, just the first, as far as I can tell, in science fiction.

However, even in the delineation of the sexual *mores* of Darkover, *The Bloody Sun* made statements contrary to my later view of Darkover—and once again, this was because I had no notion that there were going to be further Darkover books. I allowed Kennard to say that monogamous marriage on Darkover was a fairly recent development . . . whereas later developments have proven to me (via the novel *Stormqueen*) that it dated back at least to the Ages of Chaos!

A serious part of my "permanent concept" of the social structure of Darkover is that monogamous marriage is not integral to the structure. *Darkover Landfall*, many years later, worked with the concept of a limited gene-pool where many traits could disappear simply by genetic drift, and others be reinforced by inbreeding; and, aware of the limited nature of this gene pool (all the original colonists from Darkover, for instance, were white Northern Europeans) it seemed to me natural that maximum randomization of the gene pool would be highly desirable, and one way to enforce this would be a form of group marriage where no woman would bear more than one child to the same man—this, of course, somewhat modified by individual preferences. It also seemed to me —another of the "ground rules" for Darkover, and a part of my permanent concept of the Comyn—that they would tend to marry and reproduce among themselves, since for a telepathic caste, sex with nontelepaths would be as distasteful as mating with lower animals; sex, of course, enhancing communication via telepathy, and sex with a person who could not share in that sense, unsatisfying at best and perhaps impossible.

However, having laid out the ground rules for sex on Darkover, in the next Darkover book I abandoned any attempt to work with sexual mores and ethics, and wrote a juvenile.

During the period immediately following *The Bloody Sun*, I got my degree, and I came to Berkeley to do graduate work, and I married again, and I did commercial stuff to pay the rent, including three or four romances I can't even remember the names of, or the pen names under which I wrote them. Scott Meredith got me to doing Gothics, too, which was a great improvement over even the relatively decorous "risqué" novels I was writing then for Monarch Books. I wrote a couple of Gothics, and when he suggested it was about time I try another science fiction book, my creative energies were at a fairly low ebb; so instead of inventing a whole new world, I decided to write another Darkover novel, a juvenile this time.

I had written one other juvenile, for Monarch, which had been killed off by poor distribution—Monarch's reputation was for "adult romances", so when people saw the Monarch name, they ignored it—and had had the final quietus put on it by a cover indicating that the book was intended for the 5-9 year-old audience instead of being, as it was, written for teenagers and young adults. But I had enjoyed writing a teenage novel, bearing always in mind the dictate of Robert Heinlein: "make your hero seventeen years old, and write the story otherwise exactly as you would write any other novel."

Since I had mentioned that Lew Alton's mother was a Montray, and related to the Aldaran family, in *The Sword of Aldones,* I decided that in *Star of Danger* I would try to indicate when the Montray family had come to Darkover; whereupon my young hero became Larry Montray, born on Darkover.

I have always been a great believer in the Mary Roberts Rinehart method of telling a story on two levels; the outer story, known to the reader, and the inner story, known to the writer and revealed only slowly and by degrees to the reader. Somewhere in *Star of Danger* I had Larry recall that his mother had died before he was old enough to remember her; but this, as I made apparent later (in *Heritage of Hastur,* to be exact) was simply what Larry *believed;* it is clear at the end of *Star of Danger* that his father had lied to him, at least once, about the circumstances of his birth and family background, which I felt was enough of a doorway left open so that I might indicate that Larry's mother had been a kinswoman of the Aldarans and that she might even have survived the end of the marriage, without Larry's knowledge; also that there might have been a sister whose very existence was unknown to Larry, if the separation was so early in his life that he did not remember her.

For a character contrasted to Larry, I chose a Darkovan youth, and because I had already established the existence of Kennard, in *The Bloody Sun,* I decided that

Kennard as a boy might well have had contact with the Terrans.

One other element went into the plotting of *Star of Danger* which needs a little explanation. By this time, *The Planet Savers* had appeared in one of those German reprint editions, in a magazine-pulp format. *The Planet Savers* is a *very* short novel, not long enough to fill up a book, although as the flip side of an Ace Double it was long enough; therefore the German pulp-writer hack who translated the thing for its German incarnation had blithely added an extra chapter! I read German very poorly, so for years I didn't even bother going through the German edition; but one day when I did, several months before writing *Star of Danger*, I discovered an illustration which did not seem to fit into *The Planet Savers* at all; an illustration which showed Jason, Kyla and the other members of the expedition to the trailmen all hung up in a giant net or bag of some sort. I couldn't remember writing anything like that; a quick look through the printed version told me I *hadn't* written anything like that.

I corresponded for a little while, most unsatisfactorily, with the German translator, who couldn't imagine why I was incensed about it—he told me that he took it for granted that if a book wasn't long enough he would provide wordage to order to bring up the story to the "proper" length. It never occurred to him that I could have any reservations about this kind of unauthorized collaboration! I don't remember the translator's name, and I finally decided that (a) he meant no harm, (b) translators were paid so little that he certainly hadn't made enough money from this edition that I could justly accuse him of profiteering, and (c) the whole thing wasn't worth worrying about anyhow. However, I decided that when I wrote the NEXT Darkover book—and already it was fairly obvious that all my books would be resold for German translation—I was going to mess up that translator very thoroughly by including the scene which he had written into *The Planet Savers*, in *Star of Danger*. My German wasn't good enough to *translate* the episode, and Walter was too busy to read it to me, but I studied the illustration, and created the episode where Larry and Kennard are captured by the trailmen, by the method of using a big net!

Well, after *Star of Danger*, I decided I was through with Darkover. It didn't sell very well, and I imagined that the readers were bored with the stories. I had had two children somewhat too close together—not entirely by choice—Walter had suffered a long illness, and we had gone broke and had to put our beautiful big Berkeley house on the market for sale as our last ditch attempt to avoid bankruptcy. (It has since been cut up for a student rooming house and we have never again lived in a house which was really big enough to hold all our books and records—alas!) We moved to New York on the promise of a job from an old employer of Walter's, but the job did not materialize, and during the next few years Walter worked very irregularly, due to illness and a shortage of work in his specialized field, and I kept the whole shebang together with my typewriter. I wrote Gothics and mysteries and romances and astrology articles—including, during one dreadful year, daily horoscopes for an astrology monthly magazine—and reviewed books for underground newspapers, and did columns for them, and any other damn thing I could do to make something approaching a living for us and the little kids. The only science fiction novel I wrote during that dreadful time was another teenage novel, called *The Brass Dragon*, for which my inspiration burned so low that during one long and terrible blank stretch I even asked my 18-year-old son David to provide some scenes and chapters for it, in return for a small but definite percentage of possible royalties some day. The book was not, to put it mildly, a world-beater; in fact, *The Brass Dragon* got such poor reviews that I resolved to stop writing science fiction entirely and concentrate on Gothics.

During this time, I took a job as features editor of the aforesaid astrology magazine. The publisher was one of the old-time kind who bragged that he paid his writers less than any publisher in the business. In 1968, or was it '69, he was still insisting that fifteen dollars a page was plenty to pay his writers; and he gave Walter and me somewhat less than a thousand dollars a month to produce the whole package. This meant that we could not afford to buy material from reputable writers, and most agents laughed in our faces, so we were left with two choices; buy material from the slush pile and rewrite it, paying the incompetents almost nothing except the pleasure of seeing their names in print, or write the entire contents of the magazine ourselves. We needed the money so badly that we opted to write it all ourselves, under several pen names; so every month I wrote a woman's column, a teenage column, "Occultism for You," "The Astrologer's Bookshelf" and a variety of informative articles and similar claptrap; not to mention the damn daily horoscopes!

In retrospect this was an education in itself. It gave me some insight into the seamy underside of the publishing business; it made me realize that most editors were not tough hard-headed bastards, but the same sort of overworked and hard-driven wage-slaves as the worst of us; it taught me to proofread; and last but certainly not least, it showed me how VERY much an editor depends on his writers, and what a delight it is to an editor to find something even halfway literate in the slush pile! It also gave me considerable confidence in my own abilities as a writer; if this was the level of the competition, why was I worrying?

But I had never believed that any supposedly creative job, like writing, could be so appallingly, soul-destroyingly BORING. I was turning out, every month, the equivalent in wordage of a full-length novel; and not getting paid novel rates, or anything like them. My work wasn't selling, and I had a pro desk man at Scott Meredith's, for the first and last time, who didn't seem able to sell ANYTHING I wrote. He convinced me that no editor would buy any of my work if I crawled to him on my knees. I was just about resolved to quit writing and try to get a better editorial job somewhere in the city— I could hardly have had a *worse* one—but as a sort of last resort, I went up to the old Ace offices one day, drank a cup of coffee with Don Wollheim, and confided to him our circumstances and the shape I was in. He had quite a bit of good advice for me, but he was very firm in telling me that I should not consider giving up writing; and he put his money where his mouth was, offering to buy a novel; whereupon I sent off a presentation, and got back a contract, and a check, for what was to become *The Winds of Darkover*.

I was so utterly, absolutely sick of astrology that the idea of doing a good, serious, straightforward, action-packed science fantasy novel delighted me. In *Star of Danger* I had postulated bandit raids; it struck me that this would make a good background for the story. I felt I had written too much about the Comyn and the Seven Domains, that everybody must be dreadfully sick of them; but *The Brass Dragon* had turned out such a failure that I didn't quite dare abandon Darkover altogether. So I decided to write a Darkovan story about the far mountains. Also, having just read an Andre Norton novel that I liked—maybe it was *Witch World,* maybe it was *Dread Companion*, it might even have been *Ice Crown* —I resolved to try a female protagonist.

I had intended at first to make the heroine a Free Ama-

zon, hired to fight bandits in the hills of Darkover. I
played for some time with that idea, but somehow it never managed to jell. I was not to write successfully about
the Free Amazons again for another seven or eight years.
Being unable to manage a Free Amazon protagonist, I
thought about the matter for a while, and decided that
most sword-and-sorcery novels deal with the barbarian
business of conquest; all too often that means the conquest of women as well as castles. This is simply the
seamy underside of heroic fiction; and having seen the
seamy underside of something else about which I had
illusions—the publishing business—I was in a mood to
write a very disillusioned story. So my heroine became
one of the women who suffered from a bandit attack.
Actually there were two women to start with; Melitta,
the younger and more spirited, and Allira, the eldest,
raped and summarily married off to a bandit chief. Allira
turned out to be a washout as a heroine. Try as I might
to infuse her with heroic spirit, all she did was cry; so the
burden of rescue fell, willy-nilly, on Melitta, who turned
out to be courageous enough to climb down the castle
wall and escape though a tunnel of fungus and horrible
little beasties. I wanted to contrast Melitta's bravery with
the ordinary life of women on Darkover, so in addition to
her jelly-spined sister, I allowed her to go into the Dry
Towns, where women are chained, lawful property of
some man.

During this time, my major recreation was working
with the local Kingdom of the Society for Creative
Anachronism, a medievalist group given to researching
ancient methods of sword play, ancient music and dancing; they also give tournaments, the winner being ceremoniously crowned as King, and installing his chosen
Lady as Queen; and they hold Twelfth Night revels and
musical events. For a time I served as Seneschal, and
came into contact with many lovers of fantasy and sci-

ence fiction who had never entered into fandom as such. I discovered, in this group, many people who really enjoyed my books, "especially the ones about Darkover." This was actually the first glimmering I had that there were people who read more than one of my books, even that the books could be read as a series, or regarded as a separate entity quite apart from my other fiction. There was one young girl, however, who insisted that her favorite was *Falcons of Narabedla*—the shameless Kuttner pastiche I referred to above—and kept teasing me to write a sequel!

I couldn't figure out any way to do it—I still can't—but for Karina's sake I invented a rationale for the "falcons" and used them in Storn Castle as a way to spy on the bandits and the battles. I had actually envisioned the falcons after reading an old Sax Rohmer thriller (the maker of Fu Manchu wrote some science fiction, sometimes, between chronicling the adventures of sinister Chinese doctors and dacoits) called *The Day the World Ended*, where mechanical flying-suits via radio beam allowed the would-be dictator's men to fly in the guise of giant bats. I had used the "falcons" in *Narabedla*, and I brought them back in *Winds of Darkover* as a way for the blinded Storn to witness the battle; the original title of the story was supposed to be *Wings of Darkover*; but due to a misprint—and I still don't know whether it was mine or the Ace typist's—the contract came to me as WINDS *of Darkover*, and so I shrugged and wrote in a Ghost Wind sequence.

Because, years before, when I was writing *Birds of Prey/The Door Through Space*, I had tossed in a phrase, intended to sound colorful without meaning much of anything, about "the terrible Ya-Men, who turn cannibal when the Ghost Wind blows." Now I had no idea what I meant by that. I just thought it sounded colorful and let the reader's imagination do the rest. What the Ya-men

were, or what the Ghost Wind was, I couldn't imagine; I
suppose I picked up the phrase from looking at the masks
of Ghost Dancers in the Iriquois Museum in the Education Department in Albany, New York. But when I discovered that willy-nilly I was writing a book called
Winds of Darkover, I decided it was time for me to figure out what the Ghost Wind was and what it could do.
This was during the time when everybody was talking
about psychedelics, so the notion of a psychedelic wind
seemed a good idea; psychedelic winds—yes, but HOW?
Perhaps a psychedelic pollen which blew around at certain seasons . . . and the Ghost Wind was born. In *The
Bloody Sun* I had mentioned a liqueur called *kirian*, psy-
choactive and psi-stimulating; perhaps it was made from
this pollen? Later, I was to use this idea in *Summer of
the Ghost Wind*, which was retitled *Darkover Landfall*.
I kept the Ya-men mercifully vague, because, to be
absolutely truthful, I couldn't imagine what they would
be like; so I threw in a few phrases of description and let
the reader imagine the rest.

Most of my readers give me credit for being far more
profound than I am. I'm not profound; I simply let the
reader figure out what is terrifying to HIM and visualize
that in the blank spaces I leave in my book. Television
spectaculars, with their silly monsters, have shown us
that no one can possibly describe anything half as horrible as the reader with imagination will create for himself from your hints, if you stimulate his imagination.
And nobody reads science fiction or fantasy unless his, or
her, imagination is in good working order.

So I have no idea what the Ya-men were—or are—like.
I only know that they are very terrible indeed, with
plumes and talons and shrill yelping cries—and I am sure
that the picture in your mind seems more dreadful to you
than it would if I described them with the care of an
anatomist. After all, at least to me, the final scene of

"The Dunwich Horror" where they describe Wilbur Whately lying dead and carefully count all the peculiar-looking tentacles and suckers around his waist and under the "abundant and tightly buttoned clothing" which had enabled him to pass as human—well, that scene destroys all the horror of the rest. Because I am not horrified, personally, by physiological abnormalities. My apologies to H.P.L., but the idea of a fish-faced or "batrachian" humanoid reminds me of nothing more dreadful than the Tenniel illustrations of the fish-footman and frog-footman in *Alice in Wonderland*. Comical, perhaps. Dreadful for the poor soul who suffers from disfigurement—but then, so is a hare-lip. But horrifying? Good heavens, no!

So I prefer to leave my monsters vague, allowing the reader's imagination to create for himself, out of his *own* terrors, his very own nightmares. I have literary precedent for this. Oscar Wilde, when he was being attacked for writing of the "nameless sins" of Henry Wooton, in *The Picture of Dorian Grey*, commented that the "unspeakable sins" committed by that (un)worthy were simply those sins which the reader found most dreadful; that the reader, in his own mind, committed the sins and shuddered at them. Wilde himself had been careful not to particularize.

And I know that the Ringwraiths, in *The Lord of the Rings*, and the Balrog, are very terrible and very vague —but the recent Ralph Bakshi film has robbed the children who read *The Lord of the Rings* afterward of the shuddery pleasure of creating their own dreadful Balrogs. For I, at least, was not frightened by the Balrog at all, no more than by that charming construct of Japanese "horror" films, Godzilla, the friendly dinosaur. Indeed, who *could* be frightened by a monitor lizard with big wings? Certainly not anyone with the faintest knowledge of saurian physiology. I should, no doubt, be terrified to meet an angry monitor lizard, even without wings, in my back garden; or anywhere else where he was not securely caged. On the other hand, I have a young friend who keeps an immature specimen in her bathtub. *De gustibus.* . . . there's no arguing about tastes in monsters, or in pets. One man's monster is another's favorite zoological specimen.

Meanwhile, back on Darkover, I'd had a lot of fun in writing *Winds*, and it was a great relief after doing horoscopes, but I felt that enough was enough. I was fairly fed up with writing science fiction anyway. I felt that I hadn't read anything in science fiction that really excited and delighted me, not for ages; not since *Stranger in a Strange Land*. And in writing *Winds*, I felt that I was not doing anything new and original, but re-combining old and familiar elements for a fairly routine piece of science-fantasy. And so I resolved I was through with Darkover. I still had a drawerful of unfinished ideas about Darkovan and quasi-Darkovan characters, but I had decided that everyone must be thoroughly bored with this by now. So I resolutely closed the door on Darkover and pledged to myself that I wouldn't write any more Darkover stories; that chapter in my life was ended.

I resolved that I would think up some original ideas for a science fiction novel, or even a fantasy—fantasy was just barely beginning a respectable comeback via the Ballantine "adult fantasy" line. And if I couldn't think up some good ideas, I'd throw it all up and write Gothics! I had actually written, about that time, a couple of fairly good Gothics, one of which wasn't a Gothic at all but a horror-story packaged as a Gothic, *Dark Satanic*, in which I made use of my experience as an editor, placing much of the novel in an editorial office.

Ever since 1948 or thereabout, even before Tolkien, and probably influenced by my purchase of a copy of Yeats' *Irish Fairy and Folk Tales* and an odd volume or two of James Stephens, I had been thinking about a race of nonhumans who would be like the Irish faery folk of Gaelic legend. At one time I had started a science fiction novel about a colonist group who encountered these people, without being fully aware that they were the same as the faery folk who had supposedly landed somewhere in remote Ireland during the Pre-Christian era; forest-dwellers, post-technological, males indistinguishable from females. After reading Tolkien, my faery people unavoidably took on something of the color of Tolkien's elves. Nowhere in Tolkien does it speak of the elves as ambiguously sexed; I don't know where I picked up that idea, perhaps from one of the Theodore Sturgeon stories in which he explored the notion of legendary people who could appear as men to a woman, or as women to a man. I always thought of them, not as Tolkien's elves, warlike and magical, but more like the people who dwelt within the Norse mountains or the Irish "Faery Hills," uncanny and spellbindingly beautiful. In my early teens, about the same time that I read *The King in Yellow*, I had come across Maeterlink's *Pelleas and Melisande*, and without fully articulating it, I always thought of the mysterious Melisande as a "woman of the elf-mounds" who had strayed out of her faery homeland and could not find the way back.

I had used one of these *chieri*, as I called them, in *Star of Danger*; alien, beautiful and strange, with mysterious powers. And I had actually begun a short novel about the attempts of this lost and alien race to interbreed with humans. Influenced by Ted Sturgeon, I am sure, it had to do with an experiment, not dissimilar to that in the Vercors novel about a monkeylike half-human race, to test whether or not the monkey race was legally human, by seeing if it could crossbreed with mankind. Only in my story, it went the other way round; men, landed on an alien planet, were offered the opportunity to test their

human-ness by testing whether or not they were in-
terfertile with the "old race." Most of the book dealt
with the emotional problems of a woman scientist preg-
nant by the alien, and how her husband reacted to this
experiment. I wrote about six chapters of this garbage
and finally put it whole into the wastebasket, before it
even had a good working title. (I called it *The Human
Test*, or *Test for Humanity*, which just goes to show.)

It finally came to me that the *chieri* were, of course, a
unisex race, now male, now female, operating at different periods in time. However, I decided that the sexual element in such a story would make it difficult to
handle at all, with the kind of taboos operating in science
fiction at that time. I had no desire to write the kind of
story which would have to be published as pornography;
that seemed too high a price to pay for literary honesty.
I have always tried to handle sex as frankly in my books
as the standards of the marketplace would allow; but I
had no desire to trespass those standards. So I hadn't
done anything at all about the *chieri* novel. And then, in
1970 or so, I went to Boskone; and while there I had one
of those "What are you working on now—?" conversa-
tions with Anne McCaffrey, which all writers find valuable, and which are just about the only reason I ever go
to conventions these days.

At that time Anne was Secretary of the SFWA—Science
Fiction Writers of America—and to her, I confessed my
disillusionment and disgust with science fiction. I'd let
my SFWA membership lapse and had no intention of re-
newing it, or, for that matter, of writing any more science
fiction. I was tired of writing the same novel over and
over again. I was tired of *reading* the same novel over
and over again. I was going to throw it all up and write
Gothics. They were dumb, but then everybody *expected*
them to be dumb. And so forth. Anne, bless her, listened
patiently to this tirade, then asked if I had read Ursula Le

Guin's *The Left Hand of Darkness*, which had just been published as an Ace Special. And this, poor Anne, brought on another tirade. No, I hadn't and I didn't intend to; I had just struggled through two super-avant-garde, formless and totally unreadable "Ace Specials", *The Jagged Orbit* (I forget who wrote it—hardly John Brunner, I'd think?) [Editor's note: It was John Brunner.] and Joanna Russ's *And Chaos Died*, and I said if that was representative of really fine science fiction, I *knew* I was going to write Gothics, because the whole "New Wave" turned me off, off, off! Nobody wanted *stories* any more, just political tracts and prose poems!

Anne said this one wasn't like that, and urged me to read *Left Hand of Darkness*; she'd bet me anything I liked that there were still some good science fiction novels around. I think she even put her own copy into my coat pocket, and I read it on the plane going home that night. I was spellbound; I shook Walter awake, at 2 A.M., when I arrived home, squealing wild enthusiasms about the *marvelous* new book I'd read. Maybe there was still some good science fiction after all! Walter read *Left Hand*, and his reaction was very strange; he said "Now you can write that story about the *chieri* that you thought you couldn't write."

I let the idea simmer for a while, meanwhile reading some books on ecology, and finally I came up with a plot outline for a book to be called *The World Wreckers*. Many, many years ago, in the old pulps, Edmond Hamilton had been affectionately called "The ol' world-wrecker," because of his habit of destroying at least a planet, sometimes a solar system, and occasionally even a universe in his far-ranging space-opera. So I wondered; what would a *real* world-wrecker be? Norman Spinrad had one good idea in *The Doomsday Machine*; I decided, though, that there were subtler ways to wreck a world, such as messing up a fragile ecology.

And it also struck me that this would be a good way to finish off the Darkover series; wrap the whole thing up, reconcile them for good and all with the Terran Empire, finish up everything I had to say about Darkover in one fell swoop—and incidentally tie off the loose ends of the series so tightly that nobody could ever resurrect it. This was my moral equivalent of tossing Sherlock Holmes off the cliff at the Reichenbach Falls. Finish. No more. Full stop.

There was only one snag in the writing. Editorial taboos about sex. Halfway through the writing, I called Don Wollheim up and said "Hey, Don, I have to have at least one fairly explicit sex scene in this new book."

He wasn't pleased. But I explained to him that it was one thing to *say* that a human and an alien had sex—Burroughs managed it, and even wound up with John Carter and his Martian princess sentimentally regarding their unhatched egg—but quite another to make a sophisticated reader, in 1970, *believe* that such a thing was even anatomically possible. And I reminded him that Phil Farmer, in an old *Startling Stories* novelette in 1951, *The Lovers*, had managed to be quite graphic without offending anyone.

He extracted a promise from me that there would be no four-letter vulgarisms (unnecessary, for I dislike them quite as much as he does, if not more) and in turn I asked him for a promise that he would not cut the scene without consulting me. "If there's anything in it that you simply can't live with," I urged, "call me, and I'll cut it or change it to something you can live with. But please don't whack away at it with a blue pencil. Promise?" and he promised.

This, of course, was the scene between Keral and David which shocked some people and pleased others. Homosexuality had always been a *major* taboo in science fiction. Theodore Sturgeon had attacked the phobia against homosexuality in his story *The World Well Lost*, and later in *Affair with a Green Monkey*, but the subject itself had never actually been dealt with in a science fiction story. However, this was necessary. In *The World Wreckers*, much of the story turns upon the desire of a young *chieri*, Keral, for a child to assure the continuation of his otherwise dying race. However, his emotional sympathy is attracted only by David Hamilton, a young, male, doctor; and David has learned to love Keral in male phase. In order for the two to mate, David must first overcome his culturally-ingrained distate for a love affair with a human being of the same sex.

This curious problem in alien emotions, and in cultural interchange, faced squarely, had a curious side effect; because I was the first person to attack this problem straight on, I became known as highly sympathetic; in fact, for a time, I managed to become something like science fiction's token homosexual! I had no particular aversion for this position; but I am sure that it encouraged many other writers to stop being afraid of the subject, both in their writings and their private lives. I received a great deal of mail on the subject. And I am pleased with one side-effect of *The World Wreckers*. Having discovered, via the popularity of *The World Wreckers*, that the skies would not fall when he published a story which dealt honestly with even unconventional sexuality, Don Wollheim was encouraged to take a more straightforward view of sex in science fiction. His publisher objected to the implication of physical sex between David and Jonathan in a fantasy with a Biblical setting, called *How Are the Mighty Fallen*, by the excellent, and tragically short-lived, young writer, Thomas Burnett Swann. A few years before, I think, the publisher would have had the last word; but Don Wollheim went to bat for the artistic purpose of Swann's work, and managed to force her to back down and allow the book to be published as Swann had written it. So I felt that my last look at Darkover had achieved a useful purpose. But I was also disconcerted. Because every time I stated that this was the end of the Darkover series, the answer was an outcry of "Oh, don't DO that!" And this, not only from personal friends, but from virtual strangers and casual readers!

IV

I think it was about a year after *The World Wreckers* when, discovering that Wollheim had left Ace, due to a quarrel with the people who had bought the company from A.A. Wyn (a period of eclipse for Ace, during the time when it belonged to Charter Communications) I paid him a courtesy call at his new offices, and found him angry and disgruntled. It seems that when he had started his own publishing company, so he told me, agents and authors took that as license to send him all kinds of old rejects and unpublishable junk. Specifically, he told me that he would like to publish something of mine, but that when he informed Scott Meredith of this, they had sent him a dreadful old novelette which had obviously been making the rounds for upwards of fifteen years (*I* had believed *Mission Camouflage*, a real clunker about an interplanetary spy on Earth, had been lost or destroyed even before *Planet Stories* went out of business in the fifties) and chapters-and-outline of a dreary old end-of-the-world novel that I'd abandoned, and forgotten, after it was rejected ten years before! He told me that he'd be happy to look at something new; especially, he said, a Darkover novel. I told him I hadn't intended to do any more of them, and he protested, saying that Darkover was a known series and a popular one.

I told him I didn't think I had much more to say about

Darkover, but I'd do what I could, and went home to write him something. A couple of weeks later I came back with three presentations. One was a quasi-fantasy novel called *House Between the Worlds*, which he didn't like; I didn't sell it until six years later, and then to a hardcover publisher. One was a Brackettesque idea about a man escaping a prison planet to be betrayed and sold to the mysterious race of "Hunters" who make a fetish of trying to find bigger and better prey from all over the Galaxy. He said the prison planet idea had whiskers, it had been used so often. I'd never read it myself, but I deferred to his judgment. (A few years later, with the first scenes on the prison planet eliminated, he bought that one too, as *Hunters of the Red Moon*.)

The third was a story of the first landing of the Terran ship on a planet which would later be named Darkover; and the basic problem was something which had always vaguely intrigued me. What had changed a technologically oriented group of scientists and colonists into a vaguely feudal, sword-and-sorcery oriented world? And with this was another question which had stuck with me since my novelette, *The Climbing Wave*, published in *F & SF* in 1954; in this novel, a colonist ship returning to Earth commented that "It had taken them three generations to repair the ship so that they could return home." No sooner was that novelette in print than I began to contemplate a sequel, or rather a prequel, because it seemed to me that there would evidently be two parties, one wholly dedicated to repairing the ship and returning home; the other to abandoning the damaged ship and colonizing the new world; and that the clash between the two would be highly dramatic. I interjected into this story the "Ghost wind" which I had introduced in *Winds of Darkover*, as a disruptive force; and I called the book *The Summer of the Ghost Wind*. Darkover was nowhere mentioned in it; not until the very last line of the book.

However, Don changed the title of the book to *Darkover Landfall*, because, as mentioned earlier in this article, Darkover was a known series, and a popular one, and the distributers wanted the readers to be able to identify it.

I didn't know at that time how much influence the distributors had upon sales and marketing. But this forced me to think very seriously about continuing the Darkover books as a series—the knowledge that they had a following—and so, when he suggested another Darkover novel, I was receptive and willing.

Many, many years before—in 1948 or there about,—I had read the now-classic Jack Vance collection of short stories called *The Dying Earth*, and there was a line in one story where Pandelume, the magician, remarks to a woman, "Your sword lives. It will kill your enemies with intelligence."

Now that concept both intrigued and annoyed me. I am a great lover of fantasy, but when I grew up, fantasy was not—quite—respectable, and there always had to be some scientific rationale for how the things worked. (My *very* favorite example is in a Kuttner story where a werewolf was described as being composed of "Specialized osseous tissue—capable of almost instantaneous alteration." That made a lot more sense to me than the curse which supposedly caused lycanthropy.)

So I simply could not imagine how this could be done. How would one cause a sword to act on its own initiative? Well, suppose the sword was linked—by matrix, of course, and telepathy—to the mind of a famous swordsman who could use it? *Voìla!* Then all I had to do was devise somebody who needed rescuing—it turned out to be a Keeper, of course—and somebody who wasn't very good at using a sword but needed to rescue the damsel in distress *anyhow*.

I had intended the Earthman Andrew Carr to do the rescuing; but Damon Ridenow walked into the story, and

I allowed him to take it over. I have found out, during almost thirty years of writing, that the best characters are the ones who simply walk, unplanned, into a story, and take it over. I suppose the real explanation is that they represent the spontaneous creativity of the subconscious mind, which is less labored than the conscious mind which sits down and doggedly says "I gotta get this damn story written or the rent won't get paid." I must be getting old. I am tired of logical explanations, as with the physiologically realistic Kuttner werewolf. I prefer to think that Damon exists somewhere and demanded to be written about.

Apart from Damon's surprise appearance in *Spell Sword*, it was, and still is, a fairly routine damsel-in-distress story. However, I like it, first of all because of the catmen who appeared in it almost out of nowhere—I had used them, like the Dry Towns, in *The Door Through Space*—and because several of my friends, including my oldest son David (who is, in his twenties, both a friend and a fan of mine), have said that *Spell Sword* is a good book with which to start the reading of Darkover novels; it has the "flavor" of Darkover, and is a good, straightforward action story, devoid of ethical problems or controversial issues.

It was the only non-controversial story I wrote for years. *Darkover Landfall* stirred up a furor because some outraged feminists objected to the stand I took in the book, that the survival of the human race on Darkover could, and should, be allowed to supersede the personal convenience of any single woman in the group. I have debated this subject *ad nauseam* in the fanzines, and I absolutely refuse to debate it again, but to those who refuse to accept the tenet that "Biology is Destiny" I have begun to ask them to show me a vegetarian lion or tiger before they debate the issue further.

Not long after *Spell Sword*, I decided to attempt another Darkover novel. Many years before, while I was still writing Al-merdin fantasies, I had written a long and extended fragment about the early life of Regis Hastur, his career in the Guards, his quarrel with Dyan Ardais, his friendship with Danilo Syrtis, and so forth. Many of my friends and family had read this, under the working title of *Insolence*, and urged me to finish it and have it published, but I felt that it was not publishable as it stood. At the same time, I felt I should write about the events which had culminated in *The Sword of Aldones* —Lew Alton's love affair with Marjorie, his part in the Sharra Rebellion, and his encounter with Kadarin. However, I didn't think it could be done. Jacqueline Lichtenberg, with whom I was corresponding at that time, insisted that it could be done, and undertook to show me HOW it could be done; she actually wrote me a nine or ten page letter which contained a very lengthy chapter-by-chapter outline of the novel she thought I could make out of this book. I read the letter and exploded into screams of rage. No, no, no, a thousand times no, I cried (in a letter longer than her original). Regis Hastur could never behave like THAT, he'd have to do THIS instead. Lew Alton couldn't possibly have done so-and-so because (lengthy analysis of Lew's character and why he would have done otherwise). And after fifteen pages or so of this kind of stuff I concluded by saying that now, if she had half a brain in whatever it was she was using for a head, she would see that I couldn't *possibly* write the thing, and would she please write her own books and stop trying to tell me how to write mine? To which she replied that all she had proven was that *she* couldn't write *The Hastur Gift* (which was what she was calling it then) but that I could—and had just proved it to her by telling her how I would have done it, so why didn't I just stop fooling around and DO it.

So I began what later came to be called *The Heritage of Hastur*.

About halfway through this book I had a really major policy decision to make. Was I going to be completely consistent with *The Sword of Aldones*, thus locking myself into my fifteen-year-old's mind and my adolescent concept of Darkover? Or was I going to write *The Heritage of Hastur* as an adult, sacrificing consistency if I must, but writing the book the way I thought it should be written? I decided that I would be true to my adult self and to the best plotting and writing I could do NOW, in 1974. Out the window with consistency! I retained only the bare outlines of the story; the presence of Rafe Scott during the Sharra rebellion, the fact that Thyra later bore Lew's child (I could write a saga about the difficulty I went to, bringing Lew and Thyra together . . . in fact, I once said, flippantly, that I went to far more trouble getting that child conceived than either of the parents!) and Marjorie's tragic death, possessed by the ravening Sharra.

Well, the damned thing turned out nearly twice the length of anything I'd ever written before, and I was afraid Wollheim wouldn't want it. But he had just begun experimenting with longer novels; Tanith Lee's *The Birthgrave* was the first, and *Heritage* was the second. Despite a perfectly dreadful Gaughan cover on the first edition, it sold well; in spite of breaking every taboo in the business. Once again I had had to attack the subject of homosexuality head on; but, curiously enough, no one was upset by the picture of male homosexuals in *Heritage*, with a rather curious exception. I received a few nasty letters from confessed homosexuals in the Gay Activist movement, accusing me of prejudice because I, professing to be sympathetic toward homosexuality, had perpetrated the stereotype of the homosexual as brutal sadist, preying on young boys.

I didn't pay too much attention to this criticism. It was overbalanced by the enormous amount of fan mail I received from young people who had been touched by the

story of Danilo and Regis; one or two young people even
confessed to me that they had become more willing to
face it in themselves without guilt or suicidal impulses.
My message, of course, had not been intended to give aid
and comfort to Gay Liberation; the message, if any, had
simply been that no one can live and be healthy without
self-knowledge and self-acceptance, whatever form one's
own differences may take. I am not a crusader for anything except the right of everyone to be what he must be,
without being brutalized by the opinions of others. I regard Dyan Ardais, not as evil, but as unhappy, a man
desperately at the mercy of his own misery and his own
obsessions; and Dyan's tragedy, I have always felt, was
that he did not come to know Regis well until he had
destroyed himself irrevocably in the younger man's eyes.

I have also discovered that there are two reactions to
Heritage; those who identify, in the reading, with Regis,
and those who identify with Lew. Personally I identify
with Lew, which is why I chose the *Bleak House* technique for writing it: alternate chapters in first person
from the viewpoint character, and third person for the
adventures of the other characters, telling what the viewpoint character cannot know.

Heritage was my most popular novel to date. I received more fan mail about it than all my other novels
put together, and I still get letters about it. It is also my
favorite of my own books.

However, it lost the Hugo, missing out on the list of
finalists. It did turn up on the list of Nebula nominees for
that year, but that was only because there were 25 nominees and, that year, sfwa was experimenting with having
no "short list" but with direct voting on all recom-
mended novels. At the Nebula banquet, when C.L.
Moore, (my own childhood idol) was giving out the
Nebulas, although I had no expectation (and no real de-

sire) to win a Nebula, I still could not keep my mind from toying with the thought; just suppose I *did* win? Imagine getting a Nebula from C.L. Moore! (childish attitude, hero-worship; she'd *have* to notice me then!) I also felt that while I didn't really mind losing the Nebula (and I certainly wouldn't burst into tears, as one loser did, to my chagrin, for I was sitting next to him) I would feel awfully damned angry if I were to lose it to Chip Delaney's unwieldy *Dhalgren*, which was also on the Nebula nominee list that year, or to Joanna Russ's *The Female Man*, which I admired but did not like, having a constitutional aversion to political tracts packaged as novels.

Well, the presentation came and went, and I don't even remember who won the Nebula in question (which is why I have no great desire to win one—who, except the winner and his mother, ever remembers who won a Nebula four years later?) although I think it was Arthur C. Clarke's *Rendezvous With Rama*, which probably pleased everybody. [Editor's note: It was *The Forever War* by Joe Haldeman.] However, later that night a certain Silly Female who regarded me as a friend, God knows why, came up and cooed at me "Mrs. Bradley—ARE you disappointed?" For a minute I couldn't even remember what she was talking about; when I finally figured out that she was asking if I was sad at not winning a Nebula, I was becroggled. I finally found my voice and told her that in twenty-five years of reading and writing science fiction, I had heard a hell of a lot of gauche questions, but that really took the cake—that I might have expected it of a fourteen-year-old fan without any social *savoir-faire*, but that from a woman of my own age, who had enough sophistication to get invited to a Nebula banquet, I considered it unspeakable. Every time I have run into the woman since I have cut her dead, which is probably cruel of me.

V

Years before, long before writing *Winds of Darkover*, I had mentioned that I would like to do a book about the Free Amazons. After *Heritage*, I asked Wollheim what he thought of the idea. I can't say that he was enthusiastic; at that time, the science fiction audience was still mostly male, or at least the articulate branch of it was male. But there were more and more books with female protagonists, and he felt that if I wanted to do one, I might do it well; so he gave me the go-ahead, and signed a contract for a book to be called *Free Amazons of Darkover*. I started with a mental picture of Kindra, the Free Amazon, lurking outside the Great House of Jalak, tyrant of Shainsa, to rescue somebody . . . and then I couldn't imagine why. What importance would the sister of a Free Amazon have on Darkover? Well, maybe Kindra was somehow kin to the Comyn. No, maybe she had been employed to lead a rescue, as Kyla, the Free Amazon in *The Planet Savers*, was employed to lead a mountain-climbing expedition. That, somehow, *clicked*; and with that, Rohana Ardais walked into the story, and, as Damon Ridenow had done with *Spell Sword*, decided to take it over.

When the book was finished, Wollheim called it *The Shattered Chain*. I didn't understand why; the title didn't seem to mean much to me. He explained that it was because of the women in the book, who were casting off their chains, physical and mental, real and imaginary . . . it's a very good title, and probably a better title than mine, because, after I had finished writing the book—which originally, I had hoped to make a straightforward adventure story like *Spell Sword*—I discovered that it wasn't really about Free Amazons at all; it was about freedom in general. My thesis in the book was that most people think they are free and weight themselves with invisible chains; while Rohana, who refuses to remain with the Amazons, accepts her unwanted family responsibilities, and says at the end of the book that she has had "everything but freedom" has won a kind of freedom by accepting that she is *not* free, that nobody alive is ever completely free.

And just as in *Heritage of Hastur*, the only attack ever made on the book was from the people I believed would like it best. While some conservative male readers attacked it as "the obligatory radical feminist novel that every woman now feels compelled to write," these were greatly in a minority. Most women liked the book, liked the mix of free women and women struggling to be free; and the Amazons have certainly affected the amateur writers. Some friends of mine, under the name of the Friends of Darkover, publish several fanzines, including one devoted to amateur Darkover fiction; and from the beginning we have received more stories about Free Amazons than on all other subjects combined. I know at least four women who have legally had their names changed to the Amazon form on their checkbooks and driver's licenses; the first was a young friend of my family who now calls herself *Jaida n'ha Sandra*.

But the radical feminists, one and all, attacked me, saying that by allowing Jaelle, the heroine, to fall in love with a man in the last chapter of the book, I sold out the feminist premise—that I gave the impression that Jaelle's Amazon vows were just an adolescent stage, which vanished when she found a man she could love. I had, of course, no such theory—I only meant that *any* choice was likely to prove difficult, and that Jaelle's belief in her own freedom was just as fallacious as Magda's belief in her ability to defend herself, or her independence.

But the feminists *raged*. A whole issue of a feminist fanzine was devoted to "trashing" the Amazons as being phony feminists. I can only assume that these women had identified so deeply with the Amazons in the story that they felt I had no right to disappoint their daydreams of a feminist paradise . . . though how they ever managed to think of Darkover as a feminist paradise, even for Free Amazons (or, more accurately, Renunciates) I cannot imagine.

But by the time *The Shattered Chain* was being reviewed I didn't really care all that much (though once again I allowed myself to be lured into debating the issue in the feminist press, as I had injudiciously done with *Darkover Landfall*). I had other fish to fry.

About the time I finished *Spell Sword* (way back there in 1973) my sister-in-law, Diana Paxson, had made an offhand remark about Andrew and Callista from that book, saying, "There's a marriage that's really got three strikes against it." After a little thought, I realized that this was so. Twice, now, I had facilely used the marriage of a Keeper to an outsider, even a Terran, as a fictional device, in the best "Hero married the enchanted princess and lives happily ever after" tradition. But when I really stopped to *think* about it—no, really, it didn't sound all that easy, did it? As a nice pat fictional device, a Happy Ending, it was just fine. But for real? Come on, now, I wondered, what would that marriage *really* be like? For that matter, what kind of weddings did they have on Darkover? So one night, even before I finished *Heritage*, when I wasn't working on anything else, I rolled a sheet of paper into the typewriter and started to write about the double wedding of Andrew and Callista, Damon and Ellemir, including the scene where Leonie gave Callista permission to leave the Tower and marry.

Damon and Ellemir would be all right. Ellemir wanted children, and probably would have them, and the only real problem they would have, would be the fact that she and her husband were such close relatives that they might be, probably would be, duplicating lethal recessives. But Andrew and Callista were quite another story. I went back into the files for an episode I had written way back before *The Sword of Aldones* was in print, or even finished; the one where the Keeper Callina Aillard (who was, in that version, called Cassandra Marceau-Valeron) was attacked with Lustful Intent by a villain whose name I had all but forgotten, but who later metamorphosed into one of the three villains who merged to become Dyan Ardais. (Edric the Red Fox of Serrais? Valdrin Aldaran? I've forgotten his name, but he was definitely a Villain of the Blackest Dye, and Cassandra managed to protect herself by summoning up lightnings to strike him down!)

Well if a Keeper could be conditioned to do THAT to any man who laid a rude hand on her (and I remembered that in *The Bloody Sun*, there was a distinct taboo against touching a Keeper) suppose she could not *allow* herself to be touched, even when she wished? How would this mechanism work? And, above all, WHY? The answer to this led me into examination and research in Yoga, biofeedback, Kundalini, the imagined shock of the sex-force, Brahmacharya (the law of chastity for pious Hindus and Yogis, written about by Gandhi and others) and the tradition of virgin priestesses in pagan religions. I found myself writing about what happened when Andrew finally attempted to consummate his marriage. And what Damon and Ellemir thought about it, Callista and Ellemir being twins and in telepathic rapport. And would Callista continue to use her *laran*, and if not, why not? What *were* the laws of Arilinn about failed Keepers? Obviously, there had been many changes made in the laws of the Towers since the time of Cleindori, who was murdered by fanatics for abandoning her ritual virginity; Linnea of Arilinn, in *The World Wreckers*, made no bones about the fact that she was *not* a virgin.

By the time *The Shattered Chain* was in print, and

Wollheim was asking about the new book, I was so deeply involved in *Quadrille*, which is what I called the thick mess of manuscript, that I didn't have any wish to get involved with anything else, but I was fairly sure that it wasn't professionally publishable. I told him this, saying that it was nothing but "a love story among a bunch of telepaths" and that he wouldn't like it. But he asked to see it anyhow, so I sat down with it and tried to make it into a plotted story with some kind of purpose.

I did this by the fairly simple device of adding a story line which could take place around and through the love story; the desire of Dezi, illegitimate son of Dom Esteban, to be recognized as a son of the Alton line. To gain this, he tries first to put Andrew out of the way, then arranges the ingenious, accidental-seeming murder of the Heir to Alton, young Domenic. Like some of the Julio-Claudian emperors of Rome, he attempted to inherit by killing off everyone who might stand in his way, and when Damon discovered it, he had to act firmly to remove the menace. This was the main action plot, as against the two other threads of the story; Damon's decision to take up again the control of *laran*, which he feared, and had renounced, as Keeper of the Forbidden Tower, and Andrew and Callista's attempt to achieve a happy marriage.

And it took me longer to finish this book than any previous one, because I was seriously worried about the taboos I was breaking. I had skirted lesbianism in *The Shattered Chain*, not out of squeamishness, nor out of fear of popular-fiction taboos, but because I wished to write for ALL women, and knew that if I made any main character a lesbian, they would immediately say "This story has nothing to say to me, it's not about my kind of woman at all." Also, because for some strange reason lesbianism is regarded as "sexy and exciting" by a certain kind of man, the voyeuristically inclined who is excited by the thought of lovemaking between two women, and the idea of writing that kind of thing for a male audience revolted me more than I could say. So, although in writing about Amazons I had to touch upon the matter (for in any feminist group, as NOW has also discovered, some women whose feminism is based upon separateness from men are attracted to the movement) I forced the "lovers of women," to use the Darkovan phrase, into the background, and required them to keep a low profile. I did not want to do this; but I preferred it to writing a sensational book for the audience that would say "Oh, wow, lesbians, goody! Oooh!" and simper.

But in *Forbidden Tower* there was no way to avoid the sexual implications of a four-way telepathic rapport between two couples, wide open to one another's sexuality. It was very difficult to write without tipping over the scales into the pornographic. I had to face the sexual themes frankly without becoming tastelessly explicit; and I have never been very much interested in fiction which treats of sex in the manner of (as the limerick says) "Who did what, and with which, and to whom."

Finally I had once again to call my editor and ask him just how far I *could* go. He surprised me by saying flatly that he believed that, since *Dhalgren*, there were really no more taboos in fiction, and that I could write anything I wished provided I handled it with good taste. I had been dawdling on *Forbidden Tower* for eight months. I finished it, after that, within the month.

It was a long way from the argument I had over *The World Wreckers*! The world had changed, and I was very glad to see it happening in science fiction.

About the most adverse comment I had on *Forbidden Tower* was in a fanzine review which said "Our attention is kept almost claustrophobically in the bedroom". But most people liked it, and once again, it was nominated for a Hugo, although not for a Nebula; I had formally requested that none of my works be considered, under any circumstances, for a Nebula. This time it went up to the final voting, and perhaps, if the Hugo committee had managed to get all the ballots out in time for the postal service to return them, the final tally might have been different. I think, also, that some harm was done to the voting because, well in advance of the final balloting, the publishers of Fred Pohl's *Gateway* were announcing in advance that *Gateway* was going to be the first novel ever to win all three of the awards—Nebula, John W. Campbell Award, and Hugo; and some voters like to be on the winning side, and will vote for a sure thing. But even so, I was told afterward that I lost the Hugo (or rather, *Forbidden Tower* lost it) by a scant handful of votes, fewer than ten. Unless one is a devotee of the Vince Lombardi thesis that winning is the "only thing" (and I am NOT) it is certainly no disgrace to come in narrowly close to a book of that kind of stature.

But losing the Hugo resulted in the same kind of amusing episode that happened at the Nebula Banquet, and makes me think that in the long run, Hugo losers have more fun than winners. The next day, a young Darkover fan with more enthusiasm than tact came up and informed me that it was unfair, dismal, horrible, dreadful. I thought she was commiserating with *my* loss—which had happened to me several times already, and was far worse than losing in the first place—but it seems that instead she felt it was a cruel and terrible injustice that Gordon Dickson's *Time Storm* had lost. Well, I hadn't (and haven't yet) read *Time Storm*, but even so, I thought that I was the wrong target for this comment; it would have been better aimed at the Hugo committee, or better yet, at Gordy himself; he would have enjoyed hearing it, and I wasn't, quite, yet able to appreciate it!

Later that night, I retailed this comment to Gordon Dickson, who complimented me on my forbearance—he

said bluntly that if any of *my* fans had come up to *him*,
and wept all over him (as this girl did on me) because
Forbidden Tower had lost a Hugo, he would forthwith
have dropped said fan out of a fourteenth story window!

VI

But, of course, by the time *Forbidden Tower* was
being voted on for a Hugo, I had already written *Stormqueen*. My fans had been badgering me to write a novel
about the Ages of Chaos, and the heyday of the Towers,
for years, and I had held off, feeling that without the
conflict and culture shock of Terran and Darkovan, the
Darkover novels would be no better than any other
barbarian-sword-and-sorcery fantasy. But I finally decided to write it, thinking of Callista striking Andrew
with lightning, and of the "anger that could kill," and
wondering what would happen if this power reposed in a
child too young to exercise discretion in its use.

But *Stormqueen* is too recent a book for me to know
what it is "about." Books are never about what I think
they are about. At the time I write them, I am interested
only in the story line and narrative. I have no idea what
their inner meaning may be, or even if they have any.
Some day, five, or perhaps seven years from now, it may
dawn on me what *Stormqueen* is "about"—aside from
being a novel of an old man's obsessive pride and his
desire to leave his estate in the hands of his dearly loved
foster-son rather than in the hands of relatives with
whom he has quarreled. I see *Stormqueen* as a tragedy of
hubris; and, once again, in the form of Allart Hastur who
could see not one but all possible futures, I worked with
the theme of the man who only wants to cultivate his
own garden, *a la* Voltaire's *Candide*, but who is drawn
unwilling into the great events of his day. Also, I wanted

to write about the heyday of the Towers, and about
Darkover fighting wars before the Compact; and of the
early days of Nevarsin monastery.

And then, after I had finished *Stormqueen*, Jim Baen
took me out to lunch one day, talking about the reprints
of the early Darkover novels, and asked me if I had ever
thought of rewriting any of the earlier ones. I couldn't
honestly say that I had, but I told him that when I wrote
The Bloody Sun, there had been less interest in Darkover and matrix mechanics, and that I had been hampered by length restrictions, back then in the sixties. And
so, although I had written fairly fully of the techniques
used for the forming of the Tower circles, and of the
matric technology of mining, and so forth, much of what
I wrote had been cut out because of rigid ideas, in those
days, that a science fiction novel should not run over
50,000 words or so.

And we ended by agreeing that I would rewrite *The
Bloody Sun* for him, putting back what had been de-
leted, and writing somewhat more frankly about the for-
mation of the Tower circle and Jeff's integration into it.

I had been thinking for some time that I would like to
write the story of Cleindori, the Keeper who ran away
from Arilinn to work outside. After *Forbidden Tower* it
was obvious to me that Damon's work had spurred
Cleindori's rebellion; for it was transparently obvious to
me that after Damon had discovered that, among other
things, men could work as Keepers, or that Keepers could
function without their ritual isolation and virginity, there
would have to be changes at Arilinn.

But why, one of my young friends asked me, would
they *accept* Cleindori at Arilinn? She was, said my
friend, absolutely *traife* (the reverse, of course, of being
kosher) having come out of the Forbidden Tower.

The answer, to me, became quickly fairly simple; she
would go to Arilinn to prove that it could be done, that

since a Keeper is responsible only to her own conscience, she, as Keeper of Arilinn, would be free to proclaim new laws for the Arilinn people. But Cleindori, in her innocent belief that people were reasonable, would not have counted on the fanaticism which thought of Keepers as sacred symbols; not just as matrix workers of a special kind.

And for this she fled from Arilinn, and was later killed.

I wanted to write this story. I even had a title for it; *The Way of Arilinn*. But it struck me that it would be altogether too grim, a story of innocent optimism brought to wreck, of betrayal and death and despair, fanaticism and murder.

And so I decided to incorporate this story into *The Bloody Sun*, to tell Cleindori's story through her son's eyes. In rewriting *The Bloody Sun*, I also added one character—Neyrissa, monitor at Arilinn, to emphasize Jeff's growing awareness and his place in the forming circle—and made it very clear just where *Bloody Sun* belonged in the chronology of Darkover; immediately following *Forbidden Tower*.

I also tried to fill in some details left blank in the earlier version of the book; the main one being this: what was it that changed Kennard from the light-hearted youngster of *Star of Danger* into the embittered and cynical man of *Heritage of Hastur*?

I didn't know, and now I do. It was his part in the rebellion during which Cleindori died. For he had believed in her, and believed in Arilinn, and believed in the honor of the Comyn and the reasonableness of most of the people on Darkover; and after Cleindori was murdered, he could no longer believe in any of those things, except with the gravest of reservations. He continued to work for the good of his world. But not with the same firm belief and optimism; only with a sort of dogged hanging-on. And so *The Bloody Sun* becomes a pivotal book in the two "sequences" of Darkover novels, which, offhandedly, I call the "Damon sequence" and the "Alton-Hastur sequence."

Will there be other Darkover novels?

Oh, certainly, as long as editors keep buying them and fans keep wanting to read them. For instance, I am in the middle of another *Ages of Chaos* novel, called *Two to Conquer*, about a historical period which I call the "Time of a Hundred Kingdoms," when what is now the Seven Domains was divided up into many, many little independent domains and kingdoms and principalities and dukedoms and shires. And I have been asked to write a post-world-wreckers novel about the child of David and Keral; and who inherited Regis Hastur's throne in that beleagured world? And I have been asked, by friends, if Lew Alton ever came back to Darkover; to which I can only say that I don't know, but that I am sure his daughter Marja did.

And somewhere in my bureau drawers I have several hundred pages of a story about what happened to Magda in the Free Amazon Guild-House; and *certainly* Jaelle could not have lived long with that turkey Peter Haldane!

And so forth and so on. . . .

But I don't know what, or when, or how I will write all these things. I never know what a book is going to be about until I have written it, and sometimes even then I'm not very sure. I never know what a book is going to be about until it walks out of some darkness at the back of my brain and says "Here I am; write me."

Oh, I can say to myself, "Dammit, I'm going to write a book about so-and-so," and force myself to write it.

But my best books force themselves upon me. And many, many of them appear in my mind in the light of the Bloody Sun, or of the four moons of Darkover. I don't exactly "wait upon inspiration." I quite agree that the best way to write a book is to apply the seat of the pants firmly to the seat of the chair, and remain there, ignoring all distractions. Genius is 10% inspiration, 90% perspiration, and "an infinite capacity for taking pains."

But you need that ten per cent of inspiration.

Now let me see. Regis adopted a son. . .

Yes, there's a book there. But don't ask me where or when it will get written.

—Marion Zimmer Bradley

MORE SCIENCE FICTION ADVENTURE!